THE BREAK

• • •

Also by Katherena Vermette
North End Love Songs (poetry)

THE BREAK

KATHERENA VERMETTE

Atlantic Books

LONDON

First published in Canada in 2016 by House of Anansi Press.
First published in Great Britain in 2017 by Atlantic,
an imprint of Atlantic Books Ltd.

1 3 5 7 9 10 8 6 4 2

A CIP catalogue record for this book is available from the British Library.

E-book ISBN: 978 1 78649 390 3
Hardback ISBN: 978 1 78649 388 0
Export trade paperback ISBN: 978 1 78649 389 7

© Jacket, Ojibwa, no date, leather beads and fur, Collection
of Glenbow, Calgary, Canada, AP 1967

Printed in Great Britain by
TJ International Ltd, Padstow, Cornwall

Atlantic
An imprint of Atlantic Books Ltd
Ormond House
26–27 Boswell Street
London
WC1N 3JZ

www.atlantic-books.co.uk

For my mother

In honour of those who have been lost.

With love to those who have found
a way through — you lead us.

FAMILY TREE

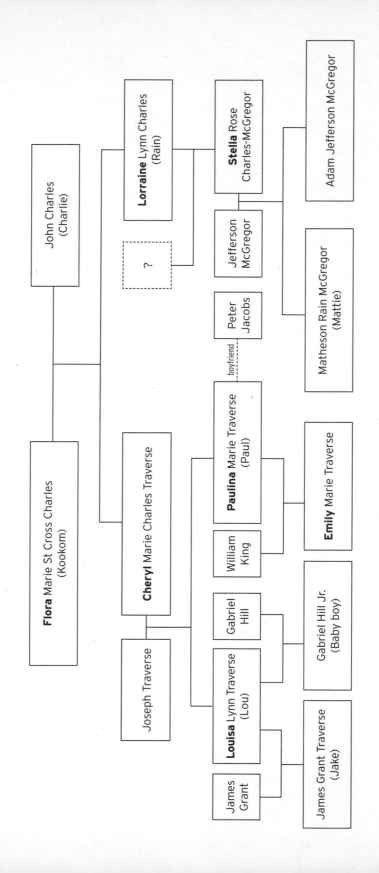

Betty, if I start to write a poem about you
it might turn out to be
about hunting season instead,
about 'open season' on native women
                                        ~ from "Helen Betty Osborne"
                                        by Marilyn Dumont

"The most common way people give up their power
is by thinking they don't have any."
                                        ~ Alice Walker

PART ONE

. . .

The Break is a piece of land just west of McPhillips Street. A narrow field about four lots wide that interrupts all the closely knit houses on either side and cuts through every avenue from Selkirk to Leila, that whole edge of the North End. Some people call it nothing and likely don't think about it at all. I never called it anything, just knew it was there. But when she moved next door, my Stella, she named it the Break, if only in her head. No one had ever told her any other name, and for whatever reason, she thought she should call it something.

It's Hydro land, was likely set aside in the days before anything was out there. When all that low land on the west side of the Red River was only tall grasses and rabbits, some bush in clusters, all the way to the lake in the north. The neighbourhood rose up around it. Houses built first for Eastern European immigrants who were pushed to that wrong side of the railway tracks, and kept away from the affluent city south. Someone once told me that North End houses were all made cheap and big, but the lots were narrow and short. That was when you had to own a certain amount of land to vote, and all those lots were made just inches smaller.

The tall, metal Hydro towers would have been built after that. Huge and grey, they stand on either side of the small piece of land, holding up two smooth silver cords high above the tallest house. The towers repeat, every two blocks, over and over, going far into the north. They might even go as far as the lake. My Stella's little girl, Mattie, named them robots when the family first moved in beside them. Robots is a good name for them. They each have a square-like head and go out a bit at the bottom like someone standing at attention, and there's the two arms overhead that hold the cords up into the sky. They are a frozen army standing guard, seeing everything. Houses built up and broken down around them, people flooding in and out.

In the sixties, Indians started moving in, once Status Indians could leave reserves and many moved to the city. That was when the Europeans slowly started creeping out of the neighbourhood like a man sneaking away from a sleeping woman in the dark. Now there are so many Indians here, big families, good people, but also gangs, hookers, drug houses, and all these big, beautiful houses somehow sagging and tired like the old people who still live in them.

The area around the Break is slightly less poor than the rest, more working class, just enough to make the hard-working people who live there think that they are out of the core and free of that drama. There are more cars in driveways than on the other side of McPhillips. It's a good neighbourhood but you can still see it, if you know what to look for. If you can see the houses with never-opened bed sheet covered windows. If you can see the cars that come late at night, park right in the middle of the Break, far away from any house, and stay only ten minutes or so before driving away again. My Stella can see it. I taught her how to look and be aware all the time. I don't know if that was right or wrong, but she's still alive so there has to be some good in it.

I've always loved the place my girl calls the Break. I used to walk through it in the summer. There is a path you can go along all the way to the edge of the city, and if you just look down at the grass, you might think you were in the country the whole way. Old people plant gardens there, big ones with tidy rows of corn and tomatoes, all nice and clean. You can't walk through it in the winter though. No one clears a way. In the winter, the Break is just a lake of wind and white, a field of cold and biting snow that blows up with the slightest gust. And when snow touches those raw Hydro wires they make this intrusive buzzing sound. It's constant and just quiet enough that you can ignore it, like a whisper you know is a voice but you can't hear the words. And even though they are more than three storeys high, when it snows those wires feel close, low, and buzz a sound that is almost like music, just not as smooth. You can ignore it. It's just white noise, and some people can ignore things like that. Some people hear it but just get used to it.

It was snowing when it happened. The sky was pink and swollen and the snow had finally started to fall. Even from inside her house, my Stella heard the buzzing, as sure as her own breath. She knows to expect it when the sky fills with clouds, but like everything she's been through, she has just learned to live with it.

STELLA

STELLA SITS AT her kitchen table with two police officers, and for one long moment, no one says a thing. They just sit, all looking down or away, for a long pause. The older officer clears his throat. He smells like old coffee and snow, and looks around Stella's home, her clean kitchen and out into her dark living room, like he's trying to find evidence of something. The younger one goes over his scribbled notes, the paper of his little coiled book flips and crumples.

Blanket over her shoulders, Stella wraps one hand around a hot mug of coffee, hoarding the warmth but still shaking. In her other hand, she balls a damp Kleenex. She stares down. Her hands look like her mom's did, older-looking hands for a young woman. Old-lady hands. Her Kookom had hands like this too, and now that she's an old lady all over, her hands are practically transparent, the skin there worn thin. Stella's aren't that bad yet, but they look too wrinkled, too old for her body, like they have aged ahead of her.

The officer breathes heavily. Stella finally looks up and

braces herself to start explaining, again. The officers both sit with shoulders up, and neither touches the steaming mugs of coffee she has poured and placed in front of them. Their uniformed jackets are still on. The radios at their shoulders spit static and muffled voices, numbers, and alerts.

She has given up trying not to cry in front of these strangers.

Officer Scott, the young one, finally breaks the silence.

"Well, we know something significant definitely happened out there." He looks at her side-eyed. His voice matter of fact, slow and hinging on the words *happened* and *out there*. His mouth frowns in a practiced sympathy that Stella knows is fake but takes anyway. The older one, Officer Christie, doesn't look at her, only agrees with a quick nod of his bearded head and another throat-clearing noise. Stella thinks he's bored, and the young one, he's so young, is eager, maybe even excited.

Officer Scott tries to look nice, again, and asks her, again, "Can you think of anything else? Anything at all?"

Stella blinks a tear and shakes her head. She looks out the window at the Break, that empty expanse of land next to her house. She doesn't have to look to know it's snowing lightly. She can hear the faint buzzing, the low drone of the Hydro towers just out of view. The sky is still bright pink in the night, swollen with more snow to come. The Break is mostly a blank slate of white stretched out to house beyond. The house's siding and the snow reflect the streetlights and the moon, but the windows are dark, of course. Everyone's windows are dark except Stella's.

The two officers had gone out there, stomped around, and made a circle around the blood, the puddle that melted the snow. Stella can just make it out from the window, a corner of it. It lies across the white ground like a dark shadow, probably frozen now. Flakes fall on top of it, wanting to cover it up. It doesn't look sinister. It doesn't look like what it really is.

Stella goes over each detail in her head, remembering everything, wanting to forget. It is probably 4 a.m. now, and Jeff will be home soon. She wants Jeff to be home more than anything. She listens for her children, ready if they wake, surprised they haven't from the all the foot stomping the officers made when they came in, but everything is quiet upstairs. The baby's been asleep since Stella finally got her kids to bed about four hours ago when she got off the phone with 911. They slept but she couldn't. She waited and stared out the window with nothing to pass the time but her anxious thoughts. So she got up and started cleaning. Everything was spotless by the time the officers finally arrived.

Her mind scatters, but she remembers everything, over and over.

"She was small, so small." Stella's shoulders shake as she finds her words again. "Like a really tiny woman, maybe five feet, not much more than that." She clings to the blanket around her. "Long straight black hair. I couldn't see her face. So small and skinny." Stella reaches for her own long black hair and remembers something else. Her voice chokes out for a minute. She knows she's repeating herself.

"Now, you only saw her through your door, right?" Scott has stopped taking notes. His pen rests on the paper pad, over his few blue scrawls. Christie finally takes a sip of coffee.

"Yes, through the screen door. The glass." Stella motions at the air. She can still see the small woman through the foggy glass, slowly moving away, finally moving down the back lane.

"That's a pretty long way away, Mrs. McGregor. Are you sure it couldn't have been a young man? You know a lot of these native boys wear their hair long."

Stella just looks at him. His too-young face still a mask of a smile, stuck there. Naïve. She thinks of the word and rolls it around in her head. Naïve.

"No, it was a girl. A woman." She looks down again, wraps her hands in the blanket but still shakes.

"Okay, okay, tell us again," Scott tries gently. "From the beginning, please. You heard noises outside..."

Stella shakes her head. "I didn't hear anything outside. The baby woke up. I went up to get him and saw out his window. I didn't know what I was seeing at first, thought it was a fight or something. It looked bad, so I called 911. But I couldn't do anything, my baby was crying so hard. He's teething."

She looks up to see this Scott officer nod and lean forward. Practiced. His partner takes another audible sip of coffee and looks at his watch. Stella turns to the old clock on the wall — 4:05. Yes, Jeff will be off shift by now and on his way home.

"911 EMERGENCY."

"Yes. Hi, there's some sort of fight going on outside my house. Looks like someone might be getting jumped."

"I'm sorry I can't hear you, ma'am. Did you say an assault? Outside your residence?"

"Yes, yes. Shhhh, Adam, shhhhh, my boy."

"And where is your residence, ma'am?"

"Magnus. 1243 Magnus. On the west side of McPhillips. Just passed that Break thingie, area."

She hears the operator sigh. "All right ma'am, is the assault still taking place?"

"Yes, I think so, or wait, I think... They're running away."

"Okay ma'am..."

"Oh no! Oh my god. Shhh, Adam, it's okay."

"Ma'am? What direction are they running?"

"McPhillips. They're running that way. But someone's hurt! It's a girl, a woman, I think. Oh my god!"

"Ma'am, I will dispatch someone right away. Ma'am?"

"Oh god oh god oh god, she's not getting up. Her legs... she's not...moving."

"Ma'am?"

"Oh god, oh my god."

"Ma'am, I can't hear you with the baby crying. I will dispatch someone right away."

"Oh my god."

"Please stay where you are, ma'am? Ma'am?"

"But she's not moving."

SCOTT TRIES AGAIN. "And then when you went to the door and watched her, the victim, get up?"

"Yeah," she chokes out, nods.

"And you didn't go out there? Or talk to the person?"

Stella shakes her head and looks down at her hands again. She can't stand how these officers look at her.

He tries again. "Did you see anything distinguishing on the attackers? Any clothing logos or something?"

Stella tries to swallow her anger and tears, her shame, and look at this officer. His skin is so young he still has a couple of pimples. He has dark freckles across his nose. Stella has always liked freckles like that, skin sprinkled with brown.

"No just, umm." Stella pauses, thinks. "Dark, baggy clothes, bomber jackets, I guess. One of them had a long black braid. The others were wearing hoods, black ones. Big dark jackets." These are all things she said already. She thinks they might be trying to trip her up, like she's lying about something.

Scott sits back. Christie just sips his coffee again, nearly says, *"Ahh,"* he does it so loud.

"If you remember anything else, Mrs. McGregor, even if you think it's not important..."

Stella shakes not just her head but her whole body. She doesn't want to think about it but can't think of anything else. It runs over and over in her head, a visual echo, the images blending together. The details are getting fuzzy already, blurry black bodies on the white snow. The muffled night outside, the baby crying, crying, crying. Stella's hushing voice, shh, baby, shh, but she's watching bodies hunched over something, what is it? What is it? Then they all jump up, suddenly, and they run away. No, not all of them. There's one. Only one. Lying there, so still, not moving, something, no someone dark and small in the snow.

"Stell? Stell?" Jeff yells as he pushes through the back door. Stella startles and goes to him before he gets louder.

"Hey." She sees his worried face. She grabs on to each side of his open parka and pulls him to her. She doesn't know where to start.

"Where are the kids?" he asks, his voice short and scared.

"Your children are fine, Mr. McGregor," Scott calls from the table. "There's nothing to worry about."

Jeff pushes Stella away gently and looks into her face. She nods and falls back against him, crying all over again. The inside of his jacket is so warm. His arms are strong around her, and for a second, they make her feel better.

"There was an incident just outside your property, Mr. McGregor," the young officer continues. "Your wife witnessed some sort of an assault."

"Assault?" Jeff asks. He takes Stella's hand and they sit at the table. She doesn't want to let go. The officers don't introduce themselves, but only speak in curt, official-sounding sentences. Jeff nods as they explain. Stella feels cold again.

"Your *wife* believes it was a *rape* of some sort." The young officer says the words as if they are questions. Wife? Rape?

"No, it was a rape. Someone *was* raped." She turns to Jeff. "It was a woman, a small, skinny woman."

Jeff only nods at her and squeezes her hand. He thinks he's helping.

"Keep in mind, Mrs. McGregor," the older officer finally pipes in. "We've been doing this a long time, and it just doesn't look like a sexual assault. It seems, unlikely?" He says his words like questions too.

"Why? Why do you say that?" Stella stammers and tries to sound firm, but she doubts herself now. It was so dark, and she is so tired.

"Well, it's outside for one, in the winter. That's highly unusual. And there's a lot of blood which means someone was, well, bleeding."

"What if she was hurt? Beaten up? Can't you test the blood or something?" Stella is stammering now.

"I know you're upset, but let's think of the facts. There was a broken beer bottle at the scene." Christie pauses, sighs. "Drinking often means fighting. Blood also means fighting. Sexual assaults don't usually happen in the cold, outside in winter. It seems . . . unlikely. I know it was probably very hard to witness. It was probably very violent. It's common to . . . panic." Christie nods and takes one last sip of his coffee as if to say the conversation is over.

Stella's tears dry in her eyes, and a familiar rage fills her. She can't find the right words. They are none that would convince them anyway.

"Well, we don't know what happened, do we? None of us

know for sure," Jeff tries. Stella sits beside him, still clutching his hand. She can tell he is relieved. She can tell he thinks everything's okay now.

Since it happened, all she wanted was for him to be here, to comfort her. Now that he's here, she doesn't feel better. She feels stunned, and he just squeezes her hand. Not helping. She wants to let go but can only loosen her grip, let her hand go limp inside his. He doesn't even notice. She looks out the window. The snow's falling harder now.

What she really wants to do is call her Kookom. She thinks of her, her beautiful grandmother undoubtedly sleeping now in her mouldy but warm basement apartment, just over on Church. Stella wants to go lie there in her wrinkled arms and have her whisper that everything is okay, the way she always did. Stella always believed it, no matter what.

"We'll let you know if there are any developments." Christie gets up. "Likely, around here, it's just some gang violence. I wouldn't worry about it. Just lock up. Keep yourselves safe."

Jeff sees them to the door, but Stella stays sitting, seething and staring out at the snow. She hears them half laugh politely, the way white men say goodbye, and it only makes her more furious.

"Oh fuck, I was so worried, hon," Jeff says as he comes back to her. He wraps his arms around her, comforting, but only himself now. "When I saw the cop car out front. Christ, I have never been so scared."

Stella just sits there, lets him hold her.

"I know what I saw," she says after a moment, knowing she only sounds defiant now. Pathetic.

"I know, hon. I know. But maybe," he pauses, rethinks. "Who knows what the hell that was?"

"I do. I know," she says, and then lowers her voice so she won't wake the kids. "I know what I saw, Jeff."

"I know, I know. But, they're right, aren't they? It seems, unlikely."

"But..."

"They know what they're talking about, Stell. And I mean," he pauses again, really trying. He sits down beside her, looks her right in the eye. "You know, Stella, maybe you did, like, dream parts of it?" He's talking in questions now too. "You haven't been sleeping very well with all Adam's fussing and teething, right?"

Stella gets up, fuming. She grabs all the stupid coffee cups and takes them to the kitchen, throws them in the sink and starts scrubbing. She puts them in the drying rack and starts wiping the counter. Jeff just sits at the table, waiting for her to talk.

"I'm not crazy," she says finally.

"I don't think you're...No one said that. I just think, maybe." He yawns. She can tell he doesn't mean to but he does. It is so late it's early. She had waited hours for the police to come. Waited shaking, thinking they would come at any moment. She was unable to stop cleaning or crying. She should have called her Kookom then. She would've been asleep, but she still would've answered. Or Aunty Cher, she would've been up. Aunty Cher would've listened. She probably would've come over, made the coffee, yelled at the cops when they started acting like they didn't believe her. But Stella didn't do any of that.

Jeff gets up, stands behind her at the sink and pulls her into his arms, forcing her into a hug. She waits until he's done so she can ring out the wet cloth.

"You were half asleep. And it's okay. It's okay. But with your past, hon, you know you could've just been dreaming. You could've just been confused."

She breaks away from him and goes to wipe the table.

"There's blood all over out there," she says over her shoulder as she storms out of the kitchen again. The wind picking up outside, knocking at the old window.

"No one says nothing happened," he sighs. "It just might be different than you think."

She doesn't say anything, just scrubs.

He stands there a moment, in the middle of the kitchen. She refuses to look up, just bends her head as she passes him, and shakes the rag out in the sink.

Defeated and tired, he goes to the bathroom and starts to get ready for bed.

Stella wipes the counter again, prepares the coffee so it's ready again in the real morning, and tidies the towels. Then she goes down to the basement and pulls the clean laundry out of the dryer and starts to fold.

By the time she gets into bed, the cold pre-dawn grey is coming up. Her whole body aches and her husband is fast asleep.

She thinks about her Kookom again and wants to call her. Her Kookom always gets up early. She would probably be up, making tea and looking out her window, "Watching day come," as she calls it. When was the last time Stella called her grandmother? It's been too long. The guilt washes over her. She chills the hot rage with more of her cold shame. But she doesn't call, she can't. She can only pull the covers up to her chin and lie there.

The grey light stretches out behind the blinds, but she doesn't do a thing. Not until she hears her daughter wake up. Then, ready, she springs back out of bed.

(2)

EMILY

EMILY HAS NEVER kissed a boy before.

There was this one time, in like grade five, when that Sam kid gave her a peck close to her lips but not on her actual lips. It shouldn't count, though — it was only a dare that happened after school with everyone gathered around. He had big, bucky-looking teeth and chapped lips. He pushed his lips out, but she turned a bit at the last second so his lips hit her cheek instead. All the kids yelled out like it was a big deal. It left a wet spot but it was nothing, really. Not like a kiss was supposed to be. Emily doesn't think it counts at all.

Her best friend Ziggy's never kissed a boy either, but she's different. Zig is tough and doesn't care, and thinks the guys at school are all morons. She's probably right, Emily thinks, but some of them, a few of them, are so, so cute.

Clayton Spence is the cutest of all of them.

Emily is thirteen. She feels ugly and fat most of the time and is positive no one has ever, ever liked her. She pretty much believes that she is repulsive and will never get a boyfriend and never get kissed for real.

She complains about it a lot to Ziggy, or at least Zig complains that she complains about it a lot. But Emily thinks it's time. Thirteen is time to have a boyfriend, or at the very least, a kiss.

This is what she is thinking about as she and Zig huddle over their binders, and brace themselves against the cold through Peanut Park, trying to get to Emily's new place as fast as possible. It is so cold they are nearly running. Emily forgot her gloves, again, and her jacket sleeves only cover so much. Her fingertips are red and numb only a block away from school. They are moving as fast as they can.

"Hey Emily," a voice, a male voice, calls from the old play structure.

Emily startles at the sound of her name. She looks at Ziggy who looks scared too, like she is about to run. But then Emily sees, so amazingly, it's him.

"Did I scare ya?" Clayton jumps down and walks up to them, his hair bouncing with his stride.

"No." Emily shrugs stupidly. Ziggy just looks at her like she's an idiot. Ziggy's glasses fog up in the cold.

"Don't lie. I totally did." Clayton laughs, but not mean. He walks right up and stands there in front of her. He smells like cigarettes, but not in a bad way. "Didn't mean to."

Emily thinks Clayton is the best-looking guy she's ever seen. She said so, when they voted. Ziggy picked Jared Padalecki from *Supernatural*. But Emily wanted to pick someone she actually kind of knew, someone she could see in person and find out what he smelled like. Clayton is older, had been held back a while ago, so he was fourteen at least, probably fifteen. He has a rough, brown shag of hair above his lip that looks so soft and shiny, and when he grins he shows all his teeth. Clayton doesn't smile, he grins, and he grins wide. He also has perfect pink lips. Emily's spent some time looking at him from a distance, but now that he's right here, she can't look at him directly. She does notice that he's tall, but not too tall. Emily is used to being taller than boys, but this is better. He's just the right height.

She shrugs again, unable to think of something to say that's not lame, so she just looks at his feet. His runners are untied, brand new, and bright clean white.

"Where ya heading?" He grins. Emily can feel it, his grin. She suddenly doesn't care that she's so cold her fingers might fall off, or that Mountain Avenue is still two blocks away. She shivers but doesn't want to move.

"Just home." She hugs her binder closer.

"Oh." He's still grinning, and somewhere someone laughs. "Hey! You wanna go to a party?" Someone laughs again, louder. It's a friend of Clayton's, but Emily doesn't know his name. Everyone knows Clayton.

"What?" She looks up all the way up at him, flinching.

"A party. You should come to this party." He seems to talk quickly. "Bring your friend." He nods to Ziggy, who only looks at him over her fogged-up glasses, no smile, nothing. Ziggy can be so embarrassing.

"K," Emily says, and then thinks. "Where?"

"On Selkirk," he says. "Got a pen?"

"Yeah sure." She opens her binder as quickly as she can, nearly dropping everything in the snow. It makes her heart stop just thinking of everything falling out, all her papers. She would've died. She manages to get out a pen, and hand it to him.

"Knew you'd have a pen." Grin again.

Emily's cheeks are hot all of a sudden, frostbite and embarrassment all together. It's a stupid, cold February and her face is probably bright red. She smiles back as best she can, and he gently pulls out her arm and holds it close to his body as he writes across her wrist, 1239. The ink doesn't come out right away so he goes back over the 1 again. Back and forth he gently rolls the tip on her skin. His fingers are so cold, but he holds her palm gently, lets go too soon.

She turns to go, feeling dumb, and turns back.

"Oh yeah, what day?"

"What day? Oh yeah, I guess any day," he laughs, "but you should go Friday. Yeah, come Friday and I'll be there."

His friend laughs again and calls out, "Come on, Clay. I'm freezing my balls off out here!"

"Friday, K?" He smiles sweetly at her, different than the grin this time. This one is nice. He is so good-looking and nice too. And he wants her to come to a party. "You'll come, right?"

Emily nods without thinking. She doesn't say yes, doesn't find her voice in time, but she knows right away that she isn't going to miss it. She isn't going to miss it for anything.

KISSES ARE SUPPOSED to be sweet. They're supposed to be gentle and full on the lips. Even wet, but just a little. They're supposed to make you excited and happy, make you forget everything and everyone. Everything becomes before and after that one moment, Emily thinks, and it's supposed to be perfect.

"There is no way Paulina is going to let you go!" Ziggy says too loudly when they get to Emily's empty, still full-of-boxes new house. Emily still can't believe it. She keeps running the scene over and over, trying to remember every little bit so it won't float away. "No way in hell."

She's right. Emily's mom will never let it happen.

"I could just say I'm sleeping over at your house," Emily suggests, her fingertips thawing and pinching but the rest of her still so warm. Clayton Spence.

"Pfft, then what are we going to tell Rita?" Ziggy says sitting on the floor and pulling her books out onto the coffee table.

"She'll be going out too. It's Friday," Emily says, feeling brave, looking out the window and thinking, thinking. This will be easy. "My mom won't check. She'll be too busy loving up Sniffer at the bar to care."

Ziggy looks at her sideways. Sniffer is Emily's nickname for Pete, the guy she and her mom just moved in with. Emily knows nothing about the guy other than he smells like gas from working on cars all day, so she calls him the Sniffer. Zig doesn't have any sympathy though. "Oh please, Paulina's not half as bad as when Rita gets a new man."

"At least your mom never moves you in with them. I mean, can't you smell it? It, like, reeks of gas like all the time, and I have to live here."

"At least he has a job. Remember Freddie? He slept on our couch for a month. He stunk too, but like BO and bad breath. I swear he never, like, even left the apartment."

"Yeah, he was gross." Emily takes out her books and then remembers Clayton again. It's like she forgets for just a second and then gets all excited again. Clayton.

"And he was always watching wrestling. I fucking hate wrestling." Ziggy sneers and looks off.

Emily wonders if her friend is jealous, if maybe Ziggy wanted to get invited out by a boy, too. Zig is totally cute and would be a babe if she just wore some makeup and got rid of her glasses. She always acts like she doesn't care but she probably does, at least a bit. Poor Zig.

"Wah, you don't like wahsling?" Emily makes a funny voice to make her best friend smile. They both laugh, at nothing really, forgetting everything, they laugh for a long time.

ONE TIME CLAYTON shared Emily's textbook in math. That was at the beginning of the year so he probably doesn't even remember it.

He forgot his book and put his hand up to tell Mr. Bell.

The teacher sighed like he was so put out.

"Can I just share yours?" He leaned over and grinned at Emily.

"S-sure?" Her voice kind of cracked out the word.

"Thanks," he said, leaning closer, looking at the page.

She couldn't say anything else. She didn't even dare to try to talk. She didn't even really breathe.

"Thanks," he said again, after he had written out all the numbers. His grin was so infectious Emily couldn't help but smile back, but she turned away quickly, sure that it was a dumb, too-happy smile.

Clayton stopped coming to class after that. Mr. Bell still said his name for a while but only for about a week. Then it was gone.

Emily missed the sound of his name and always remembered it came between Roberta Settee and Crystal Swan. And then her, Emily Traverse.

"OKAY, SO IF we're going to do this, we have to think of everything," Ziggy says, finally coming around. Their social studies
books open but not really looked at.

"It'll be okay, Zig," Emily says, trying to act cool, trying
to feel cool. "My mom wants to go out, I heard her talking to
my Aunty Lou about it. She won't check if she thinks I'm just
at your place, and your mom is going to my Kookoo's gallery
thing, right? It's all good."

"Still, I want to be back at like eleven, latest, or ten even
'cause it's all the way past McPhillips so it'll be a long walk.
We have to be so fucking careful! You never know with Reet,
she's like a ninja." Ziggy adjusts her glasses, and Emily thinks
again how good she'd look without them.

"You're such a chicken about your mom!" Emily laughs and
pushes Ziggy's arm.

"Like you're any better!" Zig pushes back but smiles too.
"You're only being brave 'cause you're so hot on *Clayton*." She
says his name like an exaggerated sigh.

"Shut up!" Em pushes her again.

"*Clayton!*" Ziggy falls to the floor. "Oh, *Clayton*."

Emily smacks at her and laughs. "I'm going to piledriver
you so bad."

"Like you even know what a piledriver is!" Ziggy laughs
and Emily sticks her elbow out and smacks it.

"*Clayton*," Ziggy cries as she rolls around on the floor. "Oh,
Clayton."

Emily laughs and play fights, badly.

She's so happy. She knows, she just knows, he's going to
kiss her.

PHOENIX

PHOENIX FALLS UP the snow-packed front stoop and jerks open the screen door. She knew it would be unlocked, but thought, in her last steps that it might not be, just this once. That would just be her luck, wouldn't it? But nah, it's open, so she can stumble in to the warmth. Thank fuck.

Her uncle's house smells like smokes, dope, and old food, but it's great to her. And warm. Phoenix takes her hands out of her jacket sleeves, and rubs them together, blowing on them to help get the feeling back. They're raw and red, but she keeps rubbing at them anyway.

Some skinny girl is passed out on the couch, and another is on the armchair. They look like they fell over in the middle of talking and no one bothered to move them or cover them up. One of them snores lightly, her face against her bare arm, drool dripping over an awful rose tattoo and track marks. Fuck. Phoenix can smell the booze from here, that ugly day-after stench. They look pretty rough, even passed out. Most people look so peaceful when they're sleeping, but these girls just look a little less used up.

No one else is in sight. The house feels asleep. Phoenix hears music coming quietly from her uncle's room so she knows he's there. He can't sleep without music playing, usually old school rock stuff, Aerosmith and AC/DC. Classics, he'll say with a smack across the head if anyone ever tries to say no one listens to that shit anymore. Phoenix has always liked the music. It reminds her of him, of back when she was small and he was a good kid, before all these other people started hanging around him and he had to get hard.

She's so fucking glad to be here.

She limps to the disgusting kitchen on her throbbing feet, stumbles into the first upright chair there, and dumps her bag down. Her ears burn. Her face thaws with pinches across her wide cheeks. She pulls off her worn runners and rubs her toes. Her feet have that sting like when they fall asleep and are waking back up. They lost feeling hours ago and became clubs on the end of her legs. She trudged like that through the whole North End for hours. She puts her feet up on another chair. They ache and twitch, and she tries not to move them.

The table is full of takeout bags, overflowing ashtrays, bottles, and empty two-four boxes. She digs through the used cigarettes and finds a long butt. There are five lighters spread out but only one works. She inhales quickly. Her head rages and then goes light. It's been so long since she had a good smoke. She leans back, takes a look at her surroundings, and tries to think warm thoughts.

The place is a total dump. The counter is all garbage and broken glasses still sticky with booze. A dark puddle hardens on the broken linoleum, and something rots on the stove. That's what she'll do, she thinks, she'll clean it all up before her uncle gets up. He likes when she does girl things like that.

She's been feeling nice like this lately. Must be all the time alone, she thinks. The Centre was so quiet most of the time. The only other kids there were freaks or fucking suicidal fucks. They don't put many 'hood rats like her in there. Most of the guys she knows go to youth lock-up. She's been there, it's rougher, but everything's easier in the girl sections. There, the most some bitch'll do is try to slap you around, or fucking scratch you. Phoenix is a big girl. She's never had a hard time getting one over and can usually just grab their wrists and pin them. She punches with a closed fist. It's easy. It's the guys who are strong and have to really fight, have to worry about getting cut and jumped and shit. Girls, they just fuck with your mind or flay out at you like they're crazy and can kill you with useless fucking slaps. The Centre was like a kiddie pool compared to lock-up, just a bunch of messed-up kids with too much time on their hands, all depressed and shit. Phoenix has never been that pathetic, not really.

She's been thinking about her uncle though, about how much she admires him. "Think of someone you admire," the counsellor had told the group in one of their hand-holding bullshit therapy things. She thought of him, Alex is his name, Alexander, like his dad, but no one calls him that now. Most people don't even know that's his name, but Phoenix knows because they're family. She always calls him Bishop in front of people, but in her head, he's still Alex.

She also thinks of Clayton, but *admire* isn't quite the right word for how she feels about him.

When her feet feel almost normal, still beating like hearts but not asleep anymore, she walks over to the fridge to see what's inside. Despite all the takeout boxes, there isn't even a dried-out piece of pizza left. She finds an old box of Chinese noodles in the cupboard, and then a pot she can clean out to boil water. While it heats, she fills old bags with all the garbage, and finds an old not-too-gross towel and wipes down the counter. She picks a couple more long butts out of the ashtrays and then cleans those too. By the time she sits down to eat her noodles, the table is clean. She eats them plain, not wanting to add the gross shrimp powder flavour. It's the best thing she's eaten in months.

One of the girls in the living room stretches and groans, and someone moves in her uncle's room. She hears someone talking. He's not alone. The light shifts outside the window and gets darker. It's late afternoon, Phoenix had been out there, walking in the cold, all day.

SHE LEFT THE Centre before anyone was up. It was the best time to take off. They call the guards "mentors" but they're still fucking guards, and they change shifts at 6 a.m., before anyone is awake. That's when they check beds and after that, there's another hour or so before other workers start coming in. Phoenix figured this out early on in her time there, knew it would be the best time to go. Friday was be the best day because it was usually Henry's shift. Henry was a lazy old fuck who really didn't give a shit. He'd be passed out in the rec by 6:30. It was a good plan. She packed her bag the night before and kept her clothes on. When they bed-checked her, she had the covers all the way up to her chin and looked asleep. Then she waited, listening at her door for the "mentor" to stop talking about all the useless things that had happened the night before and finally fucking leave. She imagined Henry, nodding like he didn't give a fuck and just wanting to go back to sleep. He did, and was snoring by quarter to seven, and Phoenix slipped out the front door like it was any other day and she was any other person. They didn't lock the doors 'cause they liked to pretend they trusted the kids. The door beeped and the pager on Henry's hip vibrated, but he was fast asleep, and no one else was close enough to notice, even if they did give a shit.

It was a good plan.

But outside it was February, and she had no phone, no money and was somewhere in the goddamn far fucking edge of south St. Vital. She tried to remember which way to go, but she also wanted to stay off the main streets in case they found out too soon she was gone. She wandered through winding streets all morning. They all curved and twisted like they were trying to confuse you. All the white yuppies got out of their fancy houses and into their cars, and glared a little too long at her in her thin army jacket, but didn't ask her anything or stop. She made a lot of turns, just in case someone called the cops, who would, in this neighbourhood, come pretty quickly, she'd bet.

She found St. Mary's Road eventually and went into the mall to warm up. Her eyes dripped and her ears felt like they were going to fall off. She ripped off a toque from the dollar store but should've grabbed something to eat or collect-called her uncle to come get her. Should've, maybe, but she wanted to do it herself and just show up at his house like magic, like she'd pulled it off with class. She wanted him to be impressed, to clap her hand and pull her close like any other of his hard-assed friends, like his equal. She wanted him to come out of his room and be surprised, happy surprised, to see her. So she kept going, through downtown, down hard-up Main Street, and all the way up Selkirk to the other side of McPhillips. Across the whole fucking city. She was proud of herself, but fucking sore.

SHE HEARS HER uncle get up and talk loudly in his room, telling someone to get the fuck up. Phoenix lights another butt, straightens her smile, and leans back in her chair, ready to see him and his impressed face.

"Phoenix, what the fuck?" he says, walking in the kitchen, his bathrobe tied up tight, one dark hickey on his neck, and sleep still on his face. It has only been a few months since she's seen him, but he looks older and greyer in his face, like he's been smoking too much. He sits across from her and pulls out a smoke from a pack in his bathrobe pocket. He's only about ten years older than her, but his hair is already falling out, his forehead longer than it was the last time she saw him. His skinny face looks older than the twenty-six it is supposed to be. He looks like a picture she has of their great grandpa. Grandpa Mac, Elsie called him. He died way before Phoenix was born but she feels like she knew him. Grandmère had so many pictures and stories. He was so handsome and funny, she said. Phoenix thinks he must've been just like this, like his grandson — Bishop. Alex.

"You can't stay here, fuck. Your worker was already calling around freaking the fuck out."

"Why the fuck was she calling?" Phoenix says. "Fucking nosy bitch."

"Because you walked out of juvy, ya fuck. If she comes here . . ." He points his smoke and a yellowed finger at her.

Phoenix nods at him, wants to smile but doesn't. She puts out her butt, grabs another.

"Ah fuck, Phoen, that's some cheap-assed gross shit. Here." He tosses his pack to her.

She grabs it, and her smile sneaks out. She lights up and takes a long, clean drag.

"How'd you get here?" He leans forward. His face has more

wrinkles. He worries a lot, has so many things he's in charge of now.

"I walked," she says, steadying her voice the best she can but pretty fucking proud of herself.

"All that fucking way? Holy shit!" He laughs.

Phoenix almost smiles again, but stops, says, "Yeah" like it was nothing, and takes another long drag. Then she thinks and says, "Who was that bitch calling?"

"She called Ang, at my old number," he spits.

"What the fuck did she say?" Phoenix spits back, shoulders up as if she's ready to fight her uncle's ex right there, if she has to.

"Ang didn't say shit, but fuck." He shakes his head. "You can't stay here. I got too much shit going on, Phoen. Can't have any extra heat right now."

She nods, knowing Angie, his baby mama, won't say anything. He trusts her. He still loves her really. Phoenix knows this. She knows he really loves Angie, but she rides him too hard when they live together, and he's got shit to do. But he pays for her apartment down on Machray, and he buys his daughter the best of everything, name brands on all her clothes. That's love, thinks Phoenix. Then she remembers why she came and thinks of what she should do. She could maybe stay with Roberta or Dez.

"Got any other place to go?" her uncle says, reading her mind.

"Yeah, I'm good." She nods and fixes her face like she does when she thinks it's going soft.

"K, good," he says, smacking the table. "I gotta jump in the shower." He gets up like he's dismissing her.

"You got a phone I can use?" she asks.

He throws her a burner without another word. He doesn't notice she cleaned up.

PHOENIX GOES DOWN into the basement to dump her stuff and see if she can find any clothes to change into. It's an old cellar with stone walls and cold puddles on the floor. Her uncle runs a dehumidifier in the corner so that the damp doesn't wreck all the shit he stores here.

Phoenix drops her stuff in a corner behind a couple of boxed TVs big enough to hide her. She can't find any clothes, though — only electronics and a bunch of unmarked plastic bins. She gives up on finding anything she needs.

"When did you feel most safe?" the mentor had asked the group yesterday. Grace, that was her name. Tall, thin, and beautiful, Grace was everything Phoenix wasn't. And rich. Grace had this shiny watch, the kind Phoenix had only seen on TV. If she was a real thief, she would have grabbed it, but she's clumsy as fuck. So, while all the kids were whining on, she thought of all the ways she could grab that fucking watch. Grace only worked during the day and would never get caught sleeping like some other "mentors." The watch seemed latched pretty good. Phoenix watched as Grace moved her hands around. Hugging kids and telling them it was all right and everything was okay. Fuck. Stealing it would be fucking impossible, she thought finally.

"When did you feel most safe?" Grace asked, looking right at her. The whole room too, every eye, on her.

Phoenix was too mad to think of anything. She just stared at the beautiful, fucking skinny woman, and sat there with her shoulders hunched like she could push out of there if she needed to. She didn't say anything, just looked at Grace. Even rich, beautiful Grace knew enough to move on.

The stuff in her bag is still cold even after being inside awhile. Phoenix sets the bag on a box and pulls out a shirt that's almost clean enough to shake out and put on. She doesn't look down at her gross, fat body as she does it, just slides off her jacket and slips off one shirt and puts on the other. This one has a bit more room in it. The fucking Centre kept making her eat three meals every day. She got so fucking fat. She keeps everything else on. These baggy pants are the best ones she has, even if they reek. She looks down at herself and tries to smooth out her clothes. She feels huge but better.

She had only a few clothes to bring along anyway. That and a few old pictures is all she had to grab. She doesn't look at the pictures, but feels around to make sure she has them before stashing the bag behind the bigger box. A couple old tarps and a rag blanket lie wet on the floor, and, thinking ahead, she pulls them over the boxes to dry them all out. She might have to sleep here after all.

It's a good enough plan.

Upstairs, her uncle has left his smokes on the table. Phoenix smiles because, when no one is looking, he's actually a really good guy. When they were growing up, he was such a good kid, so good to her. He would take her bike riding in St. John's Park, would sit her on his handlebars and ride carefully, holding on to her sides and the handles because she was small and really clumsy. Back then, before her littlest sister Sparrow was even born, when he was still Alex, they had all lived together in the brown house across the river with old Grandmère and Alex's parents, and Cedar-Sage, her other sister, who was just a little kid and always happy. Even her mom, Elsie, was around most of the time. It hurt Phoenix's bum to sit on the handlebars like that, especially when they rode over the old wooden boards of the bridge, uneven and full of bumps, but she never said a word, just held on, and Alex held on to her, too.

PHOENIX DIALS ROBERTA'S house first but the phone's not in service. She tries Dez's phone next, and of course, Dez answers on the second ring.

"Dez, fuck, how you doing?" she says with a hard laugh and takes another drag.

"Phoen?"

She can hear someone in the background, a laugh somewhere behind.

"Yeah, it's me. How the fuck you doing?" She butts out her smoke and feels suddenly nervous. It's been six months since she's seen her girls. She still calls them when she can, but she lost her Internet privileges her first month in. She's been pretty out of it, really. "What's going on?"

"Nothing, just hangin'." Dez sounds weird, distant. "What the fuck you doing? Whose phone is this?" Someone in the background says something Phoenix can't hear.

"Bishop's," she says, trying to sneer the words, sound tough. "Ship gave me a burner."

"Are you out then?" Dez has never been one for thinking or class. The person in the background says something again, sounds like a girl.

"Yeah." Phoenix sneers better this time. "That Robbie?"

"Yeah, and Cheyenne. You staying there then?" She still sounds weird, maybe just straight.

"Maybe. Don't know yet." Phoenix thinks. "Come over. I need some weed." She says it like the command it is.

"Sure." Dez rolls over the word and stops asking questions. Finally.

"Hey, you seen Clayton lately?" Phoenix says each word like it doesn't mean a thing.

"Yeah, like every day. Why?" Dez's voice is light.

"Just wondering. You should invite him over too." Phoenix

looks down at her gross body and sucks in her gut even though no one is looking.

"He'll probably be over there anyway. Usually is."

"Why'd he be over here?"

"Oh. He's been selling weed for Ship." Dez said like it was nothing. Like Phoenix should know.

But no one had told her that. It stings a bit, knowing no one told her. She hasn't been able to get a hold of Clayton for a couple months so it might be real new. She hears her uncle get out of the shower and thinks she'll ask him later. He never talks about his business, but he might let her know what's what.

"K cool," she says to Dez. "Hey, can you bring me some clothes? I got like nothing to wear. Like a hoodie or something, I'm freezing over here." The girls in the background keep talking. Phoenix wishes she knew what the fuck they were saying. She tries not to get too mad, though. Not right now anyway. Instead, she straightens her spine and takes a deep breath, just like the fucking "mentors" always said to. Fuck. Maybe her uncle will let her sell a bit too, and she can make some money. Her uncle will probably say no because he's trying to look out for her, like he's always done.

"Sure," Dez says slowly, still not sure. "I can find something."

"Cool. Thanks." Phoenix nods, even though no one can see her. "See you in a bit." Her voice is strong again, and she knows they won't be too long. Dez will bring her clothes and do her makeup, like she does. And then, by the time Clayton gets here, she'll look like any other girl, ready to party, ready for him.

Yes, she thinks, it's a good plan.

(4)

LOU

GABE LEFT LAST night, like he said he would. Like I knew he would, eventually.

It all felt so anti-climactic.

"Lou, babe, I'm just going to go back home for a bit then," he said as he pulled his clothes into his backpack. Like it was any other night and he was just going for a visit. Maybe it was. "I can, uh, catch a ride with Lester, but he wants to go tonight. He says it's going to snow tomorrow, so we, um, gotta get going. Like now."

"Okay," is all I said. I sat down because I was suddenly dizzy.

He turned at the door and said, like an afterthought, "And I love you, hey?"

Then knocked on the doorframe for some reason. The sound of it seemed to echo in our room. My room now, I guessed.

I looked up but could only nod in reply.

"I'll call you later? Like tomorrow?" It was a question he didn't know the answer to. He didn't know the new rules any more than I did.

"Okay, good. Baby boy'll wanna talk to you. Let me know you got up there okay." I said this looking at the dresser. His stuff no longer messed up the top. He took it all.

"Okay. For sure."

I knew his for sures didn't mean what they were supposed to mean, but I was done fighting about them. "Safe drive," was all I said.

I heard him talk to the boys out in the living room.

"Okay, guys, I gotta take off," he said, like it was any other goodbye and no big deal. Maybe it was.

Maybe I only want to think we're broken up for good. Forever.

I listened to him leave but just sat there on the bed. My bed. That somehow felt more empty, too. I sat there trying to feel it. The emptiness. The cold space where Gabe used to be. They say the air gets like that, cold, when ghosts pass through.

Maybe it was the same as every other time. Maybe he'll just be back one day soon like he always comes back, eventually, and I am just imagining it to be more than it is. Maybe. Or maybe he's gone forever, like I always thought he would be. Sick of me and all my bullshit. Sick of my never giving him what he wants. I don't blame him. I'm pretty sick of me too.

MY WORKDAY WEARS on, but I can't concentrate. Instead, Friday afternoon stretches out in front of me—my files are not updated, and calls are not returned. Instead, I just watch the pink sky out my office window. Lester was right, it is going to snow. The clouds seem to swell and give everything a long, dark shadow. Downtown blurs.

I look at my files, all the poor, young children already with epic stories, their mothers mean or sad. The empty space where their fathers are supposed to be. Everything blurs. I can't seem to be a social worker right now, I think. I can only be a left woman.

I am trying to feel it. Like if I can just feel it then I can describe it, give it a name and a label and then deal with it. Hurt, angry, sad, betrayed, unworthy. I am trying to fight back the tears because I don't want to cry here, not at work where I am supposed to be hard and unemotional, but I can't. I look up to the pictures pinned to my corkboard—my two boys, my family, my man—they all blur too.

GABE HILL BLEW into my life riding high on a wave of good looking and good smelling. His dimples were so big I nearly fell into them.

He was perfect.

We were backstage at some event. Rita's ex had got us tickets, and my sister Paul and I dressed up. We all knew who Gabe was. Everybody knew who Gabe was. He wore a button-up black shirt, pressed clean, and stood wide legged like a guitarist even when he wasn't playing a guitar. We were all looking at him too long, but none of us had the nerve to go up and talk to him.

I remember going up to the bar to get a beer. Walking back, I took a sip and looked up, and there he was right in front of me. He smiled sweetly, sweet and perfect, at me. I just tried to wipe my chin discreetly, hoping he didn't see the drip or drool.

I still love that first sip of Lab Lite. Even the smell of it makes me remember that.

He was the only sober man in the room. He didn't drink, he said, didn't smoke either. It didn't take much after that to convince me. Some men just have a way of looking at you.

Gabe was like that, paid attention to me all night, actually listened. It completely unnerved me.

When I first met him, I didn't know he did that to everybody. I thought I was special.

I WALK OVER to sit at Rita's desk. I want to dive into my self-indulgent self-pity and talk about my problems. Rita is my mom's best friend, and I've known her since I was a little kid. She got me this job after I finished school, and we've gotten close, too. It's the nature of the work, really. She listens to me, her face thoughtful, her body a perfectly practiced social worker pose, and when I'm done, she peers at me over the rims of her glasses and cuts right to it.

"So you think he's gone up there to poonch this woman?"

"He denies it." I shrug.

"Well, of course he denies it. What's he gonna say, like, 'Uh yeah babe, I'm, uh, poonching some chick on the rez, uh, duh, yeah.'" She laughs one of her head-back, full-body Rita laughs. She's not this way with clients—with clients she just does the listening part, and keeps her cuts to the quick to herself.

I can only smirk back. I can't laugh like she wants me to. She keeps smiling, trying to get me to smile too, but I can't. I don't even know what to say anymore. It just goes round and round. I'm mad. Yes, mad. That's the word.

Another woman, I think. Another one.

No, I'm hurt.

"They always deny it, Lou!" Rita's voice is always a bit too loud, but loving, in her rough way. She is like this about everything. She is matter of fact, black and white, done and done. It makes her very efficient.

I try to be like her, but I'm so not. I see all sides and every angle. I need to see everything, feel everything, before I can make a decision, any decision. Rita has no need for this. She is as ruthless as I am wishy-washy. She's got balls where I got only complicated girlie grey feelings about everything.

Especially about Gabe.

I perch at her desk with my head hung low.

"Well, what's his excuse for going up there all the time then?" She sways from side to side in her chair. My life is just another problem for her to methodically analyze, looking for the weak spots and points to investigate.

"I don't know. His aunt and uncle don't want to leave their house and need a lot of help. The house is falling apart. It's his home, he wants to be there."

"Sounds plausible." She nods, a practiced nod.

"But he never cared before. He only cares now." I shrug.

"True." She looks off, thinking. "He's been down here or on the road for a long time."

Rita's more suspicious than me. She lives on suspicions. She told me once her ex, Dan, was always making his way around, so she considers herself an expert. She told me this with a big hearty Rita laugh.

"Well, it kinda makes sense, in a way," I say. "His cousins are all up there now, and Lester got on council, so there's always a ride up. It's like he never got a chance to be home this much since he was a kid. And, everyone loves him up there. They treat him like he's a real celebrity."

"Pfft celebrity. His song just got some play on country radio." She laughs.

"Everybody listens to country up there, Reet!" I sigh. I pick at the papers on her desk, but I'm not focusing on anything. "It must make him feel good to be appreciated like that." I don't appreciate him, I think, but don't say.

"Oh yeah," she says. "A good looking guy with a guitar AND a song on the radio. Meat to the wolves!" She makes a pouncing motion with her hands and laughs again, even louder. I don't ask her who the wolves are in this scenario.

Her husband Dan cheated on her with one of their friends. She lived on reserve then and the whole community buzzed with rumours, including that the woman's five-year-old was really his. He denied it, but Rita still moved to the city and stopped being "so fucking traditional," as she said, and started smoking and drinking again. She said she'd only really stopped for him in the first place, and she had been dying for a drink for "ten fucking years."

I can barely smile at her. I want to stay mad. Mad feels powerful. But I can feel the tears coming again. So stupid.

"Aw, hon." She rubs my knee. "You're really broken up about this, aren't you?"

I can only nod. Rita hands me a tissue and keeps rubbing my knee.

When Rita moved back to the city, my mom got her an apartment in her and Kookom's building, and was over there every day. She told me Rita took it "real hard" but also swore me to secrecy. Rita only looked tough whenever anyone else was around.

"So, do you know this woman he's poonching?"

"Stop saying poonching!"

She laughs again. It's nearly infectious.

"Do you know who it is?"

"I think so."

"What's her name?"

"Melody."

"Melody? Pfft, stupid fucking name!" she says and laughs hard.

He probably thinks it's a nice name, like a song he can play.

THE NIGHT I met Gabe, we talked in a bubble of just him and me for hours. When I got up to leave, he gave me this great big hug. I loved the feel of him. He was the perfect shape and took up just the right amount of space. I loved the way I just sunk into him. We stood there like we were dancing, and for that long minute, we were.

It was nice out so Paul and I walked home. Well, she describes it like I stumbled home beside her. She said it was like I was pissed drunk and had this stupid grin on my face.

My whole body ached for him. Gabe. His name rolled over and over in my head, through my whole body as I walked all excited. Well, she walked. I floated.

"Gabe Fucking Hill!" I laughed, that night so warm and long ago.

"I like his song." She smiled and started singing it. I joined in too, off key but with everything I had. Not caring who heard.

The rest of it happened quickly.

He called me the next day. The very next day. In the morning even. He came over that night for a coffee. He was so polite and so attentive to Jake, who was nine at the time and around women so much any man was his hero, especially this cool, tall guy who brought a guitar and played him old country songs. I watched Gabe, in my house, this beautiful man, paying his kind attention to my lonely son. I wanted him around not just for me, but also for my boy, whose dad was long gone and not worth chasing after. All I knew for sure was that he was a great guitarist, could sing with a perfect country drawl, and had a hit song. He said he wanted to help people and be a good role model. It didn't seem like he was trying to impress me.

He slept over that night. He never really moved in. He just stayed. For five years.

UNLIKE ME, MY sister Paul has never been so happy, and if I'm honest, it's really pissing me off.

"He's so *nice*," she told me again last weekend as we wrapped her dishes in newspaper. "Like truly *nice*. To everyone."

I stacked the plates in the small box, one after the other, and didn't say anything.

"He's still so nervous around Em. He has no idea what to do with a thirteen-year-old girl. I think she scares the hell out of him."

"When he really should be scared like hell of me!" I scoffed. I was joking, but only a little bit.

"Oh he is. Don't worry." She went on: "He has such a big family, Lou. Like big big—six kids. His parents still live in the house they all grew up in out in the bush just outside his reserve. The bush! He spent his whole life there. He hunts and everything."

She beamed, repeating things she had told me a million times before. I smiled at her and thought of the picture: a real house in a real community with a real family. Real Indians! Not city half-breeds like us. I could see what Paul loved about this. I remembered loving that about Gabe—his big family, his real place. I loved going to visit everyone back home. Paul and I had it so different, our city childhoods and little family, so small and wrecked. We had a couple winters at our dad's place in the bush, but it was always lonely and too quiet.

"You don't think I'm going too fast?" Paul's voice cracked. Unsure.

I looked up, saw her face full of vulnerability and doubt. "How would I know?" was all I said, looking away. "Gabe moved in in a day."

"And look how that's turning out." I could tell she didn't mean to say it.

It was a good point, but I only shrugged. I knew she wanted words of support, words of conviction that would give her confidence and relief. Like the kind she always had for me.

I didn't have them.

But I kept packing for her.

AS I AM getting my things to go out on one last call before I'm off work, my Kookom calls.

"So how are you today, then?" She asks like she doesn't already know. The old lady has a way of knowing how I feel just by the tone of my hello.

"I'm OK, Kookoo," I say, gathering my things. "How are you doing?"

"Oh, you know," she sighs. "Still old. Are you coming for supper tomorrow, then?" This is how my grandmother asks for things. She's never mentioned supper tomorrow before.

"Sure," I say. "What do you want?"

"I would really like some fried chicken. I haven't had fried chicken since I don't know when." I can tell she's been thinking about this all day.

"Okay, we'll come by tomorrow then." I arrange the papers on my desk and pin one to my bulletin board, covering Gabe's picture.

"Good, is Gabe coming too, then? I need his help moving some things." This is her way of being nosy.

"No. Gabe had to go back home for a bit." This is all I am going to tell her. I don't have to tell her the rest. Not yet. And not if he comes home again. "Me and Jake can help you. What do you need to move?"

"Oh." The sound lingers, knowingly. "Oh, just some old

stuff down to the storage. It's not much." This is her trying to make me feel useful, able, occupied.

"We'll figure it out, my Kookom. Don't worry."

"Oh I know," she tells me. "Tell Paulina and Emily too, if they're not too busy to visit me. I haven't seen any those girls in so long." It has been about two days.

"Okay I will. I gotta go though. I'll call you later, K?"

"Okay, my girl. I love you." This is her way of telling me she knows more than I am telling her.

"Love you too." I hang up quickly, before my voice betrays me anymore.

RITA AND I make our way through the snow-covered city as the light dims and more snow falls into the white. We slip through all the way to the northwest corner, to see Luzia, one of my favourite foster mothers. She greets us with smiles and coffee. She looks at me like my Kookom does. Knowing.

Old women know.

"So whatcha gonna do then?" Rita asks as we drive back. She's not being nosy, not really.

I'm huddled into the passenger seat, and my face all cried out. I feel numb again. "I don't know."

"It's a hard one." She sighs and never takes her eyes off the road.

I nod even though she's not looking and gaze out the window as we come out of the underpass on Main. It's dark already. Somehow it's always dark in winter. The neighbourhood passes by—people stumbling out of bars too early, a girl with a stroller trying to jaywalk across the snow-covered meridian. I see it without feeling it at all. "I think I'm done. Like really, really done." My voice sounds so weak.

"I think you are too," she says quietly. "I know how that feels, my girl. I'm sorry."

We drive on in quiet, surrounded by muffled streets. I wish for something else to talk about, to think about, but can't think of a thing.

"You should come out with me," she says, banging her hand on the steering wheel. "It's Friday, you know. People go out on Fridays."

"Yeah?" I say, and think. "Where do you want to go?"

"Let's go to your mom's gallery thing. Get drunk. Have fun. Shake it off."

"Who will watch my kid though?"

"Ask Paul to keep him, or is she too loved up to babysit for too long? Or Jake? What else are teenagers for? I'll send Sunny over to keep him company. Hell, when I was his age I was watching all the kids and their cousins too."

I shrug, thinking of all the simple steps.

It never feels that simple, but it is.

I could just go out, get drunk, be a person. I could shake it off and have fun. Could.

What's the worst that could happen?

(5)

CHERYL

CHERYL WAKES UP smelling the snow. February is blowing into her small, messy bedroom as cars honk on Main Street a block away. She sort of remembers opening the window sometime late when she finally stumbled to bed. Sort of remembers wanting the wind to blow in and remind her of something she was craving. Something she can't remember in her sober morning, but can guess.

She rolls over and aches her way out of bed. Her head throbs from the rye, her dehydrated ankles scream arthritis, and every part of her needs to be warm. In the kitchen, she runs her hands under the water until it is hot and soothing, and then pops a couple painkillers. Her small body feels all bones as she leans against the counter, head down, cigarette lungs coughing up the night before in between sips of water. It doesn't take too long to feel better or at least ready to start her day.

There was a time she thought she'd have it all together by her age, that she'd have a retirement plan, would be making art and slowly fading away with a satisfied smile. But her fifties feel exactly like her forties — everything just hurts more.

She limps around her apartment trying to warm up her aged ankles, running her bent hands through her short hair. Her Kookoo hair, her girls call it because everyone seems to cut their hair when they're old. This is her ritual, walking around the morning, trying to piece the night together. An empty mickey lies on her coffee table next to an empty, sticky glass, pencils of various lengths and density, and eraser shavings sprinkled across it all like tiny grey worms. The uncooperative canvas is tilted on the floor, pushed away in disgust and tired grief.

She is trying to revive an old series of paintings. Wolf Women, she calls them, photographs embossed in acrylic paint, shape-shifter portraits. She started the series years ago, and that first set was all of her sister, Rain — all the faces and wolves she could have been. Now, Cheryl's trying to paint some of other strong women she knows. She has done one for each of her girls, Louisa and Paulina, both small, beautiful wolves, each looking just like their mother but in a different way.

Sometime in the rye last night, she started a new painting of her sister. She looked at every photo she had, but none seemed right. She finally settled on a really old one, from about '74 when Cheryl first met her ex, Joe. In the picture, Rain is barely sixteen and is sitting on Joe's old midnight blue Challenger. Taller and more shapely than her older sister, Rain wears a brown, beaded headband and fringe jacket, her long legs in bellbottom jeans and the red boots that Cheryl borrowed whenever Rain let her. Rain's full hair curled around her young face, which had not a line, not a worry. The sisters had the same soft mouth, but Rain was always more beautiful. Cheryl taped the photo on the canvas, right in the middle, and started sketching around it, but nothing felt right. She couldn't keep a stroke. And in the morning, it looked gross. The canvas was still blank around the girl on the car, only pencil etchings rubbed away, scratched lines denting the white and smudges looming like grey clouds. Her sister looked so alone.

Cheryl wishes she had a picture of her sister dancing. That's what she needs. Rain was never so alive as when she was moving. She loved swaying around. But somehow, in that whole life she had, no one had taken a picture of her dancing.

There is something about menopause, Cheryl thinks, everything seems to be coming around again. Old yearnings and memories come back, in dreams and in thoughts, all the time. She has spent hours in the night regurgitating random parts of her life, people long gone and choices long forgotten. Everything seems to be repeating, over and over. She drinks so she can sleep, or so she tells herself. But even in sleep, her ghosts all hunt her down, wanting her to look at them, remember them.

Last night, she dreamt of the birch trees, skinny and white against the snow, and the wolves howling on the horizon. She was snowshoeing, like she did when they lived out in the bush. Her city-girl legs loved every bit of it. She loved it so much that years later, and only in dreams, her legs still knew every tension, every turn. She could smell the snow, and the winter cold air.

When she lived in the bush, her sister Rain would visit. Together they would leave the girls with Joe to make forts and have snowball fights, and they'd go off for hours snowshoeing. They both took to it immediately. Joe taught them how to strap the shoes on tight, pound through with high knees, and hold the poles firmly. With mitten waves and scarf-covered faces, they were out among the birches and the wind. Cheryl loved the way the shoes made her bounce over the snow — she sank in, but not all the way. After she'd had her girls, she'd felt so heavy, like her little body was full of stones, graceless and clumsy. But when she put those shoes on, she could amble through the trees that stretched out on the north side of their little plywood-sided house. She thought she was the lightest she could ever be. She could put on her big feet and feel smaller. They wouldn't talk much, she and Rain, only breathe and look, and there wasn't another sound for miles, only the nets on their feet hitting the snow, and sometimes, the wolves far off across the trees. Cheryl loved it.

She loved the dream too. Every time she dreamt it.

And then she woke up cold and alone, with the window open. For a moment, she couldn't register where she was. This home she had had for years. For that moment, she only knew the empty ache beside her, the void where her sister was supposed to be.

WHEN CHERYL GETS to the gallery it's quiet and empty. She turns on the office lights but leaves the public space resting in its dark, comfortable dust. She looks out in to the large, shadowed space, paintings on the walls blurry in the shadows, corners creepy and underused. She loves every inch of it.

She makes coffee even though it's nearly night again. Her helpers will be in soon—they're young, so will probably be rolling out of bed and will need the caffeine. She looks at her to-do list, texts another reassurance to Lyn, and sits down at her desk, the big one at the back. She loves sitting here, the feel of it, the very weight. It faces out into the long, dusty gallery, now quiet and cloaked but, like her, waiting in the dark. She loves this job, her finally-got-here job. Not enough money, of course, but something to sink her teeth into after years of lackey contracts and raising kids. Here, she is in charge. Finally. She likes to savour these moments. Like a sweet flavour in her mouth or the magic smell of her grandchildren, she breathes it in in long breaths. She always does this when she is trying to make good things last as long as possible.

She loves these kinds of moments. The quiet ones before it all gets started. They never last long enough.

The artist on display tonight, Lyn, comes in fast with the winter on her coat and a bag full of pamphlets she printed at the last minute.

"It's snowing!" the young girl says, stating the obvious. She has a fresh bruise under her eye poorly covered up under layers of foundation and a line of silver glitter. "Does that mean people won't come?"

"They will always come." Cheryl takes the bag of pamphlets off Lyn's shoulder. "Stop worrying, it's going to be great."

Lyn only sighs. She is probably the most talented artist Cheryl has met in a long time, but she is too young and too nervous for anything to sink in fully. So, Cheryl offers her a beer and a cigarette. She remembers that feeling, that fear of what people will think of you and your art, your whole spirit up there, out there to be judged. That fear never really goes away. It can only get dulled somehow, or swallowed.

Soon the gallery is swept, every piece is checked, all the tables are set up, and Lyn's about as ready as she'll ever be, sipping another drink and chatting with friends. Cheryl shuts the office door and calls her mom to check in. Her mom's apartment is one floor below hers, and Cheryl had gone down there before she left, but she doesn't want her mom to get confused. Cheryl usually stops in around supper, once it gets dark, and her mom might worry if she doesn't.

"Can you get me some milk when you come home?"
Her mom clears her throat. Her voice creaks—she has been
sleeping.

"No, Ma, I'm not home 'til late today. It's Friday. I have that
thing, remember?" Cheryl keeps hearing herself telling her mom
to remember, even though the old woman obviously can't.

"Oh, yeah, I know. I know now." She never admits being
confused.

Cheryl knows she has no idea. "I have that opening at the
gallery. We're showing new paintings and having a little party.
That young girl you met, Lynden."

"Oh yeah, yeah." Her voice peaks and fades again. Cheryl
imagines her nodding into the phone. Cheryl finds herself
relieved every time her mother remembers something, or
pretends to. "Lorne's girl?"

"No, Ma, not Lorne's girl. She's an artist."

"Oh, oh." Cheryl can hear her mother thinking. "So, you're
not coming home then?"

"No, not 'til late. Louisa was going to stop in after work.
She should be there soon." Reminding.

"Oh yes, or no. No, I just talked to Louisa. She was going to
bring me fried chicken tomorrow. We're going to have supper
tomorrow."

"Okay. Well, she should go there soon, too."

"I don't need checking up on. I know you girls are busy."

"She wants to come, Ma. She'll get your milk so you can
have your tea in the morning."

"Fine, fine." She is gruff and tired.

"Did you eat?" Cheryl finds herself talking to her mom the
way she used to talk to her teenagers.

"Yes, of course I ate. I am not a child, you know." And her
mom talks back just like they did.

"Okay, okay. I'll come down once I'm up in the morning," Cheryl says, distracted again by the business around her. "Might sleep in a bit, but I'll come right down." To her mom, any time after 5 a.m. is sleeping in.

Her mother ignores her. "You know Gabe went back home again, eh?" she says, always one for gossip and for keeping Cheryl on the phone.

"He's just helping his family, Ma. I wouldn't worry." Cheryl knows what Rita and Louisa think but refuses to believe it. Gabe's a good man. She knows it.

"Mmmm," her mom says, like she's agreeing. "Where have I heard that before?"

"I gotta go, Ma. Sorry. It's a busy day." Cheryl knows her mom wants to say something about Joe, something about Cheryl's own aloneness, but she just can't go there, not today, not when she's still raw from her last night and has so much to do.

"Okay, okay, fine." But she says it like she wants to keep talking. "Have you talked to Stella, Cheryl?"

"No, Ma." Cheryl sighs and puts her hands over her eyes so she can better pay attention, give her mother the attention she needs when she mentions Rain's daughter. "I haven't heard from Stella in a while, Ma. I would tell you if I had. Have you?"

"Oh, okay, that's too bad." Her mother's voice goes far away again.

Lyn calls to her from in the gallery. Her voice startles Cheryl out of that darkness. She looks up, and gives the young woman a wave. "Everything's going to be okay, Ma. I am sure Stella is fine, just busy with her baby. I gotta run. I'll call you in the morning, okay? Louisa should be over there soon."

"Oh, okay, bye already." The elder changes her tone, as if Cheryl's the one who has been trying to keep her on the phone.

Cheryl texts her daughter right away to make sure she will bring the milk, to make sure her mother is taken care of, at least that the family is helping in the small ways they can.

Rita arrives a couple hours later with lipstick on and, to Cheryl's surprise, Louisa beside her. Her girls never have much interest in her work, hardly ever come to her shows. Something must be wrong.

"Where's Baby then?" she asks her daughter, trying to find out.

Her girl just shrugs. "Jake and Sunny are staying there. He's in bed already. Everything's fine, Ma." She's angry and pounds back her wine.

Rita looks at Cheryl sideways. But no one says anything more about it.

Louisa doesn't say much all evening, but Cheryl knows. Even at thirty-five her girl can still pout the way she did when she was fourteen, but Cheryl can only let her be. Her sweet Louisa, too, doesn't yet know how beautiful she is, or how good she has it.

"I FEEL SO comfortable, Ma. Like I'm home," Paulina had said when Cheryl came to help unpack her new house earlier this week. Paulina had never sounded so in love. It was good to hear.

"That's how it's supposed to feel." Cheryl was sipping coffee and just sitting there, not really helping at all.

"Yeah, I guess." Her quiet girl shrugged and put on her tough face again. Paulina was always softer than Louisa, the way Rain had been softer than Cheryl, as if in need of more protection.

Cheryl smiled, so happy her little Paulina had finally found Pete, a good man with a good job, after being so alone for so long.

"Now, if only he knew how to do the dishes. I mean, he thinks he does but really, he doesn't." Her girl shook her head and unwrapped the first dish. She was trying to be tough, but really she couldn't be. Cheryl remembered that feeling too.

"Not many do," Cheryl said. "You think you have it bad, you should've seen the men of my generation. I don't think your dad even knew what dish soap was." Cheryl laughed, remembering. "He thought it was just a big bottle of lemony soap to wash his hands with."

"Yeah, he's pretty traditional like that, hey." Paulina smiled. "Pete's not that bad." She smiled a different smile, an all loved-up one.

Cheryl watched her daughter turn back to her unpacking, and her own smile faded slowly. They were both quiet a minute. Paulina put a stack of dishes in the cupboard, neatly to the side, and opened a new box. Cheryl recognized the dishes — chipped and heavy, they were from her mom's old house, the big one on Atlantic. Paulina placed them on the counter, one by one, and looking at them made Cheryl suddenly nostalgic for something she tried not to think about anymore.

"I feel so lucky," Paulina said after a while.

"A friend told me once not to use that word. Don't say lucky, but fortunate, she said." Cheryl got up, but only to refill her cup. "It's not just blind luck, hey. You worked for this."

"How did I work for this?" her girl scoffed.

"Well, you did good, you made a healthy home, and a man took notice."

"You say that like he's a prize."

"Well, he kind of is, isn't he?" Cheryl laughed.

Paulina made a smile, a small shy one. "Fortunate, I get it, I think. I mean, he's just good, like really good. It's kind of, you know, scary."

"How is it scary?" Cheryl asked, but knew.

"Well, I don't trust it. I don't believe it. I spent so long alone or treated badly, I don't trust that he really is like that. Or that it'll last, you know?"

"Just go with it, Paulina. All you can do is enjoy it. And try to trust it."

Her girl kept unpacking. Cheryl wanted to shake her for her luck, for her good man. Cheryl could barely remember what that felt like. It had been so long since she'd been with a man, and the good times were always way too short.

AFTER A FEW more rounds, when people start to wander out of the gallery, back down the long wooden stairs to the front door, Cheryl sets to work again. There's not much to clean up, and they can leave most of it 'til Monday. Rita and Louisa help, but Louisa teeters like she's had too much wine.

"Just go home, my girl. We can do all this." Cheryl looks at her long. Her girl is so sad.

"Okay," Louisa says finally. "Fine."

Cheryl walks her out and Louisa even lets her hug her. Cheryl knows the sad she feels and wants to shake her too. Her poor wayward girls, never knowing how lucky or fortunate they really are.

"I love you, my girl," she says to the top of Louisa's head.

"You too, Ma." She wipes her face. She has been crying again. Cheryl pretends not to notice.

"Okay, call me tomorrow. We'll eat chicken with Kookoo and all will be well." Cheryl smiles down at her, but she looks away. Her tough girl.

Louisa just nods and gets into her cab. She thinks too much, that's her problem, Cheryl thinks, knowing full well she is not one to talk.

When she gets back in the gallery, she wraps up the fruit and overhears the plan to go to the bar. She tells everyone to go on ahead, so she and Rita can finish up.

Once everyone's gone, the two women hole up in the office and open the window wide.

"What the fuck happened now?" Cheryl asks, lighting up.

Rita knows exactly what she's talking about. "What Gabe? He fucking went home again. He left last night. She thinks for good." Rita nods out the window at the snowy road and takes a cigarette too.

"Heard that before." Cheryl takes a long drag, loving the dirty smoke in her throat. "He'll be back. Louisa always thinks he's going to leave for good. She thinks too much."

"I feel bad. I convinced her to come out. Thought she'd let loose and have some fun."

Cheryl just shakes her head. "Nope, not my Louisa. When she's sad, she's sad. All the way, all the time."

"She'll be fine. It's just a man. She'll get another." Rita laughs too loud.

"Gabe's just taking care of his family. He'll be back and she will be fine. She's just too damn hard on him."

Rita exhales with a look. "You really think that's all it is."

Cheryl points her fingers and cigarette at her friend. "You always think the worst of him, I always think the better, so somewhere in between we're right."

"As long as I'm right," Rita says and laughs again.

Cheryl thinks a minute, changes the subject. "My mom was asking about Stella again."

"That girl still hasn't been around?"

"Yeah, for months. I mean, what the fuck is she thinking?" Cheryl shakes her head and blows smoke out into the cold.

"She married some white guy, wants to be all better than

us now. Forget where she's from. Women can do shitty things for shitty men." Rita ashes her cigarette and looks down, looks older than her years for a moment.

Cheryl ignores the comment but not the gesture. "Yeah, but to stop seeing her Kookom, stop seeing all of us? I know she's been hurting, ever since Rain died, but still, we're her family."

"Fuck her, I say." Rita flicks her butt out the window and looks defiant, hard.

They don't say anything more about it. They both know there is so much to say, too much pain around them, that sometimes the best thing they can give each other is quiet.

Then Rita says, "Full moon tonight."

"Really?" Cheryl looks out the window but can only see the thick pinkish cloud and snow all around.

"Time to drum," Rita says to a place very far away. "You're supposed to celebrate a moon. They're powerful."

"All right then, let's get this party started!" Cheryl jokes and tosses her smoke out the window.

They both laugh, probably too hard, and get their coats to walk off to the bar. Arms interlinked they slip in the snow and laugh with mouths open and too loud because no one cares what old ladies do.

Cheryl loves these kinds of moments. The loud ones before it all gets started. The good ones never do last long enough.

6

ZEGWAN

ZIGGY IS FUCKING frozen all the way through by the time they finally find the party, by the time she and Emily get the nerve to open the door to the old rundown house that thumps with bass and rattles with people. Inside is wall-to-wall people, and the air is thick with the smoke they make. It's warm, so warm, but Ziggy still shakes.

Ziggy knows about gangs, she's not an idiot. Her brother, Sunny, knows who's who and what's what, and has told her all about it. She thinks it's all stupid, but he said it was important that she know, so she sort of listened. These guys are all red. Some wear bandanas on their heads, or in their super-low back pockets, and some have thick name-brand hoodies in the same bright colour. Ziggy knows who they are. There's a red gang and a black gang, and they don't like each other. Something dumb like that.

She hovers a little in front of Emily. Emily is so clueless she probably doesn't even realize they've just walked into a gang party. The pretty one, Ziggy calls her. Emily is so pretty and so oblivious. Em shakes with cold after their long walk here, all the way over McPhillips, but pulls her coat down a bit so everyone can see her tight T-shirt underneath.

Ziggy has another look around. No one so much as nodded when they walked in, but she isn't about to admit she is scared. She sees Roberta Settee sitting with this guy, Mitchell, in the corner. They look high and giggle with their heads all close together. Ziggy's known them since kindergarten but has barely talked to them this year. This year they all went to the big school and separated out into groups and gangs. Ziggy and Emily became geeks, good girls. Mitchell and Roberta and the others became a part of this gang.

Ziggy knows it's okay that she and Emily are here because her brother isn't connected to anyone. He says he's neutral and "beyond that shit," but really he and Jake haven't decided yet. They're only fourteen, though, and they have time. They'll have to pick something eventually. They've got to have friends somehow. Ziggy hates this shit, feels so glad she's a girl and a geek so she doesn't have to bother, for the most part.

Just when she's ready to tell Em they should get the hell out, Clayton emerges from a dark bedroom, his eyes as red as his hoodie and his grin even more exaggerated than usual.

"You made it!" he yells at Em too loud, not even looking at Zig. Emily falls over herself. She tries not to, but Ziggy can tell. People are looking at them now. Ziggy hates it when people look at her. Clayton is talking too loud and Emily is just being a mushy cow.

Clayton takes them around the living room, introduces Em to a couple of guys.

"And who the fuck are you?" The guy has hair slicked back into a long braid and looks Ziggy up and down with squinty eyes.

"Zegwan," she says with her sternest voice.

"What the hell kind of name is that?" the other long-haired guy says with a high-pitched laugh.

"Anishinaabe," Ziggy says. "Like you."

She is trying to act tough but might have been talking too quiet, and the guy just keeps on laughing.

Clayton shows Emily to an empty armchair with exaggerated gentlemanly hand sweeps.

Ziggy groans, but again, too quiet.

"Want a beer?" he asks them both. Emily nods.

When he turns away, Ziggy just stares at her friend.

"Oh, just one," Emily snaps, but quiet enough so no one else can hear.

Clayton comes back with three open beer bottles and more grins.

"Thanks." Emily smiles back, but winces as she takes a sip.

Ziggy takes one too, but just to hold and to look the part. Everyone is high or fucked up and talking too loud, trying to be heard over the music. Then Tupac chants, and they all know the words, Clayton too. Emily just smiles — she doesn't know this music any better than Ziggy does. Sunny likes it, but Rita always tells him to put his ear buds in so she doesn't have to listen to that "fuckfuck garbage."

"Doesn't he know any other words?" her mom yelled with a laugh.

Ziggy's never liked that stuff. She likes real music, like with singing and instruments.

Clayton is super high and just keeps smiling. Ziggy's not an idiot. He looks at her too long, so she takes a sip of the gross beer. It makes her retch, and she really just wants to get the hell out of here.

Emily sips and giggles at whatever Clayton says. Ziggy can't hear. She just stands there. Some girl in a tank top stares her down, so she ducks her head but keeps looking. Girls in super-tight jeans and tighter T-shirts lean against walls. Their hair slicked down, straight and black on either side of their too-much-makeup faces. Big boys in still bigger hoodies talk with huge joints in their hands. Clayton goes off to get another beer and comes back bouncing around all over the place. He seems to know everybody. He clinks his bottles to theirs and smiles even wider.

Ziggy really doesn't see the point and just wants to go. She taps Em's shoulder, but her best friend doesn't have to look at her to know what she's going to say.

"Just a few more minutes!" she snaps.

Clayton asks if Emily wants a cigarette. Emily shrugs and takes one. Ziggy just shakes her head.

Emily nervously takes a drag and coughs a little. Clayton laughs. They've only smoked a couple times before. Jake and Sunny showed them how one night at Rita's when no one was around.

"Just inhale like you're scared or something," Jake said expertly taking a drag. "Like you go—hah, real quick."

"Nah, nah, fuck, just pretend Mom's gonna see you with that smoke." Her brother Sunny laughed at her and made a scared face.

"Not even!" Ziggy had cried out.

But everyone laughed.

It had worked. She inhaled real quick and the smoke choked down her throat. She coughed and her brother kept laughing at her. She passed it to Emily who managed a drag, but the smoke came out in a puff, and Jake said she didn't even inhale.

"You can tell?"

"You're not exactly good at pretending, Em." He shrugged.

Emily kept faking her inhales, but the boys never once believed her.

Here, she's not even trying to pretend—she inhales all the way, chokes. Clayton laughs at her again like he can't stop.

A joint comes around, and then another, one after the other. Ziggy shakes her head and waves her hand, and just sits on the arm of the chair next to Em, trying not to look too uncomfortable. Emily keeps choking and inhaling for real. Everyone is coughing and choking so she is getting away with it. Her face grows red and her eyes look droopy, right away, but she smiles up at Ziggy.

Then she mumbles something to Clayton who just grins and says they should go outside. His voice is too loud, too happy. Ziggy follows them even though they don't ask her to come. She never took her jacket off. Emily still has hers, too, though it's pulled down off her shoulders.

Outside the snow is falling again. The cloud-packed sky reflects light so it is almost as bright as daytime. The snowflakes are huge. Ziggy thinks she can make out their patterns. She stands in the yard, and Clayton and Em sit on the stoop's hardened snow. The fresh cold air feels so good. She likes winter and says so.

Clayton and Em just laugh at her.

"I think youse got a fucking contact high, neech!" Clayton laughs.

A what? Ziggy tries to say but the words don't come out.

Emily just laughs harder.

"Your face!" Clayton howls.

Ziggy is mortified. And scared now too. "Emily, we gotta go," is all she can think to say. The words get all the way out this time.

"No ways, you just got here." Clayton grins at them. He

seems to talk louder as the night goes on.

"Well, I gotta get home by ten," Ziggy says bravely.

"Ten-shmen!" Clayton laughs.

"Just a few more minutes," Emily pleads.

Ziggy stands there. She wants to lie down, here in the snow even. She thinks it would feel so good, the hard snow at her cheek, the flakes softly falling on her eyelashes.

"The party's just getting started, fuck." Clayton's eyes are slits.

Ziggy stares at Emily. "We can come back another night." She tries so hard to be brave. She sees that girl in the living room window, the one who had been looking at her earlier — she's pulled back the sheet to stare out into the yard. Another girl looks out too. She looks familiar but Zig can't remember her name.

"But no, no, you can't leave me," Clayton jokes. He leans his head onto Emily's shoulder and looks at her with puppy-dog eyes.

"I gotta go, I'm staying at her place." She smiles such a big smile. The kind even Ziggy's never seen before.

Ziggy shakes a bit and then can't stop. She's cold or nervous or both.

"I'll take you!" Clayton says loudly.

"W-what?" Emily stutters.

"She can go. I'll walk you in a bit, let's just have another beer first." He slaps his hand to his baggy knee for no reason.

"K," Emily agrees before she even looks at Ziggy, and he nods like that's the end of it, and goes inside.

As soon as the door is closed, Ziggy is at her side. "I'm not leaving you here!"

"Oh you're just scared 'cause you hate walking home by yourself." Emily is trying to act all tough. She's probably fucking high. Ziggy could smack her, she's so mad, but she just looks at her.

"Come on, Zig. Stay and loosen up. It's Clayton Freaking Spence!!" Emily coos. She really is high. "And he's nice, isn't he? Isn't he nice?"

Ziggy kicks at the snow. The girls in the window drop the sheet.

"One more beer. That's it. I swear. Your mom will never know."

"I'm not worried about her!" Her voice goes a little too high.

"Like hell you aren't!" Emily giggles.

Ziggy smiles. She doesn't want to but she does. Cheyenne. That girl's name is Cheyenne. She is a year older but was held back in, like, grade four. That's when Ziggy met her. When Ziggy first moved to the city, she used to go over to Cheyenne's place to play Barbies. She had a long screened-in porch, and her mom was always laughing and fun. She made really good hamburger soup, Ziggy's favourite when she was younger.

Clayton comes back with only two beers this time, and a warm gush of air escapes from inside. He looks just at Emily, and they talk so close Ziggy can't even hear.

Ziggy stands there with her hands tucked in her pockets, swaying around, trying not to feel cold. She feels so dumb and really wants to go home. It starts to snow harder, but still light and fresh. The big snowflakes fall on her hair and stick there, cold. Ziggy looks at her boots and kicks at the snow again. The world seems slow, the snow falling thick and clumpy.

The door squeaks open and four girls stand there, Cheyenne and Roberta and two others. Ziggy looks up just as the biggest one reaches down, grabs at Emily and takes hold of her hair.

Ziggy freezes all the way through.

"What the fuck, Phoenix?" Clayton yells. He wipes his

mouth. He doesn't get up or anything, just looks back at them, and then forward again, as if it is the most annoying thing in the world.

Ziggy is petrified, the cold rattles through her. Emily shakes the way she does when she's about to cry.

"Who is this bitch?" The girl talks into Emily's ear and grabs her hair harder and pulls her up to standing. Emily starts to cry but tries to be quiet about it.

Ziggy can only stand there, her hands out as if she can do something, but she doesn't. Can't. She's frozen.

"Shit, Phoen, let her go." Clayton looks exasperated, not frightened or angry. He still doesn't get up—he just looks out into the street, the snow falling onto his hair.

Maybe he's scared too, Ziggy thinks. The other girls look so tough. Cheyenne doesn't look at her at all. Emily can only stand there too, being pulled at, trying to keep her balance. She looks pathetically down at Clayton, like he can do something. For a really long minute, the girl doesn't let go of her hair. Then, finally, she throws Emily down the stairs. Ziggy thinks quick enough to grab her friend and stop her from falling over. Their boots squeak on the snow-packed walkway.

Ziggy can't think what to do. These girls all look so mean, glaring down at them. Emily slowly stands all the way up and wipes the snow off her jeans, but she keeps her head down.

"Who the fuck do you think you are?" The first girl spits out the words. She looks so big, wide, and mad.

Emily shakes her head and keeps looking down. Snow keeps falling around them, and Ziggy still can't even think.

"You think you can just come here and hang on to other people's boyfriends?" People crowd around the open door to watch. Some guy pulls up the sheet again and looks out the front window.

Emily keeps shaking her head feebly. *Run.* The word just comes to Ziggy. *Run.* She's a bad runner and can't go that fast. But they can't fight. She's a worse fighter than she is a runner.

"Phoen!" Clayton tries, but he still just sits there with his head in his hands, leaning forward. His shoulders getting white with snow.

"Shut up, Clayton, you little slut, you little fucking male slut, douche. This is my uncle's house. You don't go making out with skanks in my uncle's house." Ziggy guesses she is eighteen, maybe older. She looks a lot older than the other girls.

She turns down to Emily who looks down and shakes with crying. Ziggy holds on to the back of her jacket.

"Yeah that's right, you little skank, what the fuck you think about that, you little skank, whore, useless slut? *Fucking look at me!*"

Emily looks up, wincing, the snow falling on her face. Clayton's hand is over his mouth, but he still looks more annoyed than anything. More faces appear at the window, the sheet pulled all the way up, and the light shines into Ziggy's eyes. One girl with a black hoodie on, the one Ziggy doesn't know, lights a smoke and looks right at her. They could run. They could at least try.

The older girl, Phoenix, keeps looking at Emily. Her glare doesn't move.

"You should answer her," the hoodie girl says to Emily.

Emily shakes her head so fast. "I didn't know," she says.

"*Didn't know?*" Phoenix's face looks even more evil when she screams. It gets all distorted. "You don't seem to know nothing."

Emily takes a deep breath. Ziggy can feel it, feel her best friend's fear beside her. A quiet falls over everything. Ziggy feels like she's waiting. Phoenix glares, and the other girls tower on the stoop. Clayton just sits there, looking small.

She looks at her best friend, who doesn't look at her but can see.

Run.

Ziggy doesn't know if someone had said it, or if she had said it, or if she just thought it, but the word echoes inside her, over and over and over—Run run run-run-run-run-run-run-run-run.

Ziggy pushes Emily in front of her, down the path to the street, turns her heel on the squeaky snow and runs behind, as fast as she can.

7

TOMMY

OFFICER TOMMY SCOTT doesn't say a word until they're in the squad car. Not until his hands are on the wheel and he can stare straight ahead and not look at his older partner. He knows Christie is going to make fun of him, but he squares his shoulders and asks anyway.

"So what the hell do you make of that?" He steadies his voice to sound as even as possible.

"It was just a fucking gang fight," Christie says, unconcerned, pulling the laptop on its metal pivot and peering into the screen. "Crazy dame. I feel for that guy."

Tommy looks back over the field — what she'd call it? The Break. The Hydro towers loom dark, four storeys high at least, narrow at the top like some sort of lookout tower. The kind in a post-apocalyptic movie or something, one where the world has all gone to shit, everything's devastated, and only the clear-headed survive. They look scary anyway, shadowed in the night. Between them, he can just make out where they inspected the scene, where a big pool of blood lies in a packed-down space of snow. Someone lost a lot of blood. He looked at it when they first got here, looked at all the blood and thought it was going to be a big case.

That was before they talked to the witness.

"Likely some fucking stab wound's gonna wander into Emerg before the night is over. I'm not going to worry about it," Christie says, and he pushes the computer back to the middle of the dash. "Let's go to Tim's."

"The one by the bridge?" Tommy says, still watching the space, the Break.

"Yeah, we'll go see how the good people live," Christie says sarcastically. Across the bridge being slightly less ghetto than on this side.

Tommy pulls out around the older model Mercury, undoubtedly Mr. McGregor's car. The guy must've rushed home and parked in a hurry—the car now sits ass end way out.

"Buddy's going to get clipped." Christie nods to the long sedan white against the white street and snow banks.

"You should call 'im," Tommy suggests, knowing Christie likes to be the nice guy when he can.

"Naw, he'll be fine." He also likes to make as little effort as possible, whenever he can. "He has enough to deal with."

Tommy fishtails the cruiser a bit as they turn on to McPhillips. The night is quiet, and the snow falls in pieces around them. The sky cloudy and low. The city reflects off it like they're all under a dome. Tommy drives up Selkirk but keeps thinking about the call. The words, the witness, her dark hair hanging limp on either side of her face. High cheekbones and almond-shaped eyes. Done up she must be pretty hot, but tonight she just sagged under an old bathrobe, baby puke on one shoulder. Her face blotchy and burrowed into tissues. She was really upset, not making-it-up upset. Or, crazy upset. Really upset.

"Crazier things have happened," he starts, slowly. "It just looked funny is all. Like something was off there."

"Ah, you getting your poll-eece in-stinked on, son?" Christie laughs. He has one of those congested smoker laughs — it sounds as if it's coming from some deep, ugly place in his over-extended gut. "I wouldn't worry about it, May-tee. She's just a crazy bitch is all. Dime a dozen, those kind."

Tommy just cringes. She was troubled, that's for sure, dishevelled and clearly emotional. Scott lists off how he would describe her on the report. Native, mid-thirties, thin, medium height, mentioned new baby several times, clearly exhausted, and distressed, crying uncontrollably. It looked as if she'd been like that for some time before they arrived. Then again, it had been about four hours since she called it in.

"I don't think it's a sex assault," Christie says, with authority. "Again, there's no evidence of anything other than a fight. Just write out her statement. If anything, they'll be a stab wound at Emerg soon."

He is probably right. He's been at this a lot longer than Tommy has. But the old guy is lazy, so lazy he didn't write down anything more than he had to. He probably didn't even write down what the witness had said. Not really.

Selkirk Avenue is mostly asleep, and all the broken-down buildings looking cleaner in the snow and winter. The officers drive on, slow like they're supposed to. Eyes always open. What cars there are fall into this same slow, careful drive, the way civilians do around police cars. Tommy always liked that, how he'd drive and the world around him seemed to straighten out, get better. Same thing happened when he wore his uniform — everyone stood up a little taller, and some would even smile and nod at him, some even looked genuine. It has been nearly a year but the feeling still hasn't gotten old.

A drunk teeters down the sidewalk. His old, bloated body edges around the tall mounds of uneven snow but doesn't fall. His jacket, ratty and ripped, falls open and his pale gut falls out of his dirty T-shirt. Christie eyes him, looking for trouble, but there isn't any. They pass a house party, lights blazing out every window even though it's getting light out. Older Natives smoke on the stoop but inside just looks like a bunch of drunks laughing and yelling at each other. Christie peers out his window and motions Tommy to slow down, but Tommy knows it's nothing, just some people having a few. Still, Christie nods at the folks on the stoop. They shiver in the cold but straighten their backs.

In the parking lot at Tim's is another cruiser. Clark and Evans are sitting in their car. Clark is doing the files and Evans is on the phone.

Tommy rolls his window down and pulls up beside them.

"What's up, my brotha?" he says as Clark's window goes down too.

"Not much, not much. You?" He keeps typing.

"Want anything?" Christie opens the passenger door.

"Naw, I'm good," Tommy says. Then thinks. "Thanks." It's best to keep Christie happy.

The old cop just grunts and walks off to the coffee shop.

Tommy turns back to Clark. "Done, I think. Just in time too. I am wiped." He runs his hands along the wheel. Two hours and he'll be in a warm bed next to Hannah. She went out tonight, drinks with friends at a cowboy bar, so she will sleep in tomorrow. Today. She texted when him when she got home at three, she's good about stuff like that. Not likely she'll still be up though, not by the time he's done. But at least tomorrow's Saturday so she'll sleep in until at least noon. That'll be nice, to stay warm in bed for a few hours. Almost perfect.

"I hear ya, it's been non-stop this way." Clark types with two fingers, still doesn't look up.

"Anything interesting?" Tommy knows the guy just wants to finish up so he can race off shift. Clark's good that way.

"Naw, just nates beating on nates. Same old." Clark's radio drones something Tommy can't hear. He turned his down when he went into the witness's house, didn't turn it back up again. He thinks of it now and adjusts the dial. "Fifteen-year-old female, five foot four inches tall, heavy set, last seen at the Migizi Centre in St. Vital." The operator pronounces it Meh-gee-zee, but Tommy knows that's wrong. Should be Meh-geh-seh. Short vowels, he remembers from his language teacher. The tall guy with the strong laugh and a grey braid that went all the way down his back, all the way to a point of perfectly looped hair. What was his name again?

Evans gets off the phone. "Old man inside?" he asks Tommy.

He nods. He has to write up that statement, should follow up at the emergency rooms nearby, just in case. Really, he probably has at least two more hours before he can get into bed.

The old men come back, laughing about something. Tommy shuts the window and cranks the heat but can still hear their bellowed tones through the glass. They stand outside and watch their young partners at the computers and keep laughing. Tommy squares his shoulders and keeps typing, and turns up his radio, listening for a sex assault, wondering if one will be reported. He's kind of hoping for it, just to prove the old guy wrong.

"He's a good little worker, this one." He can hear Christie tell Evans. "Didn't think he would be, being a May-tee and all."

"Oh they will surprise you, they will surprise you," Evans says playing along. "Not full-blooded Indians or anything. Good little horses them May-tee."

The old guys laugh again and go off to circle the parking lot and stare down civilians.

On Tommy's first day, Christie walked up, pudgy middle and greying beard. Tommy stood straight with his hand out to shake but the old guy didn't take it.

"I hear you're May-tee," he sneered.

Tommy didn't know what else to do, so he nodded.

"Well, young buck, your special treatment ends here. Got it?"

Tommy, all brushed up in his new uniform and with fresh nerves, felt suddenly dirty. He rubbed his hands together and wanted to wash them.

"You drive. I'm too old for this shit." Tommy couldn't tell what he meant and wasn't about to ask.

He's been May-tee ever since. He knew he should've never checked that fucking box. He only did it 'cause Hannah made him.

"You'll get in that way, for sure. It's like equal hiring or something. They have to call you." She nodded her blond head excitedly like she does. Tittering, that's what that's called. Hannah titters.

"But I don't have my card or anything," he had said.

"Well, get it. How hard can it be? Everyone has them." Hannah had this idea about Métis people and Tommy didn't want to correct her so he just let it go.

He had shrugged, not convinced it was that easy.

"Just show 'em a picture of your mom. They'll never doubt you then."

He looked at her side-eyed. She meant well. His mom did look Native, real Native. She was almost full blooded, but never had status 'cause her dad was Métis. They did that back then. If you were a woman and married outside your community, they just took away your status card. Even if his mom had had it, she would've lost it again when she married his white dad. The law finally changed in the eighties, and a bunch of people got their status back, but his mom said she didn't want to.

"Could've gotten it years ago, but your dad wasn't having it." His dad was a racist prick. She has always wanted Tommy to identify as Métis, like her dad, like her. She thought it was a safe choice, and apparently so did Hannah.

"Come on, Tommy. I can call, if you want. I'll help." Hannah was always so helpful. "If it'll get you the job, then it's worth it. You might even get a tax break or something."

"That's not Métis cards that's status cards, and it's not really like that."

"What's the difference?" She was actually doe-eyed—fragile and innocent with a pointy nose, like a deer. Over the years, the look seemed more and more practiced.

"Status is Indian, Métis is just Métis—half-breeds." He put it in terms she'd understand.

"Well you're not an Indian, you're just Métis, so we'll get that one."

"Actually, my mom could get her status back if she wanted to. My aunt did, after my grandma died. I could get it too, really."

"You don't need to go that far! Métis is good enough," Hannah said like they were picking paint colours. Red is too bold, just a pale pink please.

Tommy didn't say anything more about it, but he signed the papers she had filled out. The card finally arrived when he was in training. He looked at it a long time, thinking his father must be turning in his grave. Turning and swearing like hell, calling him every fucking derogatory racist name his angry ginger brain could think of.

"Holy fuck, it's cold!" Christie sits back in the car and it lurches with his weight. "Let's fucking go in, it's almost five."

Tommy finishes what he's typing and pushes the computer back without a word. He still hasn't heard any news of a stab wound or sex assault. Neither meant anything but the feeling stayed with him. Something wasn't right, and that woman, something about that witness, she was so...sincere. But he knows better than to question Christie. He meant to run it by Clark but didn't get a chance. He's a good guy, Clark, grew up poor in Elmwood so was what Christie would call "fucking sensitive," but Tommy liked picking the guy's brain on the hard stuff.

They're quiet as they drive down Main, Christie probably half asleep. Tommy is exhausted but awake. He spots a girl on the corner of Pritchard. She slinks back into the shadows as they pass but he sees her. Tight, short skirt and tall black boots. She must be cold, he thinks. Doesn't look much different than Hannah when she goes out, and she's always complaining she's freezing. Still dresses like that though.

At the station, Christie grunts, "Good night. Good morning." He lumbers his way out of the car. "See you tomorrow, In-stinked!"

In-stinked is a new one. Tommy doesn't mind it as much as May-tee, wouldn't mind if it stuck.

Clark pulls up too but only waves and makes his way in. It's the end of shift, no time for talking.

Tommy just sits there a minute, and then starts typing, the lady's voice echoing in his mind. She wasn't that old, really, same age as him probably, just looked older. Tired. His mom had that look for a lot of years too. She kind of looked like his mom, actually, but Native women always remind him of his mom.

HE'D NEVER BEEN to the North End until his first shift all those months ago. When he got behind the wheel, Christie started barking orders. They drove down Main first, then Selkirk. It all looked the way he thought it would, old and rundown.

His first-ever call was a domestic. A fat guy drunk with puke down his once-white shirt, a wife beater ironically enough, and his woman, small and skinny, face mashed with blood and beginning to swell. She didn't want to press charges, but they had to take the guy in anyway.

"Zero tolerance," Christie bit the words, and then again in the car. "Zero fucking tolerance."

The fat guy cried in the backseat, his hands cuffed and awkward behind him, his face falling into his bulging, puke-covered belly. Tommy had no sympathy, just squared his face and drove this guy in. He thought of the woman, left there in her trashed living room, face puffing out. She'd have to clean up now, she'd probably clean everything first, then take some painkillers so she could get some sleep, if she could sleep. That's what his mom always did. Cleaned up first. The woman had dark, frizzy hair, and black eyes, just like his mom.

"...assault with a weapon..." beeps on his radio and he listens close, but it's nothing like what he is looking for. They'll probably never know anyway. This case will go where the others go: far away, never to be heard of again.

This work isn't what he thought it'd be. He thought he'd be breaking down doors and always in the action. At the academy, he learned about community policing, which basically meant that he was supposed to be nice and make relationships with people, but he doesn't do that either. Mostly he just takes notes, makes reports and never thinks of them again. Or does think of them, but just never does anything about them. Incidents become reports become just words on a screen. Computer folders become numbers, filed away.

His dad was a mean drunk. No, he was an angry guy and angry guys become mean drunks. His hands, permanently stained by menial factory work, would clench into fists after only one drink. If you didn't look closely, you'd think he was only stretching out his hands, sore from early arthritis — flexing them after a day's hard work. But Tommy knew better. His dad was only getting ready. It looked so normal: his mom, Marie, smoking on one side of the couch, little Tommy on the other, and Tom Senior in his rocking armchair, getting up and going to the kitchen at every commercial break to crack open another can of beer. But Tommy knew what it was really all about. So did Marie. When he was little, she knew the exact moment to send her child to bed. By the time he was a teenager, he knew that moment too, felt it, and she stopped sending him up. Instead, his growing body became a shield between his father and mother, a tense set of squared shoulders, ready to jump.

"She's a wild one, Tommy," his dad would say when he thought she couldn't hear. "Got her off the reservation for cheap. She was on sale." This was his big joke. His discounted wife.

When his dad was alive, his mom never did anything, she just sat at home, was just a poor Native woman with an asshole white husband. Tommy used to wonder if it was the same with every white husband and red wife. When he marries Hannah they'll be white wife, pink husband, but it won't be the same. It won't be much different either. Hannah makes jokes sometimes, vague unfunny quips about her man's wild ways, how she tamed him. She doesn't mean anything by it, and he's never told her it bothers him.

He feels sorry for the lady, that's what it is. He just feels sorry for her. She's not lying, but what she's telling doesn't sound like the truth. Marie always lied when the police came to their house. She'd tell them whatever would get them out the door the fastest. The lady said she would never have called them, but she didn't know what else to do. And she was still so emotional after she waited for hours, for four hours, and she kept talking even after it was obvious they didn't believe her. There's something to that, he thinks. There must be.

He calls three hospitals, but nothing fits any scenario. The voices all drone back at him, barely registering his questions. Nothing fits. The sun comes up with cold light. Tommy finally sighs, closes the laptop, and turns off his radio and the car. It's fucking freezing tonight. But just an hour or so more and he can lie next to Hannah and get all warmed up.

PART TWO

. . .

My girl, I have been waiting, I think. I've been waiting so long I don't even know what I am waiting for. But I think I'll know it when it comes. It'll be one of those things you just know, those deep-breath kind of feelings when everything just makes sense.

It's a frustrating way to describe something, I know, but I don't know any other way. You can't grab spirit like that. You have to just let it be.

When you were born, it was like that. A deep breath. Before you came, I was so messed up and didn't think I even wanted you. I watched your aunty with little Louisa and thought I couldn't do that, all those things, not me. My hands didn't know how to wrap a little baby so tight in a blanket or tell when the bottle was warm enough. My heart had no room for all the space you would need. I didn't think I could do it.

But when you came, I only had to look at you, and I knew. There wasn't even a feeling or maybe there's just not a word big enough for all that feeling. There was so much it filled me all the way up. It was something more than knowing. More.

Whatever else I was, I loved you and you knew it. Your Kookoo knew it too. And you all loved me back. Whatever else you think or know, that is the most important thing about me. That I loved and was loved.

And still I wait.

Still I'm here.

I could never go too far from you.

(8)

STELLA

THE MORNING AFTER goes on cold and quiet, as if nothing even happened the night before. Just hours before. The sky is clear but the snow blows around the Break, covering the dark red with fresh white. Slowly, slowly. Stella watches out her kitchen window. The sun grows brighter, and the blood has all but disappeared. She looks down Magnus but sees nothing of what happened. Not even a footprint is left. The snow made everything clean, just as it always does. It sticks to branches of the skinny, naked elms and makes them white and beautiful too. These trees are smaller than the ones closer to the river. Down Atlantic Avenue where Stella lived when she was small, the trees were tall and arched over the street, all the way down, like a tunnel. When those trees would fill with snow like this, she would only have to wait for a good gust of wind, and it would snow all over again.

The day wears on, and Jeff sleeps off his shift. Stella wipes the counter, the table, and messy chins over and over. Every baby's cry is met with a swift, full hug, and little Mattie's every wish is granted as soon as it's suspected. Stella meets every need. But she's not really there. She is making a list, a list of—what was it Jeff called it? Her past? No, *a past like hers*. Yes, that was it. The words echo around in her head, sore from lack of sleep. Her eyes burn. She sips more coffee and thinks of it. Her past. Hers. She knows what he meant, what he knows, what she's shared with him in dark nights filled with memories and restlessness. She thinks of each time, every instance. One by one. It's really the past. Not even hers. Just stories that really belong to other people but were somehow passed to her for safekeeping, for her to know, forever. Incidents. Situations. They roll by in her head, factual and unemotional. Things she's seen, things her cousins told her, things her mom and Aunty Cher told her and her cousins, Lou and Paul, when they were little kids. All those big and small half-stories that make up a life. *A pattern*, she thinks of the word—like something that makes something else. *Pattern*. All those little things, those warnings to be careful, those teachings of what not to do. She always knew to be careful, always knew to look out for men, strange men, men doing strange things. That's how she was raised. On alert. One by one the scenes echo in her head, almost every day. A past like hers. Mattie gets a second cup of Cheerios and another hour of TV, and the baby needs to be rocked to sleep.

She sits upstairs and keeps rocking long after the baby finally calms. She loves his face, his soft whiffling breath on her skin. She rocks him, holds him close, and looks out the window. The snow has stopped falling but the clouds linger on the fringes, and the wind knocks against the glass. She thought it was all gone, but from here she can see a long line of foot tracks that cuts through the otherwise-untouched slate of snow.

She shivers, sits back in her chair, leans back until she can only see the bright, cold sky and the Hydro wires. She keeps rocking, tries to breathe, calm herself.

A past like hers.

The tall, metal towers stand just out of view. Mattie's *robots*. A good name — Stella can almost see the square faces frowning in firm resignation, one after another, like an image trapped in a room of mirrors.

Somewhere in the moment, Stella sleeps. Hands firm on her baby, the cartoon music just below, her little girl singing softly along, and the creak, creak of the floorboards as Stella slowly rocks herself to sleep.

In the old house on Atlantic, her bedroom closet was under the stairs. The space reached out past the hung dresses to a long, dark fort whose ceiling arched down, lower and lower. She kept an old flashlight there, and books and secrets. One afternoon, while the sun shone in the gap below the closed door, she and her cousins passed the light around their small circle. The scratchy lace bottom of her good dress, hanging above her, ran across her forehead, and her small skinny legs were crossed, knees scraped with summer. They were maybe eight. Yes, she doesn't remember an ache in her chest, so her mother must have still been alive. That summer, her cousins moved back the first time. They all lived together in the big house and Stella was so happy. Then, Lou told her the story, the first one she ever kept. Lou put the light at her chin, so her skin was glowing red there. Her forehead was bright yellow.

"I felt his thing. It was so, so gross," Lou told them. The extra *so* made all the difference. "And he was breathing deep like he was running. I would've punched him if I could've."

Paul started to cry, even though it wasn't her turn yet. Stella took the flashlight for her little cousin, but Paul only shook her head. Lou grabbed it back because she knew Paul wouldn't. Paul always let Lou talk for her.

"He smelled too. Like he needed a shower."

"What did you do?" Stella gasped out, knowing this was the most important thing she had ever heard.

"I said I had to go to the bathroom and went and locked the door." Stella swore she could see Lou's voice rise like steam in the upturned light.

"Then what happened?"

"Paul came in from outside." She nodded to her sister. "I came out, flushed the toilet so he'd think I'd really gone and thought up a story to go home, but he had Paul on his lap and they were both crying."

"He was crying? What did he do?" Stella looked right at little Paul, couldn't imagine anything bad happening to little Paul.

Lou kind of shook her head and shrugged at the same time. "Nothing. He... he just did the same thing... with his thing."

Stella wrapped an arm around Paul, and rubbed her arm like she'd seen her Kookoo do to people who needed hugs. Paul was the kind of kid you always wanted to hug. Lou never needed an arm or anything.

They were quiet a long minute. Lou's smoke-like breath was the only thing that moved in the same dark space. The *wow* never got all the way off Stella's lips.

Finally, Stella asked, "Why was he crying?"

Lou just shrugged and passed the flashlight to Stella, meaning it was her turn, her time to tell a story about being hurt. She needed something sinister, something dirty. She scratched her forehead where the dress kept touching her and couldn't think of anything. So she decided to tell knock-knock jokes until Paul laughed.

"Knock knock," she said for the fifth time, really knocking on the wall each time.

"Who's there?" Lou said, also for the fifth time, annoyed.

"Orange."

"Orange who?" the sisters said together, both confused.

"Orange you glad I didn't say . . . apple?"

Paul laughed. She was being nice, or she just really wanted to laugh.

"That's not how it goes," Lou said and didn't laugh. Instead, she grabbed the flashlight back. "You were supposed to say banana."

Lou did always know everything. Everything.

STELLA WAKES WITH a start. The sky is still clear, the sun is still out, and her baby still breathes gently on her skin. What time is it?

The cartoon music below has changed. Next show.

Stella puts Adam in his crib and goes to hold her daughter awhile, the dream still on her skin, like a film sinister and malignant.

It's been months since she's seen her family. When Mattie was first born, the two of them would visit her Kookom all the time. They would go there in the afternoons to drink tea lazily and talk about nothing in particular, like they always did. Stella would ask about Aunty Cher and Lou and Paul. Aunty now lived in the same building as Kookoo but was running a gallery so was never home. Lou was as good as married and rented a house on Cathedral. Paul finished school top of her class and got a good job at the hospital. Kookom always had so much to say, and Stella just sat on the floor and played with baby Mattie, listening to her Kookom's stories like she has always done.

She hadn't seen the rest of them because they never visited at night. The visits made Jeff nervous, he said. Now with a baby, he added. It had never seemed to bother him before. Then the afternoon visits started to make him nervous, too. His wife taking his baby on the bus to the really bad part of town, all the things that could happen, he said, and listed them, one by one. She could get mugged, she could get stabbed, she could get on the wrong side of a drug dealer, or worse. That's what he said, like that was what actually happened. Jeff didn't understand. He was a white boy who grew up in the suburbs. He had no idea what the things really were. What really happens. But she didn't want to fight, so she just didn't do anything. She started calling instead of visiting.

Adam hasn't even met any of her family yet. He is six months old.

Stella ruminates as she goes about her day, as she feeds, washes, and dresses her kids, over and over again, it seems, ignoring those images in her head, ignoring the droning that makes her head ache. She takes another painkiller and tries to forget. Everything. All those words. Those lost pictures of what she's seen.

In the late afternoon, she lies next to Mattie who pretends to nap. She should call her Kookom but doesn't want to worry her. She's so old, Stella thinks. She'll worry if I sound sad. She could call Aunty Cher, but what would she say?

So Stella just lies there instead, arm draped over her girl, thinking half thoughts that are really memories and waking herself up over and over. Kookoo. Her and her Kookom, Nokomis, her grandmother, always there even when everyone else went away. Kookoo waiting for her when she got home from school, the smell of homemade hamburger soup all over the house. Kookoo laughing at some soap opera that wasn't supposed to be funny. Kookoo tucking her in at night even after Stella insisted she didn't need it. Kookoo lying beside her when she couldn't sleep and being there when she woke up scared because Stella always had bad dreams, even before her mom died. Kookoo lightly snoring beside her, one arm draped over Stella's middle. Kookoo saying everything was going to be okay, and Stella believing her. Every time. No matter what. Even when Stella was so sad, and the hole broke open inside her and she knew it would never close again. Still Stella believed her.

Then she remembers, with a chill, the night before. She forgot it for a second, and now she is wide awake and so, so cold.

STELLA DIDN'T WANT to move here. She wanted to buy a house in the gentrified downtown neighbourhood where they were renting. But they couldn't afford a house there. Then, Jeff found this house and got excited.

"It's on the better side of McPhillips," the agent had told them when they went to look. "A great little neighbourhood on the up and up." She was a perky blonde who looked only a little uncomfortable there.

Jeff smiled politely and looked at the basement ceiling's beams like he knew what he was looking for. Stella didn't say anything. But she knew the place. This neighbourhood was so close to her old one, the same really. Too close. Her past. All of it, right there on the other side of McPhillips.

They moved in right away. Jeff really wanted to. When Adam came, Stella had a toddler and a baby. She just seemed to stop calling her Kookom, her whole family. Like how she stopped visiting—it just happened. She lived so close, still had to drive down Selkirk Avenue to get anywhere. Still had to see it all, all those things she had always seen, the places Jeff didn't want her going anymore. He didn't get it. None of it scared her. It all hurt though.

The TV goes on and on. Jeff sleeps, Adam sleeps, and Mattie gets up and plays quietly on the floor. Her little head turns up every now and then, but Stella doesn't move. Just smiles down, between spells of staring off into her tired nothing. The day wears on as if nothing happened. The blood is probably covered all the way up and if she goes out there, she probably won't even be able to tell exactly where it was. Not even her. And no one else knows it even happened.

Stella doesn't know what to do and wants to do a lot of things, at the same time. She wants to call her Kookom, she wants to be lying with her in the mouldy basement apartment that is somehow always warm and safe, but she doesn't do anything. Just lies there, alone, with her arm still stretched out where her girl used to be.

PAUL

WHEN PAUL HANGS up the phone, she doesn't think, just starts moving. That's what Paul does when something happens, she just goes. That's what they all do whenever Kookoo is really sick, or whenever something happens with the kids. They just go, figure out what needs doing and do it, don't think too much, don't feel anything, and don't freak out, just go. Take care of your family. Go.

Her first real thought is that she is thankful that she works at the hospital because she's already there. Then she calmly tells her supervisor she has to go down to Emerg because her boyfriend is bringing her daughter in.

"Oh my god, Paulina, what is it? What's wrong?" The older lady's voice rises in high octaves and good intentions.

"I don't know," is all Paul can think to say.

"Well, you let us know as soon as you do. You take as long as you need." Her supervisor's voice fades and Paul takes the familiar route downstairs, only she goes faster. As she goes, she thinks about all the things that could be wrong and what sorts of things she might need to do. If it's a bad period, she can page Dr. Froehlich. Paul saw her at the coffee shop this morning so she's probably still here. Likely that's what it is. That's all. Paul takes the stairs two at a time, grateful she can get there so quickly.

"PAUL, SOMETHING'S WRONG with Emily! I don't know what happened. I'm gonna take her to Emergency there." Pete's voice rang over the phone in an unnatural tone she had never heard before.

"What do you mean? What's wrong?" Paul immediately thought to soothe him. He had just moved in, she thought. He's probably just exaggerating. He doesn't know anything about thirteen-year-old girls.

"She just passed out. She was coming down the stairs and she fell." He paused, one of those pauses thick with his crowded thoughts. "She's bleeding, Paul."

"Bleeding how?" Paul asked. "Let me talk to her."

"She's out cold, Paul. I got her in the truck. Driving now."

"Okay, just drive safely. I'll meet you down there."

"She's bleeding, Paul. Down there. It's not good. It's everywhere."

Every possible scenario went through her head—maybe a ruptured cyst, maybe dehydration. Paul runs down the long, twisting hallway and thinks she should page Gyne right as she gets there. It's probably nothing. It can't be as bad as Pete thought. He just isn't used to it, that's all.

That's all, right?

But how can she be out cold?

And what did he mean by everywhere?

Paul checks herself and takes a breath before she pushes

through the doors. She won't start panicking. It's probably nothing. Just gotta take care of my girl, she thinks.

She grabs a wheelchair and pushes it out the sliding Emerg doors. Em will like that—a wheelchair, like a real patient.

The morning is almost nice. The snow finally stopped after falling all night. The sun's coming out and the fresh white sparkles in the light. A plow beeps across the street but all the snow makes the morning muted. Paul breathes in the fresh, crisp air. There has been so much snow this winter.

Pete's truck whips around the corner and stops with a squeal in front of the Emerg doors. Paul opens the door with another deep breath ready to calm her sick child.

Instead she bites her lips to swallow her own screaming.

Blood is really everywhere. Thick down Emily's once grey sweat pants, coated and dark over the seat fabric and pooling on the plastic floor mat. Her daughter's head has fallen to the seat. Paul touches her girl's leg and Emily moans. Paul reaches over and wipes her sweaty hair away. There's a cut on her bottom lip. Paul goes to touch it but her fingers streak blood across her girl's pale skin. Her baby's face so white it's nearly blue with lips slack and breath shallow.

"Em!" she cries finally, her voice faltering into a strange sound. "Em! Emily!" she tries again, shaking at the limp girl.

Somewhere behind her, Pete gets an attendant and a stretcher. Paul hears him yelling, and someone pulls her back.

"Paul, Paulina, move aside. Move aside." It's a nurse she knows, and another behind him. "Move aside, Paulina. We got this. We got it!"

The first checks a wrist pulse. The other calls out, "Emily? Emily, I need you to open your eyes," and shakes her small body gently.

Pete puts his arms around Paul and steps back a few feet

to give the nurses room. Paul didn't notice her body shaking until his big arms hold her close to him, until they close firmly around her and try to keep her still.

The two nurses heave Emily out of the truck and lay her limp little body on the stretcher. Paul reaches up to Pete's arm, but stops when she saw her hands, red with blood. Emily's blood. She doesn't want to touch anything. She just holds them out in the winter air. Everything is suddenly too cold.

They wheel her daughter into a closed room and shut the door. Pete sits down on one of the chairs in the hall, and gently pulls Paul to sit too.

"No," she says, dazed. "I should go wash my hands."

She wanders into the washroom and runs the cold water. Blood is stuck under her fingernails. She scrubs it with the thick pink soap. The metallic smell is so strong but she keeps scrubbing until she can only smell the grainy perfumey soap. When she looks up, she sees more blood over the hospital-issued scrubs she wears. She knows where to get another pair. Later. For now, she dabs at her pants with the brown paper towel. It only smears the blood to a deeper, darker colour and leaves bits of wadded paper behind.

She goes back to the room, the closed door, her daughter behind it, and Pete is on the phone—it sounds like he's talking to his family. Nurses hurry behind them. Someone yells, "I need suction here." And Paulina feels her legs give out as she falls onto the chair. Pete grabs her hand and squeezes.

"BP's eighty over forty."

He gets off the phone and looks at her in his silent way, waiting.

"I should call Lou," she thinks out loud. "And Mom. Mom can bring Kookoo."

"Okay, I can do that," he says, looking to her. She doesn't

look back. Only feels him, looking. "Okay. And you should move your truck. It can't sit there for too long. In front of the doors like that."

"I can go do that now. And I'll call Lou." He gets up but turns back again. "Is there anyone I can get to sit with you?"

Paul just waves him away.

"I'll be right back." He nods, understanding.

Once he is out of sight, she cries out suddenly. A harsh fit of tears, a violent roar, nearly swallowed. But the edge of it gets out before she can stop it. Then she is quiet. She is not going to lose it, wouldn't even know how if she wanted to. She's just going to sit there, waiting to be needed.

Her body numb, her mind in the room behind her, she can't see in, but she listens for each cue and feels every movement like many small earthquakes rippling through her.

"Oxygen," says the nurse, Mark, who was at the front of the stretcher.

"Ten ccs," says the other one, a young girl Paul doesn't know, at Emily's arm.

"Okay, I got it..."

Another nurse runs in with two pints of blood, another comes out with some printout to show another doc. No one sees her. But she sees everything. She sits there for a long time, until she breathes normally again and the shock becomes a dull ache, a wave of nausea she has to keep swallowing down.

Pete comes back smelling like the cold outside air and cigarettes. "Your mom's on her way," he tells her. "Getting your Kookom. I couldn't get a hold of Lou but your mom said she'd get her too." He pauses. "Anyone come out yet?"

Paul shakes her head and feels something like tears come again. Cold and fleeting, they fall down her face and she wipes them away like the nuisance they are. Pete sits down and grabs her hand. He leans toward her as if offering a shoulder, but Paul can't take it. She looks at him, waiting for her, but she can only shake her head. Can't rest or fall apart. She jumps up and tries to see inside the room, but too many bodies block her view. So she sits again, lets Pete take her hand. But she still can't rest.

They wait for another eternity. She doesn't think anymore, not real thoughts only random things: Emily on her first two-wheel bike, the annoyed look Emily gave last night, how much she looked like her Aunty Lou. Nothing sticks. Paul really feels only the chaos inside, rumbling and shaking. A doc she doesn't know runs in clutching his stethoscope. Another nurse tears off an apron soaked with blood. Pete squeezes her hand harder. It makes her cry again. She doesn't want to cry. If she lets herself keep crying she will never stop.

When Emily was born. That was probably the last time her daughter was here as a patient, not just visiting her mom's work. That spring day, long ago, Paul was so young and she trembled around the belly that was supposed to be her baby. Her mother was freaking out on one side of her, screaming for help every time Paul whimpered. Lou was there too, but just calm like she is. She had had Jake the year before and acted as if everything was okay, normal, but it was a long labour and Paul was scared. The pain, the whole new person about to come into the world, a living being she would be in charge of. It was a different fear.

The room behind her goes quiet. Something steadies and the rumble slows. Paul's whole body is ice cold, Pete's hand the only thing she feels. She doesn't breathe. After another long minute, the door finally opens, and Paul hears the steady beat of beeping inside. It is always a soothing sound, but in this moment, it is the best sound Paul has ever heard.

"Paulina?" A doc in green scrubs reaches out his hand

to Paul. "I am Doctor Lewicky. I've been looking after your daughter."

Paul only nods and takes his hand lightly as he kneels down to talk at eye level.

"We've got her stable now. She lost a lot of blood, but she's good now. You work here at the hospital?"

"Geriatrics," Paul says, her voice cracking. "I'm just an assistant."

"Well, her BP is low, and we had to infuse her. She's asleep. We had to put her out because she needed suturing."

"Suturing," Paul whispers, thinking. "Why?"

"Your daughter had several glass particles in her vaginal wall. They were small particles so we suspect the bleeding was consistent for some time before she started hemorrhaging. We also saw signs of a very recent hymen rupture, and there was a pretty nasty cut on her inner thigh. But we got her stable now. The bleeding has stopped. There will be a lot of swelling, but she will heal normally. We gave her IV antibiotics in case there's any infection. And a tetanus shot. She has a pretty nasty cut on her lip and some bruises, but she's okay. Everything should be fine, in the end."

He looks at her expectantly. Paul feels her face go white and can't think anything to say, can't take it in.

"Now, Paulina, we have to report this. In matters like this, as violent as this looks, we have to report, as you know." The doc looks over to Pete then back to Paul, who can only sit there.

After a long moment, she thinks she nods.

"The police should be here right away. They will need a statement and some information from you." The doctor stands up in finality. "For now, you can go see your daughter. As I said, she is sleeping. Triage is just waiting on a room, and then you can all go upstairs."

Paul nods but can't look up. She feels shame, for what she doesn't know. For herself or her daughter, she doesn't know.

She moves to stand up, but Pete has to help her. He holds her close and she limps her heavy legs into the room, finally into the room. A nurse in blood-smeared scrubs gives her a thin smile and closes the canister filled with bloodied rags and gloves.

Emily just lies there, eyes fluttering and oxygen tube at her nose. Her skin still very pale but doesn't have that scary hue anymore. The cut on her lip has a small bandage and there's a bruise under her eye that Paul hadn't noticed before. She studies her girl's face, needing to know every detail again. A bag of blood drips over her little head, down a small red tube into her arm. The needle pushed into her skin is unbearably huge. Paul can see the metal under the surgical tape.

Paul wipes away her annoying tears and takes her daughter's limp hand in both of hers. She squeezes, but there is no response, of course. Paul stands there, shaking. From faraway, she hears Pete sigh deeply and feels his breath on her neck. He stands quietly behind her, holding her up. After a moment, she realizes that's all she can do, all she has to do. She can only stand there, barely, and hold on.

Glass, he had said. Glass.

NO, PAUL AND her family had all been at the hospital together another time. Jake broke his arm, he was maybe seven, and they all crammed in to a cab and raced over. The driver said he couldn't fit everyone, said one of them couldn't come, not Paul or not Mom. But Cheryl just pushed her way in and told him to deal with it. Lou couldn't look. Jake's small forearm lay limp over a red bump in the middle, like a new elbow. Paul had to take charge, wrap his arm loosely with a tea towel and hold it steady as they all squished in the backseat. Emily was watchful and quiet, wedged behind her mother and against the door as the taxi bumped over the old streets to the hospital. Paul didn't let go of her nephew's arm, just held it up gently and smiled at him so he'd know everything would be okay. It was. He'd broken two bones, though. In the X-ray, they glowed like two jagged lines, cut and crooked like double zeds.

Paul doesn't let go of Emily's hand, but she can't smile down at her daughter, can't reassure anyone that anything is going to be okay. Emily doesn't wake up but Paul still doesn't let go, not until the nurses come to take Emily to a bed. Then she follows behind the stretcher to a quiet, beige room on a higher floor, with Pete behind her. He holds their coats over his arm and puts his hand on the small of her back in the elevator, so gentle she barely knows it's there.

When Emily is settled in her new bed, Paul resumes her position at her daughter's side, holding her limp hand, holding on for dear life. Pete gets her a chair and goes out to get coffees. Her mom comes in with a flurry, and her Kookom moves slow behind her. Cheryl sits her mother in the big, plush chair at the foot of the bed before she goes off:

"What the hell is wrong with this place? We were down at Information, they told us to go to Emerg. So we go, and they don't know where the hell you are." She looks down at her granddaughter, taking her small face in her bent, rough hands. She smells like booze and old cigarettes.

Paul looks at her mom's smeared makeup and unbrushed hair. She had rushed over. Paul hates it when she's like this, probably still drunk, but she only looks back down, at Emily. Emily is all that matters. Cheryl goes quiet and for a minute all she can hear is the soft drip of Emily's IV at her ear.

"What the hell happened?" Cheryl asks, taking Emily's other hand and looking around her. She does that too, looks around for something to do, some use to be. But there is nothing.

"She had glass," Paul starts, can barely start.

"Glass?" Cheryl looks at her own mother, who strains in her seat to hear.

"Glass," Paul chokes out. "In her."

"In her?" Cheryl's voice rises up unnaturally, painfully. "In there?"

Paul only nods. She can't open her mouth anymore—whenever she does, strange sounds come out, guttural cries from some place she doesn't open up anymore.

"How..." Cheryl looks around helplessly. "How did they get there?"

At that moment, Pete comes back in the room and the ladies go silent again. He carries a tray of coffees with stir sticks and creamers piled in the middle. A look of exhausted worry is on his usually unemotional face.

It is a random thought but it lingers a little too long. This isn't the first time Paul has wondered if she really knows him and what he could be capable of, if she can even imagine.

But she watches her mother get up to take the tray and wrap her arms around him. He looks so big with her small, short-haired mother in his bear hug. They talk but Paul doesn't hear. She just turns back to her daughter, to the bruise under her eye and the cut on her lip, swollen slightly under the bandage, sticking out like a small pout.

(10)

LOU

THERE'S A MOMENT when I first wake up when I only think of the good things. All the things I am grateful for run through my head, and I am happy, for a moment. I stare up at my ceiling, the rough edges where the plaster forms curves like white icing smoothed over a cake top, and I almost have a smile on my face. Then I realize I am alone here and remember what's going on. My body stiffens with all the things that have gone wrong, everything I have to worry about. The ceiling shows discoloration, small cracks that have browned with something, a leak that should be fixed. The ceiling, once beautiful and sculpture-like, shows its real self. The whole thing's probably going to fall on me one day.

I move my head and regret every glass of wine. I can feel them, sick inside of me, wanting to get out. I need painkillers, water and coffee, but I don't want to get my head off this pillow. I can only turn to the side, look away from the falling-apart ceiling. Thing's definitely going to fall on me one day.

But to the side is the empty doorway, cracked and needing to be repainted, where Gabe stood the other night. Where he knocked his knuckles on the wood. He knocked to be let in, or to be let out. The hollow sounds before and after. All the empty spaces he used to be.

I roll out of bed slowly. It's only 7:30 and I'm wide awake. I should force myself to sleep but Baby boy'll be up soon and need something, so I roll upright. Might as well.

Sunny and Jake are asleep in the living room, one on each couch, their long, teenager limbs reaching out. They're right where I left them when I came home last night. They just seem to have fallen over into sleep. When did they get this long? They seemed to have stretched since yesterday, skinny and long with thin ankles sticking out of the blankets and their oversized pants. Jake's mouth is open slightly, his upper lip darkened by hair. He looks more like his dad every day. He's growing into him slowly. Reminding me about a bunch of things I thought I forgot.

I nudge him gently. "Hey, hey," I whisper. "It's morning. Go up to your room."

My boy's eyes are bleary and dark. He gets up slow and shakes his friend rough.

"Sun. Sun, get up."

They stumble, wrapped in blankets. Good boys, really. Rita gives Sundancer a hard time, but just like my Jake, he's a good boy. My boy's also the most beautiful boy in the world. Just like his dad, James. The run-off and long-gone James. He was like Gabe. Pretty like Gabe. Never felt like mine, like Gabe. Couldn't stop running around, like Gabe. Only James left me for good, one day, out of the blue. But finally. He just put us out of our misery. Not like the agonizing misery of Gabe and me that goes on and on. No, James ripped that Band-Aid off quick.

We were so young. I thought it was just young and dumb stuff. Apparently it's just me stuff.

I SIT AT the table while the coffee brews. I swallow water and little orange pills to dull the throb in my head. I can't stand being upright too long and really should lean my head into something soft. In the morning light, the fresh snow curves over the boys' snow fort, making it soft and rounded. The old fence at the back of the yard is falling down, sagging in places from age and years of the boys kicking and climbing it. It's going to fall over soon. One day it'll just lose one more nail and melt into the ground. If it's still winter, the snow will fall on it, and I'll forget about it until spring.

"Mama?" Baby boy rubs sleep out of his eyes and wobbles straight into my lap. I take him up like breath, even with my aching arms. His curly black hair to my cheek. We sit there waking up, me waiting for the painkillers to kick in, listening to the coffee spit out too slowly. He cuddles in deeper, falling into me. I breathe him in.

"Can I have the marshmallow cereal?" He's been working up to this. I feel duped but get it for him anyway.

We snuggle up on the couch, still warm from where Jake was sleeping, Baby boy with his bowl, the pink milk slopping over the side, and me clutching my milky coffee. I lie on my side, my boy cozy in the nook I make with bent knees, and I'm asleep before the Sponge Bob theme song is over.

James was so gorgeous. Probably still is but we haven't seen anything of him in almost five years. He visited once just after Gabe came into the picture. I was pregnant, and his mom had called me. She's a sweet, gullible woman who thinks her son walks on water and just needed another chance to be a good

father. Just one more. I felt sorry for her and weepy with hor-
mones so I let him in. Just once more. James came in twitchy
and stinky from the night before. Nine-year-old Jake gave him
a polite hug and answered questions but didn't have any. He's
an old soul, my Jake. He's never known much of his dad, never
asked either, just understands somehow. He doesn't remember
when we were together, or the day his dad came home, packed
a bag, and said he was moving in with Darlene. He said it like
I knew who Darlene was, but I didn't, at first, really didn't
remember. He thought I was just being frustrating, again.

"You're just so cold, Lou, so fucking cold. You go around
like you don't need anybody, nobody can do anything for you,
or anything better than you. You're just too fucking cold for
your own good," he said as he packed.

Then I remembered Darlene from the bar. I had met her a
couple times. She was loud and fun. Two things I never was.

I never forgot that. Cold, he'd said. Fucking cold. The man
who was supposed to love me.

But the day he came over, James shuffled around nervously,
looking more immature than the kid he'd fathered and left. His
hands shook when Gabe handed him a coffee. My new man
stood over the old one, taller, wider, and I felt powerful. Then
I just felt sorry for this pretty boy who drank too much, and
now was a very old man even though he was only twenty-five.

Some time after that, a way-too-wise Jake told me, "Mama,
when I grow up, I'm going to be like Gabe and not get drunk."
He was playing a video game at the time, didn't even look up.
I was so proud I got teary eyed and was glad he couldn't see
me because he hates to see me cry.

I also still thought Gabe and I could make it. I still thought
I had warmed myself up.

"MAMA. MAMA!" BABY boy's face is in my face, milk dribbles on his chin. "Mama?" He shakes me just a bit.

"What? What!" I say, probably too rough. My head still aches.

He leans his elbow on my side and sweet-eyes me. "Can I have some juice?" He thinks a minute. "Please."

I take his face in both my hands and kiss his beautiful, milky cheek. I love him so much I just want to squeeze him.

I pour his juice into a plastic cup and warm up my coffee. I think about looking at my phone like I should, but I really don't want to. I turned it off last night in the cab home, last night at midnight when Gabe still hadn't called and I was fed up with checking the bloody thing. I fight the urge to look, to be disappointed again. Instead I sip coffee and groggily watch a couple episodes of my son's silly show.

I don't think I've really said a civil word to Gabe in months. I just gave up, my words clipped and my body stiff all the time, pulling away from him. I got cold with the misery and the winter. Gabe still tried for a long time, still said *I love you*, still looked at me long after I'd looked away. I couldn't give in. I just couldn't let him in anymore. Christmas blew by without even a pat on his shoulder. He got me a blender 'cause I asked for it. I said thank you but only half smiled. I got him a gift card.

I think he smiled, but I had turned away by then.

A couple of days ago, he said that he wanted to go live back home, could stay with his aunt and uncle and help out more. For now. He had said that a few times. For now. I just nodded, somehow got more stiff, and turned away.

When he came home from his last tour in November, I did meet him with a big smile and a warm, full-body hug. He had been gone three weeks. It was always so good when he was away. We talked every night, said *I love you* into the crackling connections. I always missed him.

He shrugged me off. "Don't get too close, babe. I need a shower so bad."

I remember laughing, so happy to have him back. Things were always so good when he came home. I took his bag for him and everything.

He was getting undressed, and I saw it. One small hickey on his collarbone, so small it could have been something else. He could have convinced me it was almost anything else. But he covered up too quick, put his big bathrobe on, and walked off with a quick grin. The Gabe grin. Just slightly too big and forced.

I put his bag down and sat on the bed, our bed. I got so cold I needed a sweater.

I still did his laundry.

I HEAR THE land line ring and ring. My stomach leaps but I don't bother to get up. Gabe would prefer to leave a message anyway. I just curl up, warm under the blanket, and hear the annoying cartoon theme music again.

I know I should do something. I know this crazy limbo between together and not together is weird and unhealthy. I'm sure it's making my boys uneasy too. They just know their dad and father figure goes off all the time, comes back whenever. What they must be thinking. Jake must just think this is what men do. At least Paul and I always knew our dad was out in the bush. He hated the city and was never around, but at least he was always in the same place. We could always call him. We never did but we knew we could.

"Ma," Jake calls from his room. "Ma! Kookoo's on the phone."

"What?" I wake up not knowing I had drifted off again.

"Kookoo's on my phone for you."

"Why the hell is she on your phone?" I trudge over, blanket wrapped around me like a shawl.

"She said she tried yours but you didn't answer."

I am suddenly way too annoyed at my mother.

"Hello?" My voice squeaks out.

"Lou. You have to come to the hospital. Now. You have to come now."

"Okay, okay, calm down, Ma. What happened?" I think of my grandmother, sweet, sweet Nokomis.

"We just got here. She's stable now, but Paulina..." Her voice cracks open. "You have to come now, Louisa."

"Okay, I know, I know. At Health Science?" Jake looks at me with sleepy eyes. I think of Paul, she'll be on shift and will probably already be down at Emerg with our grandmother.

"Yes, Kookoo and I just got here."

I'm suddenly confused. "Kookoo? What? What happened, Ma?"

"She got attacked, I guess. We don't know what happened. She was just bleeding..."

"Who was bleeding? Who's hurt?" My voice rises unnaturally. Jake's eyes grow bigger and stare at me.

"Emily. Emily's hurt. My sweet, sweet..." Her voice cracks again. I can hear Kookoo saying something soothing in the background. I can't hear the words but her voice is so even.

Emily.

My niece, so sweet and small, tiny like a precious doll. Emily.

"I'll be right there. Don't worry. I will be right there," I say and hang up. I turn off my brain. Don't let myself feel, don't let myself cry. I just go.

11

CHERYL

THE HOSPITAL ROOM is hot and full. Cheryl is weary and sits in a plastic chair next to the plush one where her old mom dozes. She can feel the heat rising inside and all around her. She pulls off her coat but still feels it, panic growing. She's sweating. She can feel the cigarette and booze seeping through her pores and feels gross. Gross and hot. She wants to pull off her clothes and throw the window open but she only breathes out, trying to slow her breath and make the gasps as quiet as she can.

Emily is still asleep, slightly propped up in the hospital bed and looking way too small in the cream-coloured covers. An IV looms over her, its thin, plastic tubes dripping clear liquid into the back of her hand. A white cuff is on her tiny finger, its machine beeping her pulse. Paulina holds on to her girl's hand. Her eyes have that glaze that comes after so much crying. Pete has finally stopped pacing, and slouches in a chair behind Paulina. He looks defeated and tired. They're all just sitting there like they don't know what to do, like they don't know what's hit them. Cheryl keeps looking at her granddaughter's face. The pale skin of her baby cheeks, her soft lips under the bandage barely coloured at all. Too small. It is one of those images she knows she will remember forever, not the good kind, the kind you don't want to remember but always will.

Louisa rushes in with that determined look on her face. She's trying to look tough but really only looks tired. Her oldest girl looks over everything like she's searching for incompetency. Cheryl knows that look. Louisa is going to try and fix everything now. She doesn't say much but goes right for the medical file with her social worker eyes, looking for answers. Somewhat satisfied, Louisa hooks the metal clipboard back on the end of the bed, and stands behind her sister rubbing her shoulders. Paulina barely registers the touch.

Paulina hasn't said a thing and hasn't let go of Emily's hand since they got here, since Pete came back with coffees that sit forgotten on the table, the floor, the windowsill, and they all started looking at the girl. Just looking and wondering how to avoid going crazy. Cheryl stares out the window to all of the neighbouring rooftops. She knows this, this waiting. She pulls at the collar of her sweater, wishing she could've grabbed a T-shirt, and hates it all.

When Pete called her, Cheryl had jumped out of bed, pulled on the first things she could find, and gone right down to her mom's apartment. Her mom was already awake but more confused. Cheryl explained in small words once they were in the cab. Bleeding. Okay. Hospital. Okay. The old lady's face broke then, but only then and only for a moment. Tears ran down her wrinkled face that pinched with unvoiced questions. But her mom was calm once she got here, and even when she looked at little Emily, still as stone, her old-lady face stayed strong. Emily, tiny, tiny Emily, was just broken.

Cheryl goes up and sits at the other side of the hospital bed, holds her granddaughter's hand. She wants to lean into Emily's shoulder, she wants to push her little face against that blanket and cry. But she grabs on to her hand, careful not to bother the finger cuff or the IV needle that she can see through the skin. She just rests it, limp and light, on top of her own. It's so small it makes Cheryl's look big. Cheryl feels so useless, only starts to whisper tiny things, small words just in case Emily can hear her: "My girl, my sweet girl, I love you. We're all here. You are good. You are safe now."

Cheryl had dreamt of snowshoeing again, in the bush, her old plywood house in the distance, Joe's house. She was with her Louisa this time — or at least she thought it was her girl. It was one of those dream creatures who is someone and then someone else. First she was Louisa, then her sister swaying on the shoes, and then a stranger. Maybe it was Emily. They all have the same shape, really, just move different. But the shadowed face kept shape-shifting in the snow.

Whoever it was, it was high-kneeing it through the bush faster than Cheryl could go. It was near sunset and the shadows were starting to stretch through the trees, the super thin ones just off the road. They stood like tall spikes sticking out of the snow, darkening there as the night grew. Louisa-then-Rain was far ahead, and Cheryl couldn't get her feet to go right, couldn't turn fast enough. Rain turned into someone else, Emily or her mom maybe, then a shadow of someone she didn't know at all. She felt the stranger, the unknown of her. She wanted to call but she didn't know what name to use, so she kept trying, moving, trying to get her feet to work right.

"Come on," the dream creature-woman-girl yelled back. "You're so slow."

"I'm coming," Cheryl panted, struggling. "Wait."

The creature was gaining distance ahead. The shadows grew. Trees became blacker, taller somehow.

"Come on," she called.

Cheryl struggled with her useless feet.

The dark image faded into the bush ahead, until Cheryl couldn't tell it from the trees.

She woke up in a hot panic, and then the phone rang. Then she didn't think—she moved.

TWO POLICE OFFICERS finally come in to the crowded hospital room. Their uniforms crisp and smelling like the outside. One is an older bearded white man, the other a very young-looking Métis. The young one looks long at Emily, still and sleeping, her eyelids pressed together like she's faking. He stands beside the bed by Paul. His body in its uniform is so wide it makes Paulina look even smaller. The older one just stands off, against the wall.

"Hello, ma'am," the young one starts, nervous and unsure. "Mrs. Traverse. I am Officer Scott and this is Officer Christie." He hands Paul his little white card. "I . . . we are sorry for what you're going through today."

Paulina only nods, looking at the card as if she's supposed to.

"You are all family members here?" He looks around and his eyes meet Cheryl's.

She stands up as tall as she can make herself, nods, and introduces everyone, explaining their connection to the pale girl who lies motionless in the bed, attached to beeping machines.

The young one looks around a bit more, but his eyes rest on Emily. He takes out an old coil notebook, the kind you find at the dollar store, and a chewed-up Bic pen. He writes for a long time.

"So," he starts again, "is there anything you can tell us? Anything unusual in Emily's behaviour? Does anything stand out?" He has light skin and hair, so young, with dark freckles across his nose but definitely Métis. In any other situation, Cheryl would ask him where he's from.

Paulina just looks at him and shakes her head, turns back to her girl.

"Do you know where your daughter was last night?" he says, standing over the girl, looking at her.

"Of course I know where she was." Paul's voice lit with a sudden edge. "She was going to sleep at her friend's house, but then she came home." Her voice cracks. "She's a good girl."

The officer pauses a moment, looks at the bed as if he was going to sit down, but just crouches down beside Paulina. "No one is disputing that, Mrs. Traverse, we just want to figure out what happened."

The other cop, the older one, Christie, just leans against the back wall and keeps surveying everyone. He looks at Pete and then Louisa, who both stare back. Defiant.

"Do you have any idea who would do this?" Officer Scott asks in a low voice, only to Paulina.

Paulina shakes her head. Cheryl shakes on the other side of the bed, and crosses her arms to hold herself in. She doesn't want to cry. She doesn't want to be even more mushy and useless. She wants to be like her Louisa and firm her lips in a tight line. No crying.

"Can you tell me where you were last night?" The cop tries again.

Paulina thinks for a minute. "We went for a drink, to the Briar. It's a pub. Until about twelve, maybe one, then came home."

"And Mr. . . . ." He looks to his notes. "Mr. Jacobs, he was with you?"

Paulina nods.

"When did your daughter come home?"

Paulina swallows. Her throat seems dry. Cheryl looks around for water for her, and nods at Louisa to get it. Paulina continues: "She must've...before we got home. She was sleeping so I just left her. I thought she was sleeping at her friend's place."

"Who is that friend?"

Paulina nods like she didn't hear. So Cheryl helps.

"Ziggy. Zegwan. She is my best friend's kid. They live in our building, where my mom and I live. She's a good girl. She'd never get Emily into any trouble. I've known her mom for years. They're traditional, very good people." She feels like she's rambling but can't stop.

"Can you put me in touch with them?" Yes, he's definitely Métis. Looks like one of Joe's brothers—same jawline, same almond-shaped eyes like those people, and, of course, the freckles.

"Of course." Cheryl thinks a minute and recites Rita's number. She will have to text Rita. How could she have forgotten to call to Rita? The heat grows inside her again.

"What time did you leave home this morning?" the older officer, Christie, interjects, looking only at Paulina.

"At six." Paulina's voice felt shaky, unsure. "Six-thirty. I got called in for a seven a.m. shift. Em was sleeping. Emily. In her room. I didn't want to wake her."

"And Mr. Jacobs reported that your daughter..." The young one looks at his little book again. "That she fainted after walking downstairs in the morning. He was in the kitchen when she 'passed out'?"

"That's what...she must have been bleeding all night..." Paulina's little voice trails off, getting smaller as it goes. She looks like a lost little girl, like she's the thirteen-year-old. Cheryl stays where she is but her hands ache to reach out to her child. Pete looks at everyone but doesn't say a thing.

"Okay, thanks, Paulina." Scott's smile is thin. "That's enough for now, I think. We'll get in touch with this friend, and then the nurses will let us know as soon as your daughter wakes up." He sort of smiles and the two officers leave, slipping out the door without so much as a sound.

Paulina nods and her eyes glaze over. She is just repeating motions and doesn't know what to do. Cheryl looks at her other daughter, who understands too. She had brought a cup of water, but just sets it aside and reaches out to touch her sister's shoulder again. At the very touch, or just when she knows the officers are gone, Paulina's tears fall over her baby, lying broken on the bed. That's when Cheryl finally gets up, her body stiff from its awkward, clenched position, and she holds on to her daughter until Paulina finally pulls away.

THE AFTERNOON MOVES in inches. Cheryl calls Rita instead of texting, too much to say, but it goes straight to voicemail. Rita never listens to her messages, but Cheryl leaves one anyway, listening to her best friend's curt, business-like voice before the beep.

"Reet. It's Cher." Does her voice really sound that rough? "Call me when you get this. It's important. It's crazy. Call me please."

Everyone in the room is all buzzing but somehow still dull with fear. Tired. She walks off to get more coffee. She follows the blue line to the cafeteria, the blank noise of people walking, talking, and chewing. Chairs scrape over linoleum and different kinds of machines beep. Crazy. Cheryl can only think of getting back there, to all her girls. She wants her mom to pat her hand the way she does, soothing and gentle. The skin on her mom's hands is so aged it's almost see-through, but she can still squeeze tight. Her mom's been so quiet on the plush chair.

Back in the room her mom looks calm but lost somehow. She never admits when she's confused. Cheryl should just take her home. But who would take care of her then?

The sun goes behind the building, and everything looks dark but it's only three. Cheryl stays at the other side of the bed. She pulls her chair up so she can rest her head next to her granddaughter's again. She sleeps in small bits and thinks of Joe. She should call the girls' father, Emily's grandfather. She wonders if anyone thought to let him know. She imagines how he'd be if he knew, futile and raging in his house on the edge of the bush. Would he come in to the city? Or just send comforting phone messages? Her older daughter paces intermittently, her mother snores lightly, and her younger daughter looks heavier and heavier but never lets go of Emily's hand. Pete goes in and out, talking on the phone, telling his family what has happened. Over and over, the crude words of this story repeat, and Cheryl tries to take it all in. Attacked. Don't know. Hasn't woken up yet. No, don't come. Not yet. He passes the messages and condolences to Paulina who doesn't seem to really hear.

"Why don't you guys go for a walk?" Cheryl suggests, looking to Pete, still pacing. "Get something to eat. The nurse said she won't wake up for a while yet."

"I can't eat, Ma." Paulina suddenly looks up, instantly angry, as if the thought itself is insulting.

Cheryl feels struck and coils back.

"Just a walk then," Louisa suggests, helping. "Get another coffee. Move a bit."

Paulina just shakes her head.

Louisa looks to Pete, who gets it.

"Come on, Paul. Just a little walk. We'll get these guys some coffee and I have my phone. They'll call if anything changes, right?"

Louisa and Cheryl nod. He has such a gentle voice and speaks to her so well, but still she shakes her head.

"Paulina. Go," her Kookom says from her chair, a soft command. No one knew she was awake. Paulina just looks at her. "Get me a tea."

She still doesn't want to, but she gets up. Pete helps her, but she doesn't look up and doesn't say a word.

As soon as they slip out the door, Louisa is whispering. "What are you thinking?" Her eyes plead. "You think he did this?" Her hands flay out, taking in the whole bed, their still-sleeping girl.

"No. Pete? No way!" Cheryl's voice low but still cutting. She had thought it for a second, but now it seems ridiculous. Doesn't fit. Isn't right. "What are you thinking? Of course, no!" Her voice is as hard as she can make it.

"Really? It's not like we know him all that well. And who else?" Louisa's eyes shift. She's in pain, Cheryl knows, so much pain.

Cheryl thinks about it a minute and speaks with measured words. "We don't know anything about him, except that Pete's a good man who makes your sister happy. Until we know anything else, we don't say anything." Cheryl makes her voice firm enough for Louisa to stop. She can't believe it, she won't.

Louisa starts to say something, but Cheryl stops her.

"You have to trust someone, Louisa. Not everyone is a monster."

They sit in grudging silence. The only sound is Cheryl's mom humming an old tune. Which one is it? It only comes to her ear in bits, over the sounds from the hall. Cheryl doesn't have the energy to ask, but she tries to think about what it could be for a lot longer than she normally would.

Louisa stews in her anger a while longer, but Cheryl won't even consider it. Pete is a good man. She knows good men. Louisa and Rita think she is just naïve. The things those two have seen, their jobs crusted with tragedy and filth. They've had to make themselves hard, shells with all their soft parts protected under layers and layers of suspicion and caution. Cheryl knows this. Rita has been this way for a long time. Louisa is growing this way too. Cheryl knew it, as soon as Louisa said she was going to be a social worker. It's the way she has to be. Hard. Cheryl's never been good at being hard. She has to feel everything. She has to be free to be weak and wrong. Social workers can't be wrong.

She watches her little Emily sleep. The girl's lips are still pale as paper, but the colour is rising slowly on her cheeks. The machines beep around her, insistent, almost harmonious, and Cheryl hardly hears them anymore. Yes, she should call Joe. He would want to know. He will say it's the city, the evil city, and they should have all stayed with him in the bush. Cheryl will want to tell him he should've stayed with his family no matter where they were, but she won't. Not today. It will be a bubble in her throat she will swallow because Joe really is a good man. He doesn't need her to spit her anger at him, still so fresh it comes out like it comes out like it's new. But, no. Not again. Not right now. Today, she will just listen to his pain, his ineffectual pain. And then she will make sure he will call his daughters to tell them something soothing.

Cheryl rests her head on the bed again, her mouth to Emily's hand, heavy with metal and plastic, and waits. She feels her granddaughter, warm and small, and thinks of good things — her lovely little Emily blessing, a quiet, fat baby, a happy child who loved to wear pink and flowers on her clothes. She dozes off and thinks of her wolves, the calm howling sounds that find her in the night and help her rest. She should make a painting for Emily. Emily with her baby face, Emily stronger than she knows. Cheryl will put a strong wolf-skin coat, black with only delicate touches of grey, around her little granddaughter to keep her safe.

Cheryl breathes out and tries to give her granddaughter strength. Wolves teach humility — they teach that we are all in this together, all a part of the same whole. If something happens to one of them, they all feel it. Cheryl breathes out deep and warm, breathes in Emily's pain and gives her back all the strength she has.

She hates these kinds of moments. The achingly painful ones. The ones that seem to last forever.

12

TOMMY

TOMMY FOLLOWS CHRISTIE into the noisy cafeteria. The old guy is "starving" and insists it's time to eat. Tommy is too riled up and doesn't want to sit down. He wants to go out, investigate, do something, police work. The old guy is always slowing him down.

"She'll wake up soon, might as well stay put," he tells Tommy. "Plus I'm fucking tired. Hate this fucking shift." The old cop looks at him for longer than he needs to. Christie often complains about the late shift. The worst shit happens on the late shift, he says, and they always seem stuck with it.

Tommy isn't hungry but doesn't have much choice. He totally fucked up that interview, and with the mood the old man is in, he is going to hear all about it. All he can do is sip on a horrible hospital coffee and take it.

"First of all, you don't fucking ask questions with the whole family there," Christie starts in, his mouth overflowing with fries. "That is not going to get you anywhere. They're all going to defend themselves and protect their own. It's just a can of worms you'd rather not open, my friend." He points a greasy finger at Tommy.

Tommy tries not to show his disgust, tries to make his face as unreactive as possible, just sips his coffee and waits for the next assault.

"And you were so fucking busy trying to be sympathetic to the mom, you didn't even notice the big fucking Nate fucker sulking and staring at her in the corner." Christie points with his cheeseburger this time.

"Yeah I did," Tommy snaps back but it sounds desperate.

"Well, you didn't take a good look. He was shifty as fuck!" Christie takes two big bites of his burger and chews in huffs.

"Yeah, but you think…" Tommy starts. "Don't you think there might be a connection to last night?" He regrets it as soon as he says it—it was too soon and he didn't say it determined enough.

"Last night? What last night? That gang-fight bullshit?" Christie just breathes in and swallows hard. "No. No, I don't. Where'd you get that idea?"

Tommy shakes his head. He's not going to say he just has a feeling. He's not going to give Christie the satisfaction of hearing him speak in clichés. He's just going to keep fucking quiet until he can prove it.

"Oh yeah, you got your *in-stinked* now, hey?" Christie chews at his fries while he talks. "Fuck me with your in-stinked. I'm too fucking tired for this shit."

Tommy didn't sleep much either but isn't about to complain. He kept thinking of that lady, woman—she kept turning into his mom in his dream. He dreamed that he saw it too, the four dark bodies, the girl beneath them. He couldn't sleep much after that. Hannah jumped out of bed before noon, went to some wedding show with her sister. She stood there at the bedroom door, like she wanted him to ask why she was going to a wedding show. He didn't have it in him to ask, so he pretended to fall back asleep. But he couldn't sleep. He kept thinking of the attack.

He went to the gym early. He told himself he just needed a workout, but really he wanted to be near the station and be ready. He went to his car as soon as he could and sat there listening to dispatch while he waited for Christie. There were two domestic calls, a couple girls missing from downtown, and some kid still gone from a detention centre in St. Vital. The only stabbing was in Central.

He was starting the car when he heard his name. Hospital had called. Aboriginal female. Blood loss. Signs of a sexual assault. He saw Christie coming toward him across the parking lot as slowly as only a fat man can go, his gloved hands wrapped around his coffee. Tommy took a quick breath and clicked on the radio button. He jumped when the passenger door opened.

"We got one. We have to take it," Tommy said too quickly.

Luckily Christie just groaned and sipped at his to-go cup. "I fucking hate this shift."

They drove in silence awhile. Christie read the doctor's report on the laptop screen, his lips moving as he read, slowly typing at the keyboard. The day was clear but cold as fuck, and the light was already starting to fade. Night again already.

Tommy went to pull into Emerg and Christie spit at him. "Wrong door. We're going to Children's, fuck." He pushed the laptop over with a shrug, and opened the door before Tommy even put it into park. "I'm going to take a fucking shit. This shit's crazy. I'll be at the coffee stand when you're done your reading."

Tommy watched the old guy through the sliding doors before he opened the computer up. The file contained the doctor's long narrative of emotionless medical jargon. It took a moment to settle in all the numbers and words one after the other. Girl. 13. Stitches. 8. Still unconscious.

AFTER HE'S DONE all his eating his crappy cafeteria food, Christie picks at his teeth with the corner of a bent business card. He just picked it up and folded it in two, opened his big, ugly mouth, and started picking. Tommy steps heavily as they walk back to the nurses' station. He talks to a pretty young blonde who tells them to wait—she gives a wave of her tiny hand toward the plastic chairs. The girl is still with the doctor, awake now, no head injury. Tommy only nods at nurse. She stands straight, looks down and smiles up, flirting with him. He only grins and walks over to his partner. Police work.

"You just keep the questions to the facts, if you can fucking manage?" Christie tells him again. He said Tommy should get more "practice" but really he's just too tired to do the questioning himself.

Tommy tries to remember everything. He stands there watching the nurses in their scrubs and trying to think of each word and how he's supposed to say it.

Hannah had wanted to be a nurse—when they met, that's what she wanted to be. She even got into nurse's school but left after six months. It was too hard, she said. She went to legal secretary school instead. It was only a year and she said it wasn't hard at all. She was a lot happier. She could still party all weekend and liked the office clothes she had to wear. She'll probably never make much, but at least she'll be happy. Besides, he was going to move up soon, be an important cop, and make lots of money. She would say this to their friends, if they asked, even if they didn't. She had it all worked out.

"You can go in." The young blond nurse smiles at him again. She's cute, but he has to concentrate.

He walks in first. The big guy leans against the windowsill and doesn't meet his eye. The old grandmother, still in the armchair, looks as if she's sleeping, her head to the side and her eyes closed. The older lady with short hair, maybe early fifties, grandmother, Cheryl, still sits on other side of the bed, so close to the girl, her granddaughter. The aunt stands behind with arms crossed. She is a young, good-looking woman, high cheekbones and shiny dark hair. And stern. That's what her look would be called. *Stern*. Tommy knows that look well. His aunts all have it, his mom too, when she wants to, but this woman is also so beautiful. The kind of woman who doesn't know she's beautiful or doesn't care, who is always serious and doesn't give a fuck what anyone thinks of her. The kind that intimidates the hell out of him.

He looks away from her and down at the girl, Emily. Her eyes are so brown they're black and have long eyelashes. She's somehow prettier than he thought she'd be. Her left cheek and bottom lip swell out, but overall she doesn't look that bad with the colour back in her skin. He smiles and sits at the foot of the bed, far enough from the mother, Paulina, but he still feels her tense up. He has a photo of his mom as a kid, and she looks just like this girl. It's his favourite picture. His mom in braids, dirty jeans, and rubber boots. His bush mama, when she was so happy. She's not smiling in the picture but you could tell. She loved her life once.

"Miss?" Tommy addresses Emily warily. "Miss, Emily. Hi. I'm Officer Scott and this is Officer Christie. We're here to help. Are you able to tell us anything about what happened?"

It's a long drawn out sigh before the girl starts.

"I . . ." She looks to her mother. "We went to a party."

"Who's we?" His voice is still soft but he feels excited for some reason. He can feel Christie tense and alert behind him.

"Zig and me." The girl wipes her hair out of her eyes, her index finger clumsy with the plastic pulse-taker thing, the back of her hand heavy with an IV needle.

"And that's where the attack took place? At this party?" he says, trying to speak slowly.

"No," Emily says, looking down at the blanket covering her. "After."

"After where, Emily?" He can't hold in his odd excitement. It all seems so real and he's going to fix it. But he feels the mother, Paulina, glaring at him.

Emily shakes her head and looks at her mother again.

"Maybe," Christie's voice bellows in strong, "maybe we should talk to Emily on her own."

"No!" Emily shakes her head, suddenly frightened.

"I think you'll find that's completely illegal, officer." The beautiful aunt talks over his head to his partner. "Her mother should be present at all times."

"Not if we think there's cause for concern," he snaps back too soon.

"If there was cause for concern, you'd have a social worker here already. As it is, you just want to get this over with, so go ahead." She is so upright and sure of herself. She crosses and re-crosses her arms. Christie just makes a grunting noise as if to say it's not worth the bother, and motions for Tommy to continue. Out of the corner of his eye, Tommy can see the other grandmother, the really old one, who sort of smiles. Tommy knows that kind of look too.

The man, the boyfriend, Peter, gets up and goes out of the room. The women just watch him go and then turn back to Tommy. They are all waiting. He clears his throat.

"Okay, Emily, please," he starts, forgetting everything. "If you can tell me anything you can remember. It was not at the party, you said."

Emily shakes her head.

"So when was it—on your way home?" he tries.

Emily's little face freezes. Her hair is messy on her pillow, she keeps brushing it out of her eyes. She's so nervous.

"Do you know who attacked you?" He leans in and tries to look as comforting as he can.

Emily shakes her head, back and forth, slow though, like she's in pain. She squeezes her eyes shut and tears fall out.

"Okay." His voice rises. "Were these people from the party? Did you see them there?"

Emily just looks at her mother who leans down and smooths the girl's hair away and smiles with so much love Tommy's heart contracts.

"Is there anything you could tell us to, um, distinguish the attackers?" he says finally. "Any tattoos, or marks or scars, or something."

Emily shakes, not so much her head, but her whole body, and turns away. It probably hurts so much to move, but still she turns away from him.

"Can we take a break?" The mother looks defeated. "She needs to rest." She is looking only at her daughter, with a sort of pride and sorrow. Tommy knows that look, too.

"I know, Paulina, but this is important." He's being so careful with his words. "Do you think they knew you, Emily? Or were they following you?" he says to the back of her small head.

The aunt cuts in. "She needs to rest."

She speaks with such authority that Tommy almost gets up to leave. But then, Christie steps forward.

"You have to give us a little more to go on, Emily. We can't help you if you don't tell us everything that happened." His voice stretches across the room, loud and confident, a man used to being listened to.

The mother just sits there, tense, and grabs onto her daughter's hand, nodding for her to go on. The aunt frowns but then looks down at her niece and her stern face softens, becoming even more beautiful. The girl turns back with a wince on her face.

"It was dark." She pulls the blankets closer.

"I know this is hard..." Tommy starts.

"Just tell them what you remember," her mother offers, helping her with the blankets, covering her up to her chin. "Just what you remember."

Emily shakes her head, one small movement over and over. "It was dark, I couldn't see them..."

"Them? Okay, how many?" Tommy tries.

"Four." Her small voice drips into the pillow. "I think."

"Four, okay, and what were they wearing?" His voice jumps. He has to swallow to keep from sounding too excited.

"Black clothes, black jackets." Her eyes open and shut, trying to blink everything away. "It was cold."

"Okay, good, Emily, that's good." Tommy can't help smiling. "You said it was cold, was it, was it outside? Did this happen outside?"

The girl nods. Tommy wants to shout but stays calm and collected.

Christie is not as patient, nor as excited. "Was there anything that made them stand out, like scars on their faces or the colour of their hair?"

Emily is quiet for a moment. Christie is about to talk again when she finally says,

"I think, I think they had long hair?" She says it like a question.

The room waits.

"One had a . . . a braid."

"Okay, okay, that's good, Emily. That's good." Tommy smiles. Elated.

"Okay, is that enough for now?" The aunt looks right at him.

He nods but thinks, and looks up to Christie.

The old cop sighs and says a quiet "Yeah."

Out in the hall, Tommy is determined not to be smug, determined not to say anything like *I told you so.* But he has to smile. The old guy looks at him, shakes his head, but Tommy just smiles.

"Congratu-fucking-lations, May-tee," he says. "You're now the proud owner of one hell of a fucked-up rape case."

Tommy's face melts down, slowly.

"And your pool of suspects is only every fucking gang-banger on the north side." He laughs one of his old smoker laughs. "How's that *in-stinked* feeling now?"

By the time they get to the elevator, Tommy is sweating so much he pulls on his collar a bit to see if it'll loosen. He tries to square his shoulders and stand tall.

Christie's name sputters over the radio at his shoulder, and the old guy calls dispatch on his phone.

Tommy's got his top button undone but keeps pulling on his collar while he waits, anxiety rising in his chest.

Hannah wants to get married. That's her new project.

"We're the last ones not married out of all our friends," she said one night, eyeing another glossy magazine. "Even my sister's getting married and she's younger than me."

He can feel her gearing up for this, her next project. Life is just series of steps for Hannah. It's simple really, one thing after another. First he's a corporal, then a sergeant. First they get married, then buy a house. Then have some babies. Tommy knows this is the way it's supposed to be, he just doesn't know how he feels about it, if he feels anything about it.

He just knows it's there, laid out in front of him. He doesn't really have to do anything, not really. He just has to go along.

"Fucking great." The old man mutters as he puts his phone down.

"What?"

Christie doesn't answer. The elevator opens and he presses the button for the main floor.

"Good thing we're already here," the old guy says with a smirk. "We gots another victim there, *in-stinked*." He slaps at Tommy's shoulder.

"What?" Tommy says again, quieter.

But he heard. The words linger and his breath slows back to normal as the floors beep down in quick succession. Another. Victim.

13

ZEGWAN

ZIGGY LIES IN the big bed, her face covered with the blanket and turned to the wall. She's hiding, all huddled and cocooned. She knows she has to get up soon, it is late morning probably, and Rita's going to start yelling any time now, but she doesn't move. Not yet. She's hot as hell but she doesn't pull the blanket down, just holds it there, her hands on her head, her phone in her hand, trying to stop all the repeating thoughts in there, trying not to move at all.

Her mom got in late. Ziggy didn't look at the clock but heard her humming and knew she had been drinking.

"I thought Emily was sleeping over," her mom half whispered to her back. That was the only thing she'd said.

Ziggy just mumbled like she was sleeping, and tried to breathe deeper. Deeply. Like she imagines she does when she's sleeping. Rita finally flopped in the bed beside her and started snoring in no time.

Ziggy tried to be as quiet as she could but couldn't stop crying and shaking. She kept looking at her phone. Nothing.

She kept telling herself there was nothing to worry about but she didn't believe it at all.

Her mother is up early like always and has been puttering around the house for hours. The radio hums in the kitchen, country music. Ziggy usually loves hearing the radio in the kitchen—it reminds her of being back home. She misses home this morning, has never wanted to be anywhere so bad in her whole life.

She can smell it. The wide-open field would be so cold and smell like clean air. Her Moshoom's wood stove burning in the morning air, that muskeg smell from the outside woodpile, and the faint crackle of the fire. They all used to get up so early on the weekends. Her grandfather in his warm layers with his red flannel on top and her dad in his worn, country jeans and sweater, ready to work. She liked getting up with them like that, listening to them talk at the table. Her Moshoom had tin cups and plates, just like the olden days. She would wrap herself in woollen blankets and sit on her grandfather's lap as he talked, his Adam's apple wobbling against the back of her head, her dad nodding and smiling down at her like he used to. She'd never felt so warm.

Not like this morning when she's hot as all hell but still can't stop shaking.

She must've fallen asleep again because the sound of her mother's phone ringing makes her jump. It's that guitar strumming sound Ziggy's heard so much she's memorized every strum and pause. It's so dumb. Ziggy's usually annoyed but today she's just frozen with that same fear. She looks at her phone, still nothing, just her screensaver of music lyrics. She waits.

Rita is through the door and shaking at her foot.

"Zig! Zegwan, wake up!" Her mom's voice squeaks unnaturally high. She must be really mad.

Ziggy stiffens but tries to groan like she's deep asleep.

"Zig, I need you to wake up right now!" She's trying to make her voice normal but it's not working.

"What?" She turns slowly under the blanket, feeling her face in every inch. This is not going to be good.

"Zig!" Her mom is exasperated and pulls at the blanket.

The cold gush of air soothes her skin, but the daylight is so bright even with her eyes closed. She covers her face before her mother can squeak again.

"What the hell happened to you?" Rita's voice breaks all the way. Ziggy doesn't have to look to know how mad her mom is now.

It was Ziggy's job to pile the wood that her Moshoom cut. It wasn't an easy job, and you had to be very careful and very strong. Sunny had had that job before but he got fired because he wasn't careful enough. Then Sunny had to shovel with dad. Not the cool on-the-tractor shovelling either — he had to use an old hand shovel. That was the kind of job you got after her Moshoom fired you from something.

"You have to make sure each piece of wood is firmly in place before getting the next one. I can't have this pile just falling over. It'll just get all wet in the snow and then . . . useless." Her Moshoom always waved his hands whenever he said *useless*. It was the worst possible thing to ever be. Sunny wasn't useless — he just made too many mistakes. He wanted to cut the wood but he wasn't ready yet. He had to be careful or else he could get useless. Ziggy was never going to be useless. Not ever.

She worked hard. Moshoom chopped wood very fast. His old red-flannel arms took the axe so high and then straight down, each piece cut all the way through on the first try. Ziggy had to be fast so the wood wouldn't sit in the snow too long, and she dusted the pieces off before setting them carefully on the others. Her old leather mitts were quick. Her small hands gripped each log. She put the sharp edges in between the rounded pieces because they stayed in place better, just like her Moshoom showed her. And when the pile got too high, she got the old wood chair from the shed and kept working. She had to go even faster then so she could step down, get the wood, and step back up.

By the time they were done, she would be breathing hard, but her Moshoom would clap his leather hand on her back and nod down at her.

"Go warm up," he'd say. "We'll clean up the kennels after lunch."

He'd wave her off to go drink hot chocolate and eat reheated stew, but he'd keep working. Her Moshoom never sat down when it was daylight. He told her that's why he liked the winter so much, because he rested more.

Rita gets a cold, wet cloth and puts it on Ziggy's face, covering her eyes with beautiful darkness. It helps. She fixes it to her face and feels her swollen eyes, one more puffed out than the other. She doesn't try to open them yet.

She hears Rita's phone beep and her brother's muffled voice on the other end of the line.

"You heard yet?" her mom says.

Sunny seems to say yeah.

"How's Jake and Baby?"

Sunny's garbled voice.

"Okay, good, tell him to call Gabe. He needs to be down here now. Then come home."

More garbles. Sunny has a high-pitched mad voice just like Rita.

"I need you here, Sundancer. Now!"

High garble.

"Because, your sister's face is smashed in, and I need you to help me take her to the fucking hospital."

The whole world seems to stop for second. Rita can exaggerate stuff sometimes, just to get the reaction she wants.

"I know, I know. Okay. I'm going to call a cab." Ziggy hears the hang-up beep and Rita's sigh, deep from the bottom of her belly. "Okay, kiddo, let's get you dressed, okay?"

Ziggy lets the cloth fall and winces her one eye open. Her left eye is still shut almost all the way and she doesn't want to force it open. It feels like a balloon of water on her eyelid and it's numb like a blister. Her right eye is better but still stings. Everything looks red, even her mom's back to her, as Rita looks through the closet, thumbing Ziggy's sweaters.

Ziggy loves being back home in the summer too. She loves the wheat fields and tall grass and bush. But when she misses home, when she misses living there, misses her dad and her Moshoom, she thinks of wintertime. When they'd be outside until it was dark, which was so early most of the time but Ziggy still felt so, so tired by the time she saw the stars. When Sunny would pull her around on the old wooden toboggan or they'd slide down the ditch that was the only hill, and it was barely longer than the toboggan itself. Still they'd slide.

She remembers once he pulled her across the road and deep into the bush. He said there was a mountain and dragged her far in. The trees were thick and dark and the snow was so shallow in some places she could see the mashed brown leaves on the ground. He took her all the way to the river. The mountain was really just a hill, but was about three toboggan-lengths high. The slide down was always too short and the walk up too hard, but they kept doing it 'til they looked around and it was completely dark. They heard their mom's high-pitched voice and saw a small light break through the trees. Rita made them both walk back, kept telling them to wiggle their toes and kept swearing as their empty toboggan hit her heels as she pulled it behind her.

When they got home, she told them to take off all their outside clothes and socks too. She poured water into the old sick bucket and made Ziggy put her feet in it as she sat in front of the fire. The water bit at her toes and burned.

Frostbite, Rita called it as she boiled water on the stove like she did when they lived at home.

When her Moshoom and dad came in, Rita told them what her "nasty children" had done and Dad scolded them for going out too far. Moshoom never got in the way when their parents gave them heck. He just sat in his chair because it was after dark and smiled knowingly at Ziggy. He rolled his eyes behind his son's head and it was all she could do not to giggle.

She wonders if Sunny remembers that. She wants to ask him as they all drive to the hospital in the back of a cab. Rita didn't trust herself to drive and didn't know how long they'd be there anyway. Better to take a cab, she'd said. Parking at the hospital is impossible. Ziggy used to love riding in cabs, like it was the best treat in the world. Today it just feels stupid. Her mother always overreacts.

When he saw her, Sunny looked down at her and smiled. "I hope the other guy looks worse."

Rita looked at him like he was in trouble but only told him to get moving.

On the side of the Children's Emergency Room there's a large wooden play structure in the shape of a tree.

"Wanna go play, Zig Zig?" Sunny teases and points.

Rita just stares at him. She's so quiet that Ziggy thinks she must really be in trouble. They wait there for so long, Rita jittering the whole time. Sunny's either cracking jokes or trying to sleep. Ziggy tries to slowly open her right eye and keeps a cold cloth to her left. She saw her face when she went to the bathroom. It's all red and poofy and pretty scary looking. Her cheek is puffed out, and her lips are so chapped they've broken open and are bleeding a bit. Her jaw is sore on the right side. She pokes at the skin. It'll probably bruise. Her fingers are still numb. Frostbite. Her right shoulder hurts too. She knows that's where she hit the hard snow.

When they finally get a bed, it's nighttime. The windows are all the way dark and they still have to wait for the doctor. Rita goes out for a smoke. Ziggy just lies down and wants to sleep, her head so heavy and throbbing now. Everything seems to hurt more as the day goes on.

"Hey, Sun," she says.

"Yeah?" He's sitting on the far chair.

"'Member that time we took off to the river and stayed too long?"

"When we were little?"

"Yeah."

"Yeah. Rita was so fucking mad." He laughs like he always does.

"Nimishomis wasn't. I think he was proud of us, somehow..." Her voice fades.

"Yeah, I bet he was."

"I miss him."

"Me too."

ZIGGY DOESN'T WANT to wake up, but she's sitting upright for some reason and someone is pushing into her cheekbone.

"Doesn't appear broken," a strange voice says. "We'll X-ray it to be sure, but it looks okay, Mrs. Sutherland."

"Okay? How the hell can that look okay?" Rita's voice goes up.

"From an ortho perspective, I mean, it doesn't look like the bone is broken."

Ziggy doesn't want to open her eyes. She wants to keep them shut and pretend she's back by the river tobogganing down the bank, only this time the way down will last longer. It'll last as long as possible.

The doctor seems to go away and Rita puts her hand on Ziggy's. Her mom's hand is so cold but feels nice, so she grabs it. Rita squeezes back and Ziggy thinks she might cry for the first time today.

She doesn't want to.

"Why don't you go get us something to eat, Sunny?" She hears the rustle of Rita's purse. "Whatever you want?"

"Zig?" her brother asks.

"Um," she says. "Fries? Maybe a drink."

"You sure that's all?" Her mother's voice so soft.

Ziggy tries to nod but it hurts in her neck now. She squeezes her right eye. Her left eye is still swollen and starting to feel itchy. But she's too scared to touch it.

"Okay. And get the nurse to come in when you go, okay?" Rita says to Sunny. "We'll get you some painkillers, okay sweetie?"

Rita doesn't call Ziggy that too often. She's a lot tougher than Paul, Emily's mom. She's even tougher than Lou, Jake's mom, though Jake thinks it's a close call. Paul's a softie though. Everyone knows that.

When she hears Sunny walk off, Rita leans in close.

"Honey." Her voice is at Ziggy's ear. "I have something to tell you."

Ziggy tries to turn as best she can.

"Mommy?" she starts. She doesn't want Rita to finish. She doesn't want to know.

"It's Emily, honey." Rita squeezes her hand tighter.

"Is she dead?"

Rita seems to swallow before she answers. "No, she's going to be okay. She's just very hurt."

Ziggy can't breathe. At least, she can't breathe for a minute.

"The police are on their way and you have to tell them what happened." She can hear Rita breathing funny. Ziggy finally opens her right eye and sees her mother crying. "Or you can tell me, if you don't want to talk to them, but you have to tell us what happened."

Ziggy doesn't move but closes her eye again. She just wants the snow, the smooth rush of sliding down on to the frozen river, the smell of cold trees. Ziggy just wants to go home.

"Zegwan? My sweet girl?" Rita huffs and her voice distorts unnaturally. "My girl, what happened?"

"We . . . we went to a party." Her voice is not much louder than a whisper.

"What party?"

"This, gang party. Emily wanted to go." Ziggy feels too close. She wants to be far away again.

"Why did Emily want to go to a gang party?" Rita doesn't let go of her hand.

"She didn't know it was a gang party. She wanted to go see this guy." Ziggy keeps her eyes shut. That helps.

"And then what happened?" Her mom's voice is a sigh.

"His . . . girlfriend saw us." The fear. That fear.

"His girlfriend?" Rita's voice goes high.

"This girl, this big girl. We tried to run away." *Her legs, pushing her legs to go.*

"And then what?" Soft again.

"This other girl, she caught me. I fell. She beat me up, Mommy." Zig is huffing now too. She opens her one eye but her mom just looks at her, not really anything, mad or sad.

"What about Emily? Did you see what happened?" is all she says.

"She ran away."

Rita chokes.

"She ran ahead of me. She got away, and then I couldn't find her." The cold, so cold.

Rita keeps making choking noises.

"Mommy?" Something's so wrong.

"She didn't get away, sweetie. Someone attacked her."

"Those girls?"

"No, honey, no. Someone, someone . . ." She talks slowly. She doesn't want to say the words. "Raped her, sweetie. She was raped."

But she does say the words, and then Ziggy has to hear them. She opens her eye again to see her mom's head hunched all the way over.

"What do you mean?" It doesn't make sense.

"I mean, Emily was attacked and . . . raped." She swallows. "She's upstairs here in the hospital. She's going to be okay now. She was hurt but she is okay now."

Ziggy doesn't think Rita is exaggerating this time.

She thinks of it all again. How that girl, Roberta, knelt over her. How she pounded on her face but it didn't feel like anything at first until she pushed her head into the hard snow. That hurt so bad she thought she was cut. Then that girl jumped off, and she and that other girl ran off.

Ziggy heard them all yell and then leave, but she could only lie there and watch the snow fall out of the pink sky.

When she finally got up, she wandered down the block, stumbling as she went. She peered down that big open field but couldn't find Emily. She called her phone but there was no answer. She called her name into the cold air in case she was hiding somewhere, but nothing. By the time she got home, her cheeks and fingers and toes burned with frostbite. She checked her phone. She'd called Emily thirty-seven times, kept texting over and over, but no answer. She didn't know what to think. But she didn't see Emily. Emily got away.

Her face thawed when she finally lay in her bed. She pulled the covers over her until she felt too hot, until she started to hurt in a whole different way.

(14)

PHOENIX

THE SMOKE STINGS her eyes, but Phoenix takes another, long
drag off her stub of a cigarette. She watches the smoke swirl off
the ember and dance in the cloudy, grey air. The room is thick
with it. Somewhere, Dez coughs. Not somewhere — she's just
over there, but the sound feels far away, echoes. Over there,
the morning breaks open with grey sun. Not over there, just
out the window. Phoenix watches it and the smoke spirals up
to the ceiling and disappears into the haze.

"What the fuck, Mitchell? Pass 'er here!" Roberta calls out.

Phoenix jumps at the voice, and then she's just annoyed.
Her peaceful silence ended. How long had it been?

Desiree's boyfriend laughs behind the grey clouds, behind
his red slit eyes, and passes the thin joint to Roberta.

"Finally, fuck." She smiles. "Look at that fucking heater.
Fucking guy." She laughs an awkward laugh, flicks the ember
on the edge of an ashtray and takes a hoot. "Argh, you slob-
bered all over it. Fuck. This joint ain't Dez, boy."

Mitchell laughs again, and Dez, slack across his lap, giggles too. Her eyes are bright red and nearly swollen shut. Roberta sucks back the smoke as hard and as long as she can, making a choking noise, holding it in.

Phoenix rubs her own eyes and tries to focus. Roberta passes the burning stub over. Phoenix's hands are heavy. She manages to pinch the small thing but burns her skin.

"Fuck."

They all laugh at her.

She takes a small hoot, and reaches out to pass the joint to Cheyenne, who takes it with expert fingers, thin and beautiful fingers, manicured looking, all painted, not a chip on them.

"That's it, Phoen?" She sort of laughs. "You losing your touch, girl?"

They all laugh again.

Phoenix ignores them and leans back into the couch, sinking in, feeling like she just ran a few blocks. She looks to her fingers, blackened. Fuck. She forgot she was wearing makeup and now it's probably all smeared across her face. Fuck it. She takes another drag off her tiny cigarette. The filter is burning, not much tobacco left, but she watches the orange light up as she inhales the last of it. It glows. Like a tiny city at night, houses lit up through a thousand windows, a neighbourhood sitting on the side of a steep, black hill. Phoenix wonders what this would be like, houses on a hill. She's never seen them except on TV or in the movies, but she thinks it would sort of look like that.

She must've passed out because when she opens her eyes again, the room is different. The light is different, bright but fading. Desiree and her man are passed out in the chair, their arms and legs all intertwined like they're one person with two of everything. Cheyenne is curled up on the other side of the couch, her tiny body in almost a circle. Her mouth is open but she still looks pretty. Roberta's nowhere to be seen.

Phoenix checks her phone. 4:30. No calls.

A picture of her and Roberta last night is on the screen, one taken early in the night when they were all dressed up, looking tough, looking good. Roberta did Phoenix's makeup. Her eyes were thick with shiny black lines that edged up at the ends, and her cheeks sparkled with red glitter. Phoenix thought she looked like a fucking goof, but everyone said she looked good. In the picture, she and Roberta are laughing like nothing bad has ever happened to them. Roberta had been acting sketchy around her too at first, but then they hung out in the bathroom, everybody putting on makeup, and it was like old times, like before she went to the Centre. Like they all remembered they were each other's girls. Always.

Phoenix's mouth feels like a butt, so she goes to the kitchen to find some water. The counter has filled up again with bottles, old fast-food bags, and used glasses. She finds a glass that's not too gross and rinses it out. She runs the water long to get it nice and cool and clear, then drinks in big gulps until her tongue feels normal and her stomach feels full.

Phoenix secretly likes quiet times like these, when everyone is sleeping and she can hear them breathing, like their breath makes the place warm. Her uncle is somewhere in his room with his music playing softly, long guitar solos so familiar they just drift by. His roommate, Kyle, is in the other room. She can hear his snoring from here. He's a good guy. They were all hanging out last night, and he kept his cool even when shit got heated. Kyle's okay, even if he does fucking snore.

When people sleep around her, Phoenix likes the look of them, how their faces relax. Most people look so different than when they are awake. When she was little she used to watch her baby sisters sleep. Back then when they were always alone and she was up and scared all night, she would lie next to Cedar-Sage and watch her for hours. Her littlest sister Sparrow would just sleep, mouth open and cute, but Cedar-Sage would talk, not real words, mostly nonsense, but it was fun to listen to her. Phoenix would lie there and ask her questions to keep her talking, and laugh because her answers never made any sense. She liked doing that, waiting for her mom to come home, waiting for the sun to come up so it wouldn't be dark anymore. She was stupid and scared like that, but she was only a little kid.

Now, the sun shines against the hedge outside, the yellow slipping between the houses and turning orange as it lights up the bare branches. Just beyond, the Hydro towers loom huge and metal. The colour splashes against them too. They look so bright, like they're lit up from the inside. Two stand there, just across the street, a couple houses down. Large and wide Xs, they look like robots with arms up. They seem to be watching, somehow, like lookout towers or something.

That's where it all went down, over there, behind those Hydro things. Phoenix sees it all again in her head, the sounds, the shapes. She sees it all like she was only watching, the way everyone was looking at her. The way her uncle looked at her. The way Clayton looked away. She braces her body as if for wind, shakes it off, and wants a smoke. She finds half of one on the table with lipstick on the filter. It must've been Roberta's. She lights up and inhales hard.

She goes back to the couch and sits down. Her spot is still warm. She takes another drag and almost feels normal again.

She wants to check her phone again, but fights the urge. She wants to see if he messaged somewhere but knows better. She doesn't expect to hear from Clayton again, and really, she doesn't blame him that much.

She isn't tired but she curls into the couch arm anyway.

Nothing to do but sleep. She thinks of her sisters, their warm little bodies sleeping next to her. She misses Cedar-Sage. She should've called her yesterday, when she got out. She knows her sister is still at that Luzia's house. Phoenix has the number written down somewhere in her bag. She should've called. Today, she doesn't much feel like it anymore. Dez shifts in her sleep and Mitchell's arms fall back around her.

Phoenix closes her eyes, listens to all the breathing, and tries to feel warm again.

She asked Cedar-Sage once, one morning, "What were you dreaming about? Do you remember?"

They were in the apartment on Arlington, the one with the really big living-room window. It made the room cold but bright. Phoenix liked that place.

"No," was all her sister had said, her little body stiff. She was trying to be snarky.

"You talk in your sleep." They were sitting on the couch eating cereal out of the box because there was no milk. Sparrow was there too, drooling on the floor, like she did. Cheerios stuck to her wet cheeks. She was probably not even two. Cedar-Sage was maybe five.

"Oh." Cedar-Sage's big brown eyes were so soft and confused, looking up to Phoenix.

"I don't know. It's like mumbling." Phoenix shrugged. "Sometimes you make sense. Sometimes you don't."

"I'll remember, Phoenix," she had said and nodded, looking like she took the task very seriously.

Phoenix wakes up when she hears someone in the kitchen. Her uncle, Bishop, shirtless, hairless and tatted, rummages through all the drawers, knocks over bottles and garbage. She gets up to go help him, but leans on the doorframe and waits for him to ask.

"You got a smoke, Phoen?" he asks, not looking at her.

"Naw." She shakes her head and looks down.

"Fuck, I had a fucking pack here. Fucking losers!" He's not really yelling. "Go look in Kyle's room. His bottom drawer."

Phoenix does what she's told, knowing her uncle has a lot of things to worry about. She doesn't knock. The room is dark with the black flag hanging over the window, the walls covered with posters of old rappers Phoenix isn't really into. Kyle, still snoring, is naked and asleep under a thin blanket with a skinny girl on either side of him. One of them wears the black shirt he was wearing last night. The other is naked too, her mouth slack, her nipples perfect, brown and small, just like the rest of her. Kyle grunts and shifts. His thin, tatted arm falls across the naked girl. The Reaper there grins at Phoenix, even in the shadows.

She finds the stash of smokes in the bottom drawer. Tied in a Safeway bag, dozens of rez smokes, some broken, all probably dry as shit. She pulls out five good ones, slips one behind her ear.

On her way to the kitchen, she lights two and drops the last two on a clean spot on the table for her uncle to have later. She passes a lit one to him. He only nods, still not looking at her, and sits hunched over, hands drawn together like he's praying. Yeah, he looks like Grandpa. He is skinny like she imagines Grandpa was, smaller than Phoenix who takes after who knows who, some fat relative. Bishop takes a couple hard drags before he looks around the table of empty beer boxes and full ashtrays.

"Someone should clean this all up, fuck," he tells her.

"I'll get Cheyenne to do it when she gets up." Phoenix sits down across from him. He slumps more, brooding. She feels something coming.

She knows Grandpa Mac only from a picture. She got it out of Elsie's shit once, and never gave it back. In it, the old man looked like Ship does here, slumped, skinny, brooding, only, in the pictures, Grandpa Mac was sitting on an old car, the old-fashioned kind with a rounded top, all shined up. Even in the dull photo the car looked shiny. And the brooding man looked somehow happy too. Bishop hasn't looked happy in a long while.

"This shit's so fucking crazy, Phoen," he says finally. "You gotta fix this, fuck."

"I know," is all she says, and they smoke in silence some more.

Genuine is tattooed across his collarbones, the large, almost-square letters. There's a large knife over his heart, the blade shiny and dripping with blood, the handle wrapped in sinew ties with a small feather hanging off the end. He has a skull with a full headdress on his right shoulder, *Monias* in army letters on his left, and *Alexandra Angelique*, his kid's name, in curvy writing across his forearm. Phoenix hasn't seen her little cousin since she was a baby. She must be three or something by now. She's always thought that tattoo was so girly and different than the rest of his ink, like it doesn't match the rest of him.

"If that chick fucking talks . . ." her uncle says and stubs out his smoke.

"She won't, Ship," she says. "Or, at least, it won't come back on us. She doesn't even know us."

"She was in this fucking house, Phoenix!" he screams. Phoenix can hear her friends in the living room waking up, their breathing no longer smooth.

Phoenix is calm though, her face without expression. "There were, like, fifty people here last night. It won't come back."

He grabs another smoke and lights it with shaky hands. He drags hard, like Phoenix does, like she imagines their grandpa did. That's how leaders do it.

"We gotta get this place cleaned. Today!" he says. "I don't want a fucking joint, not a fucking kid, fucking nothing."

Phoenix nods.

"That fucking Clayton. He's a Spence, right?"

Phoenix nods.

He keeps nodding, thinking.

"Clayton hasn't been around, Ship. He's good. He's good. Don't fucking worry."

"Don't tell me to fucking not worry. I will worry. I will fucking worry my ass off until all this goes over and is fucking done!"

The girls whisper in the living room. They better not fucking leave, Phoenix thinks.

"This shit's crazy, Phoen." Bishop gets up, stubs out his smoke. "You better fucking fix this shit. And then, you got to get the fuck out of here. For real. I mean it!"

Phoenix nods and watches him walk away.

His back says *Indian* curved over his shoulder blades in the same squared letters. Under the word is a naked girl, skinny with long straight black hair, perfect. Next to her, off to the side, is another Reaper, a sneering mouth under the hood, the scythe-thing dripping with bright red blood. His Reaper arm curves around the girl, his robe her shadow, his sharp fingers reaching over her shoulder. Phoenix can't see it, because it's around her uncle's side and under his arm, but there's a gun slung in the rope at the Reaper's waist. She can't see it but she knows it's there.

Cedar-Sage never did tell her what she was dreaming. Or Phoenix doesn't remember ever finding out. She remembers looking out that big window, down to Arlington, the street, the lights, the orange buses going up and down, hoping every time one stopped that her mother would appear from behind it. She was only, like, eight. Phoenix does know she ran to her sister every time the little girl's dreams got scary, when little Cedar-Sage started yelling. She'd leave the window to wake her up and hold her until she went back to sleep. She was a good big sister, and she didn't want Cedar-Sage to wake the baby.

IN THE BATHROOM, Phoenix throws her bag down on the floor and puts the smoke down carefully on the dry shelf. She looks at herself super long. Black eye makeup smudged across her temples, her eyes a mask like a villain from some cheesy movie. The tight shirt crumpled and riding up under her boobs, her stomach rolls squished together and falling out underneath. She takes it all off, even the stupid bra, and throws it all in the corner. Her naked, deformed body in the mirror doesn't look like a naked girl is supposed to. Her skin is red and she's gigantic, swelled out and square. Her nipples are large and flat as pancakes. She hasn't eaten anything since those Chinese noodles yesterday and still she's this fucking fat. Her stomach hangs over Dez's too-skinny jeans, so she takes those off, too.

It's all Dez and Roberta's fault. They brought these fucking clothes and said she looked good. The gauzy black shirt stretched over her stomach rolls, the ruffles hiding nothing. But she was having so much fun, getting her makeup done while the other girls sat on the bathtub's edge and talked about all the boys they thought were hot. Roberta thought Ship was "cute." Fuck, they all laughed at that one.

"What?" Roberta squealed. "It's true!"

Phoenix had smiled. She couldn't help being nervous, shy,

excited. Hopeful, maybe. She only thought of one boy but didn't say a fucking thing about it.

Roberta always looked good. Even doing Phoenix's makeup, before she even got ready, she looked good. She has a perfect body beneath her tight clothes, and perfect wavy hair. Dez and Cheyenne were nice looking. Long shiny hair. Dez always showed cleavage. Cheyenne always pulled her hair super tight back in a braid but left two long strands on either side of her face, and wore makeup in heavy, hard lines. Phoenix never did like this shit, never saw the point, until now, when she wanted to be a normal girl more than any fucking thing else.

Roberta had pulled out bottles and tubes and kept putting things on Phoenix's face, until it felt heavy and itchy. Then she said, with her over pouty perfect lips, "There! You's so hot now, babe."

Phoenix looked in the mirror but only saw herself. Her lips bright, her eyes smudged dark, her cheeks sparkly, but it was still her.

She hated the shirt they brought for her, the ruffles falling over her huge stomach, so she put her hoodie on right away, and zipped it closed. Roberta rolled her eyes but didn't say anything.

Then they shared a joint in the living room, and Phoenix sipped a beer. If anyone asked her, she'd say she was just hanging out, enjoying being fucking free, but really she was waiting for Clayton. He didn't show for the longest time. People just started coming in. Mitchell texted him but said he didn't text back. Phoenix didn't believe him, but she just sat there, had another beer and drank faster.

Kyle brought out a quarter and they all got right stoned. It'd been so long, she felt really fucking high right away. The music was turned up, and the house rumbled with so many people. By the time Clayton got there, she was fucking toast. Just sitting in her uncle's dark room listening to old music while Dez and Mitchell made out in the corner. She looked up from staring at the Internet and saw him. He loomed over her, perfect and tall in a bright new hoodie.

"Hey." She tried to smile.

"Oh, Phoen, hey!" He almost smiled. "Got any more of that smoke that's going around?"

"Yeah. Sure." She smiled back, but not too much.

They smoked, but he barely talked to her. He was nice, but Phoenix knew. She knew Clayton didn't love her, no matter how much she tried to make him or who her uncle was. She was just a fat freak, more so now than ever, and he had to be nice, but he didn't fucking care. Clayton didn't give a fuck anymore. If he ever did.

Now, in the bathroom, after she rubs all the makeup off her face, she pulls up one of her uncle's shirts off the floor and finds his deodorant on the messy shelf. It smells better than the perfumey shit anyhow. She finds her bag, her baggy pants, and runs her fingers through her hair, and by the time she puts her hoodie on she feels almost normal again. She feels around her bag for her pictures in there, just to make sure.

She grabs the smoke and lights it up. The swirls unfurl in front of her reflection. She closes her eyes just a little bit more and relaxes.

Enough of this shit, she thinks, as she steps out of the room.

In the basement, she stashes the bag in the far corner, back behind the big TV boxes. Her stuff will be safe there, she thinks. For a while. She doesn't want to look at the pictures, but thinks of them: the Grandpa Mac one, the one of Grandmère when she was young, the one with her little sisters where even

Elsie was being good and looked clean and Phoenix was young enough to still love her. She can't look at them now, though. If she does she won't have the guts to keep going.

In the living room, Cheyenne pretends to still be asleep, and Dez and Mitchell talk quietly on the chair. Bishop must've gone back to bed. There is a bit of weed left on the table so she starts to roll. She always loves doing this, breaking up the tiny leaves from the sticks and smoothing the green out until the smell stretches up to her nose. At the Centre, they taught her how to smudge properly. They taught her about medicines and what they do and how to burn them for ceremony. The smoke is supposed to cleanse you, they said. When she first broke up the sage it reminded her of breaking up weed. She felt embarrassed. She thought the Elder would know what she was thinking about and ban her from doing it or something. But he didn't. She did the same thing she's doing now, breaking off the tiny leaves and pressing them in her fingers. Only instead of rolling it in a ball and putting it a smudge bowl, she sprinkles the weed apart and into a paper, then rolls it in her fingers until it makes an even joint.

With smudge, she took the ball of sage in the bowl and lit it up with a match, waved her hand over it until the medicine smoked. She loved that smell. She smudged a lot in the months she was there.

She never felt cleansed though.

She lights up her joint and leans back. Her stomach lurches and she's so fucking hungry, but she ignores it. Dez looks up like she wants a hoot but Phoenix isn't sharing this little guy. Bitch can wait. Mitchell's phone rings and he answers it, still trying to be quiet. Phoenix listens but doesn't care. She knows it's Clayton by the way they are talking. She can tell by the way Mitchell laughs. Fucking guy laughs too damn much. But when he gets off the phone, Phoenix doesn't do anything. Not just yet.

She finishes her joint and lights her cigarette. It's really fucking dry but will have to do. She'll get more from Kyle's bag. Maybe she'll make Dez go through it and pick out all the good ones. The naked girl comes out of Kyle's room, wearing another one of his shirts and looking fucking pleased with herself. Fucking slut. Roberta tries to slip out of Ship's room but Dez and Mitchell sneer and laugh at her. Roberta just looks at Phoenix but Phoenix doesn't let on what she is thinking. She just takes another hard drag and doesn't say a fucking thing.

When she's finally ready, she gets up and pulls Mitchell's phone off the table before anyone notices, and she's in the kitchen before anyone can even say anything.

"What's up, my brother?" He sounds so happy. "Forget something?"

Phoenix takes another hard drag before speaking. "It's Phoenix," she says finally.

"Phoen . . . hey . . ." He's unsure but not scared. Not yet. "What's up?"

She lets the question hang there awhile. "You took off pretty quick last night." She takes another drag.

"Yeah." He still wasn't scared. "Something came up. I just had to go. Sorry."

She lets the air out of her teeth with the smoke, slowly, letting him think a minute.

"Listen, Phoen," he started. "I'm sorry. I didn't mean, I didn't think you still thought we were . . ." He stammers like a little kid. She just lets him talk. "Sorry," he says again.

"Yeah," she says finally. "About that." She lets the words out slow. "I don't really, like, give a fuck. I mean, you're a nice guy and all, but I don't really give a fuck."

On the other end, he sighs.

"My uncle though," she starts and smiles. "He, uh, he feels a little disrespected?" She poses it like a question, and stops.

On the other end, he doesn't make a sound.

Then finally, "Phoen, I, I didn't mean to be disrespectful..."

"I know, I know."

"It's just that, well, I don't know. I really like you like..."

"I know, hey, I get it. It ain't no thing to me but, well, shit got pretty crazy last night, hey?" She's trying to sneer out her words. She's trying not to think about those pictures, the images she sees.

"Yeah, um." He's quiet a minute, like he's thinking. "Yeah."

"And you taking off like that. After what you did? It's just, not cool, man. I mean, I don't care, but my uncle." She takes another long drag and feels his breathing on the other end. "I just don't think you should, um, come around here for awhile." She does sneer.

His voice is small. "K."

"Just thought I would, you know, let you know."

"K," is all he says, again. But she hears it. He's scared now. She smiles. "Watch out for yourself now."

Phoenix tries to laugh, just a little laugh to show him how much she really doesn't care, and hangs up.

She doesn't think about it, just throws the last of her smoke into the half-full sink. The water's so slimy and gross. She'll get Roberta to clean it up later.

She straightens her shoulders and drops Mitchell's phone back on the table. No one says a word. Roberta sits in her spot, but moves over to make room. Cheyenne wakes up and sits up too. They're all waiting. But she knows. She'll get them all to clean this place up, and then, when her uncle wakes up, they'll make plans. Phoenix and her uncle, no one else. Everyone else will just listen. Then they'll all fuck off to Dez's or Roberta's and her girls will take care of her, like they're supposed to. Like they should have last night.

First she'll get Mitchell to go get her some fucking food. She is fucking starving. Then the girls can clean.

This place is going to be spotless, as if nothing ever happened, and no one will ever find a thing.

PART THREE

. . .

I used to think spirits envied their lost skin. That ghosts swayed in shadows, just out of the corners of living eyes, loving and admiring bodies, waiting to be let back in.

But I have never missed my body. Not really. Mostly it was a useless, limited thing with too many needs and not near enough strength.

I do miss other people's bodies though. The feel of someone's skin against my skin. The way I knew someone else was close by warmth of them. I miss you, my girl, I miss you in my arms. Your cheek to my cheek when we slept in the same bed until that very last night. I felt you grow beside me until your feet kicked at my knees in sleep. Your hand always reached out to feel me, the skin on your fingertips sweeter than butterfly kisses. I can still feel your hot baby's breath on my neck even in this cold, cold winter.

I miss, too, your Kookoo's old-lady hands. They were old looking even when she was young, wrinkled and dry from work, nails bitten to stubs. She would always hold my hand so hard, like she wanted me to know she'd never let go, so hard I could feel the bones in them. I think she holds hands like that so we would know how much she loves us.

I did.

I always did.

If nothing else, I knew that.

My body is only a memory. But sometimes, memories are the most real of all. And even though I am gone, you remember and love me. So really, there is nothing to envy the living.

The dead don't hang on, the living do. The dead don't have anything to hang on to. Our bodies become nothing, and we just float around the people who love us. We go back to nothing. That is all we ever were or should ever be.

To me, it feels like being in a dream. Things move imperceptibly, change uncontrollably, but ripple long after they are gone, like an echo, hollow and slow to fade. It goes on and on and then, something waves, and it all blurs and curls into something else.

The living hang on, the dead long to.

STELLA

STELLA GETS OUT of bed before the sun rises. She had actually slept, though fitfully, between Adam waking up at midnight, and Jeff getting home after four. Her dreams were really memories of the girl, the snow, her cousins, herself. Winter. Yes, she had been dreaming of winter, or was she just cold because she felt it through the old window. They should get new windows, better ones.

She turns on the coffee and watches the outside as the machine coughs and spits. It's still dark, no stars, just sky through the thin, naked trees swaying in the wind. The branches black against the dark. She pours a cup before the pot is full. She knows where the sun will rise, where the east creeps up outside her window. She looks there and will look again while she waits for the pale light to come.

Her baby will hopefully sleep awhile longer, she thinks as she limps to the bathroom. Her whole body aches with winter, but she washes her face with cold, jarring water and then gazes at her reflection in the mirror as her skin drips and chills.

She looks so familiar, she thinks. She dries her face and remembers with a start who she looks like. She's now older than her mother had ever been, just by a bit, a year, but by enough. She looks older than her mother ever looked.

Jeff almost stayed home last night. Almost. He thought about it out loud as they ate, then dismissed the idea.

"Can't call in sick just for that," he told her as he packed his lunch. "I mean, it's not like anything happened to us or anything."

Stella tries to remind herself of this too. Nothing actually happened to her. She wasn't hurt, her family wasn't hurt, not at all.

When Jeff left, she promptly set the alarm behind him. Once the kids were finally asleep, she went right to bed. She pulled the covers up and lay there, flat and straight for hours. She couldn't read, couldn't relax, and TV annoyed her. She didn't want to take the sleeping pills Jeff bought her "just in case." She was worried the baby would wake up and she wouldn't be able to hear him, so she just lay there, and got up when he cried. She must have slept at some point and long enough to remember and to feel the winter all the way inside her.

Stella finishes half her cup of coffee standing there and pours another before she wanders into the living room. Her head is clear. There is no droning, no white noise between her ears. It's going to be a clear day. That means it will be cold.

A full basket of clean laundry waits for her. She folds and sips in the quiet semi-dark, the only light from the kitchen, the day growing slowly.

The boards squeak on the old stairs. Mattie is up. Stella greets her in the kitchen, empty cup in hand.

"Morning, my girl." She smiles down.

Mattie jumps into her arms and moves her to rock awhile.

"I love you, Mommy." The three-year-old's voice is muffled

against Stella's shoulder, and they rock for another beautiful minute.

"Can I watch TV?" Mattie straightens up, fully awake now.

"Sure. You want some milk?"

Mattie only nods, and Adam calls from his bed, as if he hears them and doesn't want to be left out.

Later, while the baby naps, and Mattie plays quietly in her room, Stella stands at the kitchen sink, letting the water run longer than it should because it's warm and keeps the house from being silent.

She remembers standing here last night as her husband got ready for work.

"It's been a while, Stell," he had said, reaching around her while she washed the dishes. "I miss you."

He pressed his body against her back, but she cringed. Her whole body tensed into a board. He let go and walked away without another word. He knew what that meant, and he didn't try to reach her over the distance. He left her there, alone in her stiffened silence.

Then, someone knocked at the door. The sound made her jump out of her skin.

Jeff answered it. When she realized it was the police, she went upstairs to pick up the laundry and check on Mattie. She didn't want to deal with their doubts and excuses again. The men's voices found their way up the stairs to her ears.

"We think she might have been the victim here," she heard Officer Christie say. "She said she was coming from Selkirk Avenue."

"Listen, Stella has told you everything she knows. I don't think she can do anymore." Jeff sounded exasperated.

"I know, Mr. McGregor, we just thought..." The young one, Officer Scott, started to say.

But Stella's step squeaked on the stairs. *Dammit*, she thought, and was forced to go the rest of the way down to face them.

"You found her." Her voice sounded so weak.

Scott nodded. "A young girl. Fitting the description you provided."

Stella breathed out, something like relief. Not crazy, she thought, I'm not crazy.

Just horrible.

"She was coming from the direction of Selkirk Avenue when she was jumped."

"And she was raped?"

"There is evidence of sexual assault, yes." He nodded, more gentle looking this time. It almost looked sincere. "We can't really say any more than that."

Stella sat down. "Oh god."

"Is there anything else you remember, Mrs. McGregor? Has anything else come up since we talked to you last?" He sat across from her without being asked, looked her right in the eye. His face was so bright, different than before. He believed her now, but only because he had to. Stella didn't feel smug. She, too, wished she'd been making it up.

"The girl isn't being all that cooperative," Christie interjected from behind her, not sitting down. "She says she doesn't remember much, so anything you can tell us would be better than nothing."

Stella felt so mad all of a sudden, a fury so big she couldn't even talk. She just stared at her hands, unwilling to look up, pretending she was thinking while her cheeks grew red.

"I already told you," she finally said, when she could. "They were dressed in dark clothes. I couldn't see any faces."

The room was quiet. Stella could feel the men passing glances at each other. "Well, you have our numbers if you remember anything new, Mrs. McGregor." Officer Scott gave her a tired smile as he stood up. "Remember, no matter how insignificant you think it is."

Stella nodded at him, so grateful for this one gesture. She looked behind her, at Christie, who looked at his watch again, and at Jeff who looked at the clock.

When the officers left, Jeff kissed her forehead and said, "Well, at least that's something." He hugged her for a long time, thinking he was helping. She let him.

Then he went upstairs to say goodnight to Mattie, and Stella stood there shaking with rage. She wanted to yell but didn't know where to start, or even what words to use. She just thought she wanted to leave, that they should move, go away, go anywhere, run. I don't want to be here, she thought, rolled the words over and over in her head. Don't want to be here. Not here.

Jeff left for work with an unsure smile in her general direction. He might have said something too, but she just stood there until the baby fussed in his chair, until her daughter called to her. Then she went over and pressed the numbers into the alarm. Only after that did she go to her children.

They fell asleep quickly. By eight o'clock, the house was completely silent again. She felt okay, steady at least. Steady enough to try again.

She dialed her Kookom's number and put the kettle on for tea. She thought of all the things she wanted to ask and say, all the normal things and funny stories about her kids. Kookom will still know something's wrong but she'll like the stories. Her Kookom has always liked Stella's stories.

It rang and rang again.

No answer.

Stella counted ten rings before she hung up. She left the

kettle to shut off on its own and turned out all the lights.

She lay on her bed, under the covers, stiff as a dead thing left out too long, cold.

And sometime in the night she slept enough to dream, slept enough to be woken up with a start when baby Adam called for her. She walked through the dark to get him, and there on the stairs she remembered. Two long nights before. Just like this.

She picked up her crying baby, shh-ed him, kissed his soft head, and held him close to her. He was so warm. She looked out into the cold, white Break. The low shadow of what is left of the scene, nothing really, everything hidden somewhere under the snow. The wind pounded on her windows and made them rattle.

AFTER NAPTIME, STELLA takes the kids outside. She wraps them up in all their winter gear and lets her girl pull the baby around in his mini toboggan. They both squeal through the snow.

Her hands free, Stella picks up the shovel and starts to break through the high white drifts that have blown over the walk-way. This close to the open field, they are always shovelling, no matter what the forecast. The wind constantly pushes the snow into the yard, like a long hand trying to bury them.

She makes her way through to the back, around the shed, and back to the front again. It's such a long yard, shovelling it always makes her sweaty. When she's done, she stretches out, takes off her toque and wipes her forehead. She smiles over at the babies, still playing, but doesn't feel the smile. She looks to the field, the drifts piled so high around her fence. Long curves of sculpted snow form the length of the Break and reach out into the street. On mild days like this, with the snow glittering a million different colours, the land looks beautiful, harmless.

It was night in her dream. She was on Bannerman with Lou and Paul. Their plaid sleeves pulled over their hands. They clutched oversized Big Gulp cups, sipped at their cold drinks even as the snow fell. The wind pushed their long hair in their faces. How old were they? Maybe fourteen. No, thirteen. After mom died. She remembers the ache in her chest, so it was after. It was so bad for so long. The car pulled up slowly to let them pass, so they walked across, quick in the cold, but careless, at first.

"What the fuck, guy?" Lou muttered but not loud to the car that didn't move, just sat there for a long while.

They walked on, shivering home. Lou looked back.

Finally the car went into drive, and passed them slowly, its driver looking out. Stella saw round glasses, a long nose. At first, Stella thought the face was a mask, like one of those fake glasses with eyebrows and an oversized nose, but no — that was how he looked.

"What was that guy doing?" Paul asked.

They all got nervous at the same time. The car turned right on Aikins.

As they got to the street, another car came up, behind them this time, and passed by in that slow, deliberate way. This time Stella didn't look.

"Was that the same guy?" she asked.

Lou's face got firm the way it did when she was serious. "Let's cut through Guy's yard and go that way."

They snuck through the narrow slip between houses. It wasn't shovelled and the snow was pretty deep. Stella held on to the rough siding for balance. They hopped the low fence and the back lane was quiet. A car pulled up suddenly down the way, near where the guy would've gone. They didn't wait to see who it was. They just ran.

Paul chucked her cup in the snow bank, and Stella fell right away. She slipped on the ice and smashed her knee into the hard snow and twisted down. Her cup spilled all over her jacket, but she just gripped the cold ground with her bare hands. Lou pulled her up, and she limped on an aching ankle. She tried to run, Lou pulling her along the ice. They turned tail on Salter just as the car lights swept behind them, and then they saw it wasn't the guy after all.

"Aw man, I lost my Gulp for that?" Paul sighed. Then she smiled in relief.

"At least you didn't get yours all over you!" Stella cried, her blue jacket dark with cola.

"Well, at least you smell good," Lou laughed. They all laughed, more nervous and freezing than anything.

Another set of headlight swooped over them just as Paul said, "Come on, let's get home." Her words grew stern. She sounded like her mom.

Stella winced as she walked, and leaned into Lou. She kept thinking, it's okay, it's a busy street, we're okay. The car turned in front of them down Atlantic but went toward Main. Okay, good, she thought, we're going the other way.

They crossed Salter and the pain in Stella's ankle got worse. Lou struggled under her weight.

"Help me, Paul," she said and they pulled Stella over the curb, one cousin on either side.

"I'm sorry, guys. This fucking sucks," Stella told them.

"Let's just get home. Kookoo will fix it," Paul said into Stella's sleeve.

The two blocks never felt so far. A car passed, then another, and finally a third, and they thought they could finally breathe.

Paul opened the gate as another set of headlights came up. They all froze, and knew it was him. The car was tan coloured, Stella saw now, the headlight rounded, and the guy white, tall, curly hair, round glasses. He passed by slowly looking right at them, leering. Stella didn't know the word yet, but when she did hear it, years later, she knew exactly what it meant. He *leered* at them. Lou and Stella just stood there looking at him. Lou was trying to look tough, but Stella was just scared. Paul pulled at their sleeves, "Let's go, let's go."

Her cousins pulled her up the stairs and slammed the door behind them.

"What're you slamming that door for? Come on!" Aunty Cher yelled from the living room.

The girls dragged Stella into the warm room and dropped her on the couch.

"What the hell did you do?" Aunty Cher reached out to her young niece.

Stella went to take off her shoe but winced, the pain huge and red.

"She twisted her ankle," Lou told her.

"Did you fall?" Cher nodded to Stella's stained jacket as she kneeled to take off the girl's shoe.

Stella nodded but kept hissing at the pain.

"It's okay, it's okay." Aunty Cher unlaced the runner gently, her warm fingers burning against Stella's inflamed skin. "Louisa, go get some ice."

"But she's freezing," Lou whined. She moved to go anyway.

"Never mind." Aunty Cher got the shoe off as Stella cried out. "And put the kettle on!"

Stella whimpered a bit, under her breath, of course, trying to hide it.

"It's okay, my girl. What happened?" Aunty Cher looked just like her mom. They had the same eyes, but Cheryl was a different colour, lighter. Her hair almost red where Rain's was jet black. Stella wanted to cry, but felt like a baby.

"Some creeper was following us," Paul blurted out.

Lou walked back in the room with a towel full of ice and a glare for her sister.

"Some old guy in a yellow car." Paul was only twelve.

"What? What happened?" Aunty Cher looked from girl to girl, her soft eyes now hard. "Louisa?"

"It was nothing," Lou started.

"Like hell it was nothing. What was it?" She didn't stop looking.

No one said a word. Stella squirmed, hoping to get her leg feeling better somehow.

"It was just a creepy old guy. He didn't do anything. Just followed us around." Paul was trying to make it better, looking at Lou.

"Louisa?"

"It was . . . we . . . we just got freaked is all." Lou was pleading now.

"Like hell," Aunty Cher said again, and she took the towel-wrapped ice and put it on Stella's ankle. Stella remembers that her aunty's touch was really gentle even though she was so mad. She pulled the table in front and propped Stella's foot up with a smile. The kind of smile she always gave Stella, ever since her mom died anyway. Then she turned to her girls and her face went hard again. "I'm calling the fucking cops."

"No, Mama, don't. It was nothing." Lou went back to whining and followed her mom into the kitchen. "It wasn't a big deal."

Stella just sat there. Paul leaned against the doorframe, head slung down. Lou would give it to her later. If there was anything Lou hated, it was making something a big deal.

"You okay, Paul?" Stella looked at her younger cousin.

"Yeah," she said slowly. "Lou's gonna be pissed."

Stella only nodded. The TV droned on, some sappy movie, the kind her aunty loved.

In the other room, Aunty Cher's voice went higher as she spoke into the phone. "Hello, police, my girls were followed. Some pervert is creeping around my neighbourhood." The phone cord stretched as she paced, and Lou leaned into the counter with an exasperated look on her face. "Some pervert!" She had said.

If there was anything Aunty Cher could do well, it was to make something a very big deal.

MATTIE CALLS OUT. Stella's just standing there in the wind and the baby, having fallen out of the toboggan, is crying in the snow. His little snowsuit legs kick out like he's a turtle stuck on his back. Stella stifles a laugh.

He stops crying pretty quickly, but she keeps holding him, not ready to let go.

Aunty really did make a big deal. They had to all stay up so late that Kookoo got out of bed and made tea. Kookoo always made tea. She gave Stella a cup with lots of milk and sugar, just the way she liked it, and Paul fell asleep cuddling her mom because she was still a little kid. But the rest of them didn't go to sleep. They waited for the police to come. When they finally did, Kookoo was snoring and *The Munsters* theme music was playing because it was that late. Paul got woken up and they just told the story over and over. Lou told it like she wasn't scared, which she probably wasn't anymore.

The cops told Aunty Cheryl she probably shouldn't let the girls go to the store all by themselves, like that was the answer to everything.

When they left, she just stood at the door awhile, her hand on the knob like she was going to run out after them.

Kookoo just patted her on the shoulder and said to them, "Okay, let's get off to bed, you three."

Lou helped Stella limp up the stairs, and her aunty just stood there, staring at the door, her face blotched red with angry tears.

When the baby goes down for a nap, and Mattie's occupied with not-so-hot chocolate and the TV, Stella picks up the phone and tries again. Only two rings this time. She takes a deep, deep breath.

"Hello?"

"Hello, Kookoo. It's Stella."

"Hello, my girl." Kookoo's voice is wide and open like always, but also sad? Maybe.

"How are you?" Stella's voice is stiff but even. Kookom's voice always makes her emotional.

"Oh, my girl. I'm okay. I'm okay. How are you?" Kookom's voice is big as a sigh.

"I'm good, Kookoo. How are you feeling?" Stella wipes the counter and cleans up while she talks, distracting herself from crying.

"Oh. Old. Nothing new here," her grandmother says simply. "How's the babies?"

"Good." Stella swallows the cracks her voice wants to make. "Big. Little Adam is sitting up now. A fat, little baby." She pauses. "We have to come and see you soon."

"Yeah, you do." Her Kookoo doesn't mince words.

"So..." Stella feels at a loss suddenly. "So, is everything okay? You sound sad."

"Oh well," Kookom starts, "terrible thing. Emily, Paul's girl. You remember Emily?"

"Of course."

"She got attacked, my Stella. Raped. It is a terrible thing, such a horrible, terrible thing." The old lady sounds so fragile, her voice quaking.

"What?"

"She went to a house. A party. Some place on Selkirk. Up on the other side of McPhillips there. And these people, these awful men attacked her."

Stella feels her whole body give way. Her legs bend. She has to sit, but only has the floor. She falls there. Her stomach comes down last.

"Oh." Her voice is so small.

"I know. Poor girl. Such a good girl. She's still in the hospital. She had glass inside of her. They raped her with a beer bottle. A beer bottle. Can you imagine? My poor, poor baby. Thirteen she is. Thirteen!"

Stella feels it now. She's shaking. She wants to howl and punch something and curl up into a ball and die. Finally, she mumbles something like, "Wow," and tries to cry quietly so that her Kookom won't hear.

She doesn't seem to notice and keeps talking. "You should come by, visit. Come home, my Stella. Please."

Stella breathes over and over, trying to come to. A sudden panic wakes her. "I will, Kookoo, I will."

"I want you here, Stella." Kookom is crying now. She never cries. She sounds so old and small. She has never asked for anything.

Stella hears a bang upstairs and a howl from Mattie. "Oh, Kookom, I'm sorry. Mattie fell. She's crying, Kookoo. I got to go. I'll come there. I'll come."

"Okay. Okay. Don't apologize." The old lady's voice is almost normal again. "Call me back."

"Okay. Okay. I love you," Stella says, distracted.

Her Kookom is saying something, but Stella hangs up too

quickly and misses it. She looks at the phone a second, the empty space where her Kookom was, but has to go to Mattie. The little girl holds her head. Her hazel eyes bulge with tears, a small chair overturned beside her. Stella wraps her arms around her little girl and holds her close. They both shake and cry for a long time.

WHEN SHE HUNG up with 911, she put the baby down. He cried and cried but she left him. She ran downstairs but then stood, frozen in the kitchen. She knew the attackers had run off, but they could come back, and the woman was lying there, bottom naked, maybe dead, maybe alive. Maybe she needed help. But Stella stood there, staring at her back door, unable to open it. She paused there, remembering something she hadn't thought of in a long time.

She slipped her feet into Jeff's big work boots but Adam cried. She pulled the door open and the alarm stopped her. It rang and rang and she couldn't get the numbers straight, her fingers shaking over the buttons, so many buttons.

"Mama," Mattie called, awake.

"It's okay, honey," she managed. "Go back to bed. I'll be right there."

"Adam's crying."

"I know, honey. Just let him cry. I just... I'll be right there." She pulled the door open and stopped again. The woman was sitting up, alone. Emily was sitting up alone in the snow, pulling on her pants. But Stella just watched her, watched Emily through glass, fogged by the cold. The girl was lit by the street-light as she winced and pulled and finally turned her head up to the sky. The snow was falling silently around her.

Stella stopped again, the cold handle in her shaking hand.

"Mama!" Mattie was upset. Adam was getting worse, worse. Stella never let him cry. "Mama!"

"Okay, it's okay." She shook her head. Knowing she should do something, not knowing what to do. What could she do?

She saw the woman, girl, Emily, saw her get up, so slow, and limp a step. For a second, her face was aglow in the light and the snow dancing around her, and Stella wanted to scream.

But she didn't. She just stood there.

Both her kids were crying now, inconsolable, loud. Their voices pulled at her as sure as hands. The phone, silent, still in her hand. The police will come soon, she had thought. The police will help the woman, the girl. Emily.

She slipped off Jeff's boots and ran back up the squeaky stairs to her screaming kids.

(16)

LOU

THE HOUSE IS dark when I get back, the blue green glow of Jake's video game the only light inside. It beeps and voices ring from my boy's headset. Commands. He twitches his shoulders to the moves on the screen but doesn't say a word.

"Hey." My voice sounds so far away.

"Hey." His head twitches back in my direction.

"Baby boy go to sleep all right?" I fall on to the couch, my jacket still on, and think about falling asleep right there. I wasn't so tired a minute ago.

"Yeah." His usual one word answers, but there's something new in his voice too. Another edge.

I nod even though he can't see me, and sit there another minute, watching him play. The voices on his headset are muffled and demanding.

The whole day weighs down on me—like water it waves in heavy, then retreats. What else can I do? Emily is sedated and will probably sleep 'til morning. Paul is lodged safely on a cot between Emily and Pete. Mom took Kookoo home. Ziggy was discharged after her face got stitched up.

I took the cab back with Rita and her kids. Rita was beside herself, really, and I wanted to make sure they got in okay. The ride was eerily quiet. I sat in the front next to the driver but kept looking back, looking for something to do. A way to help. Ziggy's little face all white bandages. Her eyes hazy with drugs. She sat slack, leaning against her mother who just held her tight, and stared straight ahead. Sunny didn't say a word. He just stared out the side window. His young face seemed to have aged.

We have all been broken in one way or another.

"Did you eat anything?" I call across the great abyss to my son.

He moves his head as if to shake it, and the light hits his eyes, bloodshot and sore. Bright red blotches around his beautiful brown eyes. His face pale in its pain. I see it for only a second but then it's everywhere. All around the room.

I crawl down behind him and wrap my jacket arms around my lean, long boy, and hold him tight. I press my face between his bony shoulder blade wings and hold on as he tries to cry as quietly as he can. His hands limp. His game beeping off.

EVENTUALLY, WE INCH to separate couches. I wrap thin blankets around him, and he lets me tuck them around his feet. He puts a movie on, then another. I doze on and off on the other couch. The sounds and characters stream together and we try to sleep. I think of my niece's pale lips, her skin like paper. My sister's vibrating body curved around her child, arms wrapped gently closed. My mother's face struck red, wet and folded into itself. My grandmother, my Kookom, was too quiet. Tomorrow we will all have to make sure she is okay.

I fall asleep and wake up thinking of something else. That last call I made Friday... was it only Friday? The old lady Luzia filling us with more tea as we talked. Her foster charges sat reluctantly at the table. She had two. One of them, Destiny, had a file that read like a police report. She was the sort of child who was permanently bruised yet jutted her chin out to the world, willing it to hit her again. And the other, Cedar-Sage, same experience, same heartache, but she sat there like a turtle, hunched into herself, bracing for the next onslaught. These are the two ways we go about the world, I think. I always tried to be like Destiny, hold my head up and go forward. I don't know if I've always succeeded but I am always ready to fight. Paul has always been more turtle-like. She seems the more protected of the two of us. Or at least, she always used to be.

I GET UP before Baby and decide to make breakfast. I lay out the bacon on the oven tray, and I make lots of pancakes, extra to bring for Pete and Paul, even for Emily, if she's up for it. She's always liked my pancakes. Somehow the act of making food always feels like doing something when we are helpless to do anything else. I message Paul and tell her I'll head over after I feed my kids.

Jake sits up and takes a plate, but he and I only pick at the food. Baby boy eats a bit and then lies on his stomach on the floor, his sticky chin propped up by his palm, just like the other day. Just like any other day.

I keep looking over at my older son, but try not to. I know he wants to talk, wants to tell me something. His face is a mask of hardness. He's trying to be tough. I can only look at him sideways. My back to the arm of the couch, I can turn to the

TV or look out the window, but I can't look at my teenager and I can't talk first. This is how it works. If I say anything first, I'll wreck it. I have to wait for him to start. I pick at my food and pretend to watch the show and the street. My eyes sweep over him, but only when he can't see.

Finally, he says, "I think I know where they went."

"Oh." I make the word as short as possible. The morning light is somehow grey and offers no warmth at all.

"This guy, Bishop, lives that way, and everyone always parties at his place." He puts down his plate and crosses his arms in front of himself.

"Who's everyone?" I look down and pick at my food. Can't look yet.

"His people." Jake's narrow shoulders shrug.

I don't question this. He's leaving out things deliberately. "Have you ever gone there?" is all I ask.

"Naw. Sun and I aren't into that shit. It's pretty heavy shit." His face grows red again. He pulls up his black hood over his face and leans back.

I wait a moment. "So how did Em and Ziggy end up there?"

"Someone must've told them, I guess. Or they just went." He wouldn't talk if he didn't want to, but he doesn't want it to be emotional.

But then I think of something. "You think this was on purpose, like they wanted to get initiated or something?"

"Girls don't get initiated, Mom." His chin makes a sad smirk. I can see his dark hair there too. My boy is almost a man.

"Well, what happens to girls?" I put my plate on the floor, the pancakes cold and picked at. The moist crumbs are soaking up the brown syrup, already getting hard.

"They get, well, s-e-x-ed in, you know. Like that." He waves his hands, like this isn't a traumatizing thing to say. Spells out the words, so Baby boy doesn't even notice that his brother is saying the worst thing he could possibly say.

It takes me a minute to swallow. "You think that's what happened?"

"I don't know. It's doesn't, like, make sense." His hands disappear under his hood, rub at his tired, almost-a-man face. He sits up, looks right at me. Like a grown-up. "Like, I know girls who, did that or do that, but that's what they wanted, right? It's not like they have to force anyone to do that."

"Oh."

"That's just how it's done. It's that or nothing." He pauses. "At least that's what I heard. And I can't see Em and Zig going in for something like that. They don't really know anything about that stuff. Like, nothing."

We're quiet for a long moment.

"You're right," I say, even though I have so many questions. "It doesn't sound like something Emily and Ziggy would do."

He only shrugs.

"I wonder what they were doing there then," is all I say.

He shrugs again and I know the spell has passed. My boy goes and puts his plate in the sink without me even asking. He gets up and holds his head up, high like I do. He juts his chin out to the world, just like me.

I watch him with pride, at first. Then with thick fear.

I think of Gabe for the first time in hours, wanting him to come home, to take care of the boys and to help me convince them everything is going to be okay. I think of telling Jake to call him so Gabe can talk to him in his Gabe way and make things better. But I stop before I say anything out loud. Gabe hasn't called at all. He left Thursday, now it's Sunday, and he hasn't called at all.

THE ROOM IS full when we get to the hospital. I couldn't keep Jake away another day and Baby boy is good medicine for everyone. He goes right to our Kookom's lap. Jake greets his grandmothers and goes right to Emily, her bed raised to sitting. Her face has more colour this morning. They talk close and she smiles. Paul moves away for what looks like the first time all night. I fill a Styrofoam plate with food for Kookoo, cutting everything up for her, just like I did for Baby boy. She nibbles kindly and shares with him. My mom and Paul don't eat and I don't ask them to.

"Where's Pete?" I ask my family.

Mom looks back and forth. "He went to clean up."

"Oh," is all I say because my mom is like my boy and I'm going to have to wait.

"I am going to get a coffee. Does anyone want one?" Paul stretches up and gets her wallet.

"I can go," I chime in.

"No, I need the walk." She looks over at Emily who just looks at her cousin. My sister's mouth makes a thin line where a smile used to be.

Once she's gone, Mom pulls me out into hall. I still can hear my Kookom singing an old song to Baby. It soothes me, too.

"She's a wreck!" My mom will not be soothed. "Your sister's a fucking mess."

My mother is a big believer in stating the obvious. "Well, of course she is, Ma. How else is she supposed to be? You'd be a mess too. You are a mess."

"Well, I wouldn't be so fucking nice to that fucking sorry excuse for a doctor, I tell you that."

"What happened?"

"They want to discharge her. Her. Emily. After all this, they want to discharge her today. Or maybe tomorrow, they said.

Maybe. They already want to get rid of her, can you believe it?"

"Well, they have to be quick, Ma. If the doctor says she's good to go then she's going to be okay." I want to reach out, put a hand on her arm or something, but my wrecked mother would only flinch, and that would hurt both of us.

"I don't believe it for a second. They're just trying to push us out."

"Why would they do that, Ma?" I cross my arms in front of me instead.

"Because that's what they do. They don't care."

I look at her long, my poor mom and all she's been through. How this must feel for her. "Let's just see what the doctor says, okay?"

She scoffs a bit and looks down the hall. The beeping and the noise is everywhere. The smell, too, gets into everything.

My Kookoo starts another song.

I think of my aunty and how she died. What my mom and grandmother must be thinking now. Here at the hospital, the same hospital that wants to release their girl, their other girl.

"They didn't even treat her. Just put her right back out in the street. Didn't even look, just thought she was another drunk and didn't care," my mom says under her breath. She's talking about her sister now, feeling her sister's loss and her grand-daughter's pain at the same time.

"I know, Ma. I know." I can see it, my aunty's skinny body and her beautiful face, dirty and worn. She had this permanent rough look to her in the end like her skin was etched and carved into only one broken expression. "But they took care of Emily. They're taking care of Emily."

"I know, I know." She nods and nods. She does know, but she doesn't.

I reach out and put my hand on her arm, and she lets me. I

know she's been thinking about the hospital and that familiar fear for a long time.

Paul comes back with a tray of coffees. She knows how each of us likes ours, always gets it right. I go over to Emily to look at her for a long time. She smiles up at me, an apologetic smile that makes me want to cry all over again. Jake leaves with Mom, who takes our Kookom home and wants to go check on Rita. Ziggy had slept well, and seems to be feeling better. Everyone is supposed to be healing now.

The doctor comes in and wants to do another test, for infections, but says Emily should be able to go home tomorrow. And that everything is getting better. Healing. Pete comes back from cleaning up his truck. Mom had brought him extra blankets before, blankets to spread out over all the bloodstains he couldn't get out of the upholstery. The old blankets, she calls them, threadbare ones from gone and forgotten relatives.

I sit around and wait for something to do. I hold my Baby on my lap and read him old, worn storybooks as we wait. Finally, Baby yawns and Pete says he can take us home. I'm putting on Baby's snowsuit when Paul's phone rings. She goes out into the hall to answer. Pete doesn't look up. He just looks down at his folded hands — they're calloused and clean but the dry creases are stained from work. His nails are small worn stubs.

Paul comes back in with a huff. "The police are on their way over." Her voice shakes a bit, and our backs collectively stiffen. Pete sticks his chin out a bit. The smallest gesture, but I catch it.

I take off Baby's scarf.

"I can stay," I say without even asking.

17

PAUL

THE WIND PICKS up the snow and rattles the window. Paul sits down beside her daughter as the two police officers walk into the room. She leans over, studies her girl for a moment, to make sure she's safe and okay as she can be. All of Emily looks so small. The bed is adjusted to upright, but her shoulders are low on the pillows. Her face seems so tiny, the wounds there bigger somehow. The bruise under her eye has darkened, and the cut on her lip swells under the bandage. Paul feels useless and exposed. She can still smell the blood. That thick metallic scent goes over everything every time she rubs her nose, and her nose is red and raw from rubbing. Her body is stiff from all the sitting, but still she sits there, places herself between the uniformed men and her girl.

"Okay let's start again at the beginning." Scott flips his little book open and pulls a chair up to the bed. "So you and your friend Zegwan went to this house party on Selkirk Avenue, is that right?"

Emily looks startled but nods, looking down.

Paul reaches out to hold her girl's hand as lightly as she can. Lou, in the chair, doesn't say a word. Baby sits on her lap, playing a game on her phone, even the sound is turned off. Pete still isn't back. He didn't come up. He said he'd go get some food, more food they won't eat.

"You were invited there by a schoolmate?" Scott asks. Christie just stands there, leaning against the wall, looking on. Emily doesn't really hold her mom's hand, just lets hers be held.

"Emily?" the officer repeats.

"Yeah," Emily says finally, "I guess."

"Do you remember the address?"

Emily shakes her head, slowly, painfully, and whispers a quiet "No."

Scott sighs like he doesn't believe her. "Okay, so," he tries again, "you were headed home anyway, from somewhere on Selkirk?"

Emily nods.

"And you were jumped from behind?"

Another, smaller nod, like an echo of the first one.

"You didn't know they were coming?"

Emily shakes her head slowly. Paul knows something isn't right, she feels the tension rise in her shoulders again. Her daughter is sinking lower. Trying to hide something.

"But Emily . . ." The young officer leans in, his arms folded on the bed, too close to Emily's legs. "Why were you going through that field? The snow was knee deep."

Paul doesn't realize what's going on until Emily's eyes get big and she turns away from all of them. Paul doesn't let go of her hand and can feel her girl start to cry even though she tries to hide her broken face. She knows Emily doesn't want to be upset in front of these strangers. She also knows her girl can't help it anymore. They are all like this, not their real selves anymore, more like shadows, turned inside out.

Paul looks from her daughter's hand to the back of her head. So afraid. Hiding something. Paul can't figure out the what or why of anything anymore. She knows it all doesn't really matter. The only thing that matters is her tiny girl and her girl's big, swollen pain. But Paul feels her helplessness all over, this great big unknown like a weight on her, like it's breaking her.

Lou moves slowly along the edge of the room. She puts Baby on the chair and walks to the bedside. Pete's still not here. He wanted them to get a lawyer, to make sure the police were doing everything they were supposed to.

"We have to be careful, Paul," he told her in the dark of Emily's hospital room last night as they lay on the uncomfortable cot the nurse set up for her. "They will grab on to anything you say. Things can get messy real fast."

"But it's Emily. Emily!" Paul had just cried. "I don't give a shit what they do as long as she doesn't hurt anymore. And what if those guys come back? What if they hurt her again?"

She sobbed uncontrollably then, awkward cries escaping her even though she was trying so hard to be quiet. She felt like she howled into his chest as she pressed against him. He wasn't going to stay but he did, for as long as he could.

"Just be careful, Paul. Just be real careful." His soft words as her cries got quiet and she listened for her daughter's sleeping breath and monitors again.

She held on to him for a long time. Her inside-out self still doubted him, still wondered why he wanted her to be so careful, but she held him for a long time. All the whys and whats messed up in her head, and nothing was making sense anymore.

"I was going to Ziggy's, my friend Ziggy's." Emily turns and says finally, almost defiantly, to the cops there.

"Through the field?" The young one's dark eyebrow goes up. Even Paul doesn't believe the story.

Emily nods weakly. Paul feels a panic growing.

"Okay, let's start over," the officer starts again and checks his little book. "You went there to see a boy named, Clayton, is that right?" He emphasizes the word, Clayton, like it means something.

Paul is surprised at the name. This is the first time she is hearing this. Clayton. The name repeats in her head without familiarity. Clayton. It is like they are walking in circles, each time picking up something new that only made everything more confused. Emily looks wide-eyed at the officer, surprised too.

"Do you know Clayton's last name, Emily?"

Emily just shakes her head frantically and looks to her mom for help.

"But you go to school with him, right?" the young officer tries.

"He didn't do anything wrong!" Emily cries out, too loud.

Lou reaches out and puts a hand on her niece's shoulder. She looks like she's about to say something, her social worker face hard and thinking, but she stays quiet.

"We just need you to confirm this information, Emily. Do you go to school with him?" Scott's voice rises too.

"He doesn't even know!" Emily just shakes. Paul can feel it. Her daughter's hand gets so cold before she pulls it away. Lou, at the other side of the bed, looks at Paul with that firm look she's supposed to understand, but Paul doesn't meet her eyes.

She only stiffens again. A boy. What boy?

"We just want to talk to him Emily, you never know . . ."

"But he didn't . . ." Emily doesn't finish.

Paul only thinks it. A boy. A mean boy, a cruel boy. That makes sense to her. She has known cruel boys.

"Do you mean Clayton, Jesse Spence's boy?" Paul says the words before she thinks it through.

Emily shakes her head, faster now, and begs at her mom with her eyes. She is hiding something. Lou makes a sound and Paul knows what it means, but she can't hear it all the way. Her mind going too fast.

The young cop leans over her. "Do you know this boy, Paulina?"

"Think so." Paul's words are like slow footprints, and she wants to swallow them back as she says them. "Maybe. I don't know."

"You said Jesse. Who is Jesse?" Christie, the old one, pipes in. He is excited too.

"I don't even know if that's his name," Paul backpedals as quickly as she can. "I don't know. The boy I am thinking of is only fifteen. If that."

"You said Spence, right?" he asks again.

"If he's the kid I'm thinking of . . . I don't know." The words fall out of her, and she tries to mess them up with other words. "Maybe Sinclair, I don't know."

The officers look satisfied. Paul shuts up, presses her lips together. She looks up. Her sister and daughter are both staring at her.

The young officer gets up. The old one has a smug look growing on his face. They are saying other things, but Paul hears their words only halfway. Be in touch. Talk soon.

What have I done? is all she can think.

She sits back down and her eyes meet her sister's. Lou looks like she was going to say something again, and then thinks better of it.

What have I done?

PAUL HAD MET Pete at the Briar Pub a little over two years ago. He was big man in a white T-shirt and she had seen him walk in, but looked down to avoid his eyes. Lou was there with her, and Rita was dancing to old country. Her thin legs bent to the music and knew every move. Paul always wanted to dance like that but never did. Only sat at the bar sipping her second rye and Coke. She never did like the taste of it, only the nerve and attitude that seemed to come with it.

"Can I buy you another drink?" He was beside her but she could only glance at him. His voice was deep, seemed gentle and shy. He didn't really look at her either.

But she nodded with all the fake nerve she had sipped, and his face grew softer, his smile more crooked. He smelled so good. She looked up all the way, finally, but forgot to smile.

He relaxed a bit too and leaned into the bar. His bare fore-arms stretched out, thick and long. He asked a few, smooth questions, and she didn't even have to think to smile, eventually.

She knew better than to trust him but she did, almost immediately.

"I SHOULDN'T HAVE said anything," Paul says again, as she comes into their still-unpacked bedroom. Pete had brought her home so she could shower and change into fresh, comfortable clothes. Lou stayed with Em, who had pretended to fall back asleep. Her tiny eyelashes wet and her bandage pouting. The unopened paper food bags on the side table.

Pete sits on the bed, not taking his eyes off Paul. She still pulls her clothes off and robe on quickly, when he is in the room. "It'll be all right. They'll probably just question him is all. He's a young kid. If he doesn't know anything, they'll probably let him go."

She tries to believe him but doesn't.

"And if they don't? If Em is telling the truth and he didn't do anything? I've known his mom forever." She spits out her guilt. What have I done?

"That doesn't mean he's a good kid." Pete's hands, folded on his lap, open when she sits beside him, open to take hers in. She lets him but doesn't really hold his hand back, only lets hers be held.

"I don't think he could've done something like this." She tries to sound sure. Is she?

She remembers the girl, Jesse, in plaid shirts and baggy jeans. She had a mean face, but wasn't all bad, just tougher than Paul, even tougher than Lou.

They didn't know much about her, but for years, they were always in the same class, and then after, just around. They knew enough to know she was an artist now. A few years ago, she had painted the mural in the high school. The four colours in a soft circle: red, black, yellow, white. A brown bear in one corner, its eyes gentle, its lines rounded. She couldn't have raised a boy who could do this.

Right?

WHEN THEY PULL up to the hospital, the sky is purple and clear. The cold growing. She says good night to Pete as if they were dating again.

"I'll call you in the morning." Her hand rests on the door handle. She's anxious to be back in the room with her girl.

His leans over and kisses the top of her head. "I love you, baby. Everything is going to be all right."

She doesn't believe him, but it is nice to hear.

Back in the room, Emily is still asleep. Baby too. Lou holds her child and rocks him gently on the big chair.

"Feel better?" her sister asks, not looking at her.

Paul just makes a sound that's like agreeing but not really.

"Need anything before I go?" Lou reaches for her son's snowsuit for the second time that day.

"Pete's in the front, in the loading zone," she tells her.

"Yeah, okay." Lou gets up.

"I know you think he did this." Paul tries to keep her voice firm. She doesn't know why she says this, until she does.

"I don't think anything, Paul." Lou doesn't look up, just moves her little boy's sleeping body gently into his snowsuit.

"No, don't feel bad. That was the first thing I thought of too." She makes a sound that's like laughing, but not.

"Well then, we're both as fucked up as each other." Her words an exaggerated whisper over Baby's sleeping head.

"But he didn't." Paul's voice shakes and she knows it's true.

"No, I know. I don't think he did it either."

"Someone else did." Paul's words tiptoe across the room.

"And we will find who did and they will go to jail and never do it again." Lou is looking right at her now, that serious look Paul knows so well.

She nods back.

Lou kisses the top of her sister's head, right where Pete had, and walks off with her oversized Baby in her arms.

Paul curls up against her daughter, careful not to nudge or disturb her. Her small legs are warm under the blanket.

When Emily was born, Paul took her home from the hospital and had no idea what to do. Her Kookom had shown her how to wrap her up in a blanket, one side, the bottom, then the other side, tight.

"Like she is still inside you," she whispered as the brand-new Emily slept comfortably. She still did this, wrapped her girl up tight, rubbed her feet to make her even warmer.

"Mom?" Emily's voice in the dark is quiet and sleepy.

"Yes, baby." Paul wipes her own face, and then fixes the blanket around her girl again.

"He really didn't do anything, Mommy. Clayton didn't do anything." Her voice rises up as far as it can go.

"I know. I know," Paul says, but thinks. "Are you, are you absolutely sure?"

"He didn't. He didn't!" Emily starts to shake her head but stops.

"Okay, okay. I..." Paul starts.

"No, Mom, no. Mom, it wasn't..." Emily voice cracks a bit but holds firm.

Paul doesn't know what to believe anymore. *Check your gut*, that's what her mom would say. Cheryl's answer to everything is always to check your gut.

Her girl turns away.

"Emily?" Paul reaches out in the dark. "Tell me then, Emily, tell me. Tell me who did this."

Emily just cries as quietly as she can. Paul doesn't know what her gut is saying. She can barely remember to breathe.

"Please tell me," Paul sobs, wanting to yell, feeling like she needs to know. Like not knowing was the worst thing. "Who did this, baby?"

Emily sobs but her voice is even. "It wasn't him. It wasn't him, Mom. He didn't. He didn't do anything."

Paul's thoughts scatter. Doubt. Suspicion. Love.

Quiet. Safe. Okay.

"Okay, okay." Her words across the night.

"He didn't do anything. Don't make him get into trouble, please." Emily's soft voice turned away.

"Okay, but who, Emily? Who did this? Who?" Quieter now, only pleading.

Emily just shakes. Hiding so many things.

But Paul knows Emily can't say it. Not yet. She also thinks maybe she can't hear it. It doesn't matter yet. These details, the story, what happened. They both know what happened well enough anyway. It's the big dark thing in the room, always there. They don't have to see it to know it, to know they don't want to look at it.

And Paul remembers she doesn't really care what or why. The only thing that matters is her girl and her big, shaking pain.

"I'll fix it," Paul says. She sighs. "I'll call the police. I'll make sure he doesn't get into trouble."

She doesn't need to know yet. She can't. She can only straighten her back, hold her girl tight, comfort her, keep her from further harm. She can only look out the window at the dark sky, and hold her girl for as long as she and her broken body will let her.

That's what she has to do right now. Don't think too much, don't freak out, just take care of your girl.

WHEN PETE FINALLY told her he loved her, he cried. The light was low in her old living room and they had just finished an extra large pizza when he leaned over to put her head on his shoulder. He couldn't look at her but she felt his body at her cheek.

"I love you, Paul. I love you so much. And I know you don't trust me. I know you've been through so much and have no reason to trust me. But I promise, I will never hurt you. I will always be here for you, no matter what."

They'd been going out for months. For months, she kept him at arm's length and he only slept over if Emily was out. For months, he let her call the shots and make the rules with no complaint, only his shy smile and warm hugs.

"I love you too," she whispered into the sweet smell of him.

She knew it was true. She breathed him in and knew she didn't want to trust him.

But she did, almost completely.

18

STELLA

STELLA WOULD KNOW the way blindfolded, down Burrows to Salter, Salter to Church, past the school and the four-way stop, and there. And even though she thinks she doesn't want to go and it will take her forever, she's somehow packed up the kids and is en route in less than half an hour.

She passes Powers and thinks of Elsie. She hasn't thought about Elsie in forever but always thinks of Elsie when she sees Powers. She forgot about Elsie's story, will have to add it to her list of "pasts like hers," another story that didn't happen to her but that she keeps and remembers. It was right down there where that one happened.

She pulls up to the tall, brick walk-up where Kookoo has lived since she was a teenager and chirps a cheerful "We're here" to her kids.

The building still looks so beautiful, though a bit more rundown than last time. It's only four floors up but old, so the stories are taller than newer walk-ups. The first floor is so high that Kookoo's basement windows are big and still bright sometimes. Her Kookom moved to this little apartment when Lou and Paul finally left home and Aunty Cher went back up north for a while. Stella had lived with her on and off—off whenever she could afford to be anywhere else. Aunty came back home too, though not at the same time. She eventually got a suite of her own, when she moved back for good. Stella can see the window next to the big, arching front entrance, an oversized canvas there, turned to an angle. She heard Cher had moved her best friend Rita in here too but doesn't know where. Kookom's place is around the other side, facing the back lane. Her Kookom doesn't mind. The old lady doesn't mind, says, "At least it's east." Kookoo has a thing for sunrises.

With Mattie behind her and Adam in her arms, Stella knocks at Kookoo's door, but then just walks in. An older lady with short hair stands there, her back to Stella.

"Oh, sorry," Stella says quickly, too polite.

"Stelly!" Her aunty turns with a smile. Her hair is cropped and sprinkled with grey at her temples. Stella has never seen her with short hair and it is striking. Her cheeks look more angled and aged. Her eyes have more cigarette wrinkles and are puffy from crying.

"Aunty!" Stella says like a breath.

"Look at these babies!" Aunty Cher's sad face makes a smile as she throws her arms around Stella and Adam. She pulls away and looks Stella up and down, examining her the way Kookoo does. "How are ya?"

"Oh, you know." Stella looks down. Aunty looks more like Kookoo than she did the last time Stella saw her, like a sharp version of soft Kookoo. So does Stella though. It's like they're turning into her. No, they just all look alike: Cheryl, Rain, Stella, Paul, Lou, and Emily too. The youngest girl looks just like them all too.

Mattie comes up from behind.

"Oh, hello, you." Aunty's voice brightens. "You probably don't remember me. I'm your Aunty Cheryl."

Her aunty kneels down and shakes Mattie's hand in feigned formality. Her little girl giggles and hides behind Stella again. Cheryl stands up with a bit of groan. Stella's about to ask if she's okay, but Cher beats her to it.

"Just getting old, my dear." Cheryl exaggerates a moan then laughs.

"I am so sorry, Aunty," Stella says, an apology blanketing so much.

"It's okay, it's okay, Stelly. She's going to be okay."

"But I . . ." No, she can't tell her. How can she tell her? Her own cousin's kid. Her own family. Stella can't say it. She can only shake her head and push the tears back, again.

Aunty Cher takes Adam, "Oh, look at you!" she coos, and brings him into the living room. "Come in, come in, girls."

Kookoo's living room always looks the same and is set up just like it was when it was in a big, old house. The furniture is in the same places, only older and more worn out. The macramé plant hangers are in the corner by the window. The couch sits too low to the ground and against the far wall. When they moved her in here, the couch was missing a leg, so Kookoo got them to take them all off so it would sit even, just closer to the floor. Kookoo sits in her old, worn, velour-covered rocker.

"How are you? My girl. It's so good to see you!" Kookom's whole face is joy. She doesn't get up. She's probably so tired.

Stella leans down to hug her. Mattie clings to Stella's hand.

"Mattie. It's Kookoo," she tells her.

The old lady smiles, but even the smile looks faded somehow, the colour drained from her.

Her aunt unravels the baby from his snowsuit. He fusses a bit but then she gives him to Kookoo.

"Hello, my dear!" The old woman gives him a gummy grin. Probably lost her teeth again, Stella thinks. Kookoo never liked her dentures, always left them by her bed or in the bathroom.

Her baby is unsure but looks up at his Kookom. He could cry, or not. Stella takes off Mattie's coat, but is ready to dive in if she needs to.

"I'm so glad you came." Kookom's cloudy grey eyes look up to Stella, all seeing.

Stella looks away quickly. "I'll make some tea."

"I am going to leave you to it, my girl. I really need to have a shower or something," Aunty Cher pipes in, still standing by the door.

"Of course, of course." Stella feels her voice too formal, too late.

"I'll come back in a bit." She looks at Stella too long, too weary.

"Okay. Good." Stella tries to smile.

Mattie follows her to the kitchen, clinging to her pant leg. The same things are in the same places. The old, big fork and spoon on the wall are thick with dust. The kettle is new but the teapot is the same one Stella bought, how many Christmases ago? The cupboards need a paint job but are pretty clean.

Stella feels a pang of missing the old house on Atlantic. She loved that house. The kitchen was set up just the same too. Fork and spoon over the stove, cutlery drawer to the left, tea towels to the right because Kookoo liked things just so. That house was set up perfectly except for Stella and her mom's room. Their double bed was never made and blankets were always in piles on the mattress, and their clothes lay on the floor or in a laundry basket that was never emptied, because Rain was never just so. Stella's pretty lady lamp sat on the wooden end table. The lamp was really a doll, fancier looking than a typical Barbie, with delicate blond hair in a bun and a long stick up her back. Her hat and gown were pink, and the matching pink parasol also housed a small, bright bulb. Stella would watch the pretty lady when her mom told her stories. The ones she said out loud and knew by heart and the ones that only floated in the air and had no pictures. After she died, Stella still looked at the pretty lady, trying to remember every story. She eventually gave it away, when she got too old for doll lamps.

Back then, her big double bed was perfect for sleepovers. Her mom always suggested it and said she would sleep on the couch, but Stella was too shy, and only had one friend come over, but she came over a lot. Elsie. Little Elsie Stranger. They were inseparable for so long.

"I've missed you, my Stella," Kookoo tells her as she rocks the baby to an easy sleep.

Stella passes her some tea, just the way she likes it with too much sugar. "I've missed you too, Kookoo. How are you feeling?"

"Oh good, good. Just old," Kookoo says looking down at the baby who is mesmerized by this magical old lady giving him another shiny, gummy smile.

Her Kookom's face is so much older than the last time Stella saw it. Stella can barely keep everything in. She knows Kookoo senses something is really wrong, but neither of them say anything.

"You seem tired, my girl," is all Kookoo says. The words make Stella miserable all over. It's Kookoo who looks so tired.

"How's Paul and her girl?" Stella manages to ask.

"As good as they can be. How are you?"

"Just tired, tired." So tired.

"You should call your cousin. When she's home. I know she would love to hear from you." Kookoo always thinks everyone would love to hear from Stella.

Stella only nods her head, and hot tears swell in her eyes. She's certain no one would love to hear from her, especially now.

They talk about nothing. They talk about everything. Adam's eyes slowly pinch shut as his Kookom rocks him gently in her still-strong-enough arms. Mattie too sits at Stella's side and grows more and more still. They are all so tired.

Last night, Adam woke up again right at midnight—he needed to be fed and comforted for at least an hour. Stella sat there, feeding her baby with no choice but to look out into the empty field of the Break next to her house and remember, trying not to. It all echoed there. Black bodies on the white snow. How do shadows move like that?

Mattie wants to watch an old DVD. Stella goes to put it in but cringes at the name on the cover, in marker—*Emily Traverse*. She puts it in quickly and tries to think of something else to talk about.

She sits back on the low couch that smells a bit like mould and a lot like home.

"You ever think of moving, Kookoo? Like going into a home or something?" She's asked before but figures she'd try again.

Kookoo only laughs. "How can I leave? I have always lived around here."

She had, for as long as anyone remembers. Stella always said she would run away with Kookoo, if Kookoo would come— they'd go far, far away from this place.

"I'm going to take you to Australia, Kookoo!" she used to say.

"It's too hot there."

"How about Italy? It's supposed to be pretty there."

"Too many people."

"How about Asia? Or India, somewhere in the quiet mountains."

"What would we eat?"

"Indian food, it's good."

"Naw, I've never taken to that curry stuff. Hate that kind of rice too. It's not right."

Stella went to Mexico once, when she was in university. She took so many pictures of the beach, the islands, the ruins and sculptures. She took a whole roll of film of the ocean waves, wanted to capture how the water foamed at the sand. None of them turned out right but she showed them all to Kookom, explaining what she was trying to do.

"Sounds exhausting," was all her grandmother said.

She wasn't wrong.

Kookoo holds the baby and hums a song with no name that Stella knows as well as her own heartbeat. Her head feels so heavy. It's the most natural thing to lie here, to watch Mattie sit cross-legged on the floor, bumping along with the dancing cats. Adam is fast asleep, of course, but Kookoo isn't going to put him down.

"It never feels like home until you are here." Kookoo's voice is soothing.

Stella doesn't know if she is talking to her or the baby. The baby she just met and should have known.

"I'm sorry, Kookoo." Stella could cry so easily, fall into tears and never get up.

"It's okay, my girl. It's okay." Her answer for everything.

They are quiet for a long while, the droning voices on the TV, the room warm. Her Kookoo starts to hum another quiet lullaby and Stella leans into the pillows a little more.

ELSIE WAS SO beautiful. Blue eyes so rare, and full curly dark hair she called her Métis 'fro. Stella loved it though Elsie envied her best friend's straight hair, and, as soon as she was old enough, she piled hers with gels and creams, anything to get it poker straight. Stella would never do that, if that hair were hers.

They had been best friends since grade four, when Stella started at her school, when Kookoo changed her schools after her mom dies, and they were always together all the way through junior high. Elsie was her someone special. Paul and Lou always had each other, and Stella always felt left out of their sisterhood. She didn't have anyone, not until she had Elsie. Elsie lived with her grandparents too. They owned a house on the other side of the Redwood Bridge, and didn't want Elsie to have to change schools, so her Grandpa Mac would drive her, every morning, in his old gold car, the long, square kind. Stella thought it looked like a limo. Grandpa Mac was so nice. He would drive Stella home when he thought it was too cold, and when Stella walked over to their house, he was always cooking a big meal, always meat, like ribs or roasts. Her Grandmère was kind, too, though Elsie always called her strict.

Grandpa Mac died when they were in grade six. Elsie never even told Stella, her best friend, she just didn't show up at school for a week. Stella tried to call but no one ever answered. Elsie finally came back one morning. Stella saw her walking down from Main Street.

"Where's your limo?" Stella shouted at her. Feeling like her best friend was so far away.

Elsie just shrugged like it was an ordinary day.

It wasn't until a few weeks later, when Stella slept over, that she found out.

"Where's Grandpa Mac?" She looked around the house that didn't smell like food.

"He died." Elsie didn't even look sad.

Stella should have known how weird Elsie was then. How easily her family could just cut themselves off.

By the time Lou and Paul moved back, Elsie and Stella were back to normal, and they became a foursome. Elsie had no sisters, only little brothers who lived with her mom and her mom's new husband by Kildonan Park. She never talked about them either.

They went by there once, in the summer during junior high when they'd walk to the park to go to the pool. Elsie just pointed one day and said, "That's where my mom lives." A house they had passed a dozen times. It looked like it needed to be cleaned, and had a motorcycle in the overgrown yard.

"Do you see her ever?" Lou asked because she didn't know Elsie like Stella did.

"She visits sometimes," Elsie said, looking away. "She'll move back in with me some day."

Stella changed the subject because she knew Elsie would want her to.

The party on Powers Street was at the Other Mike's house. They called him the Other Mike not to confuse him with Mike Bruyere. Stella didn't know why they didn't just call this Mike by his last name too, but he was always the Other Mike. And in grade nine, his place was the party place. You could get anything there, and if you were a girl, you could bring five bucks and drink and smoke all you want. Every Friday, when Aunty Cher gave the girls ten bucks each, they would pool their money together. Elsie never had any money, but they could spot her and still have enough for a pack of smokes to share.

That night, they planned on sleeping at Elsie's so they could drink more. Her Grandmère was always asleep early so it was the best place to go. Even Paul was high that night, and she was usually the responsible one. Lou's boyfriend James was there, too. They were all pretty blasted. Elsie was playing cards in the kitchen with the Other Mike and some guys they didn't know. She'd been trying to get the Other Mike to notice her for weeks, so Stella was surprised but not unhappy when she saw them walk upstairs together. She didn't notice all the other guys following.

Stella didn't know how long they were up there. Looking back, it must have been a while, but none of the girls noticed. Not until a stupid stoned guy came up to James and said, "Dude, you have to go upstairs. Some girl is just giving it away." He ran away with a laugh.

Stella felt cold all over and looked at Lou who had her serious face on. Two guys came down the stairs laughing. Lou got up, all determined, and Stella followed, suddenly scared, suddenly sober. Going up the stairs took so long, and another guy came down as they went. The bedroom door was open. The bed was against the far wall so Elsie was the first thing they saw once they turned the corner. Elsie's beautiful curly hair pressed to her face by a large hand. The scene became clearer with every step. She was on her stomach. Some guy on top of her. His hand keeping her head down. The Other Mike stood with another guy, laughing and talking like nothing else was going on. The other guy had his hand on his belt buckle. He staggered with drink.

Stella couldn't move. It was Lou who did something.

"What the fuck? Get off her! Get off her!" She ran in and started pushing at him.

"Chill, bitch, chill," the Other Mike said with his hand up. "Chill. She said..."

"Get the fuck off." Lou didn't chill, and the guy was drunk enough to get pushed back and into the wall. His penis dangling, somehow erect and limp. That was the first penis Stella had ever seen.

"Get off!" Lou screamed, and grabbed at a blanket to cover Elsie's bare bum.

That's when Stella kind of woke up, moved. "Elsie! Elsie!" she screamed but her best friend didn't move.

"She wanted to. She said," the Other Mike said with a laugh. "She said." His cartoony laugh seemed to echo.

"Get the fuck out of here," Lou screamed again, hovering over Elsie as if to protect her from blows.

Stella only watched Elsie's face, still pressed into the pillow, her mouth open, her hair damp.

"What the fuck, Mike?" Stella heard one guy say, as Lou sprang up and pushed them all out the door. "Fuck! *Fuck!*" Her cousin kept screaming.

"So fucking serious," Stella heard the Other Mike say before the door slammed on his cackling laugh.

"Elsie, are you okay?" Lou tried to pull Elsie up. "Else?"

Lou propped her up but Elsie was just limp, like she was passed out but her eyes were open.

Stella just started crying. "What's wrong with her?"

"I don't know!" Lou was still screaming, trying to turn her over.

"Is she breathing? Is she dead?" Stella started hyperventilating.

"She's breathing. She's breathing."

"Why isn't she moving?"

"Go get James. And Paul."

That Stella could do, and she ran down the stairs. The other two were already coming up. She pulled at Paul's sleeves to make her move faster.

James and Lou got Elsie dressed, and she sat up. Paul just stood there with Stella, crying like an idiot.

"Elsie, what the fuck? What happened?" Lou said, tying up her shoes.

Elsie didn't say anything, just looked off at nothing. Her eyes looked dead.

"Can you get up? Get up, Elsie."

She did put some weight into her steps, and walked with Lou and James on either side of her. "Okay, let's go. Let's get you home."

"Shouldn't we take her to the hospital?" Paul piped in behind them.

"I don't know. Elsie?" Lou's voice was gentler now but Elsie still didn't answer.

When they got down the stairs, no one looked up and everyone was partying again like nothing happened. Someone tried to pass a joint to Stella but she just pushed it away. It was the longest walk to the front door.

Once they were outside, Elsie started walking on her own. Stella ran up beside her and tried to get her to say something, but she wouldn't. She just closed her mouth and pulled her jacket around her. No one said a word, even though they walked her all the way home.

"Do you want us to stay?" Stella asked but Elsie just kept walking. She looked back a little and shook her head. Stella went to follow anyway, but Paul held her arm. They all watched Elsie limp up the stairs and close the old door behind her.

Paul pulled on her sleeve and slipped her arm under Stella's for the walk home. James and Lou walked ahead. He held his arm across her shoulders while Lou shook.

That was one of the few times Stella had ever seen Lou cry.

SHE WAKES UP with a start and it's dark, the room empty and the TV burning a blank blue screen.

Kookoo talks quietly in the kitchen.

Mattie answers.

Something in the cupboard rattles.

Stella gets up to see. Adam sleeps between pillows on the carpet.

"Oh, you're up. Good, good?" Kookoo leans down and carries her old cast iron pan with two old hands. Mattie gives Stella a quick hug before resuming her position of helper.

"Here, let me get that, Kookoo." Stella reaches across the small room to take the pan from Kookoo's struggling hands.

"Oh I got it, I got it. Was going to make your girl a grilled cheese," she says, but hands it over.

"I can do that, Kookoo. You just sit down." Stella pats her back.

"Don't go making a fuss," she says as she finds her chair. "It's not like I don't do it every day."

Stella butters the bread, puts it on the pan and waits. She never did find out what happened to Elsie, she never saw her best friend again. When she called there was either no answer or it was Grandmère's soft voice.

"No, *m'petite*," she told Stella. "Elsie is not well today."

She was not well for a long time. Then she was gone. A man who finally answered one day said Elsie had gone to stay with family. Stella never did find out who he was. Or why any of it had happened at all. There were big, blank spaces where all the answers should be.

A few months later, she heard that Elsie had gone to one of those homes for pregnant girls and was going to have a baby. A few years later, someone had seen her with a toddler in a park across the bridge. But Stella never heard from her, her best friend. The person who had been all hers never called her again. Stella stayed far away, at first out of respect, and then out of habit.

Stella finds the spatula and looks around her Kookom's kitchen again, this time noticing that things are not as clean as they usually are: pans sit in a stack on the counter, probably so she doesn't have to bend down, and the sink is full of dishes crusted with dry food. She sets to work. She knows better than to ask first—she just runs the water to soak the dishes and wipes the counter.

Mattie unwraps the cheese slices carefully, and hands them up one by one.

"Want one, Kookom?" Stella asks as she sets Mattie's plate down.

Her elder startles out of sleep.

"Okay, come on, Kookoo." She nudges her gently. "Kookoo-ookoo?" She uses her old name and her grandmother smiles up at her and lets Stella pull her up.

"I can do it. I can do it." Kookoo slaps her hands away, but gently.

They walk into her dark bedroom, and Stella snaps on the light. There are clothes piled on the old chair, across the dresser, some obviously in need of a wash. A grey layer of dust lies over the side table, making all of Kookoo's treasured jewellery looked smudged.

Stella's heart breaks. She can't believe it has got this bad. She feels a spark of anger at Aunty Cher for not looking after her properly, but then no, guilt. Just guilt. This is Stella's fault.

"Let's get you to bed," she says like she hasn't seen a thing.

"I'll clean it tomorrow," Kookoo says because she knows.

"I'll help you," Stella starts.

"You'll be here. Are you going to stay?" The old lady's face lights up like a child's, like Mattie's, hopeful.

"Yeah, Kookoo. We'll stay." Stella pulls the sweater off her grandmother's shoulders and holds her there for just a moment, a beautiful moment, before she lays her down as she would her child.

Adam wakes up as soon as she walks through to the kitchen. She sits to feed him and looks more closely around the living room. Dust is piled up, but an old playpen is pushed against the wall. She only has to set it up.

Stella knows she doesn't want to leave, and thinks of all the steps, everything to do. She needs to call Jeff to sort it out.

She doesn't wait for her husband to say anything but hello.

"Jeff, I'm at Kookoo's and we're going to stay here."

SHE SAW ELSIE on the street once. It was downtown and crowded, but she knew who it was right away. It was the way Elsie walked, even if the face looked older than it should have. Stella passed by real close, so their eyes could meet. Elsie saw her but there was no recognition, her eyes were as blank as they had been that night.

Still dead.

19

ZEGWAN

ZIGGY HASN'T DONE anything but lie on the couch since she got home. When they got into the apartment, it was super late, but Rita set her down on the couch like she was a sick little kid. Rita delicately propped up pillows around Ziggy's head so she could lean into them, and brought her favourite blanket from her room. And the whole time, her mother didn't look directly at her. She was real quiet with her face screwed up like she was going to cry, and that scared Ziggy even more than if her mom was mad.

"Your dad's going to come first thing in the morning," her mother told her.

"Nimishomis too?" Ziggy hadn't meant to sound like a little kid but knew she did.

"Yup, first thing. Before you get up." Rita kind of smiled but it wasn't a real smile. "You want anything? Or do you just want to sleep?"

"Can I watch something? For a bit." Ziggy moved her head carefully into the pillows, wanting to get it right so she wouldn't have to move it again. Her mother winced but handed her the remote and went to make hot chocolate.

Sunny had put his headphones on and went off to his room. He'd been messaging Jake for hours. It's just like usual. Ziggy kind of wanted him to watch TV with her, but he said he was going out. She checked her phone, no messages.

"I'm going out for a smoke," her mom said, and handed her a cup too hot to sip.

She was gone for a while. No doubt puffing away like an old lady on the cold building stoop. Ziggy lay there propped up and kind of lonely.

It had been a lonely kind of day, the whole quiet and waiting. Waiting for doctors, for the police, to get to go up to see Emily, who didn't even talk to her. When Ziggy finally got to go up to the hospital room, her best friend lay there with her eyes tight shut, like she was pretending to sleep. Cheryl had said she needed to sleep so she would be able to go home soon. Cheryl has an exaggerated way about her, like Rita but the opposite, like everything is a little sweeter, a little more talking-like-I'm-a-little-kid than Ziggy would like. Cheryl means well. Everyone looked so tired and puffy faced from crying. Everyone told her Emily was okay now, but Ziggy would've felt better if she could have talked to her best friend herself. To tell her she was sorry she lost her. But Emily didn't wake up.

Ziggy lies there changing channels all alone. She looks forward to seeing her dad and Moshoom. They'll make her feel better, she thinks. They'll make her forget this scared feeling, this shame.

Ziggy hasn't seen her dad in over a month. He usually comes up every second weekend to get them and bring them home, back to the old house with the wood stove. Sunny has been trying to get out of it, lately, though. A few weeks ago, he didn't show up when Dad came. Dad tried calling him but finally they left without him. It was a boring weekend and her dad was moody the whole time. When they got home, Sunny acted like he didn't care. She thought he'd have been sad to have missed the trip home, but he never said anything, and neither did Rita. Then, Dad skipped out on his last weekend. He said he had to work, but Ziggy knew he was just trying to act like he didn't care either.

Rita comes back from her smoke, or smokes, and slouches at the other end of the couch, ready to help when Ziggy whimpers. It hurts so much. More when she falls asleep, when she dreams she is scared and moves to run away. She flinches as if she can actually do something, as if her brain is trying to remake what happened and change the ending. A choose-your-own-adventure kind of dream, over and over. Every time she wakes herself up, Rita is there, hand to forehead, or hand to ankle, like some weird dance in the dark.

"AANIIN!" HER DAD'S voice fills the whole living room. "How is my girl?"

Rita is still in her housecoat, pulling it tight around her to cover up.

Her Moshoom is behind him but her dad comes right in and kneels in front of Ziggy, while her grandfather greets her mom with a big hug. She can't help but cry when she sees her dad's face so close. He had bellowed her awake and now he is here. He smells like a fresh shower, strong coffee, and his old truck. The highway is long. He must've gotten up very early.

"Oh my girl!" His brown eyes are so soft, like he's going to cry too, but he fixes himself. "I hope the other guy looks worse!" He laughs. When her dad laughs, the whole room wants to laugh too.

He picks up the two plastic bags he dropped at the door and gives them to Rita. "Stopped by the store on our way in."

"Thanks." Rita nods, polite and awkward. She pulls her messy hair down with her free hand.

Her Moshoom comes over and hugs Ziggy for a long time. He smells like the lodge. He always smells like the lodge, like he lives in cedar all the time.

"Does it hurt, my granddaughter?" he asks in their language.

"Not bad," she replies in English. She is too shy to speak their language to him. He'll know she's forgetting it, losing what she has always known. Her tongue doesn't turn the words over like it used to. They come out rough and bitten.

Her Moshoom nods though because he knows, and stays on the floor holding her hand.

They watch Ziggy's parents stand away from each other. Rita holds the bags, and her dad's hands plunge deep in his pockets. They used to love each other so much. Ziggy remembers Rita used to sit on his lap with her arms around his neck and laugh. But Ziggy can't imagine her doing that now.

"I better get this cooked up then," Rita says, flustered. She turns to the kitchen. "Want some coffee?" she calls behind her.

"I'll help you make it." Ziggy's dad smiles one more time at his girl and goes off too.

Her Moshoom turns back to her. She can see now he's been crying. He sat there holding her hand and crying. "I am so sad this has happened, my granddaughter."

"Me too," she answers, still in English, though she thinks the words first in her language.

He keeps sitting there, holding her hand. She hears Sunny

get up and greet his father. They don't seem mad at each other. That's how it is when something bad happens — nothing else seems wrong anymore.

They all sit around all day, talking, and trying to laugh. Dad had brought bacon and eggs so they eat 'til they're full. Ziggy eats as much as she can, but her jaw aches with every bite. Rita looks more at ease after she's showered and brushed her hair. Even Sunny is being good.

It helps for a while. It helps to hear her family talking, to hear about what's happening at home and how much they miss her. Then the pain comes back and Rita runs to get more drugs. Then the shame comes back and her Moshoom squeezes her hand harder, as if he knows it helps.

But it doesn't go away, not all the way.

WHEN THE AFTERNOON gets quiet, Rita and Moshoom talk quietly in the kitchen. Sunny goes to his room. Ziggy lies there with her dad all to herself. He sits on the other end of the couch, and they half-heartedly watch some show. He laughs when he's supposed to, but it's not as hearty as it was in the morning. He keeps looking at her, and Ziggy knows this look. It's the same side-eyed look he had when they moved to the city. Ziggy knows what's coming.

"You okay, my girl," he starts, finally.

"Yeah," is all she can say. "I guess."

"Pretty scary stuff, eh?"

"I guess."

"I know your mom's pretty freaked out."

"Yeah." She thinks a moment. "But she's tough."

"Yeah, she is." He pauses. "But you're her baby. It's harder when it's your baby."

Ziggy hunches her shoulders to a shrug, but it hurts so she winces instead.

"It hurts a lot, doesn't it?" He reaches over and touches her bandages lightly and readjusts her blankets for her.

"I guess." She feels so tired, doesn't want to talk about it. Or think about it.

"I bet you're worried about your friend."

"Yeah."

"She's going to be all right, you know. Your mom told us. Emily is going to be fine. She just needs to get better first."

Without moving her head, Ziggy moves her hand to wipe away the tear coming from her good eye. She doesn't want to cry anymore. Her bad eye is starting to sting. She wants to think of happy things and forget this ever happened. She wants to talk to Emily and hear her go on and on about boys again. Or she just wants to talk to her.

"I love you, my girl." Her dad rubs her knee. Both her parents do this. Like they learned it from each other.

"I know." She thinks a minute, wonders where her phone is. "I just feel so, so ashamed." She says it before she thinks about it, but knows it has been there all along.

"Ashamed? Why are you ashamed?" His voice stays low, serious.

"I dunno," she says, retreating.

"Yeah you do, why are you ashamed?" He pushes her as only he can.

"Well, it's like," she says slowly, "I couldn't do anything. I didn't do anything."

Her dad goes over to wipe her tear now, and looks at her, right in the eye like he does. "What could you have done?"

"I dunno," she says quietly, trying not to shrug.

He keeps looking at her. Why do parents always look at you

harder when they're being serious? "I know what it feels like to feel shame. It's the worst feeling. But you have nothing to feel ashamed of. There was nothing you could've done."

"I know," Ziggy says finally, even if she doesn't mean it.

"Emily needs her friend right now, just be her friend. That's how you get rid of shame, you be there for her. And know there was nothing you could have done."

He nods and sits up. Like he's finished his fatherly advice. But then he looks out, facing the window but looking farther.

"Can we go see her again? Can we go see Emily?"

"Let's ask your mom." Her dad always says that, Rita being the last word on everything.

"How about we go tomorrow, first thing?" Rita says when she comes back in, her face still screwed up like that, but red and blotchy too. She was talking to Ziggy's Moshoom for a long time. "Once you've rested some more. Everything's fine over there. Emily is fine. We can see her tomorrow."

Ziggy just wants to talk to her best friend. "Mom? Where's my phone?"

Emily hasn't messaged or anything. Her last message just sits there, from Friday, 6:47 p.m., before she went over to go to the stupid party. So fucking stupid.

When it gets dark, her dad and Moshoom get ready to go. Rita says she's going to walk them to the truck but doesn't come back for a long while. Ziggy sits, alone again, still on the couch. Eventually, her brother comes out of his room, talking on his phone now.

"Yep, I got it. We got it," he says. "We'll be there in like a half hour...K...K."

Ziggy's curious but doesn't ask, just waits for Sun to finish his text and look up.

"How you doing, Zig Zig?" Sometimes his attention is so

nice, it's like all the cool kids saying hi to her at the same time.

"All right. You?" She burrows her arms under the blanket but tries not to move her head.

"Meh." He's on his phone again. "Where's Rita?"

"Smoking. Maybe she went to Aunty Cher's, who knows."

"She'll be back. She's just stressing."

"I don't know why. I'm fine."

He looks at her squarely. Serious big brother face. "You got your face kicked in by gangbangers after going to a gang party. I wouldn't be surprised if they're not convincing her to ship us back to the rez." He points his chin to the window.

"They wouldn't. Would they?" Ziggy pictures it, living back at home all the time. The bush, and the real dark of nighttime.

"I wouldn't put it past them. They're not exactly fans of the 'hood life, ya know?" He looks at his phone one last time and sits down, taps her knee with his fist, but gentle. "It's all good, Zig Zig."

"You think they'll make us go?" Ziggy doesn't remember much about going to school there, or even what high school looks like. Where would she go?

"Might do. Daddy will do anything for his little Ziggy Poo." He reaches out and lightly pinches her good cheek. He is just faking but she winces anyway, pulls away and gasps in pain.

"Sorry," Sun says with a face twisted up like how Rita's gets.

"It's okay," Ziggy says, fixing herself again. If she pushes her good side to the pillow a bit, everything feels still and almost good. But the painkillers seem to be wearing off.

Rita comes back in with her hood up. She's red cheeked. "It's getting fricking cold out there, my babies."

"You were long," Ziggy says, sounding more like a little kid than she wants to.

"I'm sorry." Rita shivers out of her coat, rubs her hands

together so she can check Ziggy's forehead. They stink sharply of cigarettes. "You need anything, my girl?"

Ziggy goes to shake her head but stops just before her face throbs again. "It hurts," she says instead.

"I know, I know." Her mom rubs Ziggy's hands now. "Might be time for another T3. I'll go look."

Rita gives Sun a funny look as she gets up.

"What was that?" Ziggy asks him, without thinking.

"Nothing. She's just worried." Sun looks at his phone again.

"Where you going then?" Ziggy changes the subject.

"Just out. With Jake."

"It's freezing. Where you guys going to go?"

"Nowhere! Fuck!" Ziggy can't tell if he's really mad or just sarcastically mad, but he gets up. "I'm going to jump in the shower."

Rita comes with the two big pills and a glass of water. It's still hard to swallow them. Then Ziggy waits for the relief to kick in.

She checks her phone again. Still nothing. Her last message from Emily is still the one from Friday.

"Bring your red top for me," it says. She was so happy. So excited.

So fucking stupid.

Why the hell did Ziggy go along with it? She knows better. Sunny had told her and she should have known better. He told her when they started grade seven because they'd be going to the big school and would need to know.

"Basically, you got two main gangs right now," he told her very seriously. "One is red and one is black, just look for red or black. You're not supposed to have colours at school but there's ways of getting around that. Black hats, red sweaters, stuff like that. And bandanas, of course, but they're usually in the back pocket, or hoodie pocket, hidden most of the time. You know?"

"But what about black hoodies, is that the black gang?"

"No, fuck, that's just a black hoodie." He scoffed like she was a moron. "Everyone has those." He pulled at his own black zip-up.

"But I thought the red gang wears red hoodies, so why wouldn't the—"

"Fuck, you're so messed. Red hoodies—yes. Black hoodies—no. It's not like fucking dress code uniforms at private schools, fuck."

"It would make more sense, is all." Ziggy hid her smile.

"It doesn't make sense, that's the point. There's logos too."

"This is really fucking dumb. I just want to go to school." They had gotten all their school supplies already. Rita had got a pile of slightly used binders from work, but all Ziggy's pencils and pens were new. She even had a new back pack too.

"It's important." Sunny was relentless. "You got to pay attention, if only a bit, so's you can keep out of trouble."

"Like I would get into any trouble." Ziggy gave him her best smirk.

"Yeah that is true, you're a fucking geek, but still." He tapped her knee with his fist the way he always did. "It's fucking stupid but just pay attention, hey?"

"What about you? Do you have to pay attention?"

"Me? Yeah. It's different for guys. Guys have to pay attention."

"So which gang are you in?"

"Pfft, yeah right, never mind. It's complicated is all!"

Rita says the same thing when she doesn't want to explain something. *It's complicated*. It was complicated when they moved to the city, complicated when she moved that stinking Freddie in, complicated when he left.

Emily thought Jake and Sun were too smart to get into

that shit, but Em's so naïve she walked herself into that gang party without even knowing it. Maybe she thought red was just Clayton's favourite colour.

But now, Ziggy doesn't know what to do or what's next. How will they act at school? Does this mean they're in the gang now? Or do they have to stay clear?

It is complicated.

"How about some pizza for supper?" Rita comes in with phone in hand.

"Sure," Ziggy says because she knows Rita would be mad if she didn't eat.

Sunny comes in with wet hair, clean clothes on.

"What do you want on your pizza?" his mom asks him.

"Naw, nothing."

"Where you going?" Her voice sounds worried again.

"I'm just going out."

"Like hell you are. Not tonight, my friend." Rita can get angry really quick. Ziggy just sits there and tries not to move her head.

"Settle down, Ma," he says, rolling his eyes like it's no big deal.

"Your sister just got her face bashed in, and her friend was fucking attacked. Where the hell do you need to go right now?" Her voice is so high now.

He just looks at her and turns to get his jacket.

"No, Sunny, no." Rita goes after him, pulls on his coat sleeves. "Don't go being stupid, Sunny. Just leave it."

"We're just going out," he yells, but his voice kind of cracks. It still does sometimes, and usually Ziggy laughs at him.

"Sunny? Sun?" Rita tries to get him to look at her.

"I'm not going to be stupid, Ma."

"I don't believe you."

"Believe what you like," he says and pushes the door open, pushes her off him, but not hard. Sunny wouldn't push her hard.

Rita just stands there a minute. Ziggy wants to ask but doesn't want to.

"Mom?"

"Just a second, baby."

Rita is on her phone, "Hi, it's me. How far away are you?... Can you come back? Sundancer just went out...I don't know where he went. Just, like, go around and look for him?...He's just left...I don't know where. Go around Selkirk Avenue there, or something...I don't know...I don't know!...I know! Okay. Bye."

She looks at her phone for a while, just stands there.

"Mom?" Ziggy's own voice cracks.

"What, my girl?" Like she's miles away.

"What's going on?"

Rita sits on the couch, not taking her eyes off her phone, texting, to Sunny, no doubt. "I'm just...I'm just worried about your brother. Worried he's going to do something stupid."

"Like what?"

"Like go after those guys, those guys who did this to you?"

"Girls did this to me," she says and huddles under the blanket even more.

"You know what I mean." And Ziggy does but doesn't say it. She meant who attacked Emily, who raped her.

"Sunny wouldn't do anything. He hates that shit. That stuff." She checks herself.

"I know, baby. I know he says that but—" Rita's face twists again, that scary way it does.

"No, really. Him and Jake stay clear of that. They don't do that gang stuff. They just play video games."

"I know, Ziggy," she says with that you're-just-a-little-kid look.

"It's true, Mom. They're good. We're all good." She pulls her head off the pillow, slow, steady, and reaches out to her mom's arms.

Rita grabs Ziggy's hand, still worried, but rubs it like she does.

"We still getting pizza?" Ziggy moves back slow, her head so heavy.

"Yeah." Rita's phone is still in her hand. "Yeah, sure. I'm just going to call Lou first."

"Okay." Ziggy thinks a minute. "That was Dad, right? Dad's coming back."

"Yes, baby. He'll find Sunny. Don't worry." She smiles down at her daughter. It's too sweet but Ziggy takes it.

She doesn't dare tell her mom she saw it—the black bandana that slipped out of his hoodie pocket when he pushed at Rita. She saw it and knew what it was. She's not an idiot.

But she wasn't worried, not really. Not until her mom told her not to be.

20

TOMMY

TOMMY REVIEWS HIS notes in his head as he drives north up Main Street. In his head, all those women blend into one, their faces so similar. The young girl, poor Emily, tiny and broken in the hospital bed, her aunt with the haunting eyes, looking so carefully, and the witness lady, so relieved they didn't think she was crazy anymore. They all look the same—same long dark hair, straight and shiny, same almond eyes, almost.

He's so fucking tired. Had to come in early again, dragged Christie in early again. He really will never hear the end of it. He hopes, somewhere in there, his partner admires his eagerness, and it will reflect well on him. He has painstakingly written and rewritten all his notes. They're meeting with the Sergeant later and he wants everything to look as it should, all the numbers marked and right, all the notes clean and detailed. He's never done anything so important. So far, his reports have been pretty basic, but this case is different. Everything has to be right.

He wants to do one more interview tonight—there's one more place he wants to check out. Christie thinks it's just to rule it out, but Tommy has a feeling. This is what Tommy tells Hannah at supper, trying to make it sound less desperate than it really is.

"I know it's the house. I just gotta get one person to say the wrong thing, just one." He cuts his meat firmly. He's really not that hungry, but Hannah likes Sunday dinners, even if they're early and before he goes to work.

"Well, that's not likely to happen, is it? I mean, they don't like to talk to the police, do they?" Hannah eats delicately, chews slowly like she's really not enjoying her food at all. For Sunday dinners she always makes pot roast or roasts a chicken.

"You have to ask the right questions the right way, babe." He likes to think she thinks he's tough, but she just looks at him with pity.

"They're gangsters, Tommy. They're, like, sadistic and don't give a crap. They're not going to, like, feel sorry for some girl. It doesn't happen like on TV. They're killers and rapists and drug dealers."

Tommy wishes he could look at her with the same kind of pity but he knows better. She would catch him and then go off. She always catches his looks, so he only thinks them now.

"I mean they don't care about anyone. They're just thugs and criminals. You can't *reason* with them." She says reason like it's the craziest idea of all.

Tommy wants her to be wrong. He wants to prove her wrong. He doesn't quite know why, but it bugs him. She has a lot of opinions about people and places she has never known or been to. He's already told her way too much about the case and reminds her to keep it to herself.

"I won't say anything, Tom, God!" She takes both their plates. His fork is poised mid-air—he was going to take another half bite. "I mean, all my friends already know what a fucked-up city we live in. I'm not going to, like, confirm it."

He'd had to tell her—he'd needed to roll the facts over and over again out loud. They didn't make sense. Nothing made any sense. Now that he's told her, he wishes he had talked to his mother instead. That's what he really wanted to do. Marie has a way of knowing about these things. Not just thinking she knows because she reads the Sun newspaper but really knowing.

"It's just crazy gangsters, hon. They're violent. End of story. They just want to hurt everybody 'cause they think they got it so hard." She's saying it like it explains anything. "Can we talk about something else now, please?"

Hannah wants life to be simple and has no desire to understand. She wants him to arrest everybody and not think about it anymore. She only wants to have nice Sunday dinners and pleasant conversation.

Tommy pulls up to Christie's house and the old man gets in with a sigh and the reek of fried food. His belly bulges over and hides his belt completely. He couldn't outrun a perp if his life depended on it. Tommy makes a silent vow to go to the gym after shift. And to give up carbs again.

"So what's the address of this place?" Christie coughs. He even sounds full.

"Twelve something Selkirk. Can you look it up?" Tommy remembers it, has memorized it, but is trying to seem less eager. He doesn't want anyone to think he's obsessing about the case. They're supposed to report in after this last potential interview, and chances are the Sergeant will tell them to forget about it. This could be his last chance before he's back to breaking up three-day parties and the other usual Sunday night things.

The house looks rundown. Blue-green TV light comes through the bed sheet–covered windows. One sheet is patterned in zigzagged stripes, once brown maybe, now almost yellow from being bleached in the sun. Overgrown hedges surround the small yard, filled with cigarette butts and beer bottles. The stoop's railing lies broken — it must've just fallen because it's not yet buried in the snow. The stoop is all ice, thick snow just packed down and curved where a lot of feet have stepped.

Christie knocks. He's going to lead this one. He said so. Tommy didn't tell him that he was happy about it. But he was.

The door opens a crack and a young woman's face appears. The wooden door chipped and the window broken and X-ed over with duct tape holding the broken glass in place.

"Evening, mind if we come in?" Christie bellows in his deep, old cop voice. It is effective, in its way.

The girl nods against the door and a voice comes up behind her.

"Who is it?" A man, young man.

"Cops," she says, like it's nothing.

She opens the door the whole way and a young, thin Native guy sits right there, as if waiting for them. He smiles. His plaid shirt is buttoned up all the way and a cigarette dangles from his fingers. The place is poorly lit but smells like Pine-Sol. The air is thick with incense. He reaches his remote control and turns the volume down, but the pictures still dance on screen. Some reality show Tommy doesn't know.

"Hello," the young guy says, but he doesn't get up. His smile is eerie and fixed.

"Are you the owner? Renter of this house?" Christie says, looking at the guy and around the room.

Tommy looks around, too, at the mismatched couch and

chairs, no pictures on the walls. Two girls sit on the long couch, the skinny one who opened the door and now lights a smoke, and a chubby one hunched over, her hoodie covering her hair. She looks young and kind of scared. Lost. He's seen that before—kids scared of the cops. He half smiles at her but she only looks away.

"Renter, yeah." The guy keeps smiling. "What seems to be the problem?"

"There was a girl attacked, not far from here, the other night, and we're inquiring around to see if anyone knows anything." Tommy keeps his eyes on the girls, but neither has a reaction. The skinny one, clearly older, just puffs away.

"I can't say I do. It's been a pretty quiet weekend. Just me and my girlfriend, and her kid sister." His smile and eyes don't move but his arm sweeps the room, taking in the girls on the couch. The skinny one smiles. The chubby one just looks down.

"Can we see some ID from you, sir?" Christie's radio chirps something that sounds like static.

The guy digs into his pocket and pulls out a plastic card. Christie takes it and hands it over to Tommy. It's an expired Native Status Card, the old kind with photo booth pictures. Michael Hutchinson. Dog Creek Indian Reserve. Tommy writes down everything.

"And you ladies, you have any ID?"

The skinny girl ashes her cigarette and picks up her purse. The chubby one just shakes her head. She's young, real young, so Christie just asks her her name.

"Roberta. Roberta Settee." She grabs a smoke too and lights up. She moves around slowly, like she's too big or too full like Christie. There's no signs of food anywhere though.

Roberta says she lives on Pritchard and gives a number.

The other girl is an Angie Dumas and lives up on Machray. Tommy writes it all down.

"All right. Thank you. Mind if we have a look around?" Christie is unfazed by the remarkable cooperation. He pushes further.

"Be my guest," the guy says, still smiling. His eyes shift, though, onto the television screen.

Tommy walks behind his partner, taking everything in. The kitchen is clean but the floor is stained. A small child, maybe three years old, sleeps on the bed in one room. The other bedroom is unoccupied. Both are full of the same posters and flags. Young men. Even the bathroom is clean. The basement is completely empty, not even a box, only a couple old blankets, wet from the puddles on the cracking stone foundation floor.

Christie looks at his partner. Tommy can't tell what he's thinking.

"Thank you, sir," he says back at the door. "Ladies. We'll let you know if there are any developments."

Tommy walks out, watching his step on the snow-packed stoop.

"Well, that was a godawful waste of time," Christie snaps as soon as they're in the car.

Tommy pulls the computer to him and starts typing. "What do you think?"

"I think that is either the cleanest mother fucking nate ever, or he's hiding something."

"The address has had a lot of noise complaints," Tommy tries.

"Who owns the house?"

Tommy goes back to his paper notebook. "Just a numbered company."

"*Hmph*. Did you look up who owns that number?"

"No, I ..." he starts.

"I'd be curious about that." Christie chews on his lip. He's thinking. Tommy knows he's interested too. It feels like a victory. "So, who's this Hutchinson guy?"

"Michael Hutchinson. There's lots. The hockey player for one. A few on the system, doesn't look like anything major."

"What about the girls?"

"Nothing on Roberta. Oh, Angie Dumas was arrested in 2010 for possession of stolen ... but let off. Known associate of an Alex Monias."

"I know that name. Look that up."

Tommy types and stares intently. The sharp glow of the screen makes his tired eyes go out of focus. "Four of them. Alex M. Monias has a drunk driving charge, oh, but he's older. Alex D. Monias has a minor traffic violation. Here. This one did three years for aggravated assault a while back, early release. Known associates ... street name Bishop ..."

"That's the one. I know that one. He went in like ten years ago."

"Yup. Got out in 2009."

"Anything since then?"

"Minor things — suspected weapons last year, awaiting trial. Possession of stolen merch. Same arrest date as that girl. 2010. He went back in for a while." He looks up. "So that was the Monias from the girl's rap sheet."

"You're a genius, May-tee. Look up his mug shot."

Tommy does but knows before the picture comes up what he'll see. He knows exactly what Alex Monias looks like.

"Fuck!"

"Figures." Christie has somehow returned to tired old cop. "What should we do?"

"Nothing." He yawns. "Let's report and then see. We don't wanna do anything stupid like tear into this guy. All we know is he's a gangster who doesn't want us to know he's a gangster."

Tommy thinks of ways to protest. Thinks of other things he could do or questions he could ask. But there's nothing, he just has to go with it, and figure it out on the way.

"Okay, we know she was at a gang party. We know that." Christie is making his own list. "And we know this guy lied, but we don't know if he had anything to do with the . . . assault. We haven't tied him to that yet."

"There's nothing in his history to suggest it, no." Tommy looks at the file one more time, running the words over and over, hoping one will stand out.

"No physical evidence from the victim." Tommy thinks of that list again. Bruises on the wrists and ankles suggested several persons held her down, possibly. Bruised left side of her face where she was probably punched. The other victim too, was punched in the face even worse. That was by girls though. Zegwan said that—she said it was girls. Emily didn't say it was anyone. Just four gangbangers. With long hair.

21

PHOENIX

"YOU'VE GOT TO fucking go, Phoen!" Bishop screams at her from the kitchen.

Phoenix is still sitting on the couch. She didn't move after the cops left, just lit another smoke, and took a long drag. The whole thing felt close. Too close. Her uncle knows just how to handle them, but he isn't happy. After they left, he just started pacing around, fuming really. He was like one of those cartoon characters with smoke coming out of their ears. Angie got up to go talk to him but even she couldn't calm him down.

"Just get the fuck out of here, Phoen. You have to fucking go!" He screamed loud.

In his bedroom, little Alexandria starts to cry. Angie looks all torn, her hands up to touch her man, her baby crying. Bishop pushes her away, so she goes to get the baby, saying *Shhhh* the whole way like that would help.

"I need you gone," he says, quieter. He scrapes a chair across the floor and sits down. It's not his fault, it's hers. Phoenix knows that. It's all her fault.

She knows she has to go.

She finishes her smoke and gets up. She's been hurting and feeling sick all day so she really has to move slow. She goes into Kyle's bedroom, doesn't turn on the light, but pulls her bag from the top shelf in the closet, where she put it when they got all the stuff out of the basement. She feels around for what's supposed to be there. The pictures, their thick old-fashioned paper, a shirt, a pair of pants she doesn't fit into anymore. She pulls another sweater out of the laundry basket, where the girls put all the dirty clothes that were on the floor, and puts it on, her hoodie over top. That with her jacket should be warm enough, she thinks. It's snowing again so that'll mean it's not so fucking cold. She finds some extra socks, too. Can't hurt.

When she gets out Angie is sitting with Ship on the couch. He's still stressing and she's rubbing his arm. Phoenix has always liked Angie. When they were young, she used to treat Phoenix really good. When Phoenix would visit, Angie would get Slurpees and fast food, especially when she was big with Alexandra and ate all the time. You wouldn't know it now because she's so skinny again, but she used to eat a lot. Phoenix eats all the time anyway.

She doesn't say anything to either of them now, doesn't even look at them, just goes to the door, finds her shoes in the pile there, and zips her jacket up. Everything feels tighter, must be the layers, but everything's covered so she'll be okay.

"K, see ya." She looks up like it's any other day. Normal.

Angie smiles but her eyes are sad. Ship just looks sideways at her, not turning around all the way. She thinks she sees him nod. It'd be good if he would've nodded. It would've been respectful.

Outside, she reaches out for the railing before she remembers it fell over, and she almost loses her balance on the ice. But, she's a fucking expert at walking on the ice. The snow falls a bit, and blows in the wind. It's colder than she thought it would be. The night is only half dark, the stars out to one side, the moon almost full. She can't tell if it's going to be full soon or coming off of being full. She learned that in school once, but never remembers which way it's supposed to go.

Out of the bushes, around the yard, and she turns toward McPhillips. She knows things this way — coffee shops she can sit at. Maybe one or two of her good doorways are still there. It's been a while since she's been out all night, and she hates doing it in the winter, but she knows how to rest when she can, keep walking when she needs to warm up. Cardboard blocks the wind — that's all she needs. She adjusts her bag on her back, it's not heavy, it's practically empty, but it's all she cares about.

The Windmill is an old, rundown coffee shop with orange walls with dusty old pictures on them. She sits in the far booth and stretches out. She wants to stay as long as she can so she orders a hamburger and fries. Shops like this are less likely to kick you out if you've had a full meal. The waitress is an old white lady with bright red lipstick. She makes her pay up front, but Phoenix doesn't mind. The coffee has free refills and she settles in with the paper, reads every article just to pass the time.

She eats her burger way too fast and is hungry again even when her plate is empty. The old waitress frowns down at her and asks if she wants dessert. Phoenix thinks no and shakes her head. She took a twenty from Kyle's stash, only a twenty 'cause she ain't no thief. But it'll have to last her all night.

"Another refill though."

The waitress just frowns again. Her face is so wrinkled that even her red lipstick looks creased.

She reads the comics twice because they're at the end and

she'll have nothing left to do after that. She's not so hungry after another cup of coffee but wants a smoke so fucking bad. She thinks again of places she can go but knows there isn't anywhere that'll take her. Dez's mom won't let her anywhere near their place, same with Roberta's, and Clayton is totally dead to her now. Cheyenne moved again and didn't even bother telling her where. She should have checked that, but that was when she still thought her uncle would come around. That was before he freaked out, and got Kyle to put all the gear in a truck and take it away.

"If the cops come here, I swear to fucking god, Phoen!"

He was true to his word, at least. When he's mad he looks just like Grandpa. Not their great-grandpa, Grandpa Mac, but his dad, her Grandpa Sasha. Not Phoenix's real grandpa but she never knew her real one. And this one, Sasha, she remembers only mean.

"Time to go. We're closing up," the waitress spits. She takes Phoenix's half-full cup.

"I thought you were open all night," Phoenix says.

The old lady just shakes her head. "We close at nine now. No sense being open all night around here anymore. All we get is people drinking refills and trying to stay warm."

Phoenix feels herself get mad but only sneers up at the lady. "Just going to use your can." She inches her way out of the booth. It hurts to get up. She almost throws up but stops herself and walks to the old bathroom, smiling in her head. It would've been so fucking funny had she puked all over that old lady's white-assed shoes.

She uses the bathroom and restocks. She needs only the extra shirt and she can put that on. The pants don't fit her anymore anyway, so she ditches them with the empty bag for the next poor shit who comes in here. She takes her pictures out carefully though. Their edges are rough and they look kind of faded but they're still good.

The one of Grandpa Mac and the car. She thinks she must've known Grandpa Mac but she didn't. Elsie loved him though. Always told stories of him, always cried for him. That's how Phoenix knows him so well. Like he was alive even after he died.

There's one of her and Cedar-Sage and Sparrow, her sisters. She's about ten and has a bad haircut. It's Christmas, and the tree is lit up behind them. Sparrow is just a little baby with pigtails, and Cedar's about six. The long, white, brick wall behind them. That was the big house, the one in the projects. Lego Land, they called those houses. Phoenix liked that house the best, out of all the places they'd lived after they moved out of the brown house, Grandmère's house. The Lego Land house was so big and clean, and there was a huge park just next door. Sparrow started walking and talking there, and everything was good for a while. It looks that way, in the picture. Good. Phoenix's face is so young, and her hair's so poofy, but she looks happy, or like she's trying to be happy. Cedar is smiling wide too. Sparrow's not even three, and she's not looking at the camera, too distracted by all the toys she got. You'd never guess how fucked up everything was by looking at this picture.

The other picture is the same day but of Elsie. Phoenix took the photo. Elsie is bending over and laughing, not ready for her picture to be taken. She is reaching out for the wrapping paper, picking it all up off the floor. The floor was covered with it. They got so many presents that year. It was almost like Elsie knew that was going to be their last happy Christmas. Phoenix likes this picture of Elsie. She looks so real, like she did, when things were good for her. Phoenix almost feels sorry for her mama here, but checks herself and slips the photo back behind the others.

The last picture is Grandmère when she was young. It's black and white, and she's all dressed up in old-fashioned clothes and standing on some corner downtown. She looks so fancy, like she was a real important lady. Phoenix knows she really wasn't. She was just a half-breed and couldn't even go into half the stores back then. But she still dressed up to go there. She knows this 'cause Grandmère used to tell her stories of the old days. Phoenix loved those old stories, even if they all turned out sad. But it was nice, sitting there with Grandmère who was so old she could barely see but she could still talk and tell the same stories over and over. Phoenix keeps them all now, what she can remember, keeps them safe inside her. She used to think of them as good secrets only she knew. When she was a kid, she thought if she knew more good secrets than bad secrets then everything would be okay. Now that she's older she knows it's all bullshit, but she still likes to keep the good secrets close.

She puts the pictures carefully in the inside pocket of her jacket and bundles back up. When she comes out, the old waitress's frown is a glare, but Phoenix doesn't say anything, she just sticks out her chin and walks out.

She knows where she wants to go now, so she walks up Selkirk Avenue with a purpose and her head held high.

They had only one Christmas in the Lego Land house. The girls were taken away before the snow melted. That was Phoenix's fault too. She had worn her mom's baggy sweater to school, and the sleeves were too big and came down off her arms. She shouldn't have done that. She knew there were bruises there. Big long finger bruises. Not that she gave a fuck about Sparrow's fucking dad. He could fucking go to hell, but she knew everyone would blame her mama. Elsie was real good back then, but when the girls left, she got real bad. Cedar-Sage and Sparrow went to a home but they didn't have a place for Phoenix so she was stuck in a hotel with older kids. She cried that first night. She'd never do that now but she was just a little kid. She tried to hide it and just cried into her blanket. One of the older girls caught her and laughed and said, "Don't be a fucking baby. It don't make no difference if you cry or not. No one's fucking coming to get you." Phoenix stopped crying after that. But she still missed her sisters and her mama. She was happy to be away from Sparrow's dad though.

It's cold as fuck, but she's okay. It's like she's gotten used to it these past few days. You get used to the cold the more you're in it. She walks up Main and turns on to Redwood and walks over the bridge. It all feels so normal it's almost good. In her head, she's pretending she's just going home, that Grandmère and Elsie will be there waiting for her, and even Grandma Margaret will be nice to her. And Alex, Alex is there with his bike and will take her for a ride, even though it's winter. She walks up the street and thinks the big brown house will be right there, but it isn't. And just when she thinks she has remembered it all wrong, she sees the crooked porch and the bent-out window. Her old house.

It looks older but it's still brown. The curtains are closed but there's a bluish light of a TV upstairs. The porch has two big red chairs that look comfortable, like you could pull them together and get comfortable enough to sleep. If it was summer, that is. The sidewalk is all shovelled, right down to the cement, and only the few flakes that just fell lay there. Phoenix wants to still pretend she lives here, that she has always lived here and that she's just come home after a long time away. She can almost believe it. If she wasn't so cold, she'd believe it all the way.

She goes around and down the back lane, but the whole backyard looks different than how she remembers it. There's a big new garage where the old one was. It was more of a shed really, with two old wooden doors that held Alex's bike and the old lawnmower she never saw anyone use. It was always dark inside, smelled like wood and oil with drawers full of tools she'd never seen anyone use either. When she was little, Alex said Grandpa Mac was still in there, haunting the place, so she'd never go in all the way.

But it's all gone now.

She doesn't know how long she lived in that house, doesn't remember any place else until she and Elsie left. That was when Elsie was big with Sparrow. Grandmère had died and Grandma Margaret wanted to move, wanted to "sell the fucking dump." Phoenix remembers that. Elsie was mad. She didn't want to move. But they did. She couldn't afford it without her parents too, not even if Sparrow's dad moved in. So they left. They went from a big house to a small apartment, and Sparrow's dad moved in anyway. They never went back. Phoenix hasn't seen the house since they had to leave.

She turns and goes down the back lane, walking in the ruts the cars made. The river is white and flat and wide under the bridge. She thinks about how it'd feel to jump off onto the ice and snow, how much it'd hurt. She'd probably just die. But it'd hurt first. It's a weird thought. She's still feeling a little sick, and she's sad now, and cold. She pulls her toque all the way over her ears but they still burn. She slips into the drugstore and pretends to walk around the vitamin section awhile. When she's warm enough, she slips out again and walks around the big cathedral and up the Mountain. She knows a doughnut shop back at McPhillips. That one is open twenty-four hours, for sure.

Grandmère was born in the French part of town and never spoke English until she was grown up. Her *père* was a member of the Union Nationale Saint-Joseph and so proud about who he was, even when it was dangerous to say you were Métis. Even though they grew up in the city, Grandmère and her brothers and sisters would snare rabbits along the river. Grandmère could make a snare even when she was blind. She had taught Alex and he would set them up in St. John's Park. Phoenix and Alex almost caught a rabbit once — the string wrapped around its long foot but it kicked its way free. Phoenix was secretly glad it got away because she didn't want to kill a rabbit. She was just a little fucking kid.

Grandpa Mac was Métis too but half-breed Ojibway, and he spoke English, so when she met him, Grandmère started speaking that language. Grandpa Mac worked very hard and bought that house with his own money. Grandmère was very proud of him and loved her house so much she never wanted to move. She wanted it for her children, all the way down to Phoenix. They only had sons until Grandma Margaret — she was last. Everybody was so happy and loved her so much. Then Grandma Margaret had Elsie and Elsie was Grandpa Mac's favourite. Then Elsie had Phoenix who was Grandmère's favourite. That's what Phoenix remembers most of all, how Grandmère would say that, even though she had so many kids and grandkids, and Phoenix was her favourite. She doesn't remember all the stories, just the feelings and the pictures in her head. Grandmère in her chair. Grandmère smiling down at her. Grandmère's old eyes, grey with age and blindness. Grandmère in her fancy old-fashioned dress downtown. Phoenix knows there are other pictures out there. Grandmère used to show her loads, but she hasn't seen them since they left that house. Grandma Margaret must have them, or have had them, before she died, too.

She has enough to order a doughnut and a coffee. There are no refills so she gets a cup of water and sips slow, and reads one of those Coffee Time newsletters. She finds an old stubby pencil, the kind used for the lottery tickets, and draws in the empty spaces. Nothing really, a bird, a face bearded and angry, her name in cool tag letters. If it wasn't so late, she could call Cedar. She'd have to find a way to do that tomorrow. She should tell her little sister about their Grandmère. Cedar would like to know. She's smart and likes good stories.

When the clock reads after two, Phoenix figures it's time enough and starts walking. McPhillips is thick with cold wind so she turns down a side street. The walk is longer this way but at least the buildings block the wind.

She passes by the Break but doesn't look down it. She can see the tall robots, and she feels the wind stronger and colder but doesn't look up. She doesn't have to. She remembers every second.

Her uncle's house is quiet and completely dark. The TV is off and nothing moves. She knew he'd be real low key and tell everyone to keep away. She goes in from the back lane and opens the door without a sound. Inside, the kitchen is still. She can see the wrappers and a case box in the shadows. It looks like they had a good supper and a few beers. That's good. Her uncle will be asleep all night.

She slips through the basement door but doesn't turn on the light. She knows it's empty down there, and the old blankets are wet on the floor. It's okay, she's warm enough in her layers and there's room enough for her up at the top of the stairs. She is still feeling sick but better than before. She has to go pee but will hold it. It almost smells like that old shed did. Old and haunted. Phoenix isn't all that scared though. She hasn't been scared of that kind of shit in a long time.

She curls up there, leans against the door, and tries to sleep. Thinking of the old, brown house, and pretending she's always been there, just like she was supposed to be.

PART FOUR

• • •

It's only a dream, my Stella. It's something I don't know, not all the way, or understand.

And that's okay, I think. I don't think we were ever supposed to know everything. No one said we were ever supposed to know why things happen the way they do. They only said we have to take it as it comes, right?

I have never seen a white light. No one in a long coat or cape has ever shown up and told me where I am supposed to go, or what I am supposed to do now. I'm just here. It's like a dream but all the same too. Because I stay here where I have always been, with all these falling-down houses and Hydro towers, all these overgrown trees and sad women. In the old house on Atlantic with its wide unmade bed and the kitchen that always smells like five different meals at once. I stay with you, my girl. I was there when you were in my mother's arms on the old velour chair, when the two of you rocked each other to sleep. I was there.

For a long time, I waited. Waited for a light, or for someone to show me the way and what I was supposed to do.

I waited in that old house a long time after you had all gone. Then I wandered through the snow and streets hoping to find you, like you were the lost ones, not me.

When I heard you, with such pain and sadness still, and I only wanted to be near you. Still needed to be needed by you. I am the light breath and wind around you. I am the knowing that you are never really all alone. You are all of my strength and none of my weakness. You are the dream my life made. Those are the best things I can ever do for you.

A storyteller once told me our languages never had a sense of time, that past and present and future happened all at once. I think this is how it happens for me now, all the same time. I think this also is why you don't let me go, because I am still happening.

None of us ever lets go, not really. No one has ever shown us how. Or why.

But you are so strong, so much stronger than I ever was. I have no doubt you will make it through anything. You just have to take it as it comes.

And it will come.

22

CHERYL

CHERYL KNOCKS ON the door but lets herself in before Rita answers. She knows her friend is up—she can smell the coffee through the crack under the door. Rita will still welcome the cardboard tray of coffees Cheryl is bringing in though.

"Hey," Rita calls quietly from down the dark hall. Cheryl sees Ziggy sleeping on the couch, her little face bandaged up and leaning at an awkward angle.

"Hey," Cheryl whispers back and her voice breaks in ways she doesn't expect. She takes off her shoes and walks to the kitchen where the pale morning light tries to shine through the smudged window and the clouds. She puts the tray down, opens her black coffee to let it cool, and leaves her friend's Double Double for the taking.

"Oh thanks." Rita appears behind her, eyeing the familiar cup. "That's why you're my best friend." She tries to laugh but her whole face is strained. Broken.

Cheryl smiles weakly.

They hug each other tight, sighing into each other's

shoulders. Cheryl thinks she could fall apart right there, would love it, really, to be able to fall apart all the way.

"How's Ziggy?" She breathes into her friend's shoulder.

"Drugged. Sleeping." Rita doesn't really cry. She has a practiced avoidance of any kind of vulnerability. Her voice might quiver, might even crack in ways she doesn't want it to, but her eyes will stay dry.

Cheryl rubs her friend's back before she lets go. She knows there is nothing she can do, nothing really she can say. All she can do is be here. And not fall apart. Rita sighs and finally pulls away.

"Those men gone?" Cheryl asks, sitting down at the table.

"Yeah, they left after supper last night. Had to get back on the road." Rita pulls out a chair and slumps down.

"Well, at least they came to see their girl." Cheryl smiles. It somehow feels both forced and sincere. She thinks of her Joe. His placating telephone words. He said he was going to come.

Rita just shrugs.

Cheryl checks her coffee and takes a cautious sip. She knows Rita won't say anymore, not about her ex or his dad, so she can only feel her way through Rita's change of subjects.

"Everybody safely home yet?" Rita asks after a moment. Cheryl knows this social worker thing she does, checking off everyone, making sure they are all safe and ensconced somewhere. Cheryl does this too, but only with her girls and their kids.

"Yeah, well, they're safe. I'm going to see Emily later. Mom's downstairs." Cheryl blows into her paper cup. "Stella's over there."

"Stella! Fucking about time. Did she hear or something?" Rita's brows furrow. Her eyes look almost black.

"I guess. She looked pretty rough, like depressed, or

post-partum, maybe. Her kids are cute. Baby looks so much like Rain, holy smokes." Stella looks much older than the last time Cheryl saw her, and so much more like her mother. The same weathered look Rain had, only Rain's eyes were brighter.

"It's rough denying who you are, hey?" Rita is so hard.

"Be nice. She's here now." Cheryl sips and tries to believe it. Her sweet young niece still so beautiful, still so sad, still carrying everything with her. Her back's nearly bent with the weight of it all.

"Should've been here all along." To Rita everything's so cut up and dried out.

Cheryl can't argue. Rita's as right as she is wrong. She thinks of something else Rita will have an opinion about. Rita likes being angry. It distracts her.

"I called Joe, hey?" Cheryl leans back and looks around the perfectly clean kitchen, and doubts Rita has slept at all.

"What's that useless son of a bitch up to?" Rita reaches into her purse for her cigarettes.

"Same." Cheryl puts down her cup and rubs her old, sore hands. "He's gonna call Paulina this morning. Gonna come in, he says, just as soon as he's done this job he's working on."

"Yeah, right." Rita's eyebrow makes an angry arch, but even her anger is tired. "Believe that when you see it, hey?"

"Yeah, I guess." Cheryl's voice sounds far away, and she doesn't want to say any more. Rita knows better than anyone how she feels about Joe. How she feels about his saying he's coming.

Her friend scoffs.

"Mom?" Ziggy calls from down the hall.

Rita face instantly changes and she jumps up to see what's the matter.

Cheryl sits there a moment longer, thinking about Joe's useless words. His voice soft and soothing, pulling her to the bush, to his arms, and that mouldy old plywood house. He would come, when he could. When it suited him.

She opens a window, lights a smoke, and looks out to the treetops with snow sticking to the branches. She thinks of the bush. That home. The worn blankets thrown over worn furniture, snowshoes hanging on the walls beside a few of her early paintings, back when she painted trees not people.

When they moved out there, back in another life, Rain was still alive and everybody could fend for themselves. Cheryl really wanted to go. She escaped with her crazy man to the bush, with only their babies and a dream. She wanted to raise her daughters in the quiet country, have a different life. For a whole winter, it was great. She painted the trees, trying to perfect their skinny curves. She loved the dark nights.

But she couldn't hack it for long. Rain was getting worse, would go missing for weeks at a time, coming home higher and higher. Cheryl came to dread the old rotary phone's two quick rings, always her mom, flustered and alone. Her voice seemed to get so old that winter. They went back when spring set in—Cheryl took the girls to spend the summer with their cousin, told Joe it was only temporary and they would come back when her sister was better. He nodded as though he believed her.

Truth was she wanted to go back to the city. By then, she missed the place, its noise and exhaust smoke. The conveniently placed grocery stores and sometimes shovelled walkways. She wanted her mom's cranky old house on Atlantic and the kielbasa smell of the neighbourhood. That was her home. The bush was Joe's. They both knew that, and even though they went back and forth for years, neither budged from where they came from. They just started visiting each other, really. She knew she had to be with her mom, especially after her sister went. She knew she couldn't stay out in the bush. He found women from town to keep his mouldy bed warm, though none of them ever really stuck around. Cheryl found more than a few ways to get by, rye mostly.

"Could've all been yours," he told her once when she visited. When she drove up with their girls and their girls' then-new babies. He told her with love in his eyes and an exaggerated hand sweep that took in the rotting sheds and dog-shit-covered grass.

She laughed then but thinks of it often. His quiet and comforting land, his eyes at once pleading and repellent. Joe avoided being vulnerable too.

It's been five years since she last visited, last left him to the bush and whomever he could find. But that place, his place, always seems to be with her.

Rita sits back down, heavy, and sips at her coffee.

"How is she?" Cheryl asks.

"Good. Well, sore, but well." She sighs.

"Nothing's broken."

"Nothing's broken." They say it like a mantra of relief, as though it could possibly be true.

"So, how's your mom? With Stella over there?" Rita changes the subject.

"She's happy but, um, she's acting funny. She's fading, Reet. She's getting more confused, more, I don't know."

"Old."

"Yeah, I don't know. I mean, should I move in there? Should I get her a full-time nurse somehow? I know she won't go to a home."

"No, she wouldn't, hey," Rita says. She turns on the ceiling fan so she can light her own smoke. "And all this. This must've really thrown her around, hey?"

"You don't even know. She's wrecked like the rest of us, but different too," Cheryl says. "She's not all there all the time. And then she comes back. I don't know. It's hard."

Rita nods but doesn't say anything.

At the hospital last night, her mom had wanted to leave.

"Cheryl, please, can we go home now? Please." She whispered her plea and her old eyes seemed to whimper. She looked like a little kid.

And when Cheryl took her into her basement apartment, her mom didn't want her to leave.

"I thought you wanted to be home," Cheryl said. "I'm just going upstairs." She was thinking of the new bottle in her purse and the quiet relief of her own empty kitchen.

The old lady only shook her head and didn't look up, said she had a bad feeling. "A bad feeling," she repeated, and her eyes filled up again.

Cheryl sighed and patted her mom's beautiful old hands. What must she be thinking? About Rain, of course. That other tragedy they had. The kind that never goes away. A child is never not dead.

"Everything's going to be okay," she told her. "Everyone is safe now. I can stay, if you want me to. I can do that."

Cheryl left her there to make tea in the kitchen. She splattered her own with a good shot of rye, and chugged back a couple swigs straight from the bottle for good measure. She put the TV on and tucked an old blanket around her mom's legs. Her mother looked up at her knowingly, but Cheryl ignored her and turned the TV to one of her silly shows. When Cheryl passed the tea, her mom patted her hand like she was the one doing the comforting, and maybe she was.

Cheryl watched her mother rock in her chair and finally fell asleep on the couch. She stretched out, smelling sweet home, and slept for the first time since she had found out about Emily.

She woke up to the knock at the door. She faintly remembered the phone ringing in her sleep. She woke up to her mom happy and alert. Her smile was so strong.

"That was Stella," she said. Cheryl got up, half asleep, and opened the door.

In Rita's kitchen, Cheryl lights up again and pushes the lump down her throat. Her fingers are still stained with pencil rubbings and aching with winter, clutching at her umpteenth cigarette. Outside, cars go down Main Street, as usual, as if nothing ever happened. The two friends are quiet. Rita looks down the darkened hall, listening for her other kid who might get up soon. The other one she worries about all the time. Cheryl thinks of her mom, thinks that she should probably check on her again soon.

"LOU IS FINE. You don't have to go back and look after her," Joe had said to her that last day five years ago. He had just got home from town, smelling of beer and cigarettes because that's what he did when things got rough. She had made up her mind and her bag was already packed and in the trunk of her old car because that's what she did.

"But that Gabe is gone all the time," she told Joe. "What the hell is she going to do when that baby comes?" It was the bottom part of winter, when spring was supposed to come but didn't. Cheryl always got restless then. Craved the city. Joe always knew and told her so.

"She's going to do the same thing she did when Jake was born—take care of him. Get by. Paul's there to help. She's going to be fine, Cher."

"You don't know how much she struggled with Jake," she said bitterly. "James was never around. And now Gabe—who knows if he's going to be either? This all happened too damn fast. We don't even know him."

"You like Gabe. He's a good guy." Joe sighed and slapped at his jeans, but he was getting exasperated. Defeated. "You just want an excuse to go home."

"I just want to look after them, that's all." Her hands out, wanting him to understand.

His voice came out quiet and hissing. "It's you that needs looking after, Cher. Just fucking admit that to yourself, at least." She hated it when he got like that, when she knew she had won. Or lost.

"What the hell is that supposed to mean?" It was an awful, ugly cry.

"It means you need help. You need to dry out and get your shit together." He spit the words at her and looked at her with thirty years of blame.

"You're one to talk." She rambled around the room, throwing her arms around to further her point. "I know what *in town* means. I know you're always at that fucking bar." She was hung over. She wasn't at her best that day. Most days.

"Whatever, Cher. Do whatever you want. You always do anyway." He pulled his old work coat off the hook. "Just stay there this time, will ya? Stop coming back here every time you want a cheap getaway. Just stay there where you belong." He threw the door open and the blast of cold hit her face like a slap, and he went out to the sounds of his barking dogs and didn't look back.

She remembered thinking she would call him once she got to her mom's, to the city. She would call and everything would be better once she got home.

It didn't really get better. It just went on. They talked less and less. He got another woman. They talked even less. Their tired, lifelong, worn-out cycle.

When she told him about Emily, his voice cracked. He would come in when he could, he had said vaguely. Got a job on the go. Can't leave. Almost done. He sounded old. His woman had moved on, he mentioned almost in passing. Cheryl's stomach lurched with an acute hunger, and she suddenly wanted that sweet plywood house, wanted to get away from all this reality. He didn't say when he would come, only that he would.

Cheryl wanted to believe him so she did.

"SO, HOW'S YOUR girl doing?" Rita says finally. Cheryl knows she means Paulina.

"She's rattled, so rattled," Cheryl says after a moment. "What else can she be?"

Rita nods. "And her girl?"

"I don't know if Em will ever be okay again."

"Who is?" she says, and lets the air out between her teeth.

They are quiet, again. Their cups nearly empty. Cheryl looks out the window at the clearing sky. It's going to be a bright day. She can still see the outline of the full moon, yellow and porous. Like a shadow.

"I think I am going to go to a sweat soon. Think I'm going to take my kids home," Rita says decisively.

"That's a good idea. I should take my kids too. We all need a little healing." Cheryl talks slow, her words footsteps to something. Somewhere. "Cleaning."

Rita nods. "Going to have to go back to clean living though. Gotta give this up," she says, nodding at the full ashtray.

"Ugh, yeah, I know. Getting too old," Cheryl says, feeling it. She wants to laugh about it but she can't.

Then they are completely silent. The sun starts to shine on Cheryl's face, and caffeine and nicotine buzz through her body, neither easing the pain.

She closes her eyes to the bright warmth and tries to breathe it in. It's one of those moments she wants to somehow forget and remember at the same time.

ONCE, WHEN RAIN was still alive and doing well, she took Cheryl to see a storyteller. It was January and he had these shows at the library. Rain loved the old stories, had to go every time. He told a story about werewolves: "Our werewolves are women. Young, beautiful women who can turn into wolves and eat the youth of young men so they can live forever."

"Imagine that," Rain had laughed as they went home, her eyes glowing. She always loved wolf stories and this one became her favourite. "Eating men. Sounds fun."

Cheryl had only grunted and shivered her way down the empty street.

"I wish I could shape-shift into a wolf. No one messes with a wolf." Rain laughed and tilted her head up to the falling snow. She was happy, having a great day. They walked down the middle of Atlantic, each in a tire-marked pathway under the winter naked trees. Rain danced as they went, her mukluk feet pounding silently on the frozen ground. Her feet were always so sure. She never slipped. Cheryl trudged beside her in her old Sorels, careful of every step and huddled into her scarf. *No one messes with a wolf.* It was a throwaway comment in the flurry of a winter walk, but it stayed with Cheryl through all Rain's bad times. Her sister was always at the mercy of her body, weak to the drink and drugs or to some man or another. Rain would have made a good real wolf.

Wouldn't they all.

23

STELLA

STELLA OPENS HER eyes, not knowing if she'd been sleeping or just remembering. She smells the mouldy warm smell of the couch under her and hears her Kookom in the kitchen. It is like it always was, every morning, when she was a kid—Kookoo in the kitchen, up long before the sun, coffee perking, and the oven open to heat up the house. Stella used to lie awake and listen first, to hear her in the kitchen and know everything would be warm soon.

This room feels like home, full of silent memories and echoes. They slip in and out of her mind, one by one. Like the pictures on her walls, this is where her memories are housed. Stella doesn't have to look at them. But, of course, she does. And remembers. All the things here that she's tried to forget, and all the things that just happened over there, that she can't ever forget.

Stella only remembers bits and pieces about when she and her mom didn't live with Kookoo. Times spent in cold apartments where she didn't wake up to her grandmother's smiling face and the smell of fresh coffee. Stella was so happy when she and her mom moved into that big old house one last time. She knew she'd never have to leave, even when her mom said it was only temporary.

"'Til I get back on my feet," she had said. Stella doesn't remember Rain ever being on her feet.

Stella's lived a whole life since her mom died. She graduated high school, went to university, travelled, had good jobs, married a nice guy, planned her babies — all the things she didn't ever think she could do. She became the kind of woman she had never known before. And yet, here she is, the exact same kid, even on the exact same couch, with the same pictures looking down on her from the wall. Small, cold, scared, alone, housed within the five square blocks she'd lived in most of her life.

When Stella moved out to live with friends by the university, Kookoo finally gave up the big house on Atlantic. Aunty Cher went up north to live with Uncle Joe again, Lou was living with her boyfriend and baby, and Paul went to stay with them for a while. Kookoo said there was no point keeping the big house. She moved four blocks over to the building on Church. The one she walked past for years and always said was pretty. Lou and Paul stayed close by too. It was Stella who went two buses away. She would've gone farther too. She wanted to but somehow never did.

"Hey, Kookoo." Stella wraps her sweater close and stands by the open oven door. The element inside glows orange, just like a real fire.

"Good morning. Your kids are good little sleepers, you're lucky." She pours a steaming cup for herself, her thumb over the lip of the cup so she doesn't pour too much. Stella waves her to the table and stirs the sugar in for her.

"He was up in the night, but just a bit." The baby too, had slept better than he had in a while. They all had. "How you feeling?"

"Good, good. It's warmer today, I think."

"Think so?" Stella looks out the dark window but can't see anything but the empty back lane. The most she can tell is that it isn't snowing.

"Yeah, I think so. It's been so cold this winter. We need a break now." Her Kookom blows on her coffee. "It's going to be warmer today. I think the worst of it is over with."

Stella sits and pulls her knees up on the chair and watches her Kookom, just like she always did. Kookoo always talks about the weather as though she knows it better than anyone else does. She's always right. Stella can't believe how much she missed this. It makes her want to cry all over again. But the morning is too perfect for anything like that.

"I'm so sorry, Kookoo," she says into the morning.

"You're here now." The elder looks off and far away.

"I'll clean up for you today." Stella swallows her uselessness. "I'll do all the cupboards and stuff too."

"You trying to say my place is dirty?" Kookoo says, smiling.

It takes Stella a moment to realize she is joking, and then she smirks back. How many things can Stella feel guilty about?

They are quiet for long, comfortable moments.

SHE CLEANS AND sleeps on and off all day. Later, Adam is asleep in the playpen, and the living room is shrouded in the evening. She hears Kookoo in the kitchen, talking gently to Mattie.

"You don't play with the dough too much, just enough." Kookoo, poised with the plastic scoop, sits across from Mattie, whose elbows are white with flour and hands are caked with sticky, beige dough. Kookoo sprinkles more flour in. "Go on. Mix it up."

"Mommy, I'm making bannock."

"You sure are!" Stella feels so happy all of a sudden, so glad to be here.

She washes her hands and helps Mattie knead out the dough. Then they press it into the old glass pie dish, the same one Kookoo has always had.

"Now prick the top so the air can go through," she tells her daughter, handing her a fork.

"Why?"

"So it can cook."

"Oh!" Everything is amazing as her little girl jabs at the top in a mash of fork prints.

They put the dish in the oven and Kookoo gets a can of soup to open.

"I can do that, Kookoo," Stella says but her grandmother just waves her away, so she helps Mattie clean her hands. She then watches how her Kookoo takes the pot off the stove, guides the milk in the can with her finger over the lip, and struggles to place the now heavier pot back on the stove.

"Now, go sit." Stella takes over. Kookoo is tired enough to feel that she's done something.

"Thank you, my girl." Kookoo sits on the chair and Mattie walks off to watch a DVD again, promising to be quiet for her brother.

Stella pours tea and makes Kookoo a cup just how she likes it.

"I'm glad you're here, my Stella," her Kookom says, looking off somewhere.

Stella looks at her for a long time, her old eyes cloudy but smiling. "I am too, Kookoo."

Later, Stella lies on the couch feeding her baby, dozing off in the shadows of the living room. In the dark of her closed eyes, she sees them again, those blurred, black bodies on the white snow of the Break. Adam is crying, crying. She is screaming, screaming. Emily. Emily is screaming, down there, in the snow, under those other bodies, Stella can hear her now. No, that's not right. She didn't hear a thing.

She wakes up with a jump. Adam jumps too but settles again, and eats in his sleep, his little lips curling in and out with each tiny breath. Mattie sits on the carpet playing and watching, her hair almost dry and curling again. Her Kookom rocks in her chair. Stella can't tell if her eyes, behind her glasses, are opened or closed. She pulls her baby close and stares at him for a while, forgetting that when she looks up, she doesn't have to face out that fucking window.

When she lifts her head, it's her family she sees. Their pictures on the wall behind her Kookom's chair: Emily small and pigtailed, Lou and Paul, before kids, their cheeks squeezed together and smiling, her mom and Aunty about the same age, faces framed with thick, hide headbands, and Stella, all alone, with only a shy smile and a shroud of long hair. There's another picture of her mom, an extra one of just her. It's a glamour shot from the eighties and she's made up and glittery, her hair freshly permed, her smile stretched a little too far. That photo was never Kookom's favourite—it was just the last good one she got.

Her Kookom fills the sink in the kitchen.

"I'll do that," Stella tells her.

"Oh, thank you my girl," Kookoo says and shuffles off out of the room.

A minute later she calls from the bedroom, "Rain. Rain! Have you seen my blue sweater, the one with the flowers?"

Stella startles and runs over with soapy hands and the dishtowel. "Kookoo?" Adam stirs at the voice and gets ready to wail.

"My blue sweater. The flowers. It's warm." The old lady stands in front of her closet, looking sad and lost.

"I don't know, Kookoo." Stella wipes her hands on her jeans and reaches out.

Adam wails in the living room.

Something breaks in the old lady's face. "Go get your girl, never mind me." She looks down, defeated.

Stella doesn't know what to do, so she runs to get the baby. She rocks him and opens her shirt to nurse, and then looks back toward the open bedroom door. This isn't the first time Kookoo has called her by her mom's name. She used to mix them up all the time, especially Lou, Paul, and Stella, or call out all their names at once: "Cher-Rai-Lou-Pau-Stella!"

"I'm Stella, Kookoo!" she would tell her.

"Oh whatever," Kookoo would laugh back, busy with whatever she was doing.

Rain's name was never off that list, even after she died. But after, when it came like that, uninvited, it was followed with a thick silence instead of a laugh.

This confusion feels different.

After a minute, her grandmother comes out of the bedroom, sweater on. Not the blue one with flowers, though. A black, woollen one.

HER MOTHER WAS so many things. She was beautiful, and she loved to dance. She was smart, really, quick witted and mouthy. That's what everyone said. "Boy, that Rain has a mouth on her." Stella always knew that, but she knew more too. Her mother was also very, very funny. No one could make Stella laugh like her mom could. Kookoo, too, was always smiling at Rain. Even when Kookoo tried to be mad, Rain could always make her smile. Rain did things like make bedtime stories better. She would do voices and change the endings. She and Stella would lie side by side with the cartoon picture book between them, the pretty lady lamp turned on with a good idea under her parasol. "Sleeping Beauty" was their favourite. Maleficent scared Stella and gave her those bottom-of-the-stomach flutters, but she still wanted to look. Rain would give the horned queen a funny voice and would end the story in a different way each time.

"And then they lived happily ever after . . . because Sleeping Beauty told the prince to bug off because she had a good home in the bush and wanted to raise dogs and live a peaceful life. She didn't want no stinking itchy gowns and girdles. 'Have you ever worn a girdle?' she asked the prince. And he shook his head because he was really very dumb and didn't have an original thought in his pretty little head. 'Well,' Sleeping Beauty scoffed. 'It ain't no fun.' And she shook her finger in his face and turned to her fairy aunties and said, 'Come on, girls. We're outta here!' And out they went, walking all the way back to their little house. It was a long way, but they didn't care because you can only breathe right in the bush, and after all those days in the palace they were so happy to be home. The End."

"But didn't she get married, Mama," Stella said, knowing even then that they were all supposed to get married in the end.

"Naw, I mean. She dated a few, you know, wood cutters, but she never seemed to find the right fella."

"Wasn't she lonely?"

"Why would she be lonely? She had her aunties and a bunch of dogs."

"What kind of dogs?"

"The kind that look like wolves. Big ones. Grey ones. And a big black one too. She called him King because he was better than that stinky, boring prince."

Stella always laughed. Sometimes Sleeping Beauty got married, sometimes she had a smart little daughter or a sister and nieces, and they all lived together in a big house, but every time Sleeping Beauty was happy. Always happily ever after.

STELLA CLEANS AND Kookoo sits, telling her all the gossip she's missed out on. Who had run off with whom, and what's happened in the neighbourhood since she's been away. There's been a string of break-ins, broken windows, and the gangs are so bad! The facts muddle together in Kookoo's mind and come out all at once.

"Don't you ever want to move, Kookoo?" Stella asks after a bit. "Just leave and go some place else?"

"Leave and go where? This is my home. I grew up over there." She points her chin toward the river, somewhere out there around the corner and down the block. "You grew up that way." She points in the other direction. "I have always lived here."

"I know, but it's a bad neighbourhood, Kookoo. Maybe we should go and live some place else." She uses the *we* in case it would convince her. Maybe if Stella just goes first, the old lady will follow willingly.

"Good or bad, a neighbourhood is just a neighbourhood."

Stella shakes her head. "It's not. Lots of stuff just doesn't happen in good neighbourhoods."

Kookoo laughs but not unkindly. "It's just different there, my Stella. Just different, or they hide it. It just looks different, but bad stuff happens everywhere."

"My Kookom." She looks at her grandmother, serious and straight. "Girls don't get attacked in good neighbourhoods."

Kookoo looks right back, just as hard, no harder, even with her near-blind eyes. "My Stella, girls get attacked everywhere."

They sit quiet for a second. Stella thinks. Kookoo sips.

"I miss my mom." Stella says it because it's true. Every day.

"Me too, my girl. Me too." Kookoo sighs. She reaches out to take Stella's hand. Stella puts the rag down and holds on. Kookom's hand is soft and wrinkly just like her bannock dough.

HER KOOKOM WAS always there, even when Rain was not. Rain would go off—Stella never really knew where. "To a friend's place," Kookoo would tell her, and she would understand. Her mom needed to be out sometimes but always came back home.

Some of their best times were out at Uncle Joe's place. Rain loved it out there. She loved the trees and the space. Stella didn't like how dark it got at night, but at least she could see all the stars. She would sleep with her cousins, taking turns in Lou's and Paul's beds. They would stay up late and talk for as long as they wanted because their parents couldn't hear them on the other side of the house. They would all go hiking through trees. They'd pick berries and the girls would be real quiet while their moms gossiped. One time Aunty Cheryl pointed out a flattened spot of grass.

"A bear must have been sleeping here," she told them.

Stella was awestruck. A real bear.

"Let's lie there, just like the bear did!" Rain laughed.

And they all did it. The grass was warm from the sun but Stella thought it was still warm from the bear. They ate their mucky handfuls of berries and Rain started the game—Stella's favourite—where you look at the clouds and imagine all the things they could be.

"That one looks like a train." Her mom pointed her chin to a big square cloud.

"That one's a flower." Paul pointed a purple finger to a bunch of white blobs.

"No, it isn't!" Lou yelled too loud. "It's a building exploding in slow motion!"

Stella liked it because if you looked real hard, you could really see what everyone else could see.

Stella never wanted to leave. Her mom was happy out there too. For a while. But they never stayed long enough. Rain would want to go home, as though she was being pulled back to the city. Stella never knew why—Rain never did much when she got there, would just go out. As a grown-up Stella knew her mom was an addict and that pull was everything she thought she needed. But as a kid, Stella only knew her mom needed something she couldn't give her.

STELLA LEANS THE full laundry basket in to her hip when she hears her aunty come in.

"Hello?" Cheryl's voice calls. "Oh, hello beautiful baby."

Adam lies on the blanket next to his sister, who is stretched out on her stomach. She hands him toys that he grabs and drops over and over.

"Hi." Her little girl looks up shyly but goes back to her playing.

"Where's your Kookoo?" Cheryl looks as though she just got up and smells like coffee and cigarettes. She wears sweats and an old shirt covered with paint.

"Lying down." Stella pats all the laundry down in the basket and sets it by the door. "She said she was feeling tired."

"Oh, how is she?" Cheryl lowers her voice.

Stella can hear Kookoo getting up, the bed springs straining under her.

"Come help me, my girl," she calls, asking for Cheryl.

"What's up, Ma? You sick?"

"No, no, I'm just old," she says as she moves to her chair. "Now tell me, how's my Emily today?"

"She's okay, getting stronger." Cheryl sits down on the couch, the pictures of her grandchildren on the wall behind her. Emily and Jake in matching school pictures. A photo studio picture of the youngest one, Gabriel. The ones of Stella's kids are smaller, and old: Mattie as a baby and a small, cut-out one of Adam from months ago. "They might let her go home tomorrow, if she keeps getting better. You want to go there today?"

"Later. After lunch, maybe." Her grandmother smiles down at Mattie.

"Kookoo." Mattie says the name slowly. "Can you read me this?" She holds up one of her picture books.

"Oh my eyes." She looks off. "Why not ask your Kookoo?"

Cheryl looks at Stella. Neither knows what to do for a second.

"Yes, Mattie, you want your Aunty Cheryl to read it to you?" Aunty Cher says.

The girl is confused but goes to the strange woman who smiles wide and opens her arms.

Stella returns to her work. Mattie sinks into her aunty's lap a little more with each page.

"Is she asleep again?" Stella whispers about an hour later. Kookoo just sits in the chair. Stella checks that she's still breathing. "Is she always like this?"

"She's getting tired." Cheryl waves it off. "She's healthy,

for the most part. A bit of angina but her doc says it's nothing really to worry about. Her cataracts are bad but surgery would be worse now."

"Should we...should we think about getting her in some place?" Stella starts but knows the answer as soon as she says it. Adam starts to fuss on the floor.

"She'd never go." Cheryl puts a blanket over her mother and brushes the grey hair out of her face, just the way she would with one of her kids.

"Maybe a nurse for home care." Stella puts her baby to her breast again.

"She has someone come in a couple days a week, to help her bathe. She won't let me help her." Cheryl looks tired too.

"You still painting, Aunty?" Stella nods at her shirt.

"Oh," she scoffs. "Not as much as I should."

They're quiet for a minute. Only Adam's soft suckling noise.

"You look so much like your mom," her aunt says finally. Stella knew she would say that.

"I know." She looks down at her baby to keep from making eye contact. "I'm older now, hey? Than she was."

"I know." Cheryl slouches into the couch as though she's been defeated. Aunty could never be defeated.

"Been thinking about her again, being here. She comes and goes, hey?"

"She's always here, Stelly." Aunty Cher's eyes go somewhere faraway. "She should still be here."

Stella nods, happy somehow, thinking of her mom. Dancing.

"Well, I better get ready to go to the hospital."

Stella is knocked out of feeling good. The room is quiet except for the playful music of Mattie's show. Stella's head is clear now.

"You okay, Stelly?" Her aunt stops and pats her niece's arm.

"Aunty, I have to tell you something." Stella says it like a sigh, quickly, before she thinks about it too much. "Aunty, I have to tell you I'm sorry. I am so, so sorry. I hurt every day and I am so sorry." It all comes out faster than Stella can think about it. She's crying before she knew she would.

"*Shh*, what's up? It's okay, Stell. What do you have to be sorry for?" Aunty Cher sits beside her again.

"It was me. I saw it. I saw it and I didn't do anything about it. I was too scared. I was so scared." Her throat catches over each word. The tears fall.

"What are you . . ."

"I thought they would attack me, or get me, or my kids. And my baby was crying and then Mattie woke up, and they were so scared. I was afraid, afraid they'd come back. But I wasn't thinking. I wasn't. I didn't know it was Emily. I didn't know. And I am so sorry."

"What? Why?"

"I didn't do anything." Her voice wails too loud. Her voice catches and she looks over, but Kookoo doesn't stir. Mattie watches out of the corner of her eye but pretends not to.

"About what?" Aunty Cher just looks.

"About Emily. About what happened to Emily. I saw it. It was outside my house. I saw it and didn't do anything but call the cops."

For the longest moment Stella has ever known, her aunt is silent. Stella can't look up. Mattie gets up and hugs at her legs. Adam falls asleep.

Finally, her aunt sighs. "Oh Stelly. How? What?"

"I should have done more," Stella breathes. She stumbles on. "I should have gone out there. And yelled and screamed and chased after them. I should have run out and made her get into my house and kept her safe but I just let her go." Stella breathes a low cry. "I didn't know what to do."

"Oh Stelly," her aunt says again. "I didn't even know...I didn't even know you lived around there."

Stella nods and nods. Mattie pats at her leg. Stella pulls her daughter to her side to reassure her everything is okay. She had told Kookoo about the house, but not where it was, only promised vaguely to take her to see it one day. That was the last time she talked to her. Just after Adam was born. How could that have been the last time?

Stella wants to sink her face into Cher's paint-splattered shoulder and go to sleep. She thinks she would go straight to sleep.

"But you called the cops. That's something." Her aunt's words are small but strong.

"That's not enough."

Her aunt sighs again. "What do you expect? It's okay that you were scared. It's okay that you didn't know what to do. Who would?"

"But I just kept thinking of myself. And my kids. I didn't think about Paul's kid. I didn't think I would know her. If I knew it was Paul's kid..."

"I know, I know. These things...happen. I mean, it's unreal, but they happen. How were you to know?" Her voice sounds unsure but she pats Stella's shoulder, awkwardly but lovingly.

"I will regret it forever."

"Yeah, that happens too."

Stella just cries now. And her aunt pulls her close. Cher smells like her mom—cigarettes and clean hair. Stella keeps crying and can't stop.

Her aunt whispers, "It's okay, Stella. You did the best you could, Stelly. You did the best you could." And rubs circles in her back, just like her Kookoo does, just like her mom did.

Where did they learn that?

She doesn't fall asleep but she cries herself out. All the way. Squeezed between her aunt and children.

Kookoo breaks the silence with a deep snore in her chair.

Aunty Cher laughs. "She's so happy that you're here, Stelly." She pauses, her face growing serious. Stella doesn't know when her aunt started looking so old. "I am so happy you're here too."

"Thank you. Thank you so much, Aunty." She swallows.

"Just stay for a while, okay? Take care of her and let her take care of you." Cheryl reaches her hand over and doesn't so much take Stella's hand as she clutches on to it, for a while.

"Okay." Stella chokes on the word.

"Stelly?"

"Yeah?"

"I know you did the best you could." Her eyes are deep, dark brown, and completely honest.

"Okay." But Stella can't look at her for too long.

"I love you. I will always love you."

And that was all she needed. At that moment, that was everything.

"I love you too, Aunty. I am so sorry this all happened." She moves her other hand around her aunt's old one. Cher's old-lady hand, just like Stella's mom's, just like her Kookom's.

"Me too, Stelly. Me too."

HER MOM "NEEDED to go out." Her words. That's all Stella remembers. It was a normal day—winter, cold. Normal. When Stella looked up from the TV, she saw her mom take her smokes from their place on the coffee table and a twenty from Kookoo's hiding place, and go upstairs to get ready. It wasn't unusual, not really. It was just that no one else was home. Stella didn't say anything, just kept watching her show because her mom used her mad voice, the one that meant Stella shouldn't say anything back, just be quiet. Stella was always good at being quiet.

"Be good," she said at the door. Her hair done up high, her makeup sparkling. She didn't make eye contact though. The laugh track stopped just then, the canned laughter of an audience, and the whiny voices of the sitcom. Stella heard the slam of the front door. The brief cold pushed at her little body from the outside and then it was all gone.

Kookom came home from work hours later. "Where's your mom?"

"She had to go out." Stella had turned all the lights on in the house and marooned herself on the couch with junk food. The phone right there on the coffee table, just in case.

Kookoo muttered things under her breath but didn't scold Stella for eating Cheetos for supper or for wasting electricity. She only called Aunty Cher, who was somewhere with her girls but caught the next bus home. Stella knew something was wrong when they came in. Even though her mom left all the time, something was different this time, something in the air stung.

A few days later Stella and her cousins were sent home from school. Her and Lou's names were called over the intercom.

"Miss Perlmutter?"

"Yes?" Their grade four teacher had a singing kind of voice. Stella remembers it singing whenever the PA called her back.

"Can you send Stella and Louisa Traverse home, please? They are wanted at home right away, please."

"Okay," she replied. She turned to them. "I do hope everything is okay." She twittered to the girls while helping them with their backpacks and smiled them out of the cloakroom. They picked Paul up down the hall.

"I wonder what happened," Paul said, always so clueless. "I hope it's not Kookoo!"

Lou just looked at Stella. They exchanged looks because there wasn't anything they could say.

They just told her she died. That's how they said it: "I am so sorry Stelly, but your mom has died." Died.

That's all they said.

Only when Stella found a newspaper did she learn what had happened. Her mother's body was found behind a dumpster. She had her pants around her ankles. There was a grainy picture in black and white: a big square dumpster in front of a tall, brick wall, something covered up on the concrete. It looked like just a blanket, fallen down, left behind.

She showed the article to Kookoo, pointing without words.

"Oh, Stelly, give me that." Kookoo took the page and folded it closed. Her face was swollen with her own sorrow but she still knelt down and told Stella: "Your mom was at a bar. She was dancing, you know how your mom loved to dance. Well, she was there alone and danced with the wrong fella. He was mean to her, Stelly." That was the word she used, *mean*.

The real story came out in parts and bits, at times when Stella kept herself really quiet when the adults were talking, especially if they were sad and drinking. Her mom was talking tough at the bar. She was always so mouthy. She must've told the wrong people her wrong opinions. Some white guy was chatting her up, and they went to his truck. Police later found blood in the cab, and they thought he beat her half to death in there without even leaving the parking lot. No one saw that or saw how she wandered, half conscious, to the hospital. Some nurse just saw her, drunk and bloody. The nurse rolled her eyes and told Stella's mom to wait. That was what the file said. She was there long enough to make a file. They thought she was just drunk, had made her own head injury, and could wait. But she didn't wait. Even though it was so cold, even though she must've been half frozen. They figured she got tired of waiting and was walking home when she went to take a pee in the alley. That's when she lost consciousness altogether. Froze to death in the end. That's all it took. Winter. She had recently had sex, no signs that it wasn't consensual. The guy said it was, when they picked him up—he said it was consensual and she was crazy. He had hit her but he was sorry. She had a record and he didn't. He only got a suspended sentence. She wouldn't have died if she hadn't been drinking. If it hadn't been winter, if she would've waited, if she hadn't been so stupid. The head injury was only one part of it after all.

Stella learned all the facts. She gathered them like bits of debris and glued them together as if they could stick again. She asked her aunt to tell her everything, but Cheryl told her only some. She asked her Kookom to tell her more and she told her some more. She learned everything she could until she put everything together, wedging each piece side by side with the others. The bar. The hospital. The street. The back lane. It wasn't a night out anymore. It was a timeline. Her mom wasn't a person anymore. She was a story. And it all didn't matter anyway. When Stella knew everything she knew the details weren't even all that important—it was what it meant that mattered. It meant that it was all her mom's fault. All her mom's fault. Her mom was dead and it was all her own fault.

For a long time, that was all that really mattered.

AFTER HER AUNT leaves, the sun fades from the window and the walls wrap themselves in grey light. Stella sits in the dark, every part of her exhausted. Kookoo naps in her bed again, this time with Mattie snuggled beside her. The baby kicks in the playpen, gurgling, but doesn't need Stella. Stella has sat in silence for years. She left her family, moved in with a man who didn't ask questions, and was just silent for as long as she could be. She thought she could heal there, but she was only resting, she was only standing still waiting for the real work to begin. Waiting 'til she found the words.

Stella leans in to the soft couch, the smell of it soothing, perfect, imperfect, home, and falls asleep to the coos of her child and the gentle snoring of her Kookom, and in the shadow of her mother's face. And for the first time she feels she is exactly where she is supposed to be.

That night Stella dreams of winter. She is in the Break walking down a long perfect white path, going north. It is not hard to walk, her feet are sure and the path is even. The towers and houses blur off in the fog. She feels alone, but, as always when she is alone, she's never fully alone. Her mother is there, near and watching. Stella can smell her on the wind and feel her curled near in sleep. Her mother's arms always just out of reach.

In the dream, the Break is land like any other land, just a place covered with snow. The sky is clear, the stars are bright and blinking, and the moon is full and bright. She can see all its dents and curves, and the light that reflects back somehow feels as warm as fire. The wind is the winter kind, huge and overpowering in her ears. It's all she hears but it doesn't make her cold. Stella walks on and knows she can take this path all the way north. She can go until she reaches the end of the city where she will see the sky and snow stretch out full and empty. So her dream self walks that way, all the way, and doesn't look back.

(24)

LOU

I WASH THE dishes for Paul. There are only a few, but they have been left too long. It's something to do while I wait for her to get out of the shower. Her sink is under a wide window, and the daylight slants over her small backyard, snow untouched except for a crudely carved walkway to the garage. I imagine Pete plods along there every morning, going to work like a good man.

Before this all happened, maybe six weeks ago, I went over to Paul's old place to watch a movie. Baby boy was tired and cranky, so I held him close. He calmed down but I didn't let him go. Em and Ziggy were in Em's room—you could hear them squealing through the door. I just held my baby and listened to them. Pete sat down the couch from me. He has always come off as a shy guy, quiet and burly-like, his hands never quite clean. I never felt as if I really got to know him then. Paul was making popcorn in the kitchen, so Pete and I waited and made awkward conversation. I had no idea where Gabe was, off at some show or just out no doubt. The thing was that when Paul walked into the room, oversized bowl in her hand, old shirt and sweats on, Pete looked up at her like she was the most beautiful thing he had ever seen. His face literally lit up. I remember thinking, "Oh, that's what they mean by that phrase." He was so bright. I nearly cried. Not even for my sister, though I did feel happy for her, but I mostly felt shamefully, completely, sorry, for myself.

A good man.

I remember this as I finish the dishes, make tea for the road. Paul comes down, sits at the table with her arms extended in front of her, head slung like it's a broken hinge. I could cry, but firm up instead and reach out to help her.

She's nervous. She vibrates with it. The police are coming back to the hospital, again, because Paul couldn't hold it in and had to fix her mistake. She called that one officer late last night, when she couldn't sleep, when she couldn't stop thinking about Clayton Spence. There will be more questions, so many more questions. Pete was with Emily, wanted to go off to work, but said he'd stay for an hour or so. Long enough for Paul to go home. No one has really been in this house since it happened. My sister's new happy home now has this shroud of sadness, like someone died. Everything is shadowed and quiet.

"You okay?" I say to her, even though it's a stupid question.

"I just want this to be all over with. I want to move on already." She sighs but doesn't lift her head.

I can only nod, the days so long, but Friday so far away somehow. I stand behind her rubbing her back. "Everything's going to be okay, Paul."

"You're not supposed to say that," she snaps at me.

"What?"

"You told me you're not supposed to say that." Her head still slung, her words angry but exhausted. "When you were in school. You said social workers aren't supposed to tell people everything's going to be okay because it's a promise and you can't promise that because you don't know."

She has such anger that all I can do is be quiet. And rub her back for a minute longer.

EMILY SITS UP in the bed, propped up and looking like she wants to be anywhere else. Mom is on one side of her, Paul on the other. Our Kookom isn't feeling well and is back at home, Mom tells me, with a long look. I know there is more to the story. She'll tell me later, after the cops have come and gone, and things have calmed down again. Pete headed off to work though he looked like he didn't really want to go in the end. I just stand there with my go-mug of tea. I'm useless really, but I don't want to be anywhere else.

The officers walk in looking as tired and angry as we are. That young one looks around like a dog sniffing for danger. The old one sits down on the big chair without being asked and sighs like he'd rather be anywhere else, too.

"I'm sorry we have to keep doing this, Emily." The young one tries to sound nice but it comes off like a warning. "We want this to be over as much as you do." Scott is his name, I remember from before. The other one is Christie.

He keeps going because no one says anything. "So, your mom called me and she said it wasn't Clayton. You said Clayton had nothing to do with it? And I believe that. We talked to Clayton. He's not a suspect, okay?" His eyes are too sympathetic, like he's trying too hard.

Emily nods but doesn't look up. Paul's face full of pain.

I look out the window and try to swallow my anger. The nerve. His fucking patronizing tone. The sun is bright and strong, but not warm. Breathing, that's what they say to do. This young cop doesn't have a clue. Breathe.

"How about we go over the timeline again?" he tries. There is an odd excitement to his voice, like he knows something we don't. "Would that help?"

"No!" Emily's voice cracks around the word. "I can't."

"Can't what, Emily?"

"I can't." She shakes her head, and flinches like even this small movement hurts. Her hand is twitching nervously, still attached to a plastic tube, liquid dripping into her slowly.

"If you would just..." he starts, but I can't let him finish.

"Officer," I try with my best social work voice, "can you understand that Emily is in a really vulnerable position here? We don't know who these people are, but if she is responsible for their arrests and they turn out to be connected or gang members..."

"But if she's deliberately delaying an investigation..." he starts.

"She's thirteen, and something horrible, unthinkable, just happened to her. She isn't doing anything deliberately!" I spit out the word.

"Okay, okay," the old one pipes in. "We're trying our best to make a good arrest here. If you hear him out..."

"Hear who out?" I look to the Scott guy. "You? What have you found out?"

He looks at Emily. "Emily, we found out the house you were at belongs to a known gang leader. Did you know that?"

Emily just looks at him.

"I know you're scared, Emily." He could almost be sincere, but he's laying it on so thick. His desperation fills the room.

"She *is* scared!" I say a little too loudly. "How is she not supposed to be scared? *Gang leader.* Do you even know what that means. To us? To her, if she says anything?"

"Ms. . . . Louisa," he turns to me, the anger on his face striking. Ma is right, he could be Métis. He looks it, more so when he's passionate like this.

"No!" The words are out of my mouth before I even think them. "This has to stop. She has to heal. She can't keep getting goaded by you."

"This is an investigation." His cheeks colour and the freckles seem darker.

"Then go investigate. Go to that house, go ask those people, go do your job because if any of this looks like she said anything..." I stop. Can't even think about it.

"We can protect her—" the old one starts.

"No you can't. You can't even say that. You have no idea how to protect her."

"Well, perhaps the family can consider moving..." The young one again.

"What? Why? They just moved. They have a home. How can you say that?" He's quiet, so I go on. "Why should they run away like they've done something wrong?"

"There are ways..." But even he doesn't believe his words.

"Would you move? If this happened to your family and someone said to go run and hide, would you?" I look at him hard, his perfect dark hair, his neat fingernails, the patronizing look in his eyes. Even the freckles across his nose make me furious. "Would you?"

"No. No, I don't know that I would." It's the first truth he's said since he got here.

"Then why should they?" Quieter now, but I don't lean back.

"But I'd also fight." He points a patronizing finger at me.

"We are fighting. This is fighting." My arms flail out to take in the whole scene, my mother, my sister, my niece. These tough women.

"Okay, okay, we're getting nowhere," the old one interjects, before turning to Paul. "Ms. Traverse, if you and your daughter have anything else to contribute, let us know. We will never point the finger at her or put her in danger. We know these people are scary. We want to stop them from doing what they are doing. That's all."

"Okay. Thank you," Paul says, softly.

Emily finally nods.

When they go, Mom takes a deep, loud breath, trying to clean the room. "All right, anyone need a coffee?" She's trying to be helpful.

"I'll go get 'em," I say, needing the walk.

"No, no, I'll go, you sit." Mom's helpful always comes off as a bit annoying.

"No, I don't mind." I try not to make my words as hard as they want to be.

"No, I can..."

"For cripes' sake, Mom," Paul pipes in. "Let her go. Don't make her mad again."

We all laugh at that. Even Emily. And just like that, the room is cleared, for a moment.

"MAMA, WHEN'S DADDY coming home?" Baby says in the bath. His hair full of suds, his cheeks shiny wet.

I ran home for a quick break because Baby hates it when his brother gives him a bath. Jake just sits on the toilet barely looking up from his phone.

"Scrub, Baby, get the soap in your hair, not just on it." I am still cold from outside, so glad to be home but still thinking of the hospital. I'll just stay home to feed this one. Jake wants to run out for a bit, get out of the house.

"Mom?" my boy says, exasperated, but innocent enough. I look at his wide eyes and it hits me, he's asking about his dad, his dad is gone again. I forgot. No, I didn't. I just tried to.

"Well..." I can only start slowly. "He's just back home for a while, Baby."

"We should go up and get him." Four-year-olds have all the answers.

"Umm." I try to stay present, to think of my child and what he needs. "I want to stay with your Aunty Paul right now, and really, we don't have a car, Baby."

"Pete has a car. A great big truck." He slips down in the water and I run my fingers through his thick hair. He holds his breath even though the water is too shallow to cover his face.

I wait 'til he's back up. "Pete and Aunty are pretty busy right now taking care of Emily. She's sick, remember?"

"Oh." He thinks on this. "Can we go see Emily?"

"Yeah, I'll take you again tomorrow." My smile is thin, meaningless.

"Okay." His smile is full of so much love, so much trust.

I pull the towel open to welcome him.

"Maaaaa, where's my black hoodie?" Jake calls from down the hall.

"Um, I just washed it," I call back. I pet Baby boy's soft, clean head and rub him dry. He lets me.

"It's not in my room!" Jake yells. "Where is it?"

"Settle down," I say. I hand Baby boy his clothes and get up. "It's around there somewhere."

Rita was so worried last night. She was sure the boys were off to do something stupid, so she sent her ex Dan after them. I didn't think anything was really the matter, but watched her in her panic. We all deal with things differently, don't we? I sat with her and didn't patronize her with soothing words, but I knew everything was going to be okay. I can't think these boys would be that stupid.

Dan and his dad found the boys at the convenience store, doing nothing that they could see, but they took them out for coffee anyway. When he got home, I asked Jake what they talked about, but he said only, "Man stuff." I want to trust him. I do trust him.

Jake is at his doorway looking into the piles of clothes. His face is puffy from crying but I don't say anything. I can't embarrass him now. He looks so dishevelled. Sometimes all I see is the little kid who didn't want to go to kindergarten that first day. He needs a hug but I doubt he'd let me give him one right now.

"Geez boy, it's right there." I point to the laundry basket filled with clean clothes folded and untouched. His favourite new hoodie is tucked under his old jeans.

"Oh," he says.

I laugh.

"You're gonna clean this up when you get home." I frown at him, but not too serious.

"Fine!" he says, pulling on his sweater, fluffing his hair in the mirror before he puts his hat back on.

"Home in two hours, okay? I want to go back to the hospital tonight. And be safe. Be so, so safe." I fix his collar and look at him for as long as he lets me. When he goes to turn away, I pull him close to me. He doesn't hug me back, but he leans in and lets me hug him.

I go back to Baby boy who got himself dressed and is now standing on the bathroom stool pretending to fix his hair, even though he's not tall enough to see a reflection.

"You look great, my boy," I say, and he beams. "Hungry?"

In the kitchen, I turn on the element for grilled cheese and hear Jake at the door. "Don't forget mitts," I call.

He groans loudly.

"Do it!"

"Fine." I watch him shove his feet into his shoes. He's going to need new runners soon. I've given up trying to make him wear boots.

"Hey!" I call, reminding him. He groans again, but runs back and pecks my cheek quickly. "See you in a bit!"

"Be good. Don't be late!"

"Hey!" Baby boy tilts his head for his own kiss.

"Never mind!" Jake laughs at the door and is gone before I can say 'bye.

I know he's just going over to Sunny's place, I know Rita is there and everything is okay. I know I trust him and he's not stupid. But I'm still scared. My boy with his chin out to the world, daring the world to do something. It's all so scary.

MOM COMES IN tired and stressed. The past days have strained her. She sits at my table and asks if I have any tea.

"Sure, Ma." I put the kettle on and sit to wait.

Her lips are pursed into a thin line. They almost disappear when she's like this, when she does but doesn't want to say something.

I can only sigh and look out the window after her. The snow has been packed down by my boys, their footprints now filling slowly with new snow. Jake made a small fort with his brother last weekend. I can make out its curves in the shadows. Baby boy really wanted to make a snow fort. They had made one at daycare and he wanted one in his own backyard. Gabe said he would make it with him but never got around to it.

After a long minute Mom finally picks what she wants to talk about and says, "So, Gabe's not coming home?"

"He's not coming home, Ma. He is home." I fold my hands together in front of me, bracing in front of her. I know my body language looks defensive. I've seen it a thousand times.

"He's a good man. You're just too proud to ask for help."

"No, Ma, I just don't need him." I look out the window again. The sky is changing colour, the orange of sunset setting in. "And he wants to be needed. His family needs him right now."

I can still see her hands, stretched in front of her like she's pleading. I can't look at her face but hear her words, "You don't want to be all the way alone, my girl. Trust me." I look out the window for longer than I need to. The last of the sun still making the snow sparkle, one small patch in the yard, but I watch it dance a bit, before it starts to blur. My boys were outside for hours. They piled the snow into a half circle, just enough to come up to Baby's knees, then they bent down inside and threw snowballs at the house. The bangs scared the bejeezus out of me when they hit the window. I scolded them with a look through the glass, but they only laughed.

"It doesn't matter whether he's good or not," I say when I trust my voice not to quiver. "He's not happy here, is he? He's always away, out somewhere, on tour, partying with someone, anyone really, just not here."

"But he comes home." This is her only argument.

"I want more than someone who just comes home." I wipe my face with my palm quickly and hug my arms across my body again.

"I just want you to be sure, my girl," she says slowly, looking away again. "I don't want you to regret it."

"I think I've regretted staying so long." I can look at her when I say this, but only because I know she's looking away. "Staying in it, like this. I should have done something a long time ago. "

She nods. "You have to try everything," she says, looking out to the last of the outside light. "You really do. For those boys, for both of you, too. Your dad and I, we, I, at least, regretted it for so long."

I nod, knowing she's right. I sit back down and she's quiet. It lets me think about it awhile. Contemplate the sun going behind the houses across the back lane, the dark setting in.

"I know you haven't been happy for a while," she says, defeated, I think. It's a gift, these words.

"A long while." I nod. "I think, I have to think it might be better this way because we can't keep doing what we were doing."

"I get that, but . . . just be careful. It's pretty lonely over here." She reaches her hand over.

I take it. "It's really lonely over here too, Ma."

I made hot chocolate when the boys finally came in, their small hands and cheeks red with winter, and their laughter ringing through the kitchen. Then I made tomato soup and wrapped them up in blankets.

Gabe wasn't even up yet.

"But all that doesn't matter now, hey?" I say, wiping my face and straightening up. "We have to help Emily now, and Paul."

"Yes." She shudders but has the same tone we all do when we get down to it. "And Pete, he's going to need us to show him what to do."

"Mmm hmm." My lips a straight line.

"Are you satisfied now?" she says, stirring her tea. "That he didn't do anything? Because he didn't. He's a . . ."

"I know I know he's a . . . good man. I know it was something else, someone else. I know that. It's just where I go with these types of things. It's the first place I go. In my work, everyone is suspicious. The only thing that matters is the child."

"Well, don't got there, at least not with him." She points her crooked finger again. "I don't think he could harm a hair on either of those girls. Ever. So you stop thinking he's got something wrong with him and let me keep one good-looking son-in-law." She smiles.

I smile back. "Okay, Ma. I will." The only thing that matters is the child. The weird thing is, everybody has been a child. And sometimes, even adults are still children.

"I have to tell you something, Louisa." Her face hardens, the air changes.

I sigh, breathe, brace again.

"Your cousin Stella is at your Kookom's. That's why she didn't come today. Stella's back."

"Oh, that's good." My cousin whom I haven't seen in probably four years. "That's good. Did she hear about what happened?"

Mom takes a deep breath. "She saw it."

"What?"

"She saw the attack, she says she saw it happen. It was right outside where she's living. She was the one who called the cops."

"That's insane! What? Where?"

"Apparently their house is right there, and she saw it." She pauses. "She didn't know it was Emily, of course."

"I don't understand."

"What's to understand? She saw her own cousin get attacked and didn't know. I told her it was okay, but I was... in shock, I think. I still am. How crazy, hey? I don't even know what to say."

"Okay, wait." I wave my hands around. "Let's think for a minute. She was at home, when did she move there? But whatever, she said she saw... everything?"

"That's what she said. She called the police." She's thinking about this. "How...do you think she didn't know? I don't get it."

"No, that part makes sense, I guess. She hasn't seen Emily since she was little, what—eight? Nine?" I can't even think about it all. I just have to let it sit off to the side, not look at it directly. "That part, at least."

"It's all so much, you know. So much."

"Yeah, Ma, it really is. But, well, it just happened over there." I point out with my chin. "Imagine seeing something like that. I am glad she called the police. That's something. That was the right thing to do."

Mom just nods her head, like she can't stop.

"Ma, it's okay."

"It's too much. It's all too much." She hangs her head down, her back bent and shaking.

"I know, Ma. I know," I say. I take her hand and let her cry. I have a million other questions but can't bear to ask her. They don't really matter now anyway. Not really.

EMILY IS ASLEEP when I get back to the hospital. Paul stretches out on the big chair, and turns down the TV as I walk in.

"Where's Pete?"

"Went home for the night. Not much for him to do here." She keeps staring up at the blue green screen like she's hoping for something.

"Yeah, I guess not. Any more news?"

"Doctor say she responded well to the antibiotics." She looks to Emily now, and her face changes. "No infection now."

"They still think she can go home tomorrow?"

"Maybe. Maybe."

I sit and stare up at the silent TV with her and let her be quiet as long as she needs to.

"So is Gabe not coming home then?" She's bitter. Paul's never bitter but there's so much anger in her now.

"Who? Gabe? No, Paul. Gabe is home."

"You didn't call him? Ask him to come back?"

"Naw," is all I say. "I don't need him to come back. Not for me, anyway."

"So, that's it then?"

"Yeah," is all there is to say.

"Does he ever think about his fucking kid then?"

I look at her for a long time. Her skinny face is puckered in a frown, glowing in the flickering images. This is how we distract ourselves.

The news passes over the screen, fast images of police cars, people talking with their names underneath them.

"I think Pete's going to leave," Paul says after a while. "This is all a bit much, hey? I know I'd leave." Her voice is even, but her eyes plead.

"No you wouldn't. And neither will he. He's not that kind of person."

She scoffs. "Haven't we said that before?"

I shake my head, certain. Trying to be certain. "No, Pete loves you. He really does."

She shakes her head too, but not in the same way. "But they all can leave, Lou. They can leave even if nothing's going on, and now so much is going on. I need him. Em needs me. I just . . . I know he's going to leave."

I squeeze her hand again. "You don't want to rely on him. But you can. It's hard but you can. He's a good man."

She shakes her head but I can tell she hears me.

"He looks at you with so much love," I tell her.

"What the fuck does that mean?" she snaps at me.

"The way he looks at you, there's so much love there."

She's not convinced. "Pfft. Gabe used to look at you like that, too. It doesn't mean anything."

"But it's different." I try not to look taken aback.

"It's not," she cries. "You don't know any more than I know."

"I do though," I tell her. "Pete's different. I know it." I pause. "He looks at you longer. Gabe would look at me for a second. It was nice but was over too soon. Pete looks at you for a long time. He doesn't turn away. He won't leave."

"Not exactly proof there." She wipes her nose with her sleeve. I have assured her, if only a little. She looks up at the screen again and spits out her words. "We live in a crazy world, Lou. It's a fucked up, crazy fucking place and I don't put anything past anyone anymore."

"You trust me, you trust Emily and Kookoo." I sit straight, making my point, and smile. "Even Mom, and she's crazy."

"You guys are my family."

"Well, maybe Pete's your family now too." I nod and try to look as convincing as possible.

We're quiet for a long breath.

"We're so fucked," Paul blurts out. "We're fucked, we're all fucked." Paul gestures to the TV screen: another pipe burst, another sludge of black tar darkening a river. A scientist floats a test tube in the water, taking a sample, and frowns at the camera. "Just fucked."

I look at her, my little sister, and want to cry. Paul is always the first one to be optimistic, the first one to say everything is going to be okay. Not this time.

"We're fucked up, yeah, but not completely fucked." I push my smile out as far as it can go.

"What the fuck is that supposed to mean?"

"It means everything's going to be okay, Paul." I say finally, and reach over the hospital bed and Emily's small, covered feet, to take her hand. She takes it, weakly, but holds on. "Everything's going to be okay."

"You're not supposed to fucking say that." Her voice quiets.

"I can say what I fucking like. I'm not a social worker today. Today, I'm your sister, and your sister says everything's going to be okay." I feel so much of her pain. Not all of it, though. We can never feel all of someone else's pain, even a sister's.

She stares back at the screen. People swarm in the street, placards pushed against bodies, the blond news anchor explains why but we don't hear.

"I hope so," she says finally.

"Well, I will know for now, and you can know for later." I look to see if she's even heard me.

"Okay." It's not a smile she gives me, it's something much smaller, but it's there.

"Okay." I give her hand a squeeze. I look out the window and all I can see is the dark winter sky.

"Okay." Paul's voice fades and the images on the TV go on and on.

TOMMY

"PHOENIX ANNE STRANGER..."

Scott turns his radio down again, rubs his eyes, and tries to concentrate. He needs to get to sleep. He needs to text Hannah and tell her he's still working. No, he just needs to get an actual good night's sleep.

Christie looks straight ahead as they drive. Tommy can tell he's annoyed and wants to get this over with. Tommy's been leading him around for days. The sergeant was no help. He didn't see anything linking this Monias guy to the assault. The numbered company turned out to be in the name of Angie Dumas, the skinny girl, Monias's girlfriend, and no one was home at her residence so Christie suggested the sister.

"What was her name? Settler?"

"Settee," Tommy had said and looked up the address in his written notes. Pritchard Avenue.

They are going there now. But it is all starting to feel like a circle.

After they talked to the sergeant, Sunday night had

descended on the northside as predicted. Tired drunk people fell out of tired drunk houses. There were only two domestics, as if everyone was too tired to fight too hard. As if they were only going through the motions, passionless. Tommy had just pulled a large, handcuffed man into the squad car and looked back at the woman left behind, standing impassively.

He shivers and wants a coffee. If he doesn't find anything soon, they'll just have to leave the case unresolved, and the words will become numbers. Emily will become Case 002-121869, never to be opened again. He thinks of the other girl. Zegwan. It means spring. He thinks of his language teacher again. His face was always on the verge of a smile, a slight smirk as Tommy tried to make his tongue wrap around the strange words.

"Zeeg-wahn."

"You pronounce too much. Relax," the old guy would say, and push his long, perfect braid behind his back.

"Zeg-wihn."

"Better."

Ben. That was his name. Ben.

Ben what?

"What about the other girl? Should we maybe talk to her again?" Tommy has this idea that if he just asks the right question, everything will unravel like a thread pulled out of a sweater.

"The Sutherland kid? I don't think she knows anything else." Christie rubs his red eyes. "She was knocked out by some girls. That's all."

Tommy thinks of her small, bandaged face. It hurt to look at her. Her mother beside her, refusing to leave her side. All these women holding each other up.

So, they will ask the sister, that chubby, sad-looking thing.

Maybe she will say something without the other two around. Maybe Tommy will find the right question.

The two-storey house is in pretty good shape. Green trim and faded white siding, it stands tall in the mounds of dirty snow. A broken-down old Challenger in the driveway is covered with an old tarp, but he can see the bumper.

"That's a beautiful car," he says as they walk up.

His dad had a Challenger. Midnight blue. Tommy saw pictures. His ginger-haired dad actually looked happy, standing next to his real pride and joy. His black beast, he called it. He said he had to sell it when Tommy was born, when he couldn't get a job and Marie had to stop working because of the baby. Marie never told him he had to, but he blamed her nonetheless.

The aluminum on the screen door is bent as if it's been pushed in and out a lot. Tommy knocks on the smudged glass, and a thin teenager appears behind it.

"Is your mother at home?" Tommy uses his best police officer voice. He knows Christie will give this one to him. He knows without even asking that he's got the lead.

An older woman in a pink housecoat comes down the stairs. Her hair pulled back and her makeup smeared, she looks like she has just woken up even though it's mid-afternoon on a Monday. Come to think of it, the teenager should probably be in school, too.

"Yes?" the lady asks, and the teenager disappears.

"Hi there, ma'am." He pauses for effect. "We're looking for a Roberta Settee. We were hoping to . . ."

"What the fuck did you do now?" the lady calls into the next room.

"Ma'am?" Tommy asks.

"Come in, come in," she tells them, and turns again. "I said, what the hell, heck, did you do now, Robbie?"

"Nothing!" the girl in the next room whines.

Tommy turns into the plain room. Nothing out of the ordinary: couch, chairs, oversized TV, a large window, and a print of an eagle on the wall. *Migizi.*

The young girl slouches in her chair.

"Well, the cops ain't looking for you for no reason." The mother sounds reasonable somehow, yelling and swearing but not mean. "Go on." She sits and lights a smoke, even offers one to Tommy but he declines with a hand wave. Christie stands behind him. Tommy can feel him taking everything in.

"I'm sorry," Tommy starts. "We're looking for Roberta Settee."

"Yeah, well, you found her." The mother floats her hands toward the thin girl who just looks down at her hands, knuckles raw and red.

Tommy stops, and looks at Christie, who is already paying attention.

"You're Roberta Settee."

She nods.

"What'd she do?"

"I'm sorry, ma'am." He thinks a moment and decides to go for it. "We met a young lady yesterday who said she was Roberta Settee and gave this address."

The mother is not surprised. She just exhales. "What'd she look like?"

Tommy thinks of the best way to describe her. "Heavy-set, Aboriginal, about the same age."

"Who's that?" she asks, talking to her daughter. "Tell me Robbie, or I swear to God..."

Tommy tries another approach. "Roberta? Can you tell us where you were on Friday evening?"

She hunches further down as if trying to shape herself into a ball.

"She was out with friends. I know their names. Cheyenne and Desiree, right?"

"Mom!" she cries.

"Well, you talk or I talk. I am sick of this shit. Taking their shit and getting into trouble. Now they're giving your name . . . Who is this heavy girl? Who's it now?"

The girl only curls into herself more.

"Not Phoenix? Did she get out?" Her voice rises to a shrill cry. "Is that crazy little bitch out?"

"Who's this, ma'am?" Tommy tries to regain control.

"Is she?" The mother doesn't take her eyes off the girl.

The girl finally gives the smallest nod.

"She's the one you'll be looking for. Phoenix. Stranger is her last name. She is crazy and violent. And more crazy. No matter what it is, it'll be her."

Tommy writes it down. Phoenix Stranger. Where has he heard that name? "Why do you say that, ma'am?"

She butts out her smoke. "Because she's crazy. She's, like, certifiable. Everyone knows it but just won't say anything because of who her uncle is."

"Who's her uncle?"

"Alex. Bishop or whatever the fuck he calls himself." The mother keeps looking at her girl. "I told you to stay the fuck away from them, I fucking told you." Her words sound more sad than angry.

Tommy looks at Christie whose face is clear of its usual frown. He seems downright pleased. He lets the old guy drive the last nail in. "Where'd you get those bruised knuckles, Roberta?"

Back in the car, Tommy types in the name and the alert

comes up right away. He reads it out loud. "Phoenix Anne Stranger left Migizi Centre in south St. Vital Friday morning and hasn't been seen since...known associates include Alexander David Monias...That's her." Tommy thinks of the chubby girl, her arms wrapped around her middle like she was trying to hide her big stomach, old black hoodie with the worn cuffs pulled over her hands.

Christie motions for him to go on.

"Attacked...Fuck, she attacked a guy with a baseball bat. Broke his jaw, his arm. Witnesses said it was pretty brutal."

"Sounds like our gal."

"Really? I mean, we're looking for a rapist."

"Are we?" Christie lets go of his chewed lip. "She was assaulted with a bottle. I mean do we even know it was guys?"

"It has to be." Tommy thinks. It has to be.

"Well, May-tee," Christie says. "I hate to say it, but that's some good police work there. You've built a solid case. It's good. Now, all we gotta do is find this crazy little dame."

Tommy puts the cruiser in gear and pulls out on to Powers.

"Can you stop calling me that?" he says finally.

"What? A good police officer?" He laughs his guttural laugh.

"No. May-tee. Please," Tommy says, knowing he shouldn't have said anything.

"Well that's what you are, aren't you?"

"Yeah I know. I am. But you don't need to call me that. I don't call you Whitey or anything."

"Well you can, makes no difference to me." The old guy sighs, all loud like it's a hardship. "Settle down, kid, no need to get your panties in a bunch. I don't have to call you May-tee if you don't like it."

Tommy makes a little nod but is quiet.

Christie waits awhile and then adds, "You know I don't mean anything by it. It's not like I think of you like you're those Nates out there or anything. I don't think of you like that. You're different. I mean, you're not that different but you're some different. You're a good kid. You're even getting to be a decent cop. Nicknames don't mean shit around here."

Tommy had heard this before, these exact words and others like them, these compliments laced with insults laced with... something else. He didn't say anything. What could he say? He just kept driving.

The house on Selkirk looks empty when they drive by. They go to the station to file for a warrant. They'll go back with that. The alert already droning over and over adds a new line: "Wanted for questioning in a recent assault..."

None of it makes any sense.

"Go home," Christie tells him. "You did good."

It doesn't feel good, though. He could go home. He could watch TV and get a good night's sleep, lie next to Hannah all night long. He wants nothing more than to sleep. But it doesn't feel right.

HE PULLS UP to the old apartment building at five. He knows she'll be home. Inside the whole place smells like potatoes, everybody making supper. His mother probably isn't cooking, though. She rarely makes big meals anymore. She doesn't have to.

"My boy." She wraps her arms around him. "I was just thinking about you. You hungry? I'm making tomato soup."

Tommy nods, knowing she won't take no for an answer, even if it is just a can of soup. She plugs in the kettle and he falls onto a kitchen chair.

Marie's apartment somehow feels like home even though he's never even spent a night here. The bathroom smells like Noxzema, the kitchen smells like tea. Everything smells like her and that's what she is, home.

"You look tired, my boy. I mean you look so handsome in your uniform but tired. You just getting off or going on?" She pulls at his collar to straighten it.

"Just off," he tells her. "Been on all weekend."

"I see," she says knowingly. She settles into her chair. "Okay, tell me."

He tells her everything, more than he tells Hannah. He tells her all the details she will understand, the mom staring down at her daughter, the chubby girl who didn't look up, the young girl small, broken in her hospital bed. He can tell Marie all the unspeakable things. Nothing shocks her. She only nods, runs her hands over her frizzy hair, and lets him talk it all out. Until he stops, and they sit in silence for a minute. She gets up to pour the hot water on the tea bags, stir the lumps out of the soup.

"That is crazy." She nods, but not like Hannah. Marie knows just how crazy it all really is. "You don't want it to be this girl, hey?"

"How can it be a girl, Ma? That's insane. A girl couldn't have done that." He tries to make it a statement but it's really a question.

Marie takes out the bowls, cups, and spoons, puts them on the table. She doesn't say another word until they're eating.

She breaks off a piece of bannock and chews it slowly. Marie never adds butter—she likes the bread dry.

"When I was a girl, there was this girl, an older girl, two years ahead of me. Boy she was scary. I never went anywhere near her. She was skinny but mean, you know." She talks as slowly as she chews. Marie has always been a patient woman. "The other girls said, this girl used to pin them behind the school and, you know, stick her fingers in them. Like down there. She would do this and then laugh and let them go."

"Oh god." Tommy watches his mom, so tough. He doesn't have to ask.

"She never did anything to me. I stayed far away from her. Everybody did. Kids talk, you know. All people talk." She blows on her tea until she can take a small sip.

"Why? Why would she do that, I mean?"

"It's a power thing. Rape is about power. She wanted power."

"But why . . . why not just beat them up? If all she wanted was power."

"She was probably messed with. Kids that are messed with get messed up. You can't make sense of that sort of thing. That's why we call it crazy."

"So you think a girl could have done this? This girl could have done this?"

"I think I've heard crazier things."

Tommy does the dishes as Marie pours new cups of piping hot tea and sits down. She eats another piece of bannock while Tommy scrubs the old pot. She always taught him to do housework, even though his dad would ridicule him for doing "wifey things." Tommy never complained about chores. Helping his mom was just something he always did.

"Why'd you marry Dad?"

"What kind of question is that? Because I loved him, silly." She looks at him slyly. "You know I was knocked up, don't even try."

"But he was such a bastard. Why did you stay with him?" He knows she'd had to marry him. In those days you had to marry the guy, she'd said a hundred times. *In those days*, she'd say with a sigh.

"Your dad was complicated, yes. He was mean but he was good too, or at least, he wanted to be."

"He was a racist fuck!" He catches the big swear and apologizes with his eyes. "He was mean more than he was good."

"The drink got the better of him." She is so matter of fact.

"Why didn't you leave?" He knows the answer, but like a kid at bedtime, wants to hear it one more time.

"Because sometimes he was sober." Simple.

Tommy remembers his dad in the final days, when Tom Senior was just a skinny man with no fight left in him. When he was sick and died slowly. Yeah, even Tommy felt sorry for him then. For a bit.

"You know what Christie called me today?" He asks, knowing they can only talk so much about his dad. "He called me different. Do you get that? Do you get called different? Like, you're not like me, but you're not like them Natives either."

"White people usually think I'm just like them Natives."

"I know, but don't they treat you like you're the exception?"

She nods slowly. "Exception to what, I'd like to know?"

"It's like I'm different, and I am different, I'm a half-breed. I'll always just be a half-breed, half of both sides. Not like either." He wipes the last fork and drains the sink.

"Says who? It's not... people who say that just don't know. They don't understand."

"I've been hearing that all my life. I'm not like anything. So what am I?" He wipes his hands, unrolls his sleeves, and sits back down, across from Marie. She's looking older again. Somehow she is older every time he sees her.

She's quiet for a long time. Tommy can feel her story

growing. Marie is really careful before she starts talking. She wants to get every word right. She also wants to make sure it's safe to say what she means. That part comes from years of getting beatings when she said the wrong thing.

"You know," she starts finally, "your aunt was telling me about blood quantum, ever hear of that? It's how much Indian you are. She was saying how it was the white people who made a big deal about how much Indian you were, but Indians never cared as much. They welcomed all their family into the family, even if you were only half the same colour as them."

Tommy thinks about this, about his being half the colour of his mom. "But we were never around your family, not really. Aunty was the only one I was ever around, really." He doesn't say this like an accusation, more like an explanation.

"Yeah, that was my mistake. I regret that. But to them, you've always been family."

"Dad's family never saw us as family." Tommy can see all those redheads who never thought much of him. They'd scrunch up their faces like Tommy smelled foul. His grand-father always looked down at Tommy and his mother—he would even lift his chin up so he could literally look down his nose.

"Some did. But not all, no." She keeps thinking. "This one time this old lady I worked with she said, 'Oh Marie. You're so nice. You're so clean. I like you even though you're Injun.' She really said *Injun*, too. She was old." She laughs tentatively.

"How do you...how do you deal with that?"

"Same way you deal with anything, my boy. You just do. People are stupid. Your dad, that old lady, your fat partner— they mean well, in their way anyway, but they're stupid. You can't do nothing with stupid. Can't fix it...You just go on being who you are. They can't change you."

Tommy doesn't argue. There's no argument, really. He just listens. His mom deserves for him just to listen to her now. They are quiet for a while, and he thinks of a story to give back to her.

"When I was growing up, I didn't pretend I was only white, but it was easier not to say anything, right? I mean, I always looked different. Kids would always guess I was Greek or Asian or something, and I would just laugh it off but not say anything. I mean when I did, I said I was Scottish like dad, but that's it. It was easier. It was always a big long story if I told them I was Native, so I just avoided it. I mean, I took some classes in school, that Ojibway class, but never really felt like I belonged there or anything. And then when I got this job, I put Métis on the application only 'cause Hannah said to, but then everyone knew. It was the first time everyone knew what I was, and I felt so different. They treated me so different. So I've been feeling more . . . Indian. But Christie thinks I'm different from them, *them*, he says—all those people out there. I'm not a real Indian. So what then? I'm just in between? I'm not like anybody?"

She nods. "I always thought it was good that you could pass. People treated you normal most of the time. I could never pass."

"I know. I saw how you got treated. Hell, I saw how my father treated you. Thing is, though, I don't feel different from them. Not any of them, any of you. I see them and they remind me of you, of your sisters, of me. They're the people who look like me. They're the only people that look like you."

"They're your people, that's why." She smiles her shy smile.

"I never thought of it like that."

"I know. That's my fault. I'm sorry for that. I just wanted to protect you. I wanted you to have the best of everything. And in those days, that meant being white, so we were as white as could be."

"We should go to a sweat or something. We should do something like that." He says it and immediately really means it.

"We could, or we could just go visit your aunt."

"Yeah, we should." Tommy thinks of his old aunt, tough as nails. That expression was made for her. Then he thinks of Hannah. She's not quite like his mom and aunt, but he wants her to know. For the first time, he really wants her to see it. "We could bring Hannah."

"You think she could handle the bush, that one?" She looks at him out of the corner of her eye. Tommy knows what she means. But he also knows she'd never say anything bad against his woman, even if she really wanted to.

"Yeah, maybe. Hannah would like it." Well, maybe.

"Mmm hmm," is all his mom says.

Tommy knows what she means. "She tries real hard. She just doesn't know, hey? It's like she wants to know, but she doesn't."

"Yeah. Well, that's better than a lot of the people we've known, hey?"

"Yeah," Tommy says, and the word rings through the kitchen awhile, floats around the comfortable silence.

They're quiet again for a long time. Tommy thinks of his case again and lists it all in his head. His mom's stories make him feel better, but he is still not reassured. He wants everything to be different. He wants the simplicity of finality, but it's never like it is in the movies. It always lingers on. Like a song that ends a beat or two before it's supposed to, it feels like there should be more but there's nothing, just an empty space and a long, fading echo.

(26)

EMILY

EVERYTHING'S DIFFERENT NOW. Everything is all Before and After. Before, she was at home and just a kid in junior high. After, she is a sick person in a hospital bed. Her mom has hardly left her, and always looks at her like she's afraid Emily will break into a million pieces. Emily would, if she could, break apart and disappear into nothing. She bets it wouldn't even hurt, to fall apart like that, to become nothing. It might even feel good.

"COME ON, EMILY. We have to try and get you up and walking today." The nurse speaks so loud. Emily thinks she must be used to talking to old, deaf people or something. "Come on, just slip your feet into these slippers. Take my hand."

Emily moves her legs as slow as she can. It doesn't hurt like it did, but still hurts in a different way. Her whole bottom half from her waist down is numb. Her back aches. Her mom told her the medicine and painkillers would probably make her feel sick but she's healing. That's what she keeps saying, *healing*.

The nurse pulls the blanket off and Emily's legs are suddenly bare and cold. The bruises bright and brown. She doesn't even feel those. Her mom gasps but puts her hand to her mouth right away, like she can swallow it back in. Then she gives Emily that look again. Her eyes like a puppy's. She winces like Emily could hurt her.

Emily's feet are only half in the paper slippers before the nurse pulls her up. It feels so mean and rushed. Paul slips a housecoat over Emily's shoulders and grabs her other arm.

"You can do it, Emily." The nurse says things in such a practiced way, like she's said them a hundred times to a hundred different people.

Standing up, Emily's head rushes. Her feet feel weak, her knees start to shake uncontrollably like she's nervous. Maybe she is.

"I think I'm going to be sick," she sputters and Paul gently helps her back down.

"Okay, okay, honey, just sit down. Do you need a bucket?" She rubs her back the way she always does when Emily throws up. Emily hates throwing up. She's suddenly crying and puking and making loud gasping sounds, like she can't catch her breath, like she has been running hard.

At least they've stopped asking her about it. For a while, that was all anyone would let her talk about. How she was feeling and what her body was doing, and then what happened. Everyone wanted to know what happened. That police officer was so nice, and really good-looking, and then she had to tell him. She wanted to die. She knew it was stupid to think about her messy hair and her puffy face but she did. She wanted him to think she was pretty but she was just a mess. A victim. That's what he called her. She knew what it meant, but still, it sounded ugly.

The days seem to break into small parts between sleeps.

She keeps falling asleep. Her body has become a blob under the blankets—no feeling, just two legs and a belly, arms she keeps close. She's always cold. She doesn't want to move her hand 'cause a needle is in there, giving her fluids, her mom said. Her mom said she could come off it soon, probably today. She said it with a smile like Emily had done something. Like Emily could control this *healing.*

Every time she pees it burns. She holds it for as long as she can but then it just comes out too fast. Her mom has to bring her a bedpan. It is so embarrassing it makes Emily cry. Paul makes sure everyone leaves the room and no one knows Emily has to go to the bathroom, but she still cries. Everything seems to make her cry.

That's what After is like, sleeping and crying, in parts.

IT'S DARK WHEN she wakes up and the hospital room is empty except for Ziggy. Ziggy with her face in bandages, her open eye red and sad.

"Hey, Em," she says like she's nervous.

Emily just looks at her. Confused, kind of nauseated. "Where's my mom?" is the first thing she says.

"She just went in to the hall with Rita. Want me to get her?"

Emily shakes her head but only a little. She doesn't need her mom, was just checking.

"How're you doing?" Zig tries to smile, sitting there with slumped shoulders, looking as heavy as Emily feels.

"Okay." Emily winces as she sits up. She pushes the button to pull the bed upright behind her. Zig's poor face is all beat up. "How are you?"

"I'm okay," is all she says. There is a big empty space where the rest of her words are supposed to be. She looks at her hands.

"I wanted to come see you sooner but Rita wouldn't let me. She's pretty freaked."

Emily nods, a little. "Yeah, Paul too. So much."

"I was more scared about you." Ziggy looks up and looks at Emily closely. Not the way Paul does, but almost.

"I didn't know anything had happened to you, at first. And when Paul told me she said you got hurt but were fine." Emily looks at her friend. "I didn't know . . . Does it hurt?"

"I'm on lots of pills." Ziggy grins, but only for a second. "It's fine really. I almost fractured my cheekbone and there's a couple stitches there. It looks pretty gross under this. But the plastic surgeon says she can fix it and there'll be no scar."

"Maybe she can fix your nose while she's in there?" Emily's smile feels small.

"I was thinking liposuctioning my arse, but yeah, my nose too."

Emily laughs but too hard. It makes everything hurt again.

"I'm so sorry, Em." Ziggy's face falls. "I tried to find you. I tried . . . I went after you. I couldn't find you."

"It's okay, Zig." She reaches her needle-heavy hand toward her best friend.

"I should've made you come home. I should have . . ." She stops, her voice fading away.

"Yeah, I should have," Emily says, but really quiet, almost like she didn't say anything. "We shouldn't have gone there."

They're quiet for a long time.

"Do you think he, Clayton, like, knew?"

Emily shakes her head but looks down at her blanket.

"Sun says him and Jake are going to find who did this. Make everything right." Zig leans in and says it really low, just in case their moms can hear. "But don't say anything. Rita is super freaked."

Emily just nods. Tired again. Nothing really has any meaning. It all gets dream-like fast. She closes her eyes and hears Rita's and her mom's voices come into the room, not what they are saying, just their voices. She just feels her best friend's hand, gently squeezing her own.

She hasn't forgotten. She knows everything. She will always know each part, every detail, even though she doesn't want to say any of them out loud. Every time she says them out loud they feel bigger, so she just keeps them here, inside of her and only says what she has to. That way it's different. That way she can keep it away from her mom and everyone. So they don't have to know, not completely. Not all the way.

That's the only thing Emily can do to make any of this better.

WHEN EMILY TURNED, she fled between the overgrown bushes and almost slipped on the snow-covered sidewalk, but she didn't stop. She ran between parked cars and through a shovelled-out opening in the snow banks. She slid across the icy ground. She didn't know where she was and couldn't think — everything looked white. She went down a path and ran right into thick snow, snow that was way too deep to go through. But still she ran, or tried to, she lifted her legs up as high as they would go and came to another street and kept going. She looked around for a place to hide and almost slowed down but then she heard their voices: "Over here, I saw her." She saw red, a huge panic over everything. The girls were not far behind her, and there was no place to hide, everything was wide open and the snow was so deep. She didn't even know where she was, so she ran straight through the snow, knees up. She moved like she was in slow motion.

She fell or was tripped. Either way she was on the ground and they were on top of her. She screamed as loud as she could, and then one of them shoved her hand over Emily's mouth and nose. She couldn't breathe. She struggled for air. The snow fell into her eyes but all she could do was blink it away.

"Fucking girl." The biggest girl, Phoenix, seemed to laugh. She got on top of her. She grabbed Emily's flailing arms. Someone snorted. They all swore. Emily tried to move out from behind the other girl's hand so she could breathe. It was the one with the braid. Emily tried to scream again, but the braid girl straddled Emily's head and pinned her arms down with her knees. She shoved hard at Emily's mouth and pushed her head down into the snow. Emily could barely breathe.

Someone else pinned down her legs, and she got punched in the stomach over and over. She thought she was going to suffocate.

She couldn't hear what they were saying. They were fighting and swearing, Phoenix's voice deeper and meaner than the rest.

Emily felt cold hands on her bare skin, felt her jeans rip open. She didn't understand what was happening, but kicked out, kept moving her legs, but she got pinned again. Her legs spread far apart. There was so much weight on her ankles she thought they were going to break. She couldn't move anything, just felt the biting snow under her and falling on to her.

It hurt so bad, Emily nearly passed out. The girl's hand over her face, almost over her nose, it was so hard to breathe. She thought of that, she focused on trying to breathe. Phoenix's voice went non-stop, sometimes softer, but still just as cruel. No one else seemed to say anything, but they all still held her down. Emily cried inside, outside, everywhere, everything about her just cried.

Then her body seemed to wrench and twitch, and everything went quiet, so quiet they all heard the bottle break with a crack.

"Fuck me!" Phoenix yelled. The girl let her hand off Emily's face. Emily was too busy gasping for air to scream and she didn't want to open her eyes.

"Fuck, Phoen!" one of them screamed.

"We gotta go!" another screamed.

"Fuck, there's someone in that house." The braid girl got up, letting Emily loose, but she didn't move.

"Come on!" someone yelled, halfway down the back lane already.

Emily made a whimpering sound, reached her hands down to cover herself. Everything that didn't hurt felt numb. She turned away, coughing air and snow.

Someone gave her one final kick in her bent back and ran off. She thinks it was Phoenix but she still didn't open her eyes.

She pulled at her pants to get them back up. The snow was falling lightly on her reddened skin. All she thought of was getting her pants back on. They were inside out and stiff with cold. She sat there in the snow, getting them straight. Her skin cold but hot underneath like frostbite.

She managed to cover her legs but cried when she tried to lift her bum. Cried with pain. Sharp, biting pain inside her. A light went on in the house next door. She stiffened. She had to get out of there. What if someone caught her? What if someone found her like this? She moved as fast as she could. It wasn't fast but she got up. She couldn't do up her pants but her sweater covered her middle. She hugged her jacket around her and moved heavily. She found one boot in the snow, the other across the back lane, and pushed her feet into them. She limped along in a tire track, trying not to slip on the ice under the fresh snow.

Her feet got wet and her legs felt sticky. She knew she was bleeding, but the dark would cover it. She had to get home. She had to get home and cleaned up before her mom got home. She could take a bath and forget this ever happened. That's all she thought about, as each step pinched and scraped her, as she felt stabs up and down her, she just thought of home, her stupid, smelly home where she could be warm and where everything would go away.

NOW EVERYTHING'S BEFORE and After. Before, she liked a boy named Clayton and boy bands and social studies. Before, her first kiss was supposed to be the best thing ever. Before, she had Ziggy and it didn't matter that she didn't have any other friends. Before, she hated moving houses and called Pete "the Sniffer" and thought it was funny. Before, the saddest she ever felt was when her Kookom got sick and her Aunty Lou told her that Kookoo was old and old people had to go to the spirit world one day. Before, that was the most scared Emily had ever been, knowing her Kookom had to go soon.

Kookoo has been here, here in the hospital room. She sang Emily songs like when she was little, held her hand and made her forget, for a little while. Everyone was here for a while and then gone. Her mom is still here, and so is Pete most of the time. He's been quiet but here. He stands behind her mom and rubs her shoulders, and she reaches up and grabs his hands, and sometimes she kisses them. Her mom is different with him, Emily knows. She knows he's different. Emily remembers him grabbing her, picking her up and running with her in his arms.

She remembers it in pieces, in and out of dreams, how he held her like she weighed nothing, and she hurt but felt safe like she knew he was going to help her. And he did. Then she woke up here, and everything was numb.

Paul says she'll go home soon, and Emily knows she has to, one day, but that part feels really distant. Going home is like another After, one that's even further away than Before.

PHOENIX

"PHOENIX STRANGER." THE guard looks right at her. The old bitch leers at her as she calls her name.

Phoenix pulls herself off the plastic chair and tries to suck in her belly but it doesn't go in that much. It hurts, everything hurts, but she sticks her chin out, her chest too, like she is the toughest bitch in here. She stares down the guard as she walks up, all slow like, like she doesn't give a fuck. She holds up her hands but the lame bitch smiles and shakes her fucking head. Phoenix doesn't change her expression, just turns away and keeps walking. Her cuffed hands fall below her belly, but she doesn't touch it, not here. Not where anyone can see. Here, she just walks on, head up.

She's been in Remand nine days already and knows the score easy enough. All these fucking uniforms are fucking weak bitches trying to push their weight around, trying things like keeping her cuffed up when she doesn't need to be, and waiting for her to beg for stuff. Fuck that. Adult Women's is just like youth lock-up, full of useless bitches who would rather claw your eyes out than throw a good punch. Phoenix can manage. She's even got a cell all to herself, one of the benefits of being so young, or so fucked up.

The guard takes her time buzzing Phoenix through but when she finally pushes her way in, she wishes it would've taken longer. Elsie sits there with her shoulders curving down and fucking weepy as shit. Elsie looking skinnier than ever and blubbering into a tissue. Fucking weak-assed Elsie.

"Phoenix, Phoenix." Her mom jumps up at her. "Honey, are you all right?"

The door slams behind, and Phoenix can only go forward. Elsie babbles on, making such a show of it. Her face is puffy, like she'd been at this awhile, her bottom lip scarred and pouting. She reaches out her arms all pathetic-like, but Phoenix pulls her weighted wrists away from her mother's outstretched hands. Elsie notices, recoils, and sits down. Phoenix looks around and sits, slow, trying not to let her belly out.

She clenches her teeth to exhale as her heavy body falls into another hard, uncomfortable chair. The table is concrete. The walls are clear plastic, and she can watch all the other visitors in the next rooms. Some bleached blonde talking to her lawyer in the next one. Phoenix can spot a lawyer a mile off. Lawyers and social workers, they have a certain look and an even-more-certain smell. She can't smell this one from here, but the lady has the look of a lawyer, that's for sure.

"I tried to get here sooner, but they had to do so many checks, so many bloody checks. Like your own mom isn't good enough to get to see you." Elsie wipes her nose and dabs at her deep-set eyes, in that order, with the same tissue. Then she looks around as if to see if anyone is watching, dumps it on the table, and pulls out a fresh one from her pocket. The back of her one hand is bruised, the thick scar on her lip is a burn, and her skin is as pale as snow. Phoenix tries to remember the last time she saw her mother. A year, no, fourteen months ago. The last time she even thought of her was when she first got to the Centre. Cedar-Sage had asked about her, if Phoenix knew where she was.

"Don't you worry about her, Cedar-Sage, just take care of your own self," Phoenix had told her.

She didn't ask again but Phoenix could tell she wanted to. Cedar-Sage was still young, still loved Elsie.

"You talk to Cedar-Sage?" Phoenix asks her mom. The metal cuffs clank together as she tries to scratch her nose. "You talk to your kid?"

"Yes," Elsie blubbers. "Of course. I, I didn't tell her what happened, but, but she's fine. She's fine." Her voice trails off.

Phoenix just lets the air out between her teeth, not believing a word.

"She still with that Tannis lady?" Phoenix asks.

"Umm, yeah. She's fine, Phoenix. She gets along just fine." Elsie is talking more to herself than to her eldest daughter in front of her.

Phoenix looks away. She knows her little sister isn't with Tannis anymore. She got moved after what happened to Sparrow. Elsie's been too strung out to notice.

"So, what the fuck do you want?" Phoenix spits, trying to be as mean as she can.

"Want?" Elsie's eyes beg. "Phoenix, honey, I just wanted to see you, sweetie!" Her voice isn't all that sure though. It is quiet and broken. Words like *sweetie* and *honey* are not making their way all the way through her sore lips, and not sounding like she means them at all. "I wanted to make sure you were all right. I was so worried..."

Phoenix leans back in her chair and looks around again.

Fucking bitch guard still leers at her through the doors. She looks down but not too soon. Her hands are heavy lumps on her lap. Her belly lurches. Phoenix almost smiles but stops herself.

"I was! I was so worried, Phoen," Elsie stammers. She dumps another tissue into the pile and pulls out a fresh one. Last time Phoenix saw Elsie she was just like this, crying, crying and not doing anything. At least that was a funeral. This is just, well, this. This is just a show. What she thinks a good mother should look like.

"It's so hard baby, so fucking hard. I feel so fucking terrible, you don't understand. You don't know how people are looking at me. They know it was you. They know what you did. And after all I've been through, too! Oh my god, Phoenix. Do you have any idea? How could you do this?" Elsie's words come out like that, a trickle then a flood. Her face makes a big, ugly frown and then crumples into tears again. All her skinny wrinkles pushed around her face make her look even more sickly than she already is. If Elsie was anyone else, Phoenix would have laughed out loud, right in her face at how funny she looks, how pathetic. She wants to be that mean to Elsie, but she can't. It's still Elsie. Her mom. She still knows all the things that Elsie's been through. So she looks down at her lap, and picks a fluff off her ugly grey pants instead. Her hands rattle.

PHOENIX DIDN'T THINK Sparrow would die. She was in lock-up then, didn't hear much from her sisters and didn't know the number for the place where they were staying. Some worker said her littlest sister was sick and had to have treatments at the hospital, but the bitch didn't make it sound all that serious. "Not to worry," she had said with a useless pat on the back.

They just didn't want to give her a fucking visit. Phoenix didn't think she was going to die.

But she did.

Phoenix got to go to the funeral. No one could have kept her away. Two guards had to go with her, but they didn't cuff her or anything, just stayed close. It was the first time she'd seen Elsie in two years. She hadn't seen Cedar-Sage for longer, not since right after Phoenix wore the wrong sweater to school and they got apprehended. Then they had visits, all of them with Elsie.

At the funeral, her little sister, now her only sister, looked like she'd been punched in the face—no bruises, just hurt. She was just a little thing, skinny like Elsie, hunched over, like she was waiting to get hit. Phoenix hugged her and didn't let her go the whole time. Family came and went, uncles and aunts neither of them had seen since they lived in Grandmère's brown house. No one ever knew where she and her sisters were, except for her uncle. Elsie blubbered along, some guy hanging on to her. She didn't tell Phoenix who he was, and Phoenix didn't ask.

When she left, she gave Cedar-Sage the address and told her to write letters every day. Her uncle gave her his new number and told her to call if she needed anything. But Elsie just stared at her awhile, hugged her too long, and made a puddle of useless tears on her shoulder. Phoenix was almost glad when the fucking guards finally said, "Okay, time to go."

Cedar did write for a while. She wrote a lot, long curvy purple ink letters. In her new school, she liked the work but hated the kids. She had a new foster home, way out in the suburbs with an old lady named Luzia. Cedar was good.

Phoenix wrote her back, short letters with her rough black printing. She lost the address, though, when she got out a few months later.

She should've memorized it.

WHEN PHOENIX LOOKS up, Elsie seems smaller. She stares at the table and looks like she wants to say something. Or maybe Phoenix just wants her to say something, when really Elsie's only thinking about her next fucking hit.

"Oh Phoenix," Elsie says. "I can't believe it. You were doing so well." She lets out a sob, a meaningless slobbering noise.

Phoenix takes in a long breath, and gets angry all over again.

"Was I?" She stares at her mother, straight in the face, hard.

"I thought so," Elsie stammers, looks away. She never could hold a stare — she's too weak. "You were in that Centre, and, and...doing school, and..."

Phoenix lets out a loud sigh, surprised Elsie knows that much. She hopes Elsie doesn't know anything else. But the woman doesn't even know where Cedar-Sage is, so probably not.

Elsie fumbles, clutches at her tissue and looks down, looking strung out and done in. Behind her, the bleached blonde shakes her lawyer's hand and buzzes back to Holding.

PHOENIX WOKE UP before the door got kicked in. She couldn't hold her pee anymore so crept out of the basement door and through the house. It was early morning, the light just starting to grow. Everything looked grey but warm enough for winter. Her uncle's door was open, so she was super quiet. She looked in his room, saw the light coming through the window in thin slices, her little cousin Alexandra asleep between her parents. It looked so perfect: mommy, daddy, baby. Her tough uncle, so vulnerable and soft, curled around his kid, one arm over her so nothing could get at her. Phoenix almost cried standing there. She'd never felt so lonely.

She was still in the bathroom when the bang at the door made her jump. The baby started to cry and Phoenix heard her uncle run across the floor and the front door slam open. There was heavy foot stomping, like boots, and a deep voice yelling.

"Alex Monias. We have an arrest warrant for Phoenix Anne Stranger."

"She's not here," her uncle yelled back.

"Stay where you are, Mr. Monias." The voice was even, and the boots stomped off, to the kitchen first.

The baby kept crying. Phoenix just stood there, the window nailed shut, her belly too big to let her fit through anyhow. She moved without a sound to behind the door. Maybe they wouldn't check, maybe they wouldn't look around a bathroom.

BROKEN ALL THE way, Elsie turns back to Phoenix and reaches her weak hand across the concrete table, but Phoenix doesn't move.

"Oh Phoenix, do you know they wanna try you as an adult? You're in the bloody Remand, for Christ's sake. This is so bad."

Phoenix can tell Elsie is trying so hard, barely swearing at all, but she is too strung out to really be feeling anything at all. Phoenix knows all her mother really wants to do is go get high. She looks like she'd been clean a good day or so, so is probably just starting to feel sick. It did probably take a lot of effort to get in to see her. Phoenix wishes she hadn't bothered. Elsie's just useless and weak, just like this visit was fucking useless and weak.

"They want to charge you with assault with a weapon! Assault! Don't you know what that means?"

"Means eight to ten, don't it?" Phoenix doesn't look up

though. Her lawyer thinks, everything considered, they'll go easy on her, but Phoenix isn't so sure.

"Oh Phoenix!" Elsie blubbers. "They wanna put *sexual* charges on you! You're going to be a *sexual* offender."

She says the word like it is the worst thing ever, and Phoenix flinches because it is.

She tries not to think about that night, the snow, the bottle, that girl. She wishes she had been meaner to Elsie now, or refused the visit. She wishes a lot of things.

"And this," she says, swiping her hand at Phoenix's belly. "What the hell are you going to do with this?"

"None of your fucking business." Phoenix snaps up, suddenly defensive. She didn't know Elsie knew. How the hell does Elsie know? "Who the hell told you?"

"I am your mother, Phoenix. Like it or not, I am still your mother." Elsie opens up the used tissues in her palm and dabs at her stupid, wet chin. "That matters, you know."

Phoenix scoffs and looks down again.

"You'll see. You'll...f-ing see real soon what it's like to be a mother. Real soon!"

IT WAS THE cop that found her. The younger one opened the door and inched inside. Phoenix didn't breathe. And there he found her, standing in front of the toilet, back to the wall. He went to cuff her with rage in his eyes, too full of hate to even say anything. His hand passed over her hard belly and he turned white. Whiter. Phoenix saw it. She knew something was wrong. She knew it and everything became a blur. Her uncle yelled at her, her cousin cried, Angie held the baby, and they all became blurs as she got pulled through the house and out into the cold. Something was wrong.

"How far along are you?" The bitch nurse at Remand looked at her for like a second and talked at her like she was nothing.

"What?" Phoenix just sat there, felt sick.

"Your baby, your...how long?"

Phoenix just shrugged.

"Lie down." The bitch sighed and lay a measuring tape across Phoenix's belly with fucking rough and cold hands.

"I'd say you're about six months."

Seven, Phoenix thought but didn't say anything. It'd been seven months, since July, since Clayton, since before the Centre, before everything.

She always thought she'd be able to tell, that she'd know, but she didn't have a clue. Not until now, not until it was so fucking obvious.

"DON'T THINK I'M going to take care of it." Elsie tries to put an edge in her tone. "I mean, even if they let me, I can't do it. Won't." Her eyes look off somewhere.

"Don't worry." Phoenix moves her hand to her belly without even thinking of it, but keeps it there. She makes sure the fucking guard is looking away, and she tries to make her voice hard. "I won't let you anywhere near it."

"Well, good. 'Cause I got too much going on to raise your fucking kid!" she spits. "It'll just go into care then!"

Phoenix shrugs but doesn't think about her kid in care. She thinks about being out, about having a kid, getting a real apartment, and a stroller. She remembers Sparrow in a stroller. She'd push Sparrow along Arlington, and Cedar-Sage would hold on to the bar on the side. They'd go to the store, and she'd put the milk in the bottom part under the stroller seat. She would have to pull the stroller up all the stairs to their apartment, but

Phoenix didn't mind doing all that stuff. She liked it, really. It made her feel important. Needed.

Elsie sighs. She is cried out, and fought out, by the looks of it. She remains quiet for a long time, looking tired all the way through. That's all she's got, Phoenix thinks, just a little fight, a little cry to feel good about being a mom, and now she's just thinking about a hit.

Elsie's always been like this. Even when Elsie's clean, she's still so sad. When Phoenix was really young, Elsie got clean for a long while but still just cried all the time. When Sparrow's dad was around, and Elsie was clean for a while, she was weak as fuck. Even as a little kid, Phoenix knew she was never going to be like that.

In the room on the other side is a lady Phoenix remembers from the dining hall. This lady has big curly hair that is almost all grey and a stern face like Grandmère used to have. This lady, though, has a teardrop tattoo under her right eye and lots of homemade tattoos all over her hands and wrists. The green ink is so worn you can barely tell what any of it says. It all just looks like blurred letters, one raggedly circle crossed with thin lines — a medicine wheel, Phoenix thinks, or a cross. The lady sits at her own concrete table, across from an old man equally old and serious looking. They hold hands over the concrete. It looks like he's telling her how much he loves her, and she's nodding. She smiles at him, a serious smile, but real.

Phoenix looks down at her lap again. Her cuffed wrists. Her thumbs trace over her belly, make circles.

They took her for a scan to make sure. She lay on the table and they squirted cold jelly all over the bottom of her belly. The attendant looked so scared of the crazy convict and her guard. Phoenix would have laughed but then the room was filled with this *whosh* sound, like water. *Whosh whosh* it went, over and over.

"Heartbeat." The attendant's voice shook and she turned the monitor to Phoenix. It was black and white and as grainy as an old TV, but she could see the nose, cheeks, a hand out like it was waving. "It's a boy."

Phoenix nodded. She couldn't have said anything even if she wanted to. But good, she thought. Good that it's a boy. He'll be strong.

"I DID TRY my best." Elsie's voice breaks open. Phoenix looks up but doesn't even know if her mother is even talking to her. "I did the best I could."

Phoenix's thumbs are numb but still make circles, and her belly lurches. No, her baby moves. Her baby boy. She's going to name him Sparrow because she wants him to be just like her little Sparrow. Only strong. Healthy. Hard. Like a boy is supposed to be.

"I know," she says so quiet she doesn't think Elsie even hears.

Then Phoenix sighs. She just wants to leave now. She knows they're both too fucking tired to go on, so she gets up slowly.

"Oh Phoenix, wait!" Elsie looks up, like she just woke up. "Wait, my girl, what's going to happen? Phoenix?" She tries reaching out for her daughter's hand again, but Phoenix moves off. She doesn't want to touch her. Not today. Not now. "Oh Phoenix, what am I going to do? What can I do?"

"How the fuck am I supposed to know?" Phoenix says, more tired than mean.

Elsie looks down again, a small, skinny, useless woman. Phoenix looks away, and pounds at the buzzer to be let out. The guard picks that exact moment to not be there. Fuck.

"I can talk to your lawyer, honey. I can go to that Centre

or your old school, get some of your friends to say nice things about you." *Pathetic.*

"My friends ratted me out," Phoenix says to the wall.

Elsie reaches out again. "Oh Phoenix, I know you are not what they called you, whatever it was Desiree and them called you..."

"*Ringleader.*" Phoenix let the word fall out slow.

"I know that's not true, Phoenix," Elsie burbles.

"But it is." Phoenix fingers at the crack in the concrete wall, her wrists heavy and wanting to fall. She can smell the falling snow, the blood. Phoenix knows her old friends told the truth. She knows it's all her fault and she did all the things they said she did. She also knows they're rats, and her uncle is going to pick them off one by one and they will never say a word like that again.

But it's still true.

Elsie sighs. "Let me help. We can...fight this. I can help." The words are flat, though, like all of Elsie's words.

Phoenix slams on the buzzer again.

"Naw." Phoenix's voice is almost a whisper. "Don't worry about it."

"Please Phoenix, please. Let me do something."

She doesn't want to look at her, doesn't want to see Elsie grovelling in her Elsie way, being weak. She doesn't want to feel sorry for her, or feel anything for her.

"There's nothing to do," is all Phoenix says as the door finally buzzes open. The bitch guard stares at her, but Phoenix ignores her and just makes her face hard again.

She looks back, just over her shoulder, and sees her mother only in a small blur as she walks through the door.

She hears Elsie calling to her, but she doesn't turn around. She doesn't need to. It's over.

The bitch guard looks like she's going to say something too, but Phoenix just keeps walking like she doesn't notice, like she doesn't care at all. She just squares her shoulders, sticks out her chin, tries to suck in her gut as best she can, and walks down the hall. She walks like nothing can get to her, like she doesn't give a fuck at all.

(28)

FLORA

IN THE END, all that matters is what is right here.

I don't remember where I heard that, but I've always remembered the words. There's so much truth in them. All that matters is what is right here.

I seem to think about everything these days. Probably because I am old and bored and tired most of the time, but I've been thinking about my life and the lives of my girls around me. I think about my body and my heart, my soul and spirit and all the things they've been through. But in the end, none of it matters. There is only what is here, what we have, that matters.

Here, though, there is a secret. A new one. I can feel it with Stella and my Cheryl. They are not telling me everything. They are saying only that Emily is okay. Going home soon. All healed, down there. They say it with words like that, like I am a child. Like I don't know. It makes them feel better to think they're protecting me so I let them. We did the same when my Lorraine went, Cheryl and I — we gathered around Stella and the others, but especially Stella. We wanted to protect her. It helped us to protect her. But it didn't make any difference to her. Her mom was still gone. She still had that hole in her. And she still knew everything somehow because the details don't matter. It only mattered that Rain was gone.

I didn't know that at the time. At the time, I had so much pain and anger, too much. Pain for myself and for my family because we had to be without her, and so much anger at that man. But he didn't matter either. He was a stupid man made dangerous because he had never been taught right. I never saw his face, not once, the man they said beat my baby to death. They never showed me a picture, only told me a name and that his sentence was *suspended*, they called it. He didn't go to jail. It wasn't his fault, they said. If she hadn't done this, if she hadn't done that, all those things we all knew she shouldn't be doing. But she did them anyway. But if she hadn't, would she really be alive now? It doesn't matter. It only matters that she's not here.

LOUISA COMES TO see me. She comes in with her voice wide and loud.

"Hey Kookoo, how are you feeling?" she shouts into the room, filling it up.

I must've fallen asleep, but I am here, in my chair. I can feel the soft armrests, worn but good under my fingers. The window light darker than it was a minute ago, my hands tingling like they were just doing something. What was it?

"How you doing, Kookoo?" She plops down on the couch across from me. The laundry is off to the side, and even the playpen is folded in the corner.

"I'm good, I'm good." I think a minute. "You?" I run my tongue over my empty gums like I've forgotten something. What is it?

"I'm okay," she sighs and leans back. I can tell she isn't. She tries too hard when she's not happy. Her voice is higher, more forceful, like she's trying to interrupt what's bothering her.

She goes off to the kitchen, and I rub my hands back to life. They're so cold. I remember then that Stella went off with her kids to get groceries, and Jeff picked them up. I told her not to buy me anything, I like the store on the corner, but she said not to worry.

But I always worry, in my way.

Louisa brings me a cup but I just set it aside. We're quiet awhile but I know she wants to talk. There is a long, warm silence between us. When she does start talking, it's about her boys, those lovely boys. Baby is not feeling well and she wants to get back to him. Jake is not the same since Emily's attack. She wants to say more but she stops.

I know there's more.

"Where's Gabe?" I say. I know the answer the minute I ask, as my Louisa's face gets sad all the way. I look down, my hands cold now, and I wrap them around each other to keep them warm.

"Yeah." She looks off somewhere for a while. "He's still up north, Kookoo. He's home." I don't have to look all the way up to see tears, even with my bad eyes.

I laugh a bit, but not mean, just to clear the air, and remember something else. "Did I ever tell that story about your Grandpa Charlie? Your Moshoom?"

"Well yeah, some. You have told me about him, Kookoo."

"Yes, well, he was like that, always needing to be someplace else, hey? He had the drink, did Charlie."

"I know, Kookoo, I know. But Gabe doesn't drink. He just always runs off, runs around."

"Same thing, really. Just needing."

"He's better off at home." She sounds so far away.

I nod slowly, thinking about Charlie too long.

"You're better off now too?" I say quietly.

She's really crying now. And I remember Charlie so bad I can feel him. The sweet, sticky smell of him, hair slicked back and full of pomade, smile bigger than the sky.

"I still love Charlie sometimes." All times, I say from somewhere far in the past. "I am glad I left him though. He needed leaving."

Outside it gets so dark, we need to turn on a light.

Stella comes in with kids, bags, and noise. Jeff helps her carry stuff in and Louisa turns aside to wipe her eyes. Mattie runs right up to me to show me her new book. I want to read it but the print is too small, so Louisa offers to do it instead.

I love it when my home is alive like this.

Then it gets quiet again, and Stella tucks me into bed like I am one of her children. My Stella, my baby, Rain's baby. Her eyes are brighter but she has the same sadness. She kisses my forehead and I fall asleep in a smile.

I dream of flying again. I have been flying in my dreams these days, up out of my basement apartment, over the earth. The trees stand there beneath my feet with their proud, naked branches reaching up at me. The whole world is bright with snow and clouds and stars, and I can't even feel the cold.

Then I wake up and smell my dusty, damp room.

Somewhere in the night, I dream of Charlie. My eyes grow shadowed and permanently bruised, like they were when he was alive. Here, in my dream, he's like the tornado he was, the way he would whip my own sadness around as if he was the wind. He would tear at my spirit as if I was just brittle, dry earth. Then I floated around, broken into bits of dust dancing low in the sky. I floated, everything was a blur, and I never could look up to see the sun or stars.

Whenever I dream of Charlie I wake up in a sweat cold, chilled like I am afraid. My hands clench up like I am ready to fight. Then I remember where I am—in the leaky basement apartment on Aikins. I remember I am safe from Charlie, no more Charlie, Charlie long gone and long dead.

Then I lie back down and miss that love. I miss Charlie and feel sorry about how broken he was after I left him. How he fell apart and died too young. I think of how much he loved me. I think of him and an old wind flows through my broken body, inside that place where Charlie had been, where he seeded our children and made me feel all of his love. I sweat hot for that kind of love, the kind I only knew once.

IN THE END, all that matters is what has been given.

Another monster was here. A monster hurt Emily. I don't know who it was. To me, it looks like my Charlie, or that stupid man who hurt my girl. I know it's not them, but another monster in another person. There's always another one.

The important thing is that my Emily is okay. That she will go on and be an amazing woman. I know she will be. She is strong. She can't be anything else. That's the only thing that matters now, that she can heal. That she still has life to heal.

"WHATCHA MAKIN', KOOKOO? I'm starved!" Jake calls from the window. He comes with a breath of outside wind. The air is almost spring.

"Breakfast, what you think?" I laugh and unhook the screen. Jake likes to come through the window. He likes to be different like that.

"I smell bacon!" He licks his lips all funny and exaggerated.

His eyes light up. He has bright grey eyes like I've never seen, such a beautiful child. I thought this would be a special gift for him. His mother doesn't feed him enough meat. She likes to be healthy, but I don't think that works for growing boys.

"Where's your brother?" I ask.

"He stayed home with mom. He was being all whiny," he says with a shrug and jumps off the chair under the window. He stands tall in my little kitchen, taller than he was yesterday, I think.

Now I remember — his brother is a little sick. Louisa said so last night, or was it the other night. No, it was last night.

"I'll get the plates out." Jake pats my shoulder and wakes me from my thinking.

"Okay, my boy," I say and flip the bacon with my big fork.

"Why don't you sit down, Kookoo? I can finish this." He is looking at me sideways. I must be wandering off. I feel all right, though. I am always most awake in the morning, and then I seem to fade all day.

He leads me to my chair and gets me my cup of tea. I like to sit on this chair under the window, especially in the early morning. It faces east and it's bright there just after sunrise. It shows a little corner of the community garden across the street where people grow vegetables and tend to them so carefully, as if the plants were their precious babies.

I used to grow geraniums in there, a few years back.

Stella told me to get proper bars and locks for the windows, not just these old thin frames with rusty hooked screens.

"But who would want to rob an old woman?" I said.

Probably a lot of people, I think. "But I have nothing to steal!" I say, grinning at her, my serious child. But I know the stuff is never what matters, it's the stealing that matters. I learned that long ago.

The thick fatty smell of the meat is filling up the room when the little ones wake up.

Mattie walks in and rubs the sleep out of her eyes. She sniffs the air like a dog. "Bacon!"

"Hands off, it's mine!" Jake jokes, turning off the oven and forking out the bacon on to a paper-towel-covered plate.

Mattie's startled because she doesn't know her big cousin that well yet.

"Easy. There's enough for all of us," I chuckle from my chair.

"I'm hungry." Mattie comes to me.

"My poor starving babies!" I hold her in my arms. She is so young, so unsure, but she lets me hug her like she needs it. She doesn't know me well, but I'm so glad to know her now. The baby cries in the other room. Adam, Stella's baby. I hear her get up and talk to him. Such a good mama, my Stella, like her mother. Like her mother could have been.

I pat Mattie's arm and tell her to go get the forks, and point to which drawer.

I keep thinking of Charlie this morning. He lingers, an echo in the noise of the day. That's what happens when I dream him. He used to call me a Horror. I thought it was such a strange thing to say. It was a word he used but he didn't really know what it meant. I laughed at it once. Only once.

"Woman!" he'd say to me. "Youse a Horror to me!" He'd get all deep in his voice like a preacher. "Youse a Horror, Woman!"

Until one day I finally said, "You want a Horror, Man? I'll give you a Horror!" And I gave it to him, the big frying pan right in the groin. The old cast iron one, black from cooking meat. I gave it to him right there where he was blessed. Hard as I could. Still laugh when I think of his face at that moment, somewhere between shock and awe he was. I got his thigh mostly, never was a good shot at anything, but he didn't know what hit him. I didn't think it was so funny at the time, but I laugh now. Boy, he had it coming.

At the time, I was just fuming. I took my girls and we were out of the house before he could even get up. I got my girls and got out of there, frying pan still in my hand. Only thing I took at the time. Still have it.

What do you think I cooked the bacon in this morning?

When the kids are done eating, Jake takes Mattie into the living room. Stella walks into the kitchen, quiet. I point to the tea and she makes her way around. She's so quiet, sweet Stella. She sits at the table, the air around her thick with so many things to say.

I wait for her to talk first.

"How are you feeling?" she asks. "You must be tired."

"No, no, I'm good," I tell her. "I like doing things, you know that. I love doing things for Jake and that Mattie girl."

She shivers in her big sweater. "She really loves you, Kookoo."

"She is growing to, yes."

We are quiet for a minute, but I feel it. I can feel all the things she wishes she could tell me but just can't. She has always done this. As a child she used to keep everything bottled up too, like a fizzy pop bottle. I could feel her ready to explode. Only she waited so long, and then she would blow up, and do something big and crazy, like move away and not call for a long time. She went downtown to university and didn't come visit for years, but she came back. When she was lost, she came back with her babies. Sometimes you have to do that.

"Jeff's off tomorrow, so I might go back home tomorrow night," she says finally.

"That's okay, my girl. I don't mind," I tell her.

"Yeah," she sighs. "But I want to stay with you, Kookoo. It doesn't feel right to leave anymore." She pulls her knees up and hugs them, rests her chin there. "I just want to be here."

"I want you to be here too." I try to look at her as best I can. She is so young and beautiful, my Stella. She just doesn't know it, not yet.

"I feel so awful, Kookoo." She swallows her tears, chokes out her words. "You don't even know."

"I know you're good person. No matter what, I know that." Her hair is straight and black the way my Lorraine's was, before she would always get it permed. Stella is so much like her mom, like her mom was supposed to be.

"But I'm not, I'm not a good person at all," she spits out.

"Yes, you are, my girl. Yes you are." After Lorraine passed, I saw her in everything Stella did. It got so bad, I started calling her Rain, in my head. I called this poor child after her dead mama.

"I got way lost, Kookoo, so, so lost." She wipes her mouth with the back of her hand. I make a move to stand up to get her a tissue. She stops me and grabs one herself.

"But you came back," I say simply because it's true. She's haunted still, looks so much like her. Lorraine follows her child, sneaks into her, and changes her face to the past.

"But, Kookoo..." She stops to wipe her nose and thinks. "I don't feel like a very good person, Kookoo. I..."

Her voice trails off.

I look at her and laugh my toothless laugh. "Who does, my girl? You've always been hard on yourself. So, so hard on yourself. You're harder on yourself than anyone else will ever be."

She doesn't answer, just sort of shrugs and sips her tea. I want to keep looking at her so I will always remember who she is.

After Lorraine died, Stella and I became like one. Stella was so small then, maybe nine, yes, I think she was nine when her Mama died. We looked after each other, hung on to each other for dear life.

I can hear the singsong of a TV show and baby Adam laughing. Someone is making him laugh. Jake is in there. He's such a good boy, my Jake.

"Jeff's really good. He's a good man, Kookoo, but he just doesn't get it." Stella's voice is a little louder, a little stronger. "He just doesn't understand." She sits there with her knees pulled to her chest, protecting herself.

"None of them do." I chuckle a little and think. "It's not their job to understand."

"I don't know if I can be with someone who doesn't understand." Her young face rests on her knee, looking away.

"Then you will be alone, and that will be fine."

I go to pour more tea. Stella straightens up, takes the pot from my shaking hand, and pours it for me.

"He has other jobs to do, he doesn't have to understand, not the way you want him to. He understands in his own way."

She nods but I don't know if she knows yet, that men are good, strong, amazing and ordinary, but not everything. They can't be. They are too busy doing other things, and she should be too.

"I think I'm going to go back to school," she says because she knows what I am thinking. "I mean, I think I want to."

"Good," I tell her and mean it. "You belong there."

"I don't know," she sighs. "Sometimes I think it's all bullshit."

"You just haven't realized your purpose yet. When you do, it's not bullshit, it's passion."

"Is that what happened to you? You found your purpose?"

"Oh for me, I couldn't do much. I had your mom and aunty. I took care of them. That's what I have always done. You all became what I did, what I was supposed to do. With you, you're different. You can do anything," I tell her. "You have always been a storyteller, a story keeper, a watcher. My Stella, you have always watched the world, and you feel everything you see. You go get degrees and learn more, but you will still just be doing what you've always done."

She nods, and in the living room Adam starts to cry. Stella jumps up to go see them. So good. She will be older than her mama was. She may even grow to be older than me.

IN THE END, all that matters is what is left behind. Moments go so quick.

When I was young, I was always so sad, so woe-is-me. I was a poor girl, an abandoned girl, an orphan left. I never felt like I was a part of the family I was in. Never wanted to be. I was used, abused, treated like I was nothing. I thought I was nothing. Then I had Charlie and my girls and things to do, people to care for. I had Lorraine and Cheryl and had to lose my Lorraine but she left Stella so she was never all-the-way gone. I am glad that Charlie went before Lorraine. He wouldn't have been good after that. Men break when things like that happen. And when they were both gone, I still had Cheryl and she had me.

Now Emily has so many: Louisa, Paulina, Peter, Jake and the wee ones. Emily is alive and strong. Jake is going to be an amazing man. So much I have, so much I made from nothing. Those who had to go, Lorraine, Charlie, they wait for me on the other side, where I go, soon. Because I am old and I feel myself fading, like my old eyes. There is so much I can't see. I have to look around for a long time, around the blurry spaces.

But I know I have my people. I can feel them, even when they go away. It means so much to have people. It is everything. I have been so fortunate.

I'M ON MY chair again, and the sky is getting dark. And Cheryl has brought me doughnuts. Where is Stella? The room is quiet and cold.

I chew the one with the pudding inside. It's easy and sweet.

Cheryl brings out her computer and shows me videos there. Funny things she thinks I will like about cats and babies. Oh yes, that's right, Stella went home tonight.

"I thought you'd like that," she says as she closes the thing.

"I did, yeah."

"You've been thinking about Rain, haven't you?" she says, her voice strong, but tired.

"Yes. She is still here, you know, close to us," I say without thinking, knowing it is true.

"I feel like I should do something, but I can't think of anything else to do," she says. "My girls, the boys, I think I've done everything, and then, I think there must be something else to do." She looks so full of things, my Cheryl. She looks at me for a long time, and I can feel her secret growing on her. She doesn't want to tell me.

"It doesn't matter." I smile. I smile big sometimes and think of my silly, gummy mouth. So much of it, it really doesn't matter. I don't know if I say these words, or just think them.

Cheryl walks me to bed and lies with me, like she used to when she was young. Like I did when all of them were young.

"You want a story?" She tucks the blankets around me.

"No, just your arm," I say, like she used to say, like she has always said.

She holds me, warm, soft. It's the kind of moment that is its own story without words.

I close my eyes and fall into a dream. I am flying again. I am high above the pointy housetops and scratchy trees and somewhere in the stars. I go higher and see the streets lined up in squares below me. Square after square, the city like a patchwork quilt, all stitched together in different shades of yellow and grey. Then I go further, that long chunk of field where the Hydro towers sit, twisted like a thick white river, the land cuts right through everything.

Charlie is there, but more a feeling than anything I can see. I feel him like the black sky all around and nowhere at the same time. I feel my Lorraine. She is keeping me warm.

Her arms are so strong, she can hold me up, and I am so happy to be with her. My Rain, my sweet girl. The clouds are so bright around us, and we can fly right into them. So we do.

We fly fast, quick as a current. I think of my other girls, sweet Stella, Louisa, Paulina, poor, poor Emily, and strong Jake, and those lovely babies, but something in me knows they will be okay. They have each other. And as long as they hold on to each other, they will always be okay.

I hold on to my Lorraine, my sweet, sweet girl, and my whole body feels like nothing, like nothing else matters. Not the hurt, or the blame or the pain. It all goes away.

We point north. I see a blur of stars and the white winter moon, and we just go.

CHERYL

EVERY TIME SHE leaves the city, Cheryl takes a deep breath. She loves that last moment, the last stoplight before the highway stretches out and there's no slowing down anymore.

The land south of the city runs completely flat. The road turns, rolls outward under the long sky. That familiar cracked, grey highway, the muted land, snow melted to frozen mud, waiting for spring. It has been so long since she has seen so much sky. Cheryl lets all the things that happened this winter fall through her as she watches the white blur around them. The winter has been so long, so sad. She sits in the passenger seat, holds her forehead to the cold window, and the road speeds below the wheels as if they're finally outrunning the season.

A skilled highway driver, Rita goes too fast, especially when she is going home. The girls are in the back seat on either side of Baby boy, fast asleep in his booster seat, his neck at an awkward angle. The girls look at their phones and talk about things they find on their screens, bands and gossip. Cheryl sighs with gratitude every time she feels their resilience, but still hopes they look out their windows once in a while to see their country spill out around them. Zegwan's eye is still bruised and swollen, and a thin Band-Aid covers the biggest cut on her cheekbone. Emily still walks with a limp, and even here, with only her family around her, she sits with her body curled into itself like a turtle ready to retreat inward. She still has a long way to go, but here they are, young girls living, talking across Baby whose perfect cheeks are slack. He sighs in his untouched sleep.

Cheryl loves highway driving, this quiet space before getting there, anywhere. An hour out of the city, every direction looks different: north is all bush, west rolls out into hills, and in the east, rocks spit out of the earth and start to whisper the long Canadian Shield. But south is just flat, a long, low valley that somehow always looks yellow, like grass burnt from sun, or snow ever fading.

"I think I lost them." Rita squints out the rearview.

Cheryl looks back and doesn't see Pete's old blue truck. "You are going one forty."

"It's not my fault the boy can't keep up," Rita scoffs and laughs her big laugh. She feels it too, Cheryl can tell—her friend feels the deep, cleansing breath of land. "Oh, that could be him. Here, I'll slow down."

Pete's truck pops up on the horizon and grows bigger. Three heads bounce up inside: Pete's wide shoulders at the wheel and the identical black silhouettes of Cheryl's girls. She has always loved the look of them, how they match each other. When they were little, she used to dress them in complementary clothes, different colours but the same outfits. As babies they looked the same, the same light, wispy dark hair, the same squished eyes. She can tell the difference in pictures only by what they are wearing. Or by Stella, born in between the two of them, with a full head of thick, black hair. They were always like that—Stella in the middle and Louisa looking the way Paulina would look in a year. Louisa was slightly bigger but only until they were full-grown, then they were the same size. Only their faces, their personalities, and the feel of them sets them apart.

When the truck catches up, Rita speeds again. Cheryl looks at her and smiles.

"What? We're already late," Rita tells Cheryl.

Cheryl shakes her head. They're not late. No one will start until they get there.

Rita slows only a little bit to turn down the gravel road—she knows the turnoff so well she barely has to. The dust billows around them and the bush closes in for a few moments, like a quick greeting hug. Cheryl can smell the fire before she can see it. When the trees open, the old board house comes into view first, its porch sagging off like it wants to fall back into the earth. The yard behind is long and drooping, and surrounded by trees, the squat, round lodge is covered with a faded blue plastic tarp and long-aged hides. The fire beside it is almost as tall. Dan and his dad stand up and wave to the car, their arms resting a moment on their pitchforks. The two young boys bend over the pile of rocks, feeding them to the fire, one by one.

Dan had come out for the funeral and then brought Jake home with Sundancer. They'd been here all week, doing "man things" as they called them, old lessons that only a Moshoom could teach properly. Cheryl thought it was a good thing for her grandson. Their little family was always so full of girl things, women's work. Not better or worse, just different.

Rita stops the car and looks out to her men with a quick

smile. The boys wear long plaid sleeves and puffy hunters' vests, and look like they've been here for years. Their faces seem peaceful, their smiles wide. Pete's truck pulls up behind them and Lou gets out before it even stops all the way. Jake runs up and gives his mom a big bear hug. He looks taller somehow.

"We're here, Baby," Emily says, gently waking her cousin. Cheryl stretches.

"I'm starved. Mom, what do we have to eat?" Zegwan asks.

"You shouldn't eat before a sweat, my girl. You'll get sick." Rita opens her door to the fresh warm air.

"But I'm hungry," her girl whines.

"Well you should've eaten when I told you to. Go drink some water and say hi to your Moshoom."

Zegwan groans but does as she's told.

"You ready to go, my girl?" Cheryl leans back to Emily.

"Yeah," she says in her new, cautious way.

"It'll be good. It always feels good, after."

Cheryl can feel Emily nod even though she can't see her. Cheryl goes around to open her door. The breeze smells like fire and the sun is strong. The grass is soft underfoot. The snow is mostly melted, but holds on in the shadows. Overhead an eagle circles high. So high it's just a smudge but its movements are unmistakable.

"Thanks, Mom. Oh thank you," Cheryl whispers and no one hears, no one but the eagle in the sky.

They take turns in the bathroom. Rita's old house looks like it's been lived in by men for too long. Cheryl has a sudden ache for Joe's place, and for Joe, too. He had come to the funeral too, of course. She was glad he did, it was the respectful thing to do. His beard was fuller, whiter, the skin around it winter worn and dry. His eyes were a bit more wrinkled but still filled with tears when he held his girls, when he high-fived

Jake because the boy was shy around him. He looked long at her and held her for longer than he needed to. She wanted to talk more, but she also knew they didn't have anything they needed to say out loud.

Rita had a bunch of old skirts in a mouldy box and the girls each put one on. Emily goes into the bathroom to change alone and comes out fidgeting and self-conscious.

"Don't worry about it, Em. You look marvellous," Louisa says to her in a sarcastic but still gentle way. They are all so gentle with Emily now. It is as if she wears a shell, something protective and translucent over all of her, something that might break at any moment. Cheryl tries to sound normal with her, tries to be normal, but she's still sad, shaken, and enraged every time she looks at her so-young baby. Every time she feels her pain there. It was the same when Rain went. They were all like that with Stella, like she was something so delicate. They had to be so careful, and they were all protective of her and angry at the world.

Cheryl doesn't know when it changed, if it ever changed, and got back to normal. She just tried not to think about it, and after a while, it seemed to drift further and further away. But then, something would happen, or a dream, and it was like it had all just happened again, and she felt that jarring ache, that big that space where her sister was supposed to be. She was stitched back together, but there was always a scar. The skin there was so sensitive, she could always feel it and avoided touching it.

CHERYL HAD TO tell Rita, of course.

"So she, like, saw it happening and did nothing? I can't fucking believe that." Rita had spit out her cigarette smoke and disgust.

"She called the police." Cheryl wasn't trying to be defensive.

"But, what the fuck, she couldn't do anything? Nothing?"

"I guess she just froze, you know. Like with all she's seen and experienced in her life..."

"I don't care what the fuck has happened to her, she still should have done something." Rita's face was firm but her voice had lost an edge it used to have.

"Yeah, maybe, I mean, of course," Cheryl said and flicked the last of her cigarette away. "But she didn't. Couldn't."

"Well, she should have." Rita too flicked her smoke away in finality.

Cheryl could only shrug in reply, couldn't agree or disagree. It's Stella, Rain's baby, was all she thought, but she didn't say it.

Cheryl didn't know how to tell Paulina. Louisa insisted they had to, at first. Then her mom, their Kookoo, finally died, and everything stopped and changed again. Everything just became a series of steps for Cheryl, things to do, planning a funeral, going through her mother's things, and all that deep sorrow lay under everything.

Paulina and Emily were not ready to go to the apartment, and Louisa was busy helping them, so it was actually Stella who came by to go through everything. For days the two of them piled and packed things, so many things. Things are so useless when they no longer belong to someone. Stella didn't talk much. She just worked. She cleaned her Kookom's things. Her shame was so big it filled the room. Even at the funeral, Stella hadn't stayed long and hadn't greeted her cousins or their children. Maybe Cheryl couldn't expect it to be any other way.

They still have so much to go through, so much cleaning to do. Stella is there at Kookoo's place now. Or she might be finished and then gone, again.

But at least she's doing that much.

Cheryl knows she has to tell Paulina one day. She dreads that day, but really, what would it matter anyway. It won't change anything. They're already so broken, could they even break any more?

"If you'd like to all gather around, I think we're ready to get started." An older lady stands by the fire and holds the shell of smoking smudge.

Cheryl goes over, lets the sage smoke lick her palms and washes her face in its medicine. She smudges her eyes and ears and short hair, and moves her stiff hands over her old skin like her mother taught her so many years ago. She looks out at her family, her girls with their children wrapped in blankets, ready to go into the lodge. Jake cries discreetly, his head covered with his hood. His pale, skinny legs stick out of his oversized swimming trucks, the kind all the men wear in a sweat.

The lodge door is flung open, revealing the damp darkness and the deeply set middle where the burning rocks will go. Cheryl crawls in with everyone else circling around the empty pit. Warm already, she snuggles close between Louisa and Emily. Her granddaughter leans in but stays by the door, in case she wants to go out. The woman leading them passes out rattles and then welcomes the first grandfather rocks into the pit. The hot stones glow orange as the pitchfork digs them out of the fire and into the indented middle of the round lodge. Then the door closes and everything is dark but the glowing stones. The woman sprinkles cedar on top and the sparks burst into light and fade quickly. Cheryl breathes in the sweet medicine silently as the others hoot and call around her. The leader sounds her hand drum and starts to sing, and slowly, others join in. Cheryl knows the song but has no voice so she shakes her rattle and holds on to Emily. She hasn't breathed this deeply for a long time. The steam gets thicker and everyone sings harder. Tears mix with sweat on her face, and she just holds on.

She stays for all four rounds, singing gently. Cheryl dreams of wolves in the den she imagines for her sister. They are all there, just wolves with shed skins, warm and together. Just like they're supposed to be.

Completely soaked, she crawls out into the bright day, dirt sticking to her knees. She stands tall and stretches her back out in the sun. She's spent, refreshed, and starving. She wraps a towel around her shoulders and sits next to Louisa at the table. She wraps her sweaty arms around her girl, who yells in protest. Just like she did when she was as young as her teenage son.

"Holy, Ma. You're all wet!" She pulls away but not for real.

Rita comes over, her face red and hot, her eyes smiling as she makes two sandwiches and crunches on a chip.

"Good sweat, hey?" She nudges at Cheryl's elbow.

"Good enough," Cheryl says, her face a full smile. She looks over to watch her grandkids play in the grass.

THEY HAD JUST gotten to Paulina's house when the police called. They had just brought Emily home. Cheryl had helped her up the stairs and tucked her into bed, then lay there with her baby's baby wrapped in her Kookoo's arms like she used to when Emily was little, when she needed four stories and a song before she'd let her Kookoo go. Cheryl lay there for a long time, and hummed that old song her mom had taught her. Then she came downstairs and the phone rang.

Cheryl watched Paulina listen and just pass the phone to

her sister instead of having to tell them herself. It was Louisa who said the words.

Cheryl didn't believe it at first, it didn't make sense. *"Girls?"* she repeated the word over and over, and looked up to her girls sitting across from her in Paulina's living room. "How can it... girls?" She kept saying the word as if that would help.

"They say that this girl used a beer bottle, so that's how." Louisa kept starting her sentences like she didn't want to finish them. "We knew that. We knew about... the glass."

Paulina just looked away, her face cemented with anger. Her fingers pressed to her chin like she was holding it up.

"Girls." Cheryl said again, lower now. Not wanting Emily to hear, even though she was all the way upstairs and asleep.

"She's in custody now, this ringleader, and they think she'll plead guilty." Louisa explained everything, slowly, carefully. She didn't want to have to repeat it.

Cheryl nodded. "I can't, it's so..." Her voice trailed off.

"I know." Louisa leaned toward her, her hands pressed together like she was praying. "But it's good, I mean, at least we know right?"

Cheryl only nodded again. Paulina looked off.

"She sounds like a pretty messed-up kid. I mean, you'd have to be..." Louisa only starts.

"I don't give a fuck about her story, Lou, so you can stop that right now," Paulina said still looking off.

"I didn't mean—" her sister started.

"It's okay," Cheryl said to them, hands up so their voices didn't rise again. She felt like she was reeling, waving her hands and talking from down an abyss. "It's a lot to take in. To think about. At least she's off the street, right? She won't hurt Emily anymore."

"Yes." Louisa nodded. "That is the most important thing."

Paulina didn't nod but her face relaxed a little. The lines smoothed, if only for a second.

The most important thing.

THE SUN STARTS to set, and the fire dies down. It's time to go. Dan cleans up and his dad talks alone with Rita for a long time. Cheryl smokes another cigarette and Baby boy still runs through the bush, chased by his brother and the other teen-agers. Emily doesn't run but still waves out her arms at her little cousin, still grabs at him the way he wants her to. His laughter rings high over the trees. Louisa sits on the ground in front of her mom and takes a smoke. Cheryl doesn't question it.

"So what now?" she asks Cheryl.

"I'm going to your Kookom's tomorrow. Clean the last of it, if you want to help."

"I guess I should, hey?" Louisa watches the children. "Sorry I've been a slacker about it. I just, I wasn't ready."

"I know. I get it." Cheryl looks up, the sky empty and turning. "But I could use your help. I don't want to ask your sister."

"Okay. I'll come tomorrow." Louisa nods into the fading light, and they're quiet again.

"I saw an eagle earlier. When we got here," Cheryl says slowly.

"Good." Louisa knows what it means to see an eagle. "I knew she'd be here somewhere."

"Yeah, she is." Cheryl sighs, feeling her mother around her, not wanting to let the feeling go. She looks up again, but the sky is still empty. Even the sun is leaving it.

BABY BOY SLEEPS in the middle and Paulina and Louisa sit in the back this time. The country is black around them. When Rita drives back to the city, she goes slower.

Somewhere down the quiet highway, Rita finally speaks. "My kids are going to turn around and go back with their dad. I think they need to be home for a while."

"That's a good idea, good for them," Louisa says, but Cheryl knows she's thinking of her own boy. She can hear it in the hardening of her voice.

"I'm going to go out there next weekend, if Em and Jake want to come with me. Dan's dad said they can come stay too, but I told him you guys wouldn't really go for that."

"Yeah, but that's good of him." In the rearview mirror, Cheryl sees her girls exchange a quick look. They're both thinking of their own kids losing their best friends.

"That's a good idea. That way they can get away and see their friends right away," Cheryl tells them. "I'll go too, if they'd want me. I like it out there."

"It's a good place, hey?" Rita says. "I never realize how much I miss it 'til I go back."

"It's your home," Cheryl says with a look.

"I need ceremony again. I said so many prayers in that lodge. I said I'd give up drinking. It's time to let that go."

"Yeah, I hear that. It's time for a good let go."

"Wanna be my sober buddy? We can drink too much tea and be real Kookoms."

"I'm already a real Kookom," Cheryl says, "and tea just makes me pee."

But she thinks a minute, the idea of not drinking suddenly feels freeing and scary. But good. Warm.

"You should, it's spring. We should all give up something bad every spring," Rita says.

"Is that like some of your old-time tradition there, Reet?"

"Yes, it's called Reet-ology. You should be a believer." Rita laughs. "For only fifty bucks, I'll cure you good."

Cheryl laughs and thinks of a smoke, but Louisa would kill her if she smoked in the car with Baby.

"Think about it," Rita says a little quieter. "I'll help youse. I'll be your non-drinking buddy."

Cheryl thinks on it. The need to be clean feels almost as good as the dream of the bush. She makes only a slight nod, but Rita catches it.

"You gonna give up anything, Lou?" Rita asks, looking at her in the rearview.

"For Reet-ology?" she scoffs. "Pfft. Umm, I just gave up my man, does that count?" She laughs and Rita joins her, generously.

Cheryl looks out into the speeding-by night. Patches of light in the black. She can still smell spring coming.

"We're fucked up but not fucked," Paulina says, breaking the quiet that rested between them. And then before Cheryl can ask, she says, "I'm going to give up feeling so hopeless. Or at least, I am going to try to feel hopeful as much as I can."

"That's a good one," Cheryl says, nodding to her girl.

"We could all use a bit of that," Rita adds. "To remember that."

Cheryl looks back to see Paulina reach out to take her sister's hand. Louisa only nods and turns away, looking out into the deepening night. Cheryl can't find her voice, but yes, she thinks, hope. That is just the sort of thing they need to keep.

She looks up and can see a star and then another, blurry but solid. She thinks of the eagle and then imagines a new work. Her mother this time, yes, but not painted from a photograph. Something drawn, something about her hands and those wide brown wings of the eagle. Yes, something entirely new.

Cheryl's hands soften and she feels the restlessness of need-ing to work. Half an hour to the city and then she can sketch into the night. But first she can stay here awhile, warm in the car with her girls around her.

These are the moments she loves the most, the ones that feel good all the way, no matter what.

ACKNOWLEDGEMENTS

This book is an offering of gratitude to the community workers and helpers who save the world in a million little ways everyday. For those who lighten loads, who help without expectation, who take pain and give healing—Thank you.

For the artists who have given us our spirits back—Thank you.

This book couldn't have happened without the ferocious chaos that is the UBC Creative Writing program, especially Annabel Lyon who helped all the noise make sense. Thank you to Marilyn Biderman, my fierce advocate and agent, Janice Zawerbny for her gentle leadership, and everyone at House of Anansi for welcoming me, and my fictional sisters, into the fold.

Thank you to those who blazed the trail, Lee Maracle, Beatrice Culleton Mosionier, Eden Robinson, Rosanna Deerchild, and all the other Neechi, nearly-Neechi and other writerly folk who have helped me on the way. You are magick! And, of course, big thanks to the Indigenous Writers Collective—I don't know where I would be without you.

Thank you to my sister, Chrysta, and Anna, and Ko'ona. Thank you to all the Boulettes, and Lena—with good thoughts and memories of April and Brian.

Thank you to my mother, my father, my brother Peter, my beautiful nieces, and especially and always, to my amazing daughters who are so, so good.

Miigwetch. Marsi. Merci. Thanks.

KATHERENA VERMETTE IS a Métis writer from Treaty One territory, the heart of the Métis nation, Winnipeg, Manitoba, Canada. Her first book, *North End Love Songs* (The Muses Company) won the 2013 Governor General's Literary Award for Poetry. Her literary work has appeared in several magazines and anthologies, and she recently completed work on a short documentary, *this river* produced by the National Film Board of Canada (2016). *The Break* is her first novel.